NOW SERVING
A FRIVOLOUS FEEDING OF
FOOLISH FANTASY!

Do you find witches whimsical? Do golems make you giggle? Do demons strike you as droll? If you like your fantasy with a taste of "wry," here's a brew of belly laughs from a comical cauldron. Editor Alan Dean Foster offers an intoxicating anthology of unreality by these ace authors of fantastic fun:

Margaret Ball, Greg Costikyan, George Alec Effinger, Alan Dean Foster, Esther Friesner, Mel Gilden, Ron Goulart, Tobias Grace, Nina Kiriki Hoffman, Wolfgang Jeschke, R. A. Lafferty, Jack McDevitt, Laura Resnick, Mike Resnick, Steve Rasnic Tem, and Edward Wellen.

Read one and get entranced by fun! You'll soon be "goblin" down the rest!

BETCHA CAN'T READ
JUST ONE!

BETCHA CAN'T READ JUST ONE

EDITED BY
ALAN DEAN FOSTER

ACE BOOKS, NEW YORK

This book is an Ace original edition,
and has never been previously published.

BETCHA CAN'T READ JUST ONE

An Ace Book/published by arrangement with
the editor

PRINTING HISTORY
Ace edition/December 1993

ISBN: 0-441-24883-7

ACE®
Ace Books are published by The Berkley Publishing Group,
200 Madison Avenue, New York, NY 10016.
ACE and the "A" design are trademarks
belonging to Charter Communications, Inc.

PRINTED IN THE UNITED STATES OF AMERICA

10 9 8 7 6 5 4 3 2 1

Contents

BETCHA CAN'T READ JUST ONE

Introduction

Supposedly everything was better in the "good old days." Even fantasy. In our harsh, modern world people decry the crudity and decay they see on television, in film, and in books. They look back wistfully on a simpler, gentler era when parents read their kids soothing tales about cute animals and respectful children, or traded harmless stories about other people or faraway lands to their friends and neighbors. Stories that made them smile and, if the tale was particularly amusing, laugh out loud.

Yes, it's a damn shame we don't have classic tales like that to share anymore. Uplifting fables like Hansel and Gretel, wherein the heroic children shove the poor old witch into her own oven and roast her alive until . . .

No, no, wait a minute. That's not quite the tone we're talking here. Come to think of it, those brothers Grimm were really rather bloodthirsty.

The great Greek myths, then. Fanciful odes to the glory that was Greece, uplifting fantasies of gods and humans. Like the Rape of Europa . . . oops, no. Wrong tone again. Well, then, how about the *Iliad*? Or wasn't that about war, and slaughter, and didn't it start with a kidnaping? The *Odyssey,* then. The record of valiant Ulysses' heroic deeds. Remember how he fooled the Cyclops? After the giant had first eaten several of his men (better skip that part). After which brave Ulysses and his men escape, but not until they've first blinded the poor hermit of a giant by shoving

1

a sharpened, red-hot log into his eye until it bubbles and melts and . . .

Darn. Finding that gentle, warmhearted tone of early fantasy seems to be harder than I thought.

Maybe we're reaching too far into a past that's somewhat more rough-hewn than is often perceived. What about more modern fables, up-to-date enough to make you laugh? What about . . . Disney! What could be more good-natured than the classic all-American films of Walt Disney? Snow White, for example. Even if the witch does, uh, want her chief huntsman to cut out the poor girl's heart, even if she does starve her prisoners to death in a truly dank dungeon, even if she does die violently in the end . . .

Wrong film. Pinocchio, then. Where our cheery puppet is exploited and tormented by an abusive adult and his friend is turned into a slave-donkey, and . . .

What happened to those good old days, anyway?

Fact is that, as is usual with good old days, the good old days are now. The fantasies of yesteryear were every bit as graphic and unsettling as those of today, and in many instances not half as funny. When I'm in the mood for a little phantasmagorical amusement I'd much rather relax in the company of Tex Avery's retelling of *Little Red Riding Hood* than the original.

Of course, the best fantasy relates to its time. The humor of Washington Irving may be "timeless," but I don't doubt that it struck a more responsive chord among his contemporaries than it does today, a Disney reworking notwithstanding. The very best contemporary fantasy, humorous or otherwise, relies for its substance and effect not on centuries-old European fairy tales but on immediacy, on relevance not to medieval Europe or Persia but to the time and place in which it is being written. As with any fiction, the best fantasy drinks deep of reality. Readers connect better with what is happening around them than with what has gone before, "classic" status bedamned.

Don't get me wrong (well, half-wrong is permissible). I like dragons and gnomes and werewolves and elves and princes and princesses as much as the next guy. It's just that I get sick of seeing them go through the same motions over and over and over again. Everyone to their taste, of course. Some folks spend their whole lives in the town of their birth and are content. Some when they order ice cream get nothing but vanilla and are content.

Me, whenever a mental repast is offered, I like a little variety.

I like to be more than merely entertained. I like to be made, to be forced, to be compelled, to *think*. That's a requirement every bit as applicable to fantasy as it is to its cousin science fiction. I like writers who at least try to do something a little different, even if it's with familiar material. Sure you love your Uncle Harry, and are amused by his jokes, but it's funnier still if one day he shows up with an ostrich and proceeds to ride it around the neighborhood. And if the men in white coats who arrive to take him away run into each other and stumble in their attempts to catch him, that's funnier still.

There are no ostriches in this book, but you may catch a glimpse of someone not unlike Uncle Harry. Usually it's a writer, gleefully gallivanting about on his or her imagination, digging in the spurs in hopes of achieving a higher, wider, wilder, exhibition. I hope you enjoy the ride.

Alan Dean Foster
Prescott, Arizona
March 1992

The Wicked Old Witch

◇   •

by
George Alec Effinger

How many stories have you heard, how many did your parents read to you as a child, how many have you yourself envisioned, which involved a witch? The poor ugly old gals are the staple villains of traditional fantasies. Your kid won't drink his milk? Scare him with a witch. Need a stock villain? Conjure up a witch. As fantasy staples they're downright overworked, and most of them aren't even eligible for residuals, much less Social Security or Medicare.

If I was a witch, I'd be getting pretty sick about now of the whole weary, disparaging business.

Sandor Courane was an easygoing kind of guy, generally speaking. The daily surprises and even disasters that ambushed him usually left him in a calm, philosophic mood. He was a hard man to ruffle, either with insults or physical attacks. It was a good thing, too, because on a particular day in 1992, an ice-cream-laden eighteen-wheeler forced him off the road to the left on the Pennsylvania Turnpike near the town of Gremmage, across a drainage ditch that did no great good to the undercarriage of his eight-year-old Renault Alliance, and onto the thickly wooded median.

It was only through an unconscious but superb emergency steering technique and the best of good fortune that he didn't destroy his car and himself immediately thereafter. Nevertheless, at the very end of the primary phase of his adventure, Courane slammed the Renault into a typical northeastern deciduous tree, rendering the car inoperable, and in the process smashing his face forward into the steering wheel.

He suffered some painful injuries, particularly neck whiplash and stinging cuts and bruises in his mouth where his teeth had been forced against the inside of his lips. Immediately afterward, however, he fell backward again into the seat, in the normal driving position.

Dazed and confused, he sat there for some time, trying to figure out what had happened. His first thoughts concerned the seat belt, which he'd always been too great a man to use. It was a simple shoulder harness, but he'd long since learned to ignore it. After he thought about the seat belt, he pondered what he was supposed to do next.

He breathed slowly through his mouth; it was marginally less agonizing than breathing through his banged-up nose, but who could really tell? Who was conducting the high-level tests that determined the accuracy of this sort of statement?

"Mr. Courane, after extensive clinical comparisons, we've decided that the mouth-breathing technique costs you in discomfort only about seventy-five to eighty percent of what our nose-breathing patients experience."

Who was Sandor Courane, and why should we care about him? Well, in the first place, he's the representative of the reader, the Everyman who found himself in bizarre circumstances. Courane will soon have to deal with an even more bloodcurdling, life-threatening situation, one which the average person will never have to face unless, God forbid, the reader's as much a *schmendrik* as Courane.

This way, the reader learns how Courane will react to what he'll walk into, so that in a worst-case scenario—that is, if the reader *does* find himself in the same unlikely series of events—the reader will know exactly how to respond. This is a very important function of the story, and it could be of vital significance to somebody, someday.

In the second place, Courane was a likable sort of guy, one who'd had quite a few other chance incidents of the kind that never happened to real people. That is, *fictional* adventures. Mr. Big Shot Average Person will just have to buy the fact that crazy things happened to Sandor Courane more frequently than to most other people.

Why was Courane on the median of the Pennsylvania Turnpike, crashed against a maple-beech variety of tree? If he hadn't been so mentally impaired at the moment, he'd have realized that this was just another typical episode. He'd either end up dead or he'd have a revealing, info-packed learning experience.

Courane *hated* learning experiences. They meant that he'd have to work his way through a state of affairs he'd rather not even know about. The big trouble, at least as far as he was concerned, was that he never, in any of these exploits, had any say in the matter. Whether he dropped dead almost immediately or gained some valuable insight was completely up to the whims of some Higher Power. For that reason, he generally didn't worry overmuch. He knew that things would always turn out the way they were meant to, and all he had to do was hit his marks and speak his lines.

Well, poor, perplexed Courane was trapped in his crumpled car. He was trapped more because he was still virtually insensible than because the side panels, front end, and roof had been crushed so badly out of shape that he could barely extricate himself from his ruined vehicle.

As his mind recovered more in the way of reason, he began to feel a little warning tingle of fear. Usually, of course, the right things to say and do inevitably appeared like magic in his mind when he needed them. It was kind of spooky, the way his speeches suddenly sprang forth, fully armed, from his less-than-brilliant mind. He was forgetting about the Higher Power again.

Don't think for a moment that Courane could be so clever and charming all on his own. A top-line performer who can do that eats so far into a short story's total budget that there wouldn't be enough left over for even so much as a Renault Alliance. Some quick calculations indicate that if we'd rejected Courane and signed, oh, somebody out of Flannery O'Connor or Elmore Leonard, all we could've afforded was a '47 Chevy—and no L.A. Sunset Strip lowrider, either. Just a '47 Chevy somebody found deep beneath a massive pile of brown leaves, but which nevertheless had been in a state of near-perfect repair since the middle of the Truman administration.

See, all these seemingly unrelated aspects have to add up; it all comes down to the bottom line, where the short-fiction accountants decide if there's enough interest and funding in this emotionally charged story to continue with it.

The Higher Power that watched over Courane liked to let him believe he had control over his own life now and then, but we all know better. At this point, the Power permitted Courane's normal consciousness to return slowly to him. Courane's first responses were reactions to pain. It included—but was not limited to—his whiplashed neck, his cut and bleeding mouth, and various other aches and afflictions caused by the impact with the tree.

Let's not mince words here. Courane felt real, undiminished suffering—and he hadn't even met the antagonist yet. Hang around for the antagonist. She's about a mover, in the unfortunately immortal words of not-so-long-ago.

The adventure was starting off with unrelieved bad news, and Courane had so far been entirely passive. This was not normal. Usually, at least, he had the option to make things worse. This was not the way his typical go-for-the-price enterprises began, and it made him a little bit afraid. It made him not want to get out of his wrecked maroon Renault Alliance.

Everything considered, sitting under the tree in the car in the shade was nice enough. The immediate vicinity was quiet except for the car's radio, tuned to a station playing Sam Cooke, one of Courane's favorite singers of all time. And Courane told himself that if there were any evil things about, let them find him for a change. Why did *he* always do all the work?

Typically Courane stood around in a fog-shrouded parking garage because some heavyweight from New York City, some button man with a moronic nickname who spent too much time in clam bars—some *guy* delighted in watching Courane stew in his own anxiety, just to emphasize their relative positions in society. This was an important feature of the growth industry of the nineties, which was pushing people around.

Courane didn't want to move an inch, at least for a little while. Maybe he'd lay his hands on some good twelve-year-old bonded stuff in the glove compartment that could make things bearable, or else he simply wouldn't move an inch. Soon, at the very worst, nature would force Courane from the car, but that was in the indefinite time to come.

Okay, we fast-forward a little to the moment when Courane couldn't stand it any longer, and had to find out what kind of surreal drama he'd fallen into this time. Knowing full well that almost anything he chose to do would be a mistake, very likely a fatal one, he massaged his lacerated forehead, winced, and forced open the driver's-side door of the Renault. Crickets chirped, leaves rustled, unknown birds out of sight in the deeper woods made soothing, natural sounds.

Courane wasn't deceived for an instant. Calm, placid surroundings often meant that he was only moments away from death. He shrugged resignedly, took a deep breath and let it go, and climbed out onto the very broad median strip of the Pennsylvania Turnpike.

He hated these goddamn adventures, Courane thought. It was like running out of gas in the middle of St. Didier Parish, Louisiana, at three o'clock in the morning. He knew at those times that he could take the gas can from the trunk and walk a million miles to a filling station, and that eventually he'd get back to the car, pour the gas into the tank, and the adventure would come to an end.

The aggravating part was that it was always such a dull, meager experience to have to get through. Life was like that, not only for Sandor Courane but for millions of normal people as well. In the dark night of the crummy adventure, it's always three o'clock in the morning.

Well, it wasn't actually three A.M. in Pennsylvania. It was well past noon, and the brassy sunlight slanted in through the boughs of the trees. Courane hadn't walked far before he could almost imagine that he was in some great forest instead of a turnpike median.

He usually went about with some music playing like background underscoring in his mind. Now, for reasons he chose not to examine closely, he realized he was remembering a brief orchestral theme. It didn't take him long to place it. It was an often repeated motif from Wagner's Ring Cycle, deep in the bass section of the score. It occurred throughout the four operas, foreshadowing all sorts of mythical gruesomeness. Courane couldn't remember the actual name of the motif, but it was usually played just before Siegfried ran into a hideous dragon or something. It did not bode well.

Courane's forced stroll through the woods was less interesting than the thing he eventually discovered, so briefly imagine for yourselves the serene yet oddly threatening surroundings. What grabbed Courane's attention some ten minutes later was a clearing in the trees, one no doubt invisible from either side of the turnpike proper. In the middle of the clearing was a small-to-moderate-sized gingerbread house. It was enough to bring him to a sudden halt. He didn't know quite how to proceed.

This wasn't what he expected, he thought. He'd been anticipating Lovecraftian horrors from beyond time and space, not semi-Disney fairy-tale props. Now, Courane was experienced enough to realize that although he was confronted with an innocent-seeming gingerbread house, and not some loathsome temple to a vile and nameless god, his life and possibly his very soul were in about the same amount of danger. He didn't need to go through an obligatory discovery scene to know that the gingerbread house was probably tenanted, and very likely occupied by a wicked old witch. In all his varied adventures, Courane had never come up against a wicked old witch. He wasn't absolutely certain of the protocols involved, and so he approached the house cautiously.

The one thing he did remember from childhood was that it was bad form to start pulling off delectable chunks of house and gorging himself, although it had been quite some time since he'd last eaten and he was feeling just on the near side of voracious. Instead, he went to the front door and looked for a knocker or bell. He saw neither. In for a penny, in for a pound, so he rapped sharply on the door, hoping to be heard by the unknown supernatural dweller within. "The Dweller Within." How apt a title. It's a shame, really, that this account already has a different and less melodramatic one.

Courane discovered immediately that rapping on gingerbread produced very little in the way of sound, so he called out in a quavering voice, "Hello?"

A few moments passed, during which Courane wondered about the wisdom of attracting the attention of a wicked old witch. He decided that the only alternative was to walk back to the useless car, or try to flag down a speeding motorist. The probable result of the latter plan was not pleasant to consider. Courane pictured himself flattened on the road's shoulder like a country possum. Or an armadillo. Every Texas armadillo ever seen has been sighted dead on the side of the road. Armadillos do not exist alive in nature.

"This adventure will go nowhere unless I make the acquaintance of this witch," he muttered to himself. Once again he called "Hello?"

"Coming, coming," replied a cracked and strident voice from within. "I was in the shower. Gimme a minute."

"No hurry," said Courane. He looked around himself, at the clearing and the gingerbread house. He knew a wiser hero would get the hell out of there while he still could. Siegfried wouldn't, but Courane always thought Siegfried was on the dim side, and look what happened to him.

The gingerbread door creaked open on marzipan hinges. An ancient woman peered out. She was small in stature, but an arcane wisdom of an unwholesome kind glittered in her black eyes. To be honest, Courane knew that he couldn't actually gauge arcane wisdom from a person's eyes, but he merely assumed a frightful knowledge went along with the gingerbread house and all the other trappings. "Yes?" said the wicked old witch.

Courane coughed to clear his throat. "Well, see, I wrecked my car a little way back, and I was wondering if I could use your phone to call AAA."

The old woman laughed. It was a cackle, of course. "Never had a phone. Never had a need for one. You're welcome to come inside and rest a spell, though."

"Thank you," said Courane.

"Haven't been munching on the house, have you?" asked the wicked old witch suspiciously.

"I know better than that."

The old woman nodded. She seemed resigned to his answer. "Expected as much. Don't get many callers these days, and those who do pass by are usually pretty well informed about the do's and don'ts." She stood aside and Courane moved past her into the dark, dangerous, sweet-smelling interior of the gingerbread house. Cottage, really. Think of it as a cottage.

What was a witch, really? wondered Courane. He looked around the dimly lighted gingerbread parlor. A witch was many things, he thought. A witch was a black cape and hood. A witch was a hooked nose with a large mole with bristly hairs sticking out of it. A witch was a multitalented broomstick leaning in a corner. A witch was the speaking partner of some sort of familiar.

Courane glanced about the cottage and saw nothing that answered the description of a familiar, but he suspected that it did not need to be a cat—it could be something as difficult to see in the gloom as an evil, croaking toad full of treachery, or a praying mantis with infernally red eyes burning in the shadows of a dirt-filled corner.

"It's so kind of you to visit me in my loneliness," said the witch in her fingernail-on-the-blackboard voice. There was silence in the gingerbread house, during which Courane realized that the sentiment precisely echoed the words of the Wicked Witch of the West, who survived her sister who'd been killed by Dorothy's falling house.

These witches were not like normal people. They could be almost immortal if they worked things right. Witches lived lives very different from the lives of the general population. There was no television here, no VCR, and Courane held the unsubstantiated belief that the witch didn't get out to a lot of neighborhood movies. That's why it seemed strange to him that the gingerbread lady would quote from *The Wizard of Oz*. How did she know what the Wicked Witch of the West had said? *Unless,* he thought suspiciously, *unless* they used to play two-handed canasta together a lot or something. He would need to tread cautiously here.

"Please make yourself comfortable," said the witch in a distracted voice. "I'm sorry, I'm trying to get my thoughts together. I can hardly remember the social conventions that govern the witch-trespasser relationship. It's been so long, you know."

"Well, I should apologize for this intrusion," said Courane.

"Oh, no, not at all. In itself, it's an essential factor leading to the union-mandated wickedness."

"Union? Witches have a union?"

The witch scowled. "We're *supposed* to. I pay my dues every year. They promised all kinds of benefits, but I never seen 'em. Still, it's an organization that allows for a certain amount of communication among the member witches, communication that wouldn't happen otherwise. I just wish the officers would worry more about what unions in other trades have fought for and won, instead of trivial matters like 'Who is rightwise a witch and who deserves to belong to the WSFA?' "

"It's the same all over," contributed Courane sagely.

"First you get the old, hard-line witches. They're annoyed by the young, disrespectful newcomers who want to change everything. I can understand the point of view of the longtime members. Na'theless, listening to the kids' arguments, sometimes I can sympathize with their feelings, too. Especially when they say the hard-liners no longer represent what is meant today by 'witch' and 'witchcraft.' "

"Times change," offered Courane wisely.

The wicked old witch shrugged. "I'm seasoned enough myself

to wish that they didn't. Change, I mean. Still, you can't hold back
progress, however so much you disapprove of what you see going
on. It's the same in music and literature, to take two examples, as
it is in the clothes people wear or the school of witchcraft they
subscribe to."

Courane's expression was less than a grimace, more than a
frown. "I think maturing is a constant process of waiting for one
dumb fashion after another to go away."

The witch very nearly smiled. "As you said, things change. If
we don't change with them, we're left behind by the times. We
become foolish relics, or else we drop out of society completely,
as I have, and end up someplace like this. You've got to admit
that the median strip of the Pennsylvania Turnpike is what you
might call *out of the cultural mainstream*."

Courane coughed nervously into his hand. "I'll go so far as to
say I never expected to find a gingerbread house and an orthodox
witch of the old school here, with cars and trucks zooming by
on either side. In the depths of some glowering, primeval forest,
maybe, but not here, along a major state thoroughfare."

Courane sat on a small davenport not much larger than a love
seat, really. The witch had long ago placed a large knitted doily
on the back, but Courane leaned forward, perched on the front
two or three inches of the cushions. He was still agitated despite
the witch's sentiments, and he could not relax.

Perhaps at this moment the average reader is thinking, "Worry
and timorousness will not improve Courane's circumstances. It
would certainly be better for him to sit back comfortably, get a
good grip on his nerves, and be open and receptive to whatever
happens."

Perhaps so. However, that was not Courane's way. He was
by nature a man frequently on the edge of nervous collapse.
Sometimes he panicked nearly to the same degree during the
Chicago Cubs' pregame interviews he watched on cable television. Telling him to chill out had no noticeable beneficial effect.
And this time, in the wicked old witch's gingerbread house, he
had a valid, legitimate cause for his barely suppressed terror.

Creeping into his conscious mind was the thought that he still
needed to relieve himself. That presented a frightening etiquette
problem, too. He wished he'd made more effective use of the
ten-minute walk through the woods; but no, that would have been
the smart thing to do. If there were a way to make an adventure

more desperate, Courane could be counted on to find it.

Moments of tense silence passed, as both the witch and Courane tried to pretend that nothing out of the ordinary was happening. Courane took note of the objects on the Eisenhower-era blond wood coffee table. There was a stack of magazines—*The New Yorker, Life,* and *Vanity Fair*—all yellowed, from the 1930s. To Courane's left was a chrome-plated, Art Deco nude woman holding up a shallow, chrome-plated bowl. In the bowl was an amethyst glass insert containing dusty, cellophane-wrapped cubes of caramel. To Courane's right was a milk-glass chicken sitting on a nest. The chicken separated from the nest about halfway down. Courane lifted the chicken to reveal a double handful of rock-hard, ruined spearmint leaves and petrified candy gumdrops of many flavors and ancient age. Courane replaced the top of the glass chicken carefully, trying to make not even the smallest sound.

"Help yourself," said the witch brightly. It was her first attempt at pleasantry with him. The result was not likely what she'd intended: he grew wary and on guard. It occurred to Courane that eating a spearmint leaf could well prove fatal, as these various sucroliths might conceivably come under the same prohibition as the gingerbread clapboards of the house's exterior.

Better safe than sorry, Courane told himself. He had vague, schoolboy memories of what had befallen the Greek goddess Persephone. Her annual four-month exile to the underworld had been the penalty for eating seven crummy pomegranate seeds given to her by Hades. Reading that myth in Mrs. Cooper's class had taught Courane that the judges of Hell did not grade on the curve.

The witch seated herself in a deep, dusty, old armchair. "You realize this is a no-win situation for me," she said in a weary voice.

"How do you mean?"

"Well, take a look at yourself. You're not what any witch would choose for a victim, are you? Nothing personal, after all, but if I bake you into a pie or shrivel, wither, and blister you beyond recognition, what do I stand to gain?"

She stared through the dismal dimness of her home and sighed. "It's not your fault, I understand that. The days when the fraternal twin children of local woodcutters would pass by to be tempted are long gone. No one appreciates a good gingerbread shingle anymore. I've been thinking of having the house done over, you know. Cover the outside with a good dark chocolate, I thought. A forward-looking, progressive idea. Even got estimates from the Godiva people and Frango of Marshall Field's in Chicago." She paused to cackle bitterly. "Maybe some plutocrat witch with a gingerbread town house on Fifth Avenue could afford it, but not I. Now were you a lissome princess with flowers in your hair, or a Hero on a great white charger, it would be worthwhile to trot out the complete shadow play of wicked witchery. As it is, you make a rather scanty victim, and I don't feel inspired to give it much more than the bare minimum."

Courane felt several emotions at once, ranging from disbelief to outrage. "Well, pardon *me,* then, madam," he said. "I apologize for not being a pair of prepubic kids lost in the muttering forest. I'm a grown man and you'll just have to deal with it. You can't always get what you want, you know. I'm not overwhelmingly thrilled about being here in the first place, if I may speak freely. After a lifetime of hearing witch stories, I must admit that I'm somewhat disappointed. The terror I might have expected is completely absent. If you don't mind, I have a wrecked car that needs attention. I suppose I'll have to flag down another driver after all. I'd hoped to avoid that."

Courane stood up and took a couple of steps. "Wait," cried the wicked old witch in her hoarse voice. "I said that you'd make an unrewarding victim, but I didn't say that I'd let you walk away scot-free. I can't do that. Tradition, you see. And union rules."

Courane sat down again on the antique davenport. "I'm an unrewarding victim, and you're a pretty poor excuse for a witch. We're made for each other."

"So sad, really," she said. "This is what I've come to."

"This is what *I've* come to," said Courane. They stared at each other for a while in the growing darkness. The only sounds were the gingerbread and candy fixtures contracting as the heat of the day began to dissipate.

Finally, Courane spoke. "Well, what the hell *are* you and your gingerbread house doing on the median strip of the Pennsylvania Turnpike?"

"You're bleeding. Did you know your face is bleeding?" asked the witch.

" 'S nothing. Hit a tree."

"Well, let me take care of it." She got slowly and painfully to her feet and crossed the parlor to look closely into Courane's face. She touched him lightly on the neck and shoulders. "Does this hurt?"

"Yes, a little."

The wicked old witch nodded. She began to murmur, almost under her breath. Courane couldn't make out any words. It sounded like a chant. Or a spell—that was it, it was a magical spell. It would either ease his discomfort or turn him into a bewildered amphibian. Or both at once.

"It was several decades ago, before you were born," said the witch, digging into the grimy apron she wore around her waist. She brought out a tin of salve that looked as if she'd bought it outside the courthouse of the Scopes Monkey Trial. "I'd been living in this house for almost a hundred years. At that time, this was a great, lovely, ancient forest. Now hold still."

Courane tried to keep from flinching as the witch applied a thin layer of salve to his cuts and bruises. He was amazed when the pain vanished almost as soon as her fingers touched him. "So you had this gingerbread house here even before, say, the Civil War?"

The witch nodded. "I gave some thought to being a station along the route of the Underground Railway. As a political statement, it wouldn't have given me any personal difficulty. However, I was a great deal younger than, and a great deal more wicked. I was more active in union business, and I was informed that what I was considering was unwitchlike. So I just came back to the house and followed the course of history from my lonely outpost in the woods. Take off your shirt."

Courane did as he was told, and she applied the salve to his neck, shoulders, and back. The whiplash pain went away immediately. "I wish I could help you somehow," he said softly.

The witch replaced the lid on the salve and dropped the tin back into her apron. "Well," she said thoughtfully, "what do you do for a living?"

"I sell aluminum siding," he said.

"Uh-huh. Aluminum siding on a gingerbread house. Just what I need."

"I'm sorry," said Courane. He'd rarely felt so useless.

"So some years ago, the state decides it's going to build a great highway linking the New York State Thruway to the Ohio

Turnpike. It meant blasting tunnels through mountains and cutting down huge swaths of virgin woodland. Used to be a magic forest around here, with all kinds of supernatural critters about, elves and trolls and whatnot. And the humans lived in their frail little cabins and respected us. Not the state of Pennsylvania, though. All they cared about in Harrisburg was the highway. My friends moved away, but I couldn't. I had too much invested in gingerbread. I was stuck. They ripped down the trees to the left of me for the westbound lanes and trees to the right of me for eastbound traffic. As luck would have it, they never even discovered that I was here."

"I feel great," said Courane wonderingly. "How can a topical salve cure bone and muscle injuries?"

"It's a secret combination of seventeen herbs and spices," said the witch. "Anyway, this median strip is all that remains of that magic forest. And me. I'm still here."

Courane wore a thoughtful expression as he put his shirt back on. He didn't like the sticky feeling of the shirt on his back. It reminded him of when he was a kid, when his mother used to smear Vicks VapoRub on his chest, and then he'd have to wear his flannel pajamas over it.

"Ever thought of leaving?" he asked.

"Leaving?" said the witch. She sounded shocked. "Leave my gingerbread house? Leave the forest?"

Courane shrugged. "You said yourself nobody passes by much anymore. When was the last time you baked someone in a pie? Or ground somebody's bones to make your bread?"

"That's giants," she said, drawing herself up haughtily. "There are clear rules about that sort of thing. Why, if the WSFA ever found out that I'd ground somebody's bones to make my bread, the word would get out, and I'd have to deal with the giants' union, too. Not me, sir. I'm an honest witch, I am."

"And lonely, too."

She looked at him for several seconds before she replied. "And lonely. And exhausted. And not particularly wicked anymore, if the truth be known." There was a long silence again. It had become dark in the parlor. "I suppose I could consider moving, if I had somewhere to go," she said at last.

"I'll tell you what," said Courane. "I'm heading east. I was going to New York City, but I could make a little detour. To the Jersey Shore. You'd love the Jersey Shore. It's mile after mile of boardwalk and beach, and mile after mile of concession stands and pinball arcades and all kinds of things like that. I was thinking—"

"I could open up a little business," said the witch, testing out the idea.

"I was thinking you could open up a little business, right there on the boardwalk in Asbury Park."

"Madame Mimi's Tarot Den," she said, a little excitement in her voice. "Fortunes told, palms read, that sort of thing. And if blond brother and sister twins happen by, why, I could just pop them into my oven, just for old times' sake, and—"

"I'm not sure about that last part," said Courane. "But I don't think you'd have a problem opening a fortune-telling booth on the boardwalk. I think you'd be a big hit. And the change would do wonders for you."

"Could do with a change," she said. "And I could always come back to the gingerbread house whenever I wanted. It would be safe. I mean, you're the first person who's happened by in ages. I don't need much time to pack. How long will it take us to get to Asbury Park?"

Courane chewed his lower lip. "There is the matter of the car," he said finally. "It's smashed up against a tree. I don't even know if it can be fixed."

"Don't worry about that," said the witch confidently. "The salve will fix anything. We'll just rub it on the car, and it'll be as good as new."

"Jeez," said Courane, for the first time realizing that he might make it out of this story alive. "I'll be glad to have the company, too."

"Facing the world again is kind of intimidating," she said, "but change means growth, and I think I was just stagnating here. I've got the guts to try it, if you do."

"Just rub the salve on the car, then?" he asked. Courane felt through the gloom until he found her in her chair. "How's your night vision? Will you be able to see the car in the darkness?"

The witch cackled. "I won't, but my familiar, Monica, will. Hold out your hand."

Courane extended his hand nervously. He felt the witch put something into it. Whatever it was, it crawled around for a few moments and then jumped away.

"Minor demon, no trouble," said the witch. "Then it's all settled. We should celebrate or something. Come on, have a Collie Bar. It's on the house. No strings."

Courane took the candy bar and began to unwrap it. How odd, he thought. The story was just about finished and he was still a—

Talk Radio

✧

by
Jack McDevitt

Technology hasn't solved our storage problems: it's just enabled us to handle the far greater volume of material that modern society threatens to drown us in. First we had cave walls, then mud tablets. Papyrus was a great improvement, and subsequently paper. Printing made mass distribution of information available to the general population for the first time.

But these developments allowed only for promulgation of the printed word. The modern era has provided us with the means to make portable images and sounds in addition to words. Radio, television, film, CDs, and tape allow the transmission of visuals, voices, and music as well as words.

There's so much sheer information floating about these days that we need computers just to keep track of what's available. With so much material about it's not surprising that bits and pieces get dumped or forgotten or misplaced.

"Fort Moxie is *not* stuck in 1948, Kathie. Just because we don't have drugs and crime, people come up here and make jokes about us. If your last caller doesn't like it here, why doesn't he go back to Minneapolis?"

—You sound a trifle miffed, Hal.—

"Well, I get tired of people talking about us as if we roll the streets in at nine. They don't mind taking our money."

19

—All right, Hal. Let me ask you a question. And I want an honest answer.—

"Okay."

—Honest, now.—

"You got it."

—Do you really believe that life along the Canadian border is exciting? *Really*?—

"Sure do. We got the best hunting in the world. Gabe's is the best bar. We got the most interesting people. And we got the End-of-the-World Call-in Show."

—Well, thanks, Hal. I can see you're a person of exquisite taste. I've lived in New York, Boston, and D.C., and I wouldn't go back to any of them. Ever. In the end, it's a matter of taste. I *like* living on the high plains, I like solitude, and I can't imagine living anyplace else. This, incidentally, is KMOX, eleven-forty on your dial, Fort Moxie, North Dakota. It is three minutes after nine, and the lines are open. Phone 555-1738. Hello, Jennifer, over at City Hall.—

"Hi, Kathie. Nice to have you back."

—Thanks.—

"I thought your listeners might want to know that the semian-nual meeting of the Woodwind Society is being held here tonight. In case anyone wants to stop by."

—What is the Woodwind Society?—

"We're a musical appreciation group."

—What do you do at your meetings?—

"Tonight, we're discussing Vivaldi. And I know how that sounds. But he's actually very passionate."

—If you say so.—

"What I'd really like to do, though, is get them turned onto the New Age."

—Where are you now?—

"City Hall."

—I understand that. But you can't be in the meeting room.—

"No, I'm in charge of refreshments. I'm in the kitchen."

—Well, Jennifer, if you really want to introduce the Wood-winds to something new, stay close tonight. Okay?—

"Sure."

—Now I've got something to tell you. I was coming back through Bemidji yesterday, and I stopped at an estate sale and picked up a set of antique music boxes.—

"Music boxes isn't exactly what I had in mind, Kathie."

—*These* music boxes might be. I've mentioned on this show that I have a passion for anything that's old. Clocks. Lamps. Books. Whatever. I have two rooms full of the stuff at home. So I couldn't resist stopping. Truth is, though, I don't like estate sales very much. Wheeling and dealing with the bits and pieces of somebody's life. You know what I mean. And most of it goes for nickels and dimes. That's a *terrible* thing when you think about it: things that were priceless to the owner are sold off as junk. They depress me, but not enough to keep me from taking advantage of one. Anyway, I picked up a beautiful set of twelve onyx music boxes. Black, and engraved.—

"*Engraved* music boxes?"

—Yes. And these are music boxes with a kick. They produce sound like my Bose 601s. I haven't figured out the mechanics of them yet. I would have to take one apart to do that, and I'm reluctant. Anyhow, it's all New Age stuff: rainstorms, thundering herds, distant drums, falling snow. Strings and electronics and stuff unlike anything I've ever heard before. You set this up for the Woodwind folks, and it'll blow them out of their socks.—

"Thanks. I will."

—In fact, I think it's time to play one now. Several of the boxes are dented, crunched up a little, but they all seem to work. Now I know you think I'm exaggerating, but just settle in and hold onto something. This is New Age with a full throat. You won't believe it's coming out of a music box, but it is, so please don't call me and tell me I'm crazy, okay? I wouldn't lie to you. Now the one problem here is that we can't go on-line with them. There's no output port anywhere on these things. So I'm just going to set them in front of the microphone. First up is a set of three boxes bearing the overall title *Hymns of the Creation.* [*Music begins.*] They're titled "First Sunrise on the Aegean," "Lizard Beach," and "Paleolithic Campfire." You're listening to "Lizard Beach."—

"Wallbanger, this is Redeye. You on the circuit, old buddy?"

"Yo, I'm here. You through customs yet?"

"Yeah. The Bitch is on tonight. Boy, she really likes to harass me. I can't believe that woman."

"She hassles everybody, Clyde. I don't mind much, though. She's good to look at."

(*Unintelligible.*)

"I know what you mean, Clyde. Hey, what have you got, a storm up there?"

"Nah. It's the radio."

"Radio? Goddamn, you must be deaf."

"Yeah, I guess it *is* a little loud. It's a talk show, mostly. KMOX. I'm passing the station now."

"Is that the place that sits on the hill overtop the graveyard?"

"Yeah. That's it. Where you wanna meet?"

"How about Sonny's?"

"Okay. I'll be there in about an hour and a half."

"Jesus, Martie."

"What's the matter?"

"I got it here. Your radio station. That *is* goddamn far-out stuff."

Transcript of radio communication between the Fort Moxie Border Station and Border Patrol Unit Kilo 17, October 18 last, 9:11 p.m.

Fort Moxie:	Shep, we've got a run-through.
Patrol:	I'm nine miles west on 11. On my way, Judy.
Fort Moxie:	That's a roger.
Patrol:	Got a vehicle description?
Fort Moxie:	Not sure it *is* a vehicle.
Patrol:	Say again.
Fort Moxie:	It doesn't exactly move like a vehicle.
Patrol:	Judy—
Fort Moxie:	Uh, it's big, and it's off the road, behind the tree screen. Hard to see exactly what it is. Henry's out trying to get a look at it.
Patrol:	It must be moving pretty slow if Henry can chase it down on foot.
Fort Moxie:	That's what's so strange about it. In the dark, we can't even tell how far it is.
Patrol:	Can you see Henry?
Fort Moxie:	I can see his light moving out in the trees.
Patrol:	Okay.
Fort Moxie:	It *has* to be a tractor trailer. It's too big to be anything else. Listen, we're getting some traffic. I have to get outside.
Patrol:	Yeah. You know, Judy, I wouldn't have

thought— [*His comments are interrupted by
the clear rattle of gunfire, and the sound of
people shouting.*]

Fort Moxie: Jesus. That's Henry.
Patrol: Be careful. I'll be there in a few minutes.
Fort Moxie: Yeah. Station out.

*Transcript of telephone conversation between Michael Kotch,
who farms north of Route 11 just outside Fort Moxie, and the
police dispatcher for Cavalier County, North Dakota, October
18, 9:14 p.m.*

Kotch: Hey, Andy, what the hell's going on?
Dispatcher: What are we talking about, Mike?
Kotch: The goddamn earthquake. How bad is it?
Dispatcher: What earthquake?
Kotch: Son of a bitch, Andy. Everything's shaking out
                 here. If it ain't a quake, I sure as hell don't wanna
                 be here when we get one.
Dispatcher: I'll check on it.
Kotch: Yeah. Let me know, willya?

U.S. BORDER PATROL
Incident Report

2126. ARRIVED FORT MOXIE BORDER STATION IN RESPONSE
TO REQUEST FOR ASSISTANCE RUN-THROUGH 2111 THIS DATE.
SURVEILLANCE OF STATE HIGHWAY 11 INDICATES NO ACTIV-
ITY. NO DESCRIPTION SUBJECT VEHICLE. ASSUME RETURNED TO
CANADA. CI HENRY TASKER IS MISSING. AM ASSISTING IN SEARCH.
9200001544882.

*Transcript of telephone conversation between police dispatcher
for Cavalier County, and Mark Wainwright, Producer, KMOX,
9:27 p.m.*

Dispatcher: Mark, have you guys had any calls tonight about
                 an earthquake?
Wainwright: An earthquake? Where?
Dispatcher: Out at Mike Kotch's place. And Margaret
                 Banford, up the road, says her house is shaking.
Wainwright: You send a car up?
Dispatcher: Tod's on his way. You haven't heard anything, huh?

Wainwright: No. Nothing here.
Dispatcher: Okay. Thought I'd check.

"Hey, Kathie, that was really alive. Know what I mean?
"That really came out of a box, huh? Doesn't sound possible.
You going to play the rest of them?"
—Some tonight. Some tomorrow.—
"What's next up?"
—Well, I was thinking about "Street Scene from Ur." But I
think we need a little sex on the show tonight. First, though, let's
break away for a few commercials.—

*Transcript of radio conversation between Officer Tod Banik
and the police dispatcher for Cavalier County, 9:35 p.m.*

Banik: Everything's quiet at Kotch's place. But *some-
              thing* happened here. He's got a smashed tool-
              shed, and there are big holes all over his prop-
              erty.
Dispatcher: *Holes?*
Banik: Holes. Ditches. Whatever. Right through the
              wheat fields. Listen, they're all about the same
              size, maybe a foot or two deep, and as big around
              as the cruiser.
Dispatcher: No idea what they are?
Banik: No. But I think we might want to send somebody
              up in the morning to get a look at them from
              the air.
Dispatcher: Why?
Banik: [*Hesitates*] Andy, they look like *footprints.*

*Transcript of telephone conversation between Mrs.
Agatha Willey and the police dispatcher for Cavalier County,
9:43 p.m.*

Mrs. Willey: [*Agitated*] Andy, something's happened over
              at the Tastee-Freez.
Dispatcher: Okay, Agatha, why don't you compose yourself
              and tell me what's bothering you?
Mrs. Willey: Bobby and Carol came home *screaming* a few
              minutes ago. They went over to get some
              milkshakes. At the Tastee-Freez—and they said
              a dragon attacked it.

Dispatcher:	A *dragon*?
Mrs. Willey:	That's what they said.
Dispatcher:	Attacked the *Tastee-Freez*?
Mrs. Willey:	Andy, a half dozen kids were running through the street. I walked over: the place is in ruins, and if you want the truth, it *does* look a bit chewed on.
Dispatcher:	What does Amelia say?
Mrs. Willey:	Don't know. Bobby tells me she was the first one to take off.

—Okay, I'm back, folks. And let's lead this segment of the show off with "Siren Song" . . . Wait a minute, they're signaling me that we're going to cut away to a news break. Adrian Carr is out at the Tastee-Freez with the KMOX news team. Okay, Adrian, what have we got?—

Extract from the minutes of the Woodwind Society, meeting in the community room at City Hall, Fort Moxie, October 18.

Mr. Cicotti's views on the use of counterpoint, and the subsequent juxtaposition of dissonance during Vivaldi's later period so enraged Mr. Armstrong that Mr. Armstrong pronounced himself "completely out of sorts," and went on to declare loudly that Mr. Cicotti was a "coconuthead." Mr. Cicotti replied, with heat, that he had "no intention of standing for that kind of talk from a tone-deaf chiropractor," and demanded an apology. The two might have come to blows, but fortunately cooler heads prevailed, and, at 9:52 P.M., we adjourned for refreshments.

—Jason Avery, Secretary

—Latest word, folks, is that no one was injured at the Tastee-Freez tonight. Police now theorize that the building was struck by a hit-and-run. They have asked us to reassure all the children out there that there's no dragon running loose in Fort Moxie tonight. In an unrelated story, a customs officer apparently wandered off and got lost tonight. Customs officials have mounted a search for the missing man. No details yet on that. They have not released his name. [*Music begins.*] Now we go to the wine-dark sea and spend some time with the Sirens. If you listen closely, by the way, you can hear the sea and the wind. And the rocks. Most of all, the rocks.—

*   *   *

"Hey, Clyde. What do you think happened to the Tastee-Freez?"

"A-rabs, Martie, what else? Dumb bastards probably got through the border with something, and blew themselves up."

"You think Arab terrorists eat ice cream?"

"Why not? They're just like everybody else."

"Yeah. I guess so. You don't buy the hit-and-run, huh?"

"Hell, no. The Tastee-Freez is on the edge of town. Near the ball field. Lot of visibility. Couldn't no truck knock the damn thing down and not have somebody see it."

"Yeah. I guess not."

"Goddamn sonuvabitch, you bastard."

"What, Clyde? What's the matter?"

"Guy in a Ford station wagon just threw on his brakes in front of me."

"They're all over the road anymore. Damn dingdongs."

"He pulled off back there. Jesus H. Christ. I don't believe this."

"What?

"He's throwing a goddamn U-turn. He's going north in the southbound lane. Look at that dumb sonuvabitch."

"Truculent, this is Moxie. You there tonight?"

"Moxie, this is Truculent. Sorry I'm late. Big date night for Louisa. But she had a fight with the guy and I had to go get her."

"Everything okay now, Evelyn?"

"Yeah. She's fine. The boyfriend's a turkey and I think she's finally figured it out. And I hope she's discovered the advantage of carrying mad money. How's everything up on the border?"

"About the same as usual. We've got a crime wave in progress. Some kids drove around town last night ripping open bags of leaves and dumping them all over the streets."

"And—?"

"That's it. Pretty wild stuff for Fort Moxie. Wait a minute—"

"What was *that*?"

"A crash. Sounds like an accident outside. Listen, I'll get back to you."

RCMP transcript of radio communication between Constable Joseph L. Hotchkiss and the duty officer at the Emerson, Manitoba, detachment, 10:02 p.m.

Hotchkiss: I've got a speeder. Clocked at eighty-eight coming south out of Morris. White 1990 Honda
                Accord, Manitoba plate 3XG1154. In pursuit
                on 75.

Duty Officer: Running Manitoba three xray golf one one five
                four.

Hotchkiss: He's not slowing down. Better alert Rod.

Duty Officer: Negative on your speeder. No prior. We'll intercept north of Emerson.

Hotchkiss: My God. What the hell—?

Duty Officer: What is it, Joe? What's wrong?

Hotchkiss: I've got another one coming up behind me.
                Black Jag. The sonuvabitch is trying to pass
                me.

Extract from the minutes of the Woodwind Society.

. . . Mr. Casey Roil, who has traditionally championed conservative causes, chose the rather delicate moment of the collision
between Mrs. Vestible and Mr. Heyer to change sides. At the
height of the melee, he rose to speak, and so somber was his
appearance that all fell silent. "After long and careful consideration," he said, in a voice ringing with emotion, "I can no
longer stand aside. It should be clear to anyone who examines
the matter dispassionately that Vivaldi's *Four Seasons* is hopelessly mechanical." Mr. Heyer clapped him on the back, and
Mrs. Vestible had to be assisted back to her chair. The general
commotion rose to a roar, and the Moderator rapped energetically
for order.

                                        —Jason Avery, Secretary

"It's a wreck, Evelyn. But I sure can't figure it. I know both
cars: Mark Epworth's little red Buick and Tommy Carlisle's
Ford pickup. They're both pretty well smashed. Mark and Tommy
were out arguing when I got up there. You know, about whose
fault it was. Then Tommy got back into his pickup, but the front
axle's bent, I think. He couldn't get it running. So he climbed
back out. Mark by then had walked away. Toward the west side
of town. Tommy followed him."

"And—?"

"That's it. They're both gone. There's a radio playing in one of the cars, but other than that, they've been left."

"They must have gone to call the police."

"I guess. But there's a pay phone in the Amoco. They walked right by it."

Transcript of radio communication between Trooper Al Sakwith and Sergeant Mary Trevor, of the North Dakota Highway Patrol, 10:43 p.m.

Sakwith: This is the worst traffic jam I've ever seen up here, Mary. We've had speeders, people traveling north in the southbound lanes, people throwing U-turns. I'm amazed no one's been killed.

Trevor: Probably because everything's moving so slow up there. Listen, I'm sending Archie to help. Try to get it straightened out, huh?

Sakwith: Yeah.

Trevor: What's the matter? You sound funny.

Sakwith: Well, I've talked to a few of these guys.

Trevor: And—?

Sakwith: They're all *guys,* by the way. And they all seem to be going to the same place.

Trevor: Where?

Sakwith: Fort Moxie.

Trevor: Fort Moxie. Why?

Sakwith: They don't really want to tell me. Just out for a ride. No big thing. But it seems odd.

Trevor: Yeah. I'll let Cavalier know. They might want to put a car over there just in case.

"Evelyn, there's something else going on that I don't understand."

"What's that?"

"There's a lot of traffic tonight out on Cemetery Road."

"Is that unusual?"

"There's nothing out there except the cemetery. And the radio station. But there must be twenty cars on that road. They're completely snarled up. Nothing's moving. And that's the direction Mark and Tommy were headed. I wonder what's going on?"

Transcript of radio communication between the Fort Moxie Border Station and Border Patrol Unit Kilo 17, 10:46 p.m.

Fort Moxie:	We got another one, Shep.
Patrol:	Ah, come *on*, Judy. That's eleven. In the last fifteen minutes.
Fort Moxie:	He rolled through here at seventy. Late-model blue Saab. Manitoba plate xray seven seven one alpha four. I'm watching him now. He's slowing down, just like the others. Going to turn off at Fort Moxie. Yep, there he goes. Right at you, Shep.
Patrol:	Okay. I've got some help here now. We'll get him.
Fort Moxie:	What's happening, Shep? Where are they all going?
Patrol:	You ready for this? They're all males, and they're after Kathie Cross.
Fort Moxie:	*Who?*
Patrol:	Kathie Cross. Runs a talk show. Anyway, if any of these guys get loose, I'd say she's in for an interesting night.

Transcript of telephone conversation between Mark Wainwright of KMOX and the police dispatcher for Cavalier County, 10:48 p.m.

Wainwright:	Son of a bitch, Andy, we need some help here.
Dispatcher:	I know, Mark. We're doing everything we can.
Wainwright:	[*Sound of glass shattering*] The situation here is deteriorating. Where's the help you promised me? Chasing the goddamn dragon?
Dispatcher:	Tod's stuck in traffic. There must be eighty cars on Cemetery. What do they want?
Wainwright:	Kathie, I think.
Dispatcher:	It's going to turn out to be a communication problem. They probably think you're giving away free vacations to the first person to show up and claim one. You got a spot somewhere that might lead them to think something like that?
Wainwright:	[*The unmistakable screech of wood splintering, followed by a cheer*] Jesus, they're breaking down the doors.
Dispatcher:	Okay. Look, you got a place that's safe? That you can get into and lock?

Wainwright: The studios are up on the second floor, in the rear. I can lock them.

Dispatcher: Who else is in the building tonight?

Wainwright: Kathie.

Dispatcher: That all?

Wainwright: That's all. Why? You want to be able to identify the bodies?

Dispatcher: Lock yourself in back there. I don't think you got anything to worry about. These people seem to be out to have a good time. Border Patrol's out there too. It may not seem like it to you, but the crowd seems more excited than dangerous. Just keep out of sight until we get to you.

Wainwright: Okay. And if I see any of them in party hats [*He is interrupted by another crash, louder than the first. And by prolonged cheering. Distinctly audible in all of this is Kathie's name, which seems to ignite wild applause*], I'll let you know—
               [*Connection goes dead*]

—Hello, Janet from Winnipeg.—

"I just wanted to tell you I'm really enjoying the music boxes. Do you have any idea where I might get copies of what you've been playing?"

—No. I have no idea at all. But if anyone out there knows, or has heard any of these productions before, why don't you give us a call?—

"What's next?"

—To tell you the truth, I'm not sure. There's something going on outside . . . What's that, Mark . . . ? Okay, ladies and gentlemen, I am informed there is a major disturbance out on the parking lot. If any of you people are listening to me, please go home. Police are on their way. Is this for real, Mark? You really don't know what's going on out there? Well, this has been one hell of a night. Incidentally, there is still no word on the missing customs inspector. Okay. The show goes on, right, Janet? Let's see what's up next. Here's one called "Water Songs of Enlil." That sounds dull. How about "The Ride of the Valkyries?"—

"You've finally picked out one I've heard of."

—I don't think so. This isn't Wagner. I doubt you've ever ridden with these Valkyries. But I think we'll save it for another night. And here's one called "Party at Tenochtitlán."—

"Sounds Aztec."

—Yeah. Well, if this is a sample, the Aztecs really knew how to celebrate. Well, let's try the "Nupe Fertility Rite."—

"Guaranteed to turn you on."

—No. Not everybody. I suspect it'll only work on females.—

"Why's that?"

—Because males have no off switch to start with. Bear with me, guys, I know that was bad . . . Wait a minute, Adrian Carr is out on the KMOX parking lot. Adrian, what's going on?—

"HI, KATHIE. YOU WOULDN'T RECOGNIZE THIS PLACE. WE'VE GOT WRECKED CARS EVERYWHERE. COUPLE OF THEM EVEN WENT INTO THE CEMETERY. WHAT'S HAPPENING, THOUGH, IS KIND OF HARD TO DESCRIBE. THE MOB HAS BEEN TRYING TO BREAK INTO THE BUILDING. INTO THE KMOX OFFICES."

—Why?—

"DON'T KNOW. I'VE TRIED TALKING TO SOME OF THEM, BUT NO ONE SEEMS TO HAVE ANY IDEA WHY THERE'S A MOB HERE. THE ONES I TALKED TO SAID THEY HAD COME TO SEE YOU. ANYWAY, THEY *DID* GET IN A FEW MINUTES AGO. BUT IT LOOKS AS IF THE ONES WHO GOT IN HAVE BEEN TRYING TO KEEP EVERYBODY ELSE OUT. THERE'S A LOT OF PUSHING AND SHOVING BY THE FRONT ENTRANCE, AND MEN ARE TRYING TO CLIMB THROUGH WINDOWS ON THE SIDE OF THE BUILDING. THEY'RE MEETING RESISTANCE FROM SOMEBODY INSIDE. BY THE WAY, THERE'S A SMALL PLANE BUZZING US. CAN YOU HEAR IT? IT'S BEEN DROPPING FLOWERS FOR THE LAST FEW MINUTES. I DON'T UNDERSTAND THIS AT ALL, KATHIE. POLICE HAVE ARRIVED AND BEGUN TO MAKE ARRESTS."

—Can we talk to one of these people? Find out what's happening?—

"OKAY, LET'S TRY ANOTHER ONE. HERE'S A YOUNG MAN WITH A GHETTO BLASTER. YOU, SIR. CAN WE TALK FOR A MOMENT?"

(*Feedback from the radio. A loud, slightly skewed voice replies:*) "I'm busy right now, buddy."

"CAN I ASK YOU TO TURN DOWN YOUR RADIO, PLEASE?"

"You're kind of pushy, aren't you, pal?"

"WHY ARE YOU HERE?"

"I don't think that's any of your business, is it? Say, are you the radio reporter? Adrian what's-his-name?"

"ADRIAN CARR. KATHIE, THE PLANE IS TRYING TO LAND. IT'S COMING DOWN IN A WHEAT FIELD."

"You're talking to Kathie Cross, aren't you? Kathie, I'm coming to get you."

—Adrian . . . —

"THANK YOU VERY MUCH, SIR."

"I love you, Kathie Cross, and nothing can ever change that."

"THIS IS ADRIAN CARR ON THE KMOX PARKING LOT."

"I'm on my way."

"BACK TO YOU, KATHIE."

(*Silence.*)

—Uh, Mark . . . What is our situation? [*Another long pause, of about a minute.*] Okay, they are telling me the police think this is a good-natured crowd. They *are* into the building, but they seem not to have come upstairs. Yet. I guess we'll be staying with this breaking story whether we want to or not. [*Music begins.*] Boy, this is sure one for the books. Let's try to forget what's going on out here, put the kids to bed and make for moonlit jungles, passionate drums, and wild times. Well, under the circumstances, that might not be such a good idea. Anyway, next up: "Nupe Fertility Rite."—

Transcript of radio communication between Fort Moxie Border Station and Border Patrol Unit Kilo 17, 11:16 p.m.

Fort Moxie:	This may be a little premature, but I think they've stopped coming.
Patrol:	I'm glad to hear it. We've got nineteen aliens down here that we'll be bringing back to you for processing. Soon as I figure out the mechanics of it.
Fort Moxie:	Okay. Let us know if there's anything we can do to help.
Patrol:	Right. Put up a barricade. Have you guys found Henry yet?
Fort Moxie:	Just his gun. Five shots fired.

| Patrol: | Nothing else? |
| Fort Moxie: | A shoe. |

Extract from the minutes of the Woodwind Society.

We had just completed a discussion of the role of the piccolo in Vivaldi's "Spring" from the *Four Seasons* when Mrs. Jennifer Rickett announced it as her opinion that the classical composers were "all right within the limitations of instruments then available, but modern technology has widened our horizons," and that modern composers are producing more powerful creations. To prove her contention, she proposed to turn her radio on to KMOX, which was then (she said) playing a composition that would demonstrate her point. She then did so. Other members immediately protested that the action had not been voted nor authorized. Mr. Harkness of Drayton responded that the members would never allow it, and that the Society was composed of persons "who think no compelling piece of music has been written since the latter part of the nineteenth century." The discussion grew intense, and Mrs. Rickett increased the volume of the broadcast. Mr. Daniel Philips, one of the Charter Members, attempted to seize the instrument. And then a curious thing happened: Mrs. Louis Ponnicelli climbed onto a conference table and pinned the male members with an expression one can only describe as lascivious, and began to move with the music. At this, there were further protests. But Mrs. Ponnicelli, increasing her RPMs (so to speak), began fingering the buttons of her blouse. She removed it, and threw it in the general direction of Mr. Quimby. We were, to say the least, nonplussed.

—Jason Avery, Secretary

Transcript of radio conversation between Officer Tod Banik and the Police Dispatcher for Cavalier County, 11:21 p.m.

Dispatcher:	Tod, how are you coming up there?
Banik:	It's quieted down now, Andy. They're all standing around, looking dazed.
Dispatcher:	Okay. Listen, turn it over to Horace, okay? And get down to City Hall.
Banik:	[*Sighs*] What the hell is it now?
Dispatcher:	The Woodwind meeting has turned into a riot.
Banik:	You're nuts.
Dispatcher:	Or an orgy. Depends on which account you

believe. And be careful: it's apparently spilled
out into the street.

—We're moving down into the final segment of the Late-Night
End-of-the-World Call-in Show. The parking lot looks quiet at
last, the cemetery stones are white in the moonlight, and the
world is back to normal. [*Music begins.*] Now, folks, to finish
off the evening: "The Cry of the Phoenix."—

Deal with the Devil

✧

by
Nina Kiriki Hoffman

If witches have been and continue to be a staple of fantasy tales, their erstwhile boss St. Nick (alias Beelzebub, Mephistopheles, Satan, Lucifer, He-Who-Paints-Pictures-of-Children-With-Exophthalmic-Eyes, and Lord of the Nether Regions, which is not to be confused with South Los Angeles) is still more frequently employed.

Certainly he's a favorite with writers. How many stories featuring St. Nick were submitted to this anthology I can't begin to tell you. Sometimes the Prince of Darkness came out on top, sometimes he lost. Usually the stories weren't very inventive, which is too bad since that's a quality most people usually ascribe to the Devil.

I'm not sure who wins in this one.

"You can do anything? And you want my soul for it?" She pulled the ashtray across the Formica tabletop, settled it in front of her, and stubbed out her cigarette. A moment later, she blew her last lungful of smoke in his direction.

"I can give you anything your heart desires," he said. He smiled, a dimple appearing in his right cheek.

"Anything?"

"Anything. The world can be your oyster. Money, fame, love, success, power."

"I don't like oysters. Could you—save the whales? For the rest of eternity?"

"Uh—"

"Could you prevent nuclear war, preserve the earth and all its species in a balanced ecosystem in perpetuity, make all industries clean forever, and yet still productive, so there would be no more toxic chemical waste, no more acid rain? Could you change all cars to run off a fuel that doesn't pollute the atmosphere, and is plentiful enough and accessible enough so that its collection and processing will support all the people who now work for the oil companies? Could you give everyone on earth enough self-esteem so they can live contented and fulfilling lives? Could you restyle the food distribution so everyone has enough to eat, and inspire people to build homes so everyone who wants it has some shelter, without killing any more old-growth forests? Could you preserve all the national parklands from depredation eternally and still balance the budget of the world? Could you fix it so all these changes work to the best advantage of everybody, and I mean every man, woman, child, animal and plant and even rock on this planet, those alive now, and those alive tomorrow, and ensure that these changes continue to work for the good of everybody, now and always?"

He thought for a long moment. She watched his eyes flicker. Faint red light shone sometimes, and sometimes flashes of white. At last he faced her again. "Yes," he said. "I think I can handle all that."

"I want one more thing," she said.

"Oh, come on."

"You said anything."

He stirred the coffee in his white foam cup with his index finger. Steam rose from the cup. "Go on," he said.

"I want another soul in exchange for the one you take from me. I want the best soul you've dealt for so far, and I want it to be mine for as long as I need it—my definition of needing it, not yours."

"Lady, you charge too much," he said. He drank down his black coffee and set the foam cup on the table. When he let go of it, it was a charred black blob.

"You said anything."

"I lied. I have that reputation, you know."

"And I have a tape recorder. The spoken word is a binding

verbal contract. I'll see you in court, Nick."

"I'll see you in hell first!" he said, and vanished.

She lit another cigarette, and smoked quietly for a while. Around her, customers came and went in the diner. Somebody punched up "Wimeweh" on the jukebox. She stared at the glowing ember on the end of her cigarette. "A nonsmoking soul," she muttered, "was that too much to ask?"

Final Solution

by
Mike Resnick

Everyone knows good ol' Mike Resnick. He's the father of that famous author, Laura Resnick. When not basking in his daughter's fame, Mike occasionally turns out a tale or two of his own. Simple, easygoing, harmless amusements, the kind you never have to think about or that don't trouble you with the world's endless problems. Tales that hardly touch upon matters of real concern.
Like this one.

It started with the Jews.

One day they announced that they were emigrating to the world of New Jerusalem. Just like that. Not even so much as a by-your-leave.

"We are tired of being underappreciated and overpersecuted," said their statement. "We gave you the Old Testament and the Ten Commandments, relativity and quantum mechanics, the polio vaccine and interstellar travel, Hollywood and Miami Beach and Sandy Koufax, the Six-Day War of 1967 and the 23-Minute War of 2041, and frankly, we've had it with you guys. Live long and prosper and don't call us, we'll call you."

And the next day they were gone, every last one of them.

It was June 21, 2063. I still remember my friend Burt passing out *Earth: Love It or Leave It* T-shirts to all the guys at work, and saying that we were well rid of them and that *now* things were going to get better in a hell of a hurry.

Then, three months later, Odingo Nkomo announced that the Kikuyu were leaving for Beta Piscium IV, and then Joshua Galawanda took the Zulus to Islandhwana II, and almost before you could turn around, Africa was empty except for a few Arabs in the north and a handful of Indians who quickly booked passage back to Bombay.

Well, this didn't bother anyone very much, because nobody really cared about Africa anyway, and suddenly there were two billion fewer mouths to feed and some of the game parks started showing signs of life. But then Moses Smith demanded that the U.S. government supply transportation to all American blacks who wanted to leave, and Earl Mingus ("the Pride of Mississippi"), who had just succeeded to the presidency, agreed on the spot, and suddenly we had an all-white nation.

Well, *almost* all-white. Actually, it took another year for Harvey Running Horse to convince all his fellow Amerinds to accompany him to Alphard III, which he had renamed Little Big Horn.

"Now," said Burt, popping open a beer, "if we could just get rid of the Hispanics, and maybe the Catholics . . ."

The Hispanics headed off for Madrid III two months later, and Burt threw a big party to celebrate. "I'm finally proud to be an Amurrican agin!" he announced, and hung a huge flag outside his front door.

Of course, it wasn't just the blacks and Jews and Hispanics who were emigrating, and it wasn't just America and Africa that were getting emptier. The Chinese left the next year, followed by the Turks, the Bulgarians, the Indians, the Australians, and the French Polynesians. It didn't even make headlines when the Cook County Democratic Machine went off to Daleyworld, which figured to be the only planet that was ever turned into a smoke-filled back room.

"Great!" proclaimed Burt. "We finally got room to breathe and stretch our legs."

Things kind of settled down for a couple of years then, and life got pretty easy, and we hardly noticed that the Brits, the Germans, the Russians, the Albanians, the Sunis, and the Shiites had all gone.

"Wonderful!" said Burt on the day the Greeks and the Pakistanis left. "So maybe we still wear gas masks because of the pollution, and the water still ain't safe to drink, and we ain't quite gotten over our little problem with Eight Mile Island"—that was the problem that turned it into thirty-two Quarter Mile islands—"but, by God, what's a little inconvenience compared to a world run by and for one-hundred-percent-pure Amurricans?"

I suppose we should have seen the handwriting on the wall when the NFL moved the Alaska Timberwolves and the Louisiana Gamblers, the last two franchises still on Earth, to the Quinellus Cluster. There were other little hints, too, like using downtown Boston to test out the new J-bomb, or the day the Great Lakes finally turned solid with sludge.

That was when the *real* emigration started, right in our backyard, so to speak. Nevada, Michigan, and Florida were the first to go; then New Hampshire and Delaware, then Texas, and then it was Katie-bar-the-door. For the longest time I really thought California would stick around, but they finally located a world with a 9,000-mile beach and a native populace that specialized in making sandals and cheap gold jewelry, and suddenly the United States of America began at St. Louis and ended about 60 miles west of Council Bluffs.

"Let 'em go," counseled Burt. "We never needed 'em anyway. And there's just that much more for the rest of us, right?"

Except that things kept happening. The ice cap slipped south all the way to Minneapolis, Mount Kilimanjaro started pouring lava down onto the Serengeti Plain, the Mediterranean boiled away, the National Hockey League went bankrupt, and people kept leaving.

That was almost ten years ago.

There are only eight of us left now. Burt was pressed into duty as World President this week, because Arnie Jenkins hurt his wrist and can't sign any documents, and Sybil Miller, who was supposed to succeed Arnie, has her period and says she doesn't feel like it.

We haven't gotten any mail or supplies in close to a year now. They say that Earth is too polluted and dangerous to land on anymore, so Burt figured it was his presidential duty to take one of our two remaining ships to Mars base and pick up the mail, and bring Arnie back his yearly supply of cigarettes.

I stopped by his office this morning to return a socket wrench I had borrowed, and I saw a letter addressed to me sitting on his desk, so I opened it and read it.

I been mulling it over, and I decided that I was all wrong about this after all. I mean, being World President is all well and good, but not when your only duties are taking out the garbage and picking up the mail. A World President needs an army and navy to keep the peace, and lots of people paying taxes, and stuff like that. I hate to leave now that we're finally down to nothing but 100% pure and loyal Americans, but the fact of the matter is that there ain't no point to being President every eighth week without no perks and no fringes, so I'm off to the big wide galaxy to see if anyone out there wants a guy with presidential experience. I'll be happy to take over the reins of any government what wants me, so long as it's white and Christian and mostly American and has a football team. In fact, I don't even have to be President; I got no serious objections to hiring on as King.

Do me a favor and post this one last official message for me.

And there was a printed sign saying, WILL THE LAST PERSON TO LEAVE THE PLANET PLEASE SHUT OFF THE SUN?

I can't tell you how relieved the rest of us are. Burt was okay for a Baptist, but you know what they say about Baptists.

Now if we can just find a way to get Myrtle Bremmer and that Presbyterian claptrap she's always spouting, we'll finally have an America that *I'm* proud to be a part of.

Rainy Day in Halicarnassus

◇

by
R. A. Lafferty

When I first encountered the utterly unique, unpredictable yarns of R. A. Lafferty I was completely convinced that he had to be some whacked-out wild-eyed long-haired twenty-five-year-old prodigy who dwelt in the depths of the Haight-Ashbury district of San Francisco, feverishly pouring out his genius between midnight and dawn while subsisting on an irregular diet of inventive hallucinogens and organic nuts and vegetables.

Imagine my considerable surprise when I first had the delightful opportunity to actually meet the man, and found him to be instead a somewhat portly, balding, elderly retired engineer who ambled about the convention we were both attending quietly observing all that went on around him while manifesting the expression of a supremely content but slightly deranged gnome.

R. A. has retired from writing to pursue other interests. Writing, you see, is more than merely hard work. It is maddening, infuriating, dangerous to the health, and potentially damaging to the soul. Unlike the ultimate chocolate chip cookie, it is not a thing to be pursued lightly or necessarily forever. This is therefore likely to be one of Mr. Lafferty's last stories to be encountered on this plane of existence.

What he may be up to on other planes I cannot vouch for, except to say that I am sure it will be like nothing you or I can imagine.

It is said that the Christ accounts cannot be true because there are earlier versions of similar stories. It is said in particular that the death-of-Christ account cannot be true because there are earlier death-of-the-sage legends. But I believe that the Christ account is the most convincing of all of them. And likely the death-of-Socrates account is the least convincing of such tales.

Using arguments like those that are used against the Christ account, Socrates could not have died his fabled death because that particular death account was already well worn and centuries old. He could not have died by taking poisonous hemlock because many sages in India did die by taking poisonous hemlock in earlier centuries. The plant known mistakenly as hemlock (*koneion*) in Greece in the time of Socrates was not poisonous in any form. But the plant known correctly as hemlock in India was poisonous.

The only account of the hemlock death of Socrates was written by Plato. Plato was almost certainly kidding Socrates (who was present when Plato first read that tour de force to their circle) by comparing him to one of the old deified sages who had died in this traditional death-of-the-sage in old India. The date of this death account or death is always given as 399 B.C.

Xenophon and other biographers of Socrates do not mention any such hemlock death, or any death at all for him. But they do mention Socrates as living in Halicarnassus in Asia Minor at least ten years after this purported death. And Socrates was present, sitting on a sort of dunce's stool that was provided for him, on "opening afternoon" when Aristophanes first satirized him in his comedy *The Clouds*. There was some banter between the playwright and Socrates the butt of the play. It seems pretty clear that this was Socrates himself and not an actor playing him. This was in 395 B.C., four years after the ascribed death of Socrates.

It may be that the legend of the false or hemlock death of Socrates has persisted because we have no account of his true death. Instead of that we have—more legend.

More than one hundred years after his false or hemlock death, Socrates is mentioned as being one of a circle of sages in Halicarnassus who had whipped the dying business: but this has the smell of legend again. And Villehardouin records

it that Crusaders spoke with Socrates in the year 1191 in
Halicarnassus: but this has the smell of deep legend. And three
different Englishmen in the nineteenth century mention meeting
Socrates in Bodrum (the modern name of Halicarnassus). To
me, this does *not* have the smell of legend. For personal reasons (one of the three Englishmen was my own grandfather),
I believe it is true.

—Arpad Arutinov, *The Back Door of History*

Art Slick and Jim Boomer had been heading for the island of
Cos when they were driven onto the Turkish mainland by a sudden
squall. They put in, an hour before sunrise, at the little harbor of
Bodrum, whose ancient name had been Halicarnassus. They had
come in the twenty-two-foot motor launch the *T-Town Tornado*,
which was too dumb to know that it shouldn't have come halfway
around the world on the open seas. And Art Slick and Jim Boomer
were likewise too dumb to know that their craft was too small for
such voyaging.

When they had tied up the little ship, the wind fell by one-half
and was not as dangerous as it had been. But the rain came down
in torrents and it would not stop that day, and maybe not the
next day.

Remember that girl in Istanbul three days ago, remember how
she sang "Rainy Day in Halicarnassus, Gloom, Gloom, Gloom!"
And later when she came to the table with Art Slick and Jim
Boomer she said, "Do you know that there are three hundred
and nineteen different words for 'gloom' in Turkish? I like to tell
these little informations to gentlemen who come into our place."

"I'd sure never learn three hundred and nineteen different
Turkish words for 'gloom,' " Art Slick had said.

"You would if you ever had to spend a rainy day in
Halicarnassus," the girl told him. "You'd learn them all and
you'd use them all. That isn't half enough words for the kind
of gloom it is there when it rains."

Well, it looked as though they would spend just such a rainy
day in that town now. It was torrential, it was blustery, and it
was gloomy, except for one stocky Greek man who had an aura
of sunshine about him.

"The *Dictionary of Idiosyncrasies* gives it that the equivalent of
a 'rainy day in Halicarnassus' is a 'Sunday in Philadelphia,' " this
broken-nosed and grinny Greek seaman said. Well, maybe he was

a broken-nosed Greek boxer and not a seaman. "There is a Greek cafe, a Turkish cafe, and a Syrian cafe in this town if you want breakfast. Then there is a Greek cinema, a Turkish cinema, and a Syrian cinema. And then there is a Greek nightclub, a Turkish nightclub, and a Syrian nightclub. These presently open at six in the morning and close at six in the evening because of the curfew which is imposed because of the political turmoil. And then there is the Ancient Museum of Living Effigies that you might want to see. There isn't anything else in town, and the rain isn't going to stop today."

"Thanks, Rocky, we may just try them all," Jim Boomer told old broken-nose.

"Why do you call him Rocky when his name is Socky?" a lady asked Jim.

Art and Jim and Rocky-Socky had a breakfast at the Greek cafe. Then they had one at the Turkish cafe, and then one at the Syrian. Well, the broken-nosed Greek was a good belly-man, and Art and Jim could stay with anything for at least once around the circuit. And what else is there to do on a rainy day in a place like that?

"How come you talk such good English, Rocky?" Art Slick asked. "Have you been in the States?" You couldn't even guess how old or how young this Rocky was.

"Oh, I've been in the area where they are now, but the States hadn't arrived there yet. Back when I was young and wise I'd learn a new language every five years," said this strong, stocky fellow who was smoking a Greek pipe. "Well, I was pretty sharp-witted then and I learned things easily. And later I slowed down and learned a new tongue about every twenty years. It took me about that long to learn Old Norse when I spent a couple of saltwater decades with those Viking fellows. And more recently it takes me about fifty years to learn one really well. I've been learning English for just about fifty years now and I'm getting pretty good at it. And now I may spend about fifty years on Indonesian."

"Oh, you've been around a long while, then?"

"Quite a while, yes, but not nearly as long as some."

"Going back that far, you're probably a pagan, Rocky," Jim Boomer said.

"Nah, I switched a long time ago. Now I usher every Sunday at St. Pete's here in town."

It was still raining when they came out of the Syrian cafe. They went under leaking wooden awnings to the Greek cinema, where they saw an American western, *Rustlers of Rim-Rock Canyon.*

"Are you a movie fan, Rocky?" Jim Boomer asked.

"Yeah, from a way back. I loved them when we had them the first time. A lot of people don't remember that, but there *was* a first time. We even had westerns that first time around, though they were easterns from my viewpoint, in desert settings, and both the Gobi and the Arabian deserts were east of me. About the only difference between those and the present westerns was the pounding of dromedary hoofs in the old ones and the pounding of horse hoofs in the new ones. And we had SF movies, sort of: fantastic stuff they were. A critic wrote recently that the old *Arabian Nights* stories sounded like primitive movie scripts. He was guessing, but he was right. They did come from old movie scripts.

"Ah, we made some good movies at those old studios in Ctesiphon: at the Biograph Studio, at Palmy Days Productions, at the Lion and the Unicorn Associated Artists. But after Baghdad became the big city in the area, most of the studios moved there. Then the decline in moviemaking set in. I don't know why."

They went to the Turkish cinema and saw the American western *Guns of the Palo Duro.* Then they went to the Syrian cinema and saw the American western *Robbers' Roost on the Rio Rojo.*

"Well, that about does the town, does it, Rocky?" Art Slick asked when they came out of the Syrian cinema.

"We can always see them over again. That's what I do on rainy days here, see them over again four or five times."

"Why do you call him Rocky when his name is Socky?" a young boy asked Art.

"You told us about the three nightclubs that are only open in the daytime on account of the curfew," Jim Boomer said, "and what was the other thing, Rocky?"

"The Ancient Museum of Living Effigies. I'm really the best one in it, but overall we haven't a very good show. I wouldn't recommend it ordinarily, but on a rainy day here, yeah, guys, it's the last diversion."

They went to the Greek nightclub, where there was an American Jewish comedian, an Italian songstress, a black trumpet player, and a troupe of Arabian tumblers.

"Is this about par for it, Rocky?" Art Slick asked.

"Yes. All nightclub acts are based on old radio acts. That's why they keep nightclubs so dark that you can't see, to preserve the illusion. When I was a young man in Greece and we had radio for the first time, we had acts just about like this. The *Petrides Olive Hour* was a good show. So was the *Arcadian Honey Hour* and the *Pappageotes Pottery Hour*. The best was the *Hippodromion Wine Hour*. I used to wrangle passes to go to the studios to see the shows live. Most of the acts were better live. Except for the arabian tumblers; they were always better on the radio. I guess the radio shows faded away after the Romans came. The Romans thought they were silly, so they dropped out of fashion."

"I guess there's nothing new under the sun, huh, Rocky?" Jim Boomer said.

"*Hey, that's new!* Let me write that down. *'Nothing new under the sun.'* That's good. Into the old notebook it goes."

"Did you always carry a notebook, Rocky?"

"Always. It's part of my self-education program. But it was more cumbersome in the old days, carrying those slabs of clay around in your pockets and wetting them whenever you wanted to make a note with your stylus. Who could afford paper or parchment then? Poor scholars like myself couldn't even afford wax to write on."

"Is this *Whipping Death* jag that you fellows are on much of a trick, Rocky? And what is the secret of it?" Jim Boomer asked.

"Oh, we don't have death whipped, just delayed for a while. And if I told you the secret of it, it wouldn't be a secret any longer."

"Whooo! What was that stroke like invisible lightning coming right through the walls?" Art Slick asked. "That was one eerie jolt."

"It was just a time-inversion shock wave," the genial Greek said. "We have them here every ten years or so lately. It means we're going to have visitors."

"That sounds like a folk superstition, Rocky," Art said.

"Sort of, boys, sort of. When we had time travel the first time, we knew how to muffle the shock waves." They were drinking martinis.

"The martini is what saved the olive from extinction," broken-nosed Rocky said. "A wonderful invention, wonderful."

The Italian songstress was singing "Rainy Day in Halicarnassus, Gloom, Gloom, Gloom." No, that had been in the Turkish nightclub. No, that was in all three of them. Each of them had an Italian songstress singing it.

"Well, that about does the town, Rocky," Art Slick said when they came out of the Syrian nightclub. It wasn't noon yet. "So we're down to the Ancient Museum of Living Effigies, of which you're the star. It's that or the movies again."

"Let's see the movies again," genial rocky-face said. It was still raining. They saw the three movies again. They went to the three nightclubs again after that. And it was not yet two o'clock. Time goes slow on rainy days there.

"When does the show start at the museum, Rocky?"

"Whenever we have as many as three customers. Come along. There's you two, and maybe there will be another one."

In fact there were seven other customers waiting, a local girl and six people from a time-probe.

"Weren't you time-trippers around here ten years ago? And weren't you around here ten years before that?" rocky-face asked them.

"Kyrie Socrates, we've spent *the whole afternoon* just trying to get a serious interview with you, and it costs more than you'd think," one of the time-trippers complained. "Yes, we've been trying you every ten years here, and it takes us ten minutes to make each location. And we've seen the silly show twelve times. We're about out of patience with you. We're convinced that you are the real Socrates. We can't reach back far enough to catch you in what I might call your credible life; and you drop out of the scene again not many decades after this time, so we have a narrow place to try to catch you. Your rediscovery can well be the historical event of the ages, but you won't let it be. Why won't you give us a real interview, now, today?"

"Ah, there's so many other things to do that are more fun."

"What are they? On a rainy day like this, what are they?"

"Oh, on a rainy day I guess there really aren't any," old pudge admitted.

The local girl there was shining up to Art Slick and Jim Boomer.

"I know you were trying to get to the island of Cos when you had to put in here to Bodrum," she said. "I want to go to Cos tonight. My sister who lives there is expecting me to come and help her with the geese. Tomorrow is the first day of Goose Plucking Week, you know. And tonight is Goose-Down-Eve Fes-

tival. We really throw a banger over there on Goose-Down-Eve.
We'll take Socky too if he's decent to these visitors for once."

The show at the Ancient Museum of Living Effigies wasn't
a very good one by ordinary standards, but on a rainy day in
Halicarnassus it was at least tolerable. And it did have a good cast:
Pythagoras, Pico della Mirandola, Lama Hama Gama, Avicenna,
Prester John, Tycho Brahe, Leibniz. But Socrates was the best
of them.

"I was the youngest member once, but gradually we drop out,"
Socrates said.

The Living Effigies, the Old Sages, gave little lectures on mathematics and philosophy and history and civic duty. They played
ancient and medieval instruments; and Socrates also played several tunes on a modern harmonica. They answered catch questions
thrown at them to test whether they really were who they said they
were. And all of them seemed to be genuine.

"We really throw bangers over there on Goose-Down-Eve,"
the local girl was telling Art and Jim. "And the wind has swung
around now. It's still a gale, but it's a strong gale off the land
now and it'll put you into Cos in two hours if that skiff of
yours has any kick at all. And the party will be just starting
good when we get there. Everybody else would be too chicken
to put out in this weather, but I know that you guys aren't
chicken."

The sages slipped away as they finished their specialties, and
one of the last of them, Socrates, was still spieling:

"Back when we had aviation the first time, I was barnstorming
one autumn in a little tri-winger plane when—"

"Oh, stop giggling when you tell them, Socky," the local girl
said. "Your stories aren't that funny."

"Kyrie Socrates," one of the time-trippers said. "You are telling
lies again. You never had aviation the first time, never had it
anciently."

"Yes we did," Pythagoras supported Socrates. "Some of his
things are lies, but we did have aviation. Alexander used aircraft
with strafers. He could really mow them down with those planes.
That was the way he scattered those big, bunched-up Asiatic
armies. You'd never scatter them with a phalanx. Think about
it a minute and you'll see how silly that is."

"Well, you're *mostly* telling tall stories, Socrates," the time-tripper insisted. "And yet you are your genuine self and you could give us deep and sensational information. You work with us and we'll create the greatest archeological-historical coup ever. We have about a hundred key questions here, and if you will just use them for takeoff points—"

"Go ahead, Rocky," Art Slick said. "You'll have time. We won't be setting out for Cos for an hour yet."

"And you *haven't* anything better to do," another of the time-probers put in. "After all, this *is* a rainy day in Halicarnassus."

"It doesn't hurt to be nice to people," the local girl said, "not when they have made such long time trips to see you. Be nice to them, or we won't take you to Cos for the Goose-Down-Eve Festival. And the Cos goose down is the softest down in the world and justly famed."

"It's not softer than thumbs down, surely," Socrates said. "Thumbs-down is softer than goose-down every time. All right, folks, I open my heart and my head to you. But I wouldn't be opening them to you if it weren't such a dismal rainy day; and I wouldn't be opening them to you if only they had changed the bill at even one of the movie houses."

Then the time-trippers fell upon him joyously for the epoch-making interview.

"We'll gas up at Turkoman's Marina, Rocky," Art Slick called. "We'll see you there, but take your time and give them what they want. You owe it to the world, Rocky."

"Why do you call him Rocky when his name is Socky," the local girl asked as she went out with Art and Jim.

And the interview was a great success. The old master used the hundred or so questions as takeoff points for truly masterful illuminations. It really was the archeological-historical coup of the century.

Of which century?

Of the twenty-ninth century. That's the one the time-trippers came from. It rejuvenated the twenty-ninth century that had gone stale. It produced one of the most startling reanimations ever. It brought about the rarest of things, the Almost Perfect World.

Rocky disappeared from the Halicarnassus scene shortly after the interview. Oh, he's still around somewhere, but he had other interests and he keeps out of the public eye, so it's said. And he won't give interviews.

So we have nine centuries to wait before we can get a piece of that startling reanimation and a share of the Almost Perfect World.

You Should Pardon Me, I'm Not Making This Up

✧

by
Tobias Grace

Ethnic humor used to be a staple of comedians and comedy in general. Nowadays we're more sensitive. Unfortunately, a vaccine for inoculating people against the insidious disease known as political correctness has not yet been found, and so we are forced to suffer the absence of what used to be a wellspring of much good humor. Sure, some of it was abusive, and insensitive, and even insulting, but by blanket-banning it all we've thrown out the baby with the bathwater. But that's another story, and not to be found in this anthology.

Among the greatest sources of ethnic humor is Jewish humor, a fair portion of which has its roots in fantasy tales, you should pardon my mentioning it. When shunned and ghettoized it's natural for a people to look inward for inspiration. Even when dealing with the unreal.

A January day in New York City is not the nicest experience one could have in this life. This particular day was a good example: two inches of filthy slush, the LIRR on strike, the Sanitation Department having a sick-out, and it was bitterly cold.

Among the thousands of aggravated urbanites struggling to get to work was a balding, middle-aged gentleman named Francis X. O'Dwyer. Frank's mission in life was to anchor a corner desk in Accounts Receivable at Bently, Bently & Comforte, a medium-size brokerage house. He had been at that desk for fourteen years and fully expected to be right there for another twenty, barring hostile takeover or the untimely collection of the debt he had incurred to Mother Nature through smoking two packs a day and not getting any exercise. Once he had thought that there would be more to be had out of life, but that was now too long ago for the memory of starved expectation to be more painful than a mild toothache.

On this day, his regrets centered around not having worn galoshes. The slush had already soaked through his wing tips and he was still more than six blocks from his office.

Walking close to the buildings with his head down against the wind, he failed to see a bag lady huddled in a doorway. Her feet were on the sidewalk and Frank tripped on them. Some trips are minor affairs; a stagger and some sloshed coffee. Often these can be disguised by the quick-witted as a sort of *joie de vivre* dance step. This wasn't one of those. It was a number ten, all-hope-lost, full frontal slide in slush, with flailing arms and briefcase falling open.

Frank pushed himself to his knees, surveyed his papers blowing away, his clothes soaked in filthy water, and felt his self-control slipping.

"Oh damn," he moaned, "damn, damn, damn. I wish I had dry socks."

It may have been that this wish was expressed with more soul than dry socks usually inspire, or perhaps it was a certain, by-chance-achieved timbre in his expostulation. Maybe it was the precise numerology of the syllables in his wish, or maybe it was just that his turn had come around to get what he wanted in life. It's even possible that there was nothing mysterious about it at all. Whatever. There was a brief flash of brilliant light and the bag lady was gone.

In her place stood a short, heavily made-up grandmother type, with brightly hennaed hair, a pink, polyester pantsuit, a fake fur coat, sneakers, a huge handbag and a lot of diamonds. As his eyes cleared of colored spots from the flash of light, Frank saw she was holding a pair of black, executive-length, Banlon socks in front of his face.

"You want socks?" she asked, "so here's socks already. You want I should put them on for you too? Go ahead, take them. They don't count as a wish or anything. They're real socks. I always carry a pair or two in my bag. You never know."

Following the invariable practice of the New Yorker when confronted by someone who has the termerity to actually talk, Frank began to edge away. Since he was still on his knees, the going was a little slow and messy.

"So take the socks, will you?" the old lady insisted, "and get up, for heaven's sake. You'll catch your death down there like that."

Frank heaved himself to his feet and tried to gather up the contents of his briefcase.

"All right, so you don't want the socks," the old lady shrugged. "So maybe I should have argyle or something. Pardon *me,* a haberdasher I'm not."

"What are you, then?" asked Frank. "I thought you were a bag lady."

"A bag lady, he says!" She drew herself up to her full five feet one inch of height. "Your mother should hear you say such a thing to me, of all people. My own godchild calls me a bag lady, after all I've done. Cruel, that's what it is, *cruel.*"

"Godchild!" exclaimed Frank. "I've never seen you before in my life."

"Of course not. I haven't appeared before. That's no reason to be disrespectful, though. Remember, I'm a lot older than you. Now, come inside here"—she indicated a coffee shop—"and put these socks on right now."

With the surprising authority often mustered by little old ladies, she propelled him into the shop and pushed him into a booth in the rear. She slapped the socks on the table and pointed to his feet.

"Look," said Frank, struggling to get his shoes off, "I don't have any idea who you are . . ."

"Rosen," said the old lady quickly, "Mrs. Ethel Rosen. I'm your fairy godmother."

"My *what?*"

"Fairy godmother, and don't raise your voice like that. People will talk. They can't see me, you know. Only you can. Order hot soup. That's what you need on a day like this: hot soup."

A waitress came to the booth and, as if to confirm Mrs. Rosen's invisibility, looked right through her, speaking only to Frank. He ordered soup.

"You mean she couldn't see you at all?" asked Frank.

"See or hear unless I let, and I don't let without good reason."

"I don't understand this at all," said Frank, shaking his head. "What's the reason for letting *me* see you? Are you going to grant me three wishes?"

"Wishes, smishes—you can wish all day and get *bubkas*. You got no idea what kind of trouble that old story gives me. Everybody thinks I'm gonna give them something for nothing."

"It *is* what all the stories say fairy godmothers do," said Frank, between spoonfuls of soup.

"That's the media for you, can't get anything right. I was misquoted. It's not wishes I grant, it's *dishes*."

"Dishes?"

"*Dishes*. You want maybe a nice tureen, or a set of coffee mugs? Maybe a covered vege? Say the word. Anyway, that's just a sideline. What I really do is not wishes or dishes, it's make *arrangements*."

"Arrangements for what?" asked Frank.

"For whatever. Listen, enough about me. It's *you* I'm here about."

"I'm doing fine, thanks," said Frank, rising to leave the booth.

"Maybe not so fine," said Mrs. Rosen, pushing him back down. "A nice young boy like you, not married yet? I don't call that fine."

"Maybe I'm gay," said Frank, trying to get up again.

"You don't think there's any nice young doctors who're gay? Even a nice lawyer maybe? Anyway, you're not gay. You're my godchild and I've known you since this high. Gay you're not."

"All right, so I'm not gay. I do not want to get married. What I want is to get to my office. It's been nice chatting but if you'll excuse me I . . . ."

"Sit *down*," said Mrs. Rosen in a tone that did not brook argument. "I can't concentrate with you making like a jumping jack all the time. And you *do* want to get married. You just don't know it yet. Look at you: missing buttons, stains on your tie, all the symptoms. Anyway, you're only half the deal. I have to consider the *total* picture."

"What's the total picture?" asked Frank.

"Brigit Kelly, also my godchild, and she *does* want to get married."

"How many godchildren do you have?"

"Oh, hundreds," Mrs. Rosen said, waving a hand. "This is a full-time job, you know. I'm very busy. I haven't had a day off in . . . oh, I guess it was Teddy Roosevelt's inauguration. He was one of mine so of course I had to go. He was some kind of boy, was T. R. *Chutzpah,* that's what he had, the real thing. A *mensch!*"

"You have *hundreds* of . . . ?"

"Clients, yes, it's a heavy caseload. That's why I never appeared to you before, you understand. But I've been watching you, and now it's time I took a hand. Past time. Let me tell you about Brigit. Such a girl! Cook? You wouldn't believe . . ."

"No, frankly I wouldn't believe," Frank interrupted. "Now if you'll excuse me, I have to get to work."

Before Frank was half out of the booth, there was another flash of bright light and a loud, crashing noise. When his eyes cleared, he saw that the soup bowl was gone and in its place was an entire service for twelve of Stangle ware pottery, fiesta pattern.

"*This* could all be yours," said Mrs. Rosen, a trifle smugly.

Frank sat back down heavily. "How did you do that?" he gasped.

"Professional secret," said Mrs. Rosen. "Now, about Brigit Kelly . . ."

"No, no, no," said Frank, "parlor tricks don't change a thing. I am not interested in any Brigit Kellys. I'm perfectly happy, stains on my tie and all, and I have *no* desire to get married. You'll have to solve Ms. Kelly's problem somewhere else on your client list."

There was another flash, and the Stangle ware doubled to a service for twenty-four.

"You want I should up the ante?" asked Mrs. Rosen, "so okay, it's upped. You drive a hard bargain."

"This is beyond belief," said Frank. "Not for a thousand plates will I get married. I'm not interested. Period!"

"For your wedding I'll make it Lenox, coffee service and desserts included."

"Goodbye, Mrs. Rosen. It's been real different, meeting you."

"Gravy boat, extra veges, matching salt and pepper, butter dish . . ."

"Good*bye,* Mrs. Rosen."

"Tree-and-well platter, sauceboat, demitasse . . ."

Frank managed to push his way out of the booth and head for the door. Mrs. Rosen followed at a fast trot. As they neared the door, the waitress picked up one of the fiesta plates.

"You forgot your china," she called.

"You keep it, dear," said Mrs. Rosen, evidently suddenly visible. "Put it with your hope chest. Mr. Independent here turns up his nose."

Frank hurried out of the shop and was halfway down the block before he chanced looking behind him. Mrs. Rosen was nowhere to be seen. By the time he got to his office and settled down with the familiar security of his desk, he had half convinced himself that the entire episode had been some kind of hallucination. Frank recalled smoking a few joints back in the sixties. Do you get flashbacks from pot? He wasn't sure. At most, he thought, it had been a close encounter with one of New York's legion of accomplished crackpots. By midafternoon he was firmly focused on his receivables when the phone rang.

"Franky?" said a familiar voice. "This is Mrs. Rosen. So listen, I want you should meet Brigit after work today, maybe have a bite to eat."

Frank stared at the phone for a long minute.

"Franky? You still there? Say something. Anything at all."

"How did you get this number?" asked Frank.

"I have my sources."

"*What* sources?"

"The phone book!" said Mrs. Rosen. "You're listed, you know. Bently, Bently & Comforte is after Bennet Carpet Cleaners and right before Benito Roach Removers. This was a state secret or something? You don't want the Russians should know? Where'd you think you were getting your customers from?"

"Our *commercial correspondents* are highly respected merchant banks," said Frank.

"So fancy-schmansy, they don't use phones?"

Frank paused to take a deep breath and close his eyes for a minute.

"Primarily," he spoke with a real effort at patience, "our correspondents are *referred* to us, a practice which would slacken appreciably were it to become known that members of the accounting staff here were in the habit of whiling away the afternoon chatting with people who claim to be fairy godmothers."

"And very right too," said Mrs. Rosen, "you shouldn't be taking personal calls at the office. I understand. You're too busy to talk to me now. Me, who stood by your cradle when you was first born, so proud I was! Me, who watched you go off to kindergarten—

my little man—with those shorts that didn't fit. They were your brother's. Who do you think kept those shorts from falling off your tush when you first walked into the classroom? Nice introduction to the other kids *that* would've been! I mean, you were not what you could call popular anyway. You didn't need something like that."

"I was so popular!" Frank was shouting at the phone, and heads were beginning to turn in his direction.

"Then there was that fight after school, when you were sixteen and that slut Sally Caruthers was making eyes at every boy in school. You happened to stumble through her line of vision and thought it was true love . . ."

"Now wait a minute," Frank objected, "Sally was a real nice girl. What we had was sincere!"

"The only thing sincere was Jake Tomasello's desire to see you in intensive care so he could have Sally all to himself. Just who do you think it was put that rock behind him that he tripped over, just as he was stepping back to give you his final roundhouse punch?"

"You know about that rock? I didn't think anybody knew about that."

"Well, they won't hear it from me," said Mrs. Rosen reassuringly. "I don't tell nothing to nobody, except my friend Mrs. Bloom, and she's a clam. She doesn't know anybody you do anyway, so your secret's safe. So it's all set, then? You and Brigit? After work?"

"No, it is *not* all set! Why me? Why has it got to be me with this Brigit of yours?" Frank's tone was such that other people in the office were now plainly staring at him.

"Just making good combinations dear, like in Mah-Jongg. I'll see to it she's waiting for you."

"No, wait . . ." Frank began, but found he was talking to a dial tone.

His duties did not receive his full attention during the rest of the afternoon. The events of the morning could be written off as some kind of sleight of hand, but the phone call was another matter altogether. *Nobody* knew about the rock. Several times he almost picked up the phone to call his mother and see if Mrs. Rosen was a fellow habitué of the Senior Citizen Center, with whom Mom may have been reminiscing too freely. He didn't call, though. Even Mom didn't know about the rock.

Frank also devoted a considerable amount of the company's time to thinking about Brigit Kelly. The whole idea was absurd, of course. Brigit was probably a stout, moon-faced farm girl who wore wool skirts and work shoes and expected to have at least six children, in between going to Mass and Confession. The concept horrified him. Fortunately Mrs. Rosen had neglected to specify where the meeting was supposed to take place.

Frank did not stop for a drink after work every day. Once in a while, when he felt more than usually convivial, or if a few people from the office made up a party, he would join the happy hour at Billy's Pub. It was not a regular activity, but after this day's upsetting events, he decided he was more than justified in having a couple of quick ones. The pub was unusually crowded when he walked in. So much so that he briefly wondered if some special event was taking place. As his eyes adjusted to the dim interior, he could see there was only one table with an empty chair in the whole place. In a few minutes, he had elbowed his way to the bar for a vodka and grapefruit and had almost made it to the table when his arm was sharply jostled. It seemed almost deliberate and Frank briefly flashed anger, but the man who was responsible had already disappeared in the crowd. When Frank turned back, he saw that the drink had been spilled on the sleeve of a raincoat worn by a seated woman who was turned away from him.

As Frank began to mumble apologies, she turned to face him. She was about thirty-five, possessed of glossy black hair, perfect features and a smile that caused Frank to stumble around in his sentences as though they were darkened rooms.

"Really, it's all right," she said, standing as Frank made ineffective swipes at her sleeve with his handkerchief. "It has to go to the cleaner's anyway."

"Well, I'm very sorry," Frank went on, "let me at least get you a fresh drink. I want to do something to make up for this."

"It really isn't necessary," she said with a musical little laugh, "but all right, if you insist. By the way, my name is Brigit Kelly. What's yours?"

"Frank O' . . . *what* did you say your name was?"

"Brigit Kelly. Is something the matter?"

Something was the matter. Frank slid down into the vacant chair with a sort of low, shocked moan, staring first at Brigit, then at the ceiling, then at Brigit again. With a look of concern, she sat back down opposite him.

"I think we're related," said Frank. "We have the same fairy godmother."

"We have the same what?" Brigit asked with a blank look.

"Fairy godmother. You know, Mrs. . . ."

Just at that moment, the bartender caught Frank's eye.

"Mr. O'Dwyer?" he asked. "You have a phone call."

Frank excused himself and made his way to the bar, taking the receiver from the bartender.

"Franky"—he knew the voice at once—"Franky, is that you? Listen, you shouldn't mention me to Brigit. This is all from my mouth to your ears."

"Meddled in *her* life once too often or something?" asked Frank.

"Meddled! Is that what you call it when my every waking thought is for your welfare? Meddled! Your mother should hear that. No, she shouldn't. It would break her heart. Well, she won't hear it from me. I'll suffer in silence. Now what about Brigit? Isn't she a sweet girl? And just look at those hips! I'll have a grand-godchild before you know it."

"Mrs. Rosen," said Frank, "will you wait with the children? She doesn't even know my last name yet, or did you take care of that too?"

"*Me?* Certainly not. I wouldn't want to be accused of meddling. Anyway, I've never appeared to her, which is why you shouldn't mention me yet. No sense confusing her with details."

Frank made it back to his chair just as the drinks arrived.

"I must say, that's the most original line I've ever heard," said Brigit. "Does it work well for you?"

"I'm sorry," said Frank, "what line? The phone call got me distracted."

"About having the same fairy godmother. I've never heard that one before."

"Oh, that," Frank waffled a bit, "ah . . . just a joke. Listen, let me buy you another drink."

"I haven't even started this one yet."

"Well, let me buy you a new raincoat, then," said Frank.

"I really . . ."

"A new raincoat, drinks and dinner, my final offer, for openers."

"I'm not really looking for a date," she began.

"Mr. O'Dwyer," the bartender called out, "you have another call."

"Franky?" said Mrs. Rosen, when he had again made his way to the bar. "Don't listen to that, what she just said. She is so looking. She hasn't had a date in three months."

Frank didn't answer. He hung up and dug through the crowd to get back to the table before Brigit could finish her drink and get up.

"Listen," Frank began, "you haven't had a date in three months. Why not enjoy yourself a little?"

"How did you know that?" asked Brigit, astonished.

"We have a mutual friend. I'll tell you about it later."

Later, however, there were other topics of greater interest. Frank discovered Brigit was a serious journalist. The next day he eschewed his usual copy of the *Post* and bought the *Times* instead. She had no use for flab in either prose or people. He joined a gym. She hated half-measures and foolish shams. Frank thought of the wisps of hair he was combing carefully up from the sides of his head to lie limp and forlorn over his growing bald spot. He shaved his head. Within six months he looked a lot less like a middle-aged clerk and a lot more like Yul Brynner in his prime. The romance flourished, except for problems caused by Brigit's busy schedule. Periodically Mrs. Rosen called up to check progress.

"Listen, Franky," she said one day, "it's time to get off the pot, you should pardon my French. You can't toy with a nice girl's affections forever. You should set a date already."

"*Me*, toying with *her*? I've been trying to propose to her for weeks. I've sent her flowers every day, theater tickets, dinners, even bought her a Cuisinart!"

"Harrumph," said Mrs. Rosen, "you don't think she can buy her own gadgets? You don't think she makes any money herself? I told you, this is a smart girl. She don't need you if she wants appliances. You got to be romantic with her."

"Believe me, I've tried," said Frank, "but every time I get the mood set just right, her beeper goes off and she's gone to cover some story. We have dinner, the lights are low, the music is right and suddenly some congressman gets arrested and she's dashing to Brooklyn to get a quote for the morning edition. I can't get any time alone with her! If I could just get a few uninterrupted hours . . ."

"Well . . ." Mrs. Rosen was obviously considering possibilities. "You wouldn't mind a little inconvenience?"

"Anything, but what can I do?"

"Let me think," said Mrs. Rosen. "I'll get back to you."

The next day, Frank was approached at his desk by Mr. Bently, Mr. Bently and Mr. Comforte themselves.

"Mr. O'Dwyer," began a Mr. Bently, "would you be so good as to come with us to the conference room? There are some gentlemen here to see you."

All Frank could think of was an IRS audit, but he didn't suppose he was nearly important enough for them to come to him. When they entered the room, Frank saw three elderly men, formally dressed and rather lugubrious. One carried a loaf of bread on a silver tray. Another had a silver dish of salt and the third carried a linen hand towel. As Frank entered, they each dropped arthritically to one knee and murmured, "Your Royal Highness," in unison. Next, the one with the towel draped it over Frank's right hand, while the others placed thereon the bread and salt. Finally, the oldest and most lugubrious drew out a parchment scroll and began to read aloud.

"Whereas it has been established that Francis X. O'Dwyer is the legitimate great-grandson of Her Royal Highness, the Princess Sophia of Wittenburg, of the true line of descent from Armgard the Saxon of ancient days, and whereas the line of the Grand Dukes of Wittenburg present upon the throne having failed with the death of His Royal Highness, Grand Duke Florian VI, of blessed memory, which death having occurred Tuesday last, now therefore it is the declaration of the Volkmoot of Wittenburg that the crown be rightly come upon the same Francis X. O'Dwyer as above noted, to reign over the Duchy of Wittenburg all of his days, the heirs of his body after him forever and ever. God save the Grand Duke!"

Whereupon the old men gave three faint cheers, which in one case petered out into a hacking cough. The Bentlys and Comforte looked distinctly ill at ease. Frank was speechless.

The following events became a haze in Frank's mind. He recalled the entire staff being clustered around as the three old men ushered him out to a waiting limousine. There were reporters screaming at him and flashbulbs going off like a Fourth of July celebration. The only really clear image he later remembered was the shock on the face of Brigit Kelly as she fought with other reporters to get closer to him with questions he couldn't answer. When she recognized him, she dropped her notebook for the first time in her professional career.

Frank had never heard of the Grand Duchy of Wittenburg. He could vaguely place a great-grandmother Sophia, but otherwise this entire business was even more of a shock to him than it had been to Brigit. Late that night, in a suite at the Plaza reserved by the Wittenburg Embassy, Frank was stretched out on the bed trying to make sense of it all when the phone rang.

"So Franky, what do you think? Not bad, huh?"

"Mrs. Rosen," said Frank in a tone of infinite weariness, "is this all more of your work? Never mind, of course it is. Silly of me to ask."

"Let me tell you, Franky boy, this one was not easy. *Tsoritz* is the word, and I don't mind saying so. You want to talk arrangements? Oh boy, did I do some arranging!"

"At the risk of being ungrateful," said Frank, "why? My life wasn't complicated enough, with Brigit and everything?"

"That's just it, Franky, *Brigit*! That's the whole reason. You couldn't get her attention. She was always running after the news. So now *you're* the news. In fact, *you* are the hottest story in New York. You could be famous for a week! Maybe even two weeks, with something like this. It's very big. And when interest starts to fade, when you find yourself on the Letterman show instead of talking to Arsinio, you blow the whole thing up again by giving up the throne for Brigit—just like the Duke of Windsor. She'll melt. Who wouldn't?"

"Suppose I want Brigit *and* the throne?"

"Don't get your heart set on that," said Mrs. Rosen rather abruptly.

"Why not?"

"Just don't."

"Well, have you given any thought to what I'm going to do after I've given up the throne? B.B. & C. might find an ex-duke a bit exalted for a job as accounts clerk."

"They shouldn't be prejudiced just because you were a grand duke for a couple days," said Mrs. Rosen. "That wouldn't be American! Anyway, you'll get another job. You'll endorse perfume or something. You're a bright boy. You'll cope. Half the world should have your problems. Listen, I'd love to schmooze but I have to get off the phone. Brigit is trying to call you."

Brigit was indeed calling. Brigit was very much on the case. During the next week, Brigit rarely left Frank's side. Her series, *The Man Who Would Be Duke*, had the morning editions selling out by coffee break time. Soon, Brigit herself became the object of popular interest. Gossip columnists began to speculate about her relationship with Frank. She was invited on the *Today* show. She let her hair down with Oprah. Joan Rivers asked her if Frank was any better in bed now that he was a duke. Embarrassed, Brigit said she really didn't know. Joan assumed that meant Brigit hadn't gone to bed with him until after he became a duke and complimented her on her foresight. The pressure was building.

Finally, after more than two weeks of this, Frank called a press conference and announced he would give up the throne if she would marry him. There was no ostensible reason why he had to give up the throne, since both he and Brigit were at least nominal Catholics, Wittenburg is a Catholic country and neither of them had been married before, but who cares about nit-picking legalisms? The crowd went wild. Brigit became hysterical. The phone rang.

"Franky? Is that you? Listen, I think you got her right where you want her. You shouldn't lose time now. You only got about an hour left."

"What do you mean?" asked Frank. "An hour for what?"

"An hour before they discover they got the wrong man to be duke. The right one is a retired schoolteacher in Canarsie. Is he going to love this! I can't wait to see his face when they tell him. He's one of Mrs. Bloom's. I just sort of borrowed his fate for a while. Sometimes we do that kind of thing in the profession, trade back and forth a bit, you know, makes the world go 'round."

"You mean you knew all along this was just temporary?"

"Of course. I warned you not to get your heart set on anything but Brigit, remember?"

"You mean I'm not a duke?" Fun though it had been, there was a definite note of relief in Frank's voice.

"Darling, you're a nice boy, a good accountant and, from what I hear Brigit says, great in bed (you should pardon me saying such a thing, I don't mean to pry), but you're no duke. You don't even get to keep the loaf of bread. And if I were you, I'd check out of the Plaza toot-sweet, before you get stuck with the bill.

Wittenburg is not a big-budget operation and they're real careful with the gelt."

Frank and Brigit's two weeks in Fantasy Land did, of course, the trick. The wedding was announced as soon as the excitement died down. Brigit had timed it to stir up interest again, having become something of a media star herself by this time. In fact, she now needed Frank's accounting expertise full-time to help her sort through the book offers, movie deals and guest appearance slots.

The morning of the wedding was bright and clear. The flowers were lavish and beautiful. The awe-inspiring set of Lenox on the gift table was the most comprehensive this side of the Nancy Reagan White House. Frank was struggling with his shirt studs. The phone rang.

"Franky? Is that you? This is Mrs. Rosen."

"I know," said Frank, instantly nervous. "You haven't got any new schemes in mind, have you?"

"Schemes! Me? Franky! What a terrible thing to suggest. I just called to congratulate. You did real good, Franky, real good. May you live a hundred years and have a dozen children."

"I don't *want* a dozen children!" said Frank, horrified and dropping his studs.

"We'll see," said Mrs. Rosen, "we'll see."

"Mrs. Rosen, no! Please! . . ." but he was talking to a dial tone.

On one of the side streets near the Metropolitan Museum of Art is an elegant, beaux arts town house with a small brass plaque by the door reading, *The Solomon H. Rosen Foundation for Unique Philanthropies.* You can find the place if you look hard enough, but it's very discreet, like everything on the Upper East Side. The day after the wedding, Mrs. Rosen was in that building, at her desk. She was paying bills. At the conclusion of every Good Combination, she paid the bills. She could have put checks in the mail, of course, but she liked to have bills presented in person. She enjoyed pressing the flesh, saying a few words, looking in eyes. She experienced no difficulty in being indulged in this pleasure. When you pay bills like Mrs. Rosen's, creditors will cheerfully present them on their knees, or drop them from hot-air balloons, if such is your whim.

Today there was a long line of private investigators, P.R. people, actors and actresses, a waitress with a "vision problem," and the ambassador of the Grand Duchy of Wittenburg. (It's amazing what kind of cooperation you can get for a few thousand bucks American in a minor Balkan country where the economy consists largely of brewing slivovitz, drinking it and stealing goats.) Mrs. Rosen paid each with a flourish and a few special words of appreciation. She was in a very good mood.

Business out of the way, she went across the hall to Mrs. Bloom's office. Entering without a knock, she went to a small table in a corner where a Mah-Jongg set was laid out. She moved two pieces: one from the dragons and one from the flowers. Turning, she smiled a bit smugly at Mrs. Bloom.

Mrs. Bloom, an almost identical little old lady whose hair was perhaps just a shade bluer, smiled back ruefully.

"So how did you find out about the rock?" she asked.

Mrs. Rosen tapped her nose with a finger. "Doesn't matter. I found out, that's all. If it wasn't that, it would have been something else. It's not the deep, dark secrets you need. It's just a couple of little things like the rock that work the best. A good combination, that's what counts. It's not that hard to make magic if you plan good. So, your move?"

"My move," said Mrs. Bloom, "and wait till you see who I've got for my boy in Canarsie! You're gonna love this. Now get the book. We got to figure the score."

When the Ego Alters

by
Laura Resnick

I mentioned previously that Mike Resnick's daughter was a certain well-known and well-regarded scribe yclept Laura. Ms. Resnick has heretofore concentrated on the field of romance novels but has begun to branch out (insert your own witty metaphor here) into other genres. Among them is that of fantasy, hence her brief tale following. I believe this may be the first time in the genre that the work of a father and daughter has appeared in the same collection.

Take that, Cal Ripken.

The call she made to her agent was frantic. "Joe, it's Olive."

"I was going to call you this afternoon," he said delightedly, surprised that she had surfaced before noon. "The book has made the *Times* list this week. You've arrived!"

"I don't care about that," she snapped. "I need—"

"You don't care?" He was shocked. To secure a place on the most prestigious best-seller list with her fourth romance novel was not an accomplishment for Olive Gruberstein to sneer at. "Olympia!"

"Don't call me that!" she cried. "That's *her* name."

"*Her* name?"

"Yes, and she won't leave me alone!"

Joe cleared his throat. He'd seen this syndrome before, sudden success followed by an equally sudden mental collapse. One of his clients had once locked herself inside a suite at the Waldorf, painting the windows black and singing the theme song to *M*A*S*H* nonstop for three days before the fire department had finally saved her from herself. Now she wrote self-help books and was again a best-seller.

"Listen, darling," he said carefully, "Olympia Greco is *your* name, your pseudonym."

"That's what I used to think," Olive sobbed. "But she's *not* me. She's . . . she's this separate entity. And she's impossible! She hates my apartment, my wardrobe, the way I wear my hair, my friends, my life-style, my—"

"All right, I know you've been under a lot of stress, trying to finish the next book—"

"That's just it! I thought I could handle her constant criticism of my personal life, but I will *not* tolerate her interference in my work. She doesn't know anything about writing!"

"Do you have any tranquilizers in the house?" he asked.

"No, you know I don't take pills. I'm sure *she* does, but I refuse to ask her for anything. I've had it with her! I want her out of my life, Joe, I mean it. You're my agent, can't you do something about her?"

He frowned. "Are you saying you want to change your pseudonym?"

"No, I'm saying I want to get rid of Olympia."

"Olive, I'm sorry, but I don't understand." He paused, then asked suspiciously, "Have you been drinking?"

"No, of course not. *She's* the one who drinks, not me."

"Why don't you sit down, take a few deep breaths, and tell me what this is all about?" he suggested.

He heard a harsh, unhappy sigh. "Well, you know, when I came to you with my first manuscript and you suggested I invent a more commercial-sounding name, I didn't necessarily like it, but I could see your point. And I was willing to let you convince me to fudge the truth on my inside-cover biography."

"Of course," he said, rolling his eyes as he recalled how fiercely she had argued about Olympia's first bio. He added encouragingly, "After all, there's no need for all your readers to know that you lived with a Turkish transvestite for three years and used to work for a company that made you hand out New Age leaflets on West Forty-eighth Street while dressed in a wet suit."

"I suppose not. But listen, Joe, ever since you started telling me that promotion, publicity, and personal appearances make or break an author, she's been impossible to live with."

"But, Olive, all the promotion you've done has worked," he said soothingly. "You're a best-seller now."

"Do you think she's satisfied yet?" Olive demanded, starting to sound a little hysterical. He heard some of those quick, panting breaths she took when she was trying to calm down.

"I didn't mind too much when she started nudging me aside at book signings," Olive admitted more evenly, "because I hate those things anyhow. And I guess it was kind of a blessing when she started taking over at those lunches with editors and publicists, although I wish she wouldn't drink so much—I mean, *I'm* always the one who pays for it later," she added bitterly. "I was even *grateful* when she started doing my interviews for me, because she doesn't mind answering all those stupid questions over and over—where do you get your ideas, do you research your sex scenes personally, and how much money do you make?

"But I can't take any more," Olive continued desperately. "Now she wants me to hire a decorator for my apartment, because she's afraid someone will see her living like this."

"She's actually talked to you about this?" Joe asked. When Olive responded affirmatively, he realized that she was even sicker than he had suspected. Poor kid, he thought.

"She's even thinking of moving, because Queens doesn't suit her image. She's actually talking about moving to Dallas, for God's sake! What would *I* do in Dallas?"

"Olive, there's a very good doctor I want you to see," Joe said seriously. "He's got a pretty full schedule, but he might—"

"I don't need a doctor," she snapped. "I need an exorcist. She's finally gone too far. Now the silly slut thinks she can write!"

He glanced at the *Times* list. "So do a lot of other people," he muttered. What a waste, he thought sadly. Such talent, such promise. Such royalty checks, such film deal potential.

"Well, she can't write!" Olive cried fiercely. "*I'm* the writer around here."

"Olive, I think you're slightly confused about—"

"No, *she's* the one who's confused. Everything was fine as long as our division of labor was clear. All I ever wanted was to be left alone to write, and all she ever wanted was to preen in the limelight that *I* earned for her."

"And that didn't bother you?" he asked carefully, keeping her talking as he started to scribble a message for his secretary.

"Well, I would have preferred it if she weren't so shallow," Olive said critically. "Have you read some of the goofy things she says to journalists?"

"Yes, of course," he said, opening his office door and signaling to his secretary. "*I'm* the one who convinced you to give all those interviews." It almost made him feel guilty. But how could he have known that public notoriety would drive her over the edge like this? His secretary silently read the note he handed her, nodded, and began dialing on another line.

"Those interviews are nothing compared to what she wants to do to my book," Olive complained. "You should *see* some of the crap she's trying to force me to include. It's too much, Joe. You've got to do something about her."

His secretary held the receiver away from her ear for a moment and said in a stage whisper, "He says he'd like to assess her immediately, and he thinks he can fit her in at two o'clock today. Can you get her there?"

Joe covered the mouthpiece of his own phone. "Tell him I'll try, but she's very sick. She may fight me."

He was about to return his attention to Olive when the door to the reception area opened. In walked Olive Gruberstein, dressed as Olympia Greco. "Olive?" he said incredulously.

"Yes," said the voice on the phone. "Joe, are you listening to me?"

"I . . . I, uh . . ." Doubtfully, he repeated, "Olive?"

The woman approaching him smiled. She was not Olive as *he* knew her—grubby jeans, careless ponytail, thick glasses, heavy book bag, and mercurial temperament. No, this was the woman that Olive, at his urging, had learned to present to her public.

"Not Olive," she said, her voice smooth and melodic. "Olympia." She smiled at him, her artfully applied cosmetics giving radiance to her thirtysomething features. Her gleaming blond hair was coiled in a sleek French twist, her lavender Halston skirt and jacket brought out the color of her eyes, and her silk blouse was both elegant and feminine. Her little handbag and matching shoes completed the ensemble, which was highlighted by discreet diamond earrings and a gold wristwatch. She extended one well-manicured hand toward him, smiled reassuringly, and said, "We really must talk, Joe."

"Olympia?" he repeated, his mind a blank.

"Oh, my God!" Olive cried on the telephone. "She's *there,* isn't she? She *told* me she was going to try to make a separate deal with you. She wants to cut me out totally, Joe!"

"Olive . . ." he began.

With a smooth, graceful motion and an air of self-assurance, Olympia took the receiver from him. "He'll call you back, Olive. *Do* try to show a little grace under pressure." She entered Joe's office and hung up the phone, then turned to face him.

"Hold all my calls," Joe said to his secretary, finding his voice. He entered the office and closed his door. Staring at her, he asked, "You're really Olympia Greco?"

She smiled alluringly. "You should know. You helped invent me."

"How is this possible?" he demanded.

"There are more things in heaven and earth, Joe . . ." She sighed. "But let's get down to business."

"What do you want to talk about?" he asked warily.

"Olive," she answered promptly. "Frankly, I think she's become something of a liability, don't you?"

He blinked. "But . . . she writes the books."

She shrugged dismissively. "But *I* pose for the cover photos, do the talk-show circuits, sponsor the 'Olympia Greco Romantic Hero Look-alike Contest,' go on the author tours, give all the speeches and interviews, and sign all the autographs." She leaned forward and met his gaze squarely. "It's clear that Olive and I can't coexist anymore. The question is, Joe, which of us do you find indispensable? The one who does all the things I've just described, all the things that catapulted us to bestsellerdom? Or the one who merely writes good books?"

He stared at her. "You're serious, aren't you?"

"Absolutely. Olive has become impossible. She even slipped through my fingers last week and told a talk-show host that the source of her love scenes was none of his damn business. You can *imagine* how hard I had to work to save the rest of the interview."

"So I have to choose, is that it?" Joe said.

"That's right. Olympia or Olive. Which will it be? I needn't add, I'm sure, that without me, Olive will go back to being a midlist author with good books and paltry royalties."

It took him only a moment to decide. He buzzed his secretary and said, "Prepare a letter to Olive Gruberstein telling her that I've enjoyed our association but am obliged to cut back on my work load. I'm sure she'll have no trouble finding a new agent."

With that done he turned to Olympia Greco and smiled. "It's going to be a pleasure working with you."

Sikander Khan

by
Margaret Ball

I think it was Charlie Chaplin who sagely observed that while stepping on a banana peel is funny, stepping over a banana peel and into an open manhole is a lot funnier. I'm not sure that has any particular relevance here. Just thought you'd like to hear it.

Humor runs the gamut from stepping into open manholes through the pie-in-the-face to finely honed nuances of language and manner. Not being visual, the latter are more difficult to convey, but have their own special rewards. Sometimes the guy who doesn't get the pie in the face can be more amusing to observe than the individual so gifted. Especially if he has little or no sense of humor himself.

In Australia my wife bought a T-shirt that shows a cluster of kookaburras sitting on a limb, all laughing themselves silly. At the end of the line is a single dour-faced member of the same species who, observing this uncontrolled hilarity, comments, "I don't get it." Because of this, the joke is on him.

As Margaret Ball notes, he has company.

Peshawar, 15 September 1876

My dear Eliza,
   You will be happy to know that only three days after reporting to our father's old regiment, your brother's energy, dedication and linguistic genius have already made a sensible impression

upon Colonel Vaughan. I have been honored by the position
of Special Assistant to the Political Officer for the Afridis—
a position created by Colonel Vaughan solely on my account!
Tomorrow I leave for tribal territory.

You will be anxious to know how all this came about. My
introduction to the regiment began most felicitously with the
greetings of one of our oldest and dearest friends—Ali Gul,
our father's faithful orderly, whom you will doubtless remember
quite clearly, since you were already eight years old when we
were sent home. Still a member of this regiment, he was waiting
for me when I arrived in Peshawar Cantonments three days ago.
He made himself known to me almost immediately, and, as is the
polite custom of the country, bent the knee to place his sword and
his wealth at my feet—the sword being regulation British army
issue, laid across the palms of his hands, and the wealth being
symbolized by a few rupees balanced precariously atop the flat of
the sword blade. I touched the sword in token of my acceptance of
his offer, wondering meanwhile whether I had any right to do so—
for after all, Ali Gul could hardly do homage to me as if I were his
feudal lord; he and I are now brothers in the service of the Queen,
and his obedience is owed to Colonel Vaughan, the head of the
regiment, and not to a mere ensign fresh from Britain's shores.

The colonel himself was gracious enough to welcome me personally to the regiment at Mess that night, and I made so bold as to
raise this question with him. He explained that Ali Gul's offer was
merely a formality which I should on no account take seriously.
Once my mind was relieved on this vexing point, I was able to
engage the colonel in conversation, mentioning the latest military
theories with which I had become *au courant* at Sandhurst and
offering to share my modern knowledge of the art of war with
any of my brother officers who might require a brief refresher
course. Unfortunately, Colonel Vaughan was unable to respond
to this suggestion at once, as just at that moment he was taken with
a coughing fit of some duration. Knowing that so seemingly trivial
an accident as the lodgement of a foreign particle in the throat
may well prove fatal if it is allowed to obstruct the windpipe, I
leapt to my feet and struck the colonel a smart blow between the
shoulder blades. So vigorous was my blow, so keen my anxiety
for the colonel's life, that I actually knocked him forward into the
tureen of hot soup which stood on the table before us. He emerged
sputtering and almost purple in his countenance, which ominous

coloration reassured me that I had acted not a moment too soon.

"Pray do not thank me, Colonel Vaughan," I said at once, before he could tender those expressions of gratitude which, however proper from one gentleman to another under such circumstances, ought on no account to be voiced from the colonel of the regiment to the most junior of his officers. "I did but do my duty as I saw it."

Colonel Vaughan leapt to his feet without speaking and hurried out of the Mess, making strange gurgling sounds. I felt some concern at this behavior, for no one had mentioned to me that our colonel was subject to fits of derangement, but one of my brother officers who happened to be seated nearby assured me that the colonel was merely in a hurry to change into a clean uniform.

"And does he always make those peculiar noises when changing clothes?" I inquired.

"Invariably," came the smooth reply. I must confess that for a moment I suspected Westbrook of "roasting" a "griffin" (as newcomers to the country are called), but there was no trace of merriment on his manly countenance.

Colonel Vaughan did not return that evening, nor was I able to see him on the following day. Since the regiment is not on active duty there is little to occupy the men and officers, and I might have been tempted—had my pecuniary circumstances warranted it—to join my fellows in the meaningless games of chance and other dissipations which constitute the daily round of a subaltern's existence between campaigns. Instead I spent the mornings, after drill, in practicing my Pashto with Ali Gul. I was glad to find that the language I had lisped in babyhood returned quickly to my adult mind, rendered agile as that mind has been by the intervening years of study of Latin, Greek, mathematics and the art of fortification. Indeed, the knowledge of classical tongues which I have acquired since my last acquaintance with the Afridi dialect of Pashto brought to mind several interesting parallels between that language and the Greek. Could this be merely coincidence? Or something more? I hope to pursue this question soon; my new appointment should give me ample opportunity to study this curious resemblance in more detail.

The afternoons I spent in walking round cantonments, observing the station's state of military preparedness and the conditions of the barracks. I was able to think of several ways in which the barracks themselves, as well as the routine of the men, could be improved.

These suggestions formed the body of a brief memorandum which I conveyed to Colonel Vaughan this very morning, with an appendix setting out my tentative hypotheses regarding the descent of the Afridi tribes from the Greek army of Alexander the Great.

Colonel Vaughan's response was gratifyingly prompt. Scarcely had my memorandum been placed on the colonel's desk when I heard him loudly demanding to know more about the author of what he rightly called "this extraordinary effusion."

"Twenty-three pages!" he bellowed at poor Farraghan, his aide. "Doesn't the fellow sleep?"

Farraghan's reply was pitched too low for my ears—not, of course, that I was eavesdropping; such a thing would be quite unbecoming an officer of Her Majesty's army. It was merely that I had lingered at the outer door of the colonel's office in case he wished to commend me at once for my vigorous activity and clear thinking. However, I heard the colonel's next words quite clearly.

"Well, I can't have any more of this!" I suppose he meant to say, *I can't have too much more of this;* I had observed already that the colonel did not always choose his words well. "If Baby Sahib is so interested in the Afridis, he can jolly well take himself out to Jamrud and study the tribe in their native habitat. Tell him to assist Phelps in pacifying the tribes, or whatever the man thinks he's doing about that trouble in the Khyber."

A murmur from Farraghan was interrupted by another shout from the colonel.

"Survive? Who the devil cares if he—oh, all right; send that old rascal Ali Gul along with him. He should be able to teach the boy how to keep out of the sights of a Khyber jezail, if anybody can. After all, it's his village causing half the trouble up there."

Naturally I understood that the colonel's irascible tone proceeded only from the warmth of his nature and the desire to see me properly rewarded for my energetic dedication to duty. With that grasp of every detail, no matter how small, that characterizes the truly successful man in every field of human affairs, the colonel had found a way to reward me without actually suggesting a promotion which would have unconscionably annoyed those ensigns senior to me in the regiment, while at the same time taking advantage of my amazing linguistic ability and the fact that I had been employing my mornings in the study of the Afridi dialect. I have no doubt that my diplomatic skills, combined with Ali Gul's local knowledge of the area, will result in a speedy conclusion to whatever minor tribal conflict the colonel was referring to; thus, my dear sister, you may expect that my next letter will recount further triumphs for the McAusland family name.

But I really must persuade Ali Gul to stop calling me "the Baby Sahib."

Your loving brother,
James Robertson McAusland

Fort Jamrud, 17 September 1876

My dear Eliza,

I have time for only a brief note to reassure you that I have arrived safely at this border fort and that I anticipate a speedy success in my dealings with the local tribes. The very first thing I discovered on my arrival was that Major Phelps (I voice this criticism of a brother officer only to you, my sister, and only in strictest confidence) has done little or nothing to resolve the tribal problem, preferring to cower within the fort and cast verbal animadversions on the Afridis.

Yesterday, when I reached Jamrud, Major Phelps very kindly invited me to ride up the pass with him for a short distance so that he could show me the troubled area and explain the difficulties he had encountered. It seems that two villages of the Ali Khels—Ali Gul's very tribe—are engaged in a deadly feud over water rights. Since this feud occurs beyond British territory, it would not in the usual run of things be of much concern to us. However, it seems that some gentlemen in the Governor-General's office are most desirous of obtaining a complete survey of the Khyber Pass so that they can evaluate its suitability for troop movements in the event of a war with Afghanistan. And the constant rifle fire between these two villages is much incommoding our surveying parties, so much so that absolutely nothing has been done since April.

"Can't blame the surveyors," Major Phelps remarked as our horses picked their way along the stony ground of the Khyber. "Bloody savages have a bad habit of torturing captives. Makes the survey party nervous. Got one of our men a month or two ago when the fool went hunting and stayed out past dusk." Eliza, I will spare your feminine delicacy the details of the torments which he then proceeded to describe, ending with, "and they stand round in a circle and watch you writhe in agony."

As I gazed about the barren, rock-strewn desolation of the Khyber, reflecting that any clump of thornbushes or red-rock ridge might well conceal a tribesman with jezail at the ready, I must confess that I felt a momentary depression quite unfitting a British officer. Was the task really so hopeless?

Major Phelps seemed bent on convincing me of this. The rest of his conversation was not much more cheerful. "The climate's not too bad at this time of year. Gets below freezing in winter, of course, and in the summer it's about one hundred twenty degrees in the shade, only, of course, there is no shade. By the way, are you keen on shooting?"

"Not particularly."

"Just as well. We have to send out pickets to guard the hilltops before you have a shoot, to keep the tribesmen away, and the men resent it rather. They keep thinking about—" And he reverted to the sad tale of the soldier who had been captured some months earlier.

A bullet whined past my ears and cracked against a rock to our left. Major Phelps promptly wheeled his horse and set off at a gallop back to the fort, calling over his shoulder, "Come along, Baby Sahib! Can't you take a hint?"

We were nearly back to the gates of Fort Jamrud when the major allowed his horse to slow to a walk and Ali Gul and I caught up with him. I ventured just one question.

"Don't the tribesmen understand that a surveying party could help settle their dispute about water rights, by determining the bounds of each village?"

"Couldn't say," said Major Phelps, chewing on his ginger moustache. "Never talk to the b——rs myself. Too dangerous."

And this man is the Political Officer in charge of the region!

Your loving brother,
James Robertson McAusland

Fort Jamrud, 18 September 1876

My dear Eliza,

I am sorry to report that the situation with the feuding tribes has grown considerably worse since my last letter. I am about to depart Fort Jamrud against the express command of my superior officer, in order to make my way to an Afridi village besieged by men who would like nothing better than to torture and kill any foreigner who violates their territory.

The attitude of the Afridis within the village is not all that friendly, either.

There is, then, some small possibility that I may not return to explain my actions to Major Phelps. In that eventuality I wish at least to be sure that you, best beloved of my sisters, know the reasons which compel me to this action, and why I feel the honor both of the regiment and of our family require me to take this step.

It began just this morning, when a Pathan arrived at the gates of the fort with news relating to the very trouble I had been sent here to investigate. Major Phelps chose to interrogate the man alone, leaving me to kick my heels outside his office. Ali Gul seemed as impatient as I was, and a little questioning brought out that he had recognized the scout as a nephew of his, one Sikander by name.

"But this is altogether extraordinary!" I exclaimed, momentarily diverted from my curiosity about the political situation. "Sikander, you know, is a corruption of 'Alexander'! Imagine that your sister's son should bear the same name as the great Macedonian! It supports the hypothesis I had begun to form of your tribe's descent—"

I had barely laid out the bare bones of my theory when Ali Gul informed me that his tribe had long known of their descent from one whom he called, in his quaint native way, "Sikander Zulqarnain," or "Alexander of the Two Horns," an appellation derived no doubt from the medieval Persian romance of that title.

"I do not think that your tribe's progenitor can have been Alexander himself," I said doubtfully, "for Arrian's writings suggest that he traversed a somewhat more northerly route through these hills, by way of the areas now known as Swat and Bajaur. However, Arrian does record that he sent his beloved companion Hephaestion with a part of the army south to make a bridge across the Indus. Hephaestion's army must have marched through one of the passes in this region—if not the Gumal or the Kohat, then why not the Khyber? And what could be more probable than that Hephaestion, like Alexander, founded cities en route, leaving some of his veterans to people them?"

So excited was I by this ethnographical discovery that I leapt up from the hard bench outside Major Phelps' office and began

pacing the hall, lecturing poor Ali Gul on the many correspond-
ences I had discovered between the Afridi dialect of Pashto and
the Greek of classical times.

"Your word *storai,* for star, is practically identical with the
Greek *aster.* Greek *laura,* an alley or passage, becomes the Pashto
lar. More commonly, though, we find the first syllable of the
Greek elided in the degenerate Pashto version—"

Here Ali Gul became somewhat excited and I had to calm him
down by explaining most carefully that the notion of "degener-
acy" in a language means nothing more than the loss or transposition
of certain sounds, and has nothing to say to the character of the
speakers of that tongue.

"Certainly no one would dare to claim that the Afridis of
Khaibar have lost some of their courage, simply because their
word for plate, *kkhanak,* has lost the initial 'le' of Greek *lekane;*
or that the Pashto *chara,* or knife, is less sharp than the Greek
small sword *machaira,*" I explained. "All the same, it does seem
a pity that the glory of Greek civilization has disappeared from
this region along with the syllables that have been elided from the
vocabulary!"

Here again Ali Gul took exception to my statement. The
romances of "Sikander Zulqarnain" are hardly to be accounted
history, rather they resemble the fairy tales which in our country
amuse small children; but the natives here, themselves childlike in
their credulity, take all these tales as sober fact. Ali Gul, therefore,
assured me most solemnly that his people were in no wise inferior
to their lofty ancestor (for he clung, in defiance of all historical
probability, to the belief that his tribe had been sired by none other
than Alexander himself). In proof whereof, he spun me a long tale
of "miracles" worked by one saint, or "Pir," after another—ending
with the preposterous claim that the mullah of his very own village
could fly backwards and forwards, and this not only through space
but also in time!

"Very impressive," I said, attempting to restrain my smiles,
"but hardly—"

Perhaps it was fortunate that we were interrupted at this junc-
ture by the abrupt opening of Major Phelps' door. The native scout
lay on the floor behind him in a widening pool of blood. I ran for
the surgeon, but when we returned, the Afridi Sikander was dead,
having expired in the arms of his uncle Ali Gul, and Phelps was
explaining indignantly that the man had said not a word about

being wounded until he fell to the floor in a dead faint, which fall had caused his wound to burst open and spatter the major's uniform with blood. Major Phelps seemed equally exercised by this accident and by the news which the man had brought; the death of the man Sikander, by contrast, appeared to trouble him not at all. Ali Gul and another orderly carried the body away in mournful silence while Major Phelps chattered about the man's news of the feud.

"He died to bring us this information," I said, somewhat rudely breaking in upon Major Phelps' monologue. "Surely we can arrange to have him buried with military honors?"

"Nonsense! He died from a shot fired at him as he was escaping from his village," the major said. "The fact that he came to us with the news is irrelevant. But what news—oh, what news!" And he actually rubbed his hands together. "The Gul Mast village is *kilabund*."

This meant that it had been completely surrounded by men of the opposing party, the men of Nur Mast. No one could get in or out of Gul Mast without coming under the fire of the Nur Mast jezails—as had happened to Sikander himself. What was more, the major informed me without troubling to disguise his satisfaction, the men of Nur Mast had also seized control of the watercourse which had inspired the original feud, a minute spring in the rocks above Gul Mast which flowed through and supplied water to both villages.

"Once they have blocked the spring, the Gul Mast will have no alternative but to surrender."

"That means to be massacred," I pointed out.

"Well? The alternative will be to await a lingering death of thirst." Major Phelps did not seem at all perturbed by the fact that his conversation foreshadowed the deaths of several dozen men, women and children.

"Oh, not very many men," he corrected me cheerfully when I brought up this point. "Sikander said most of them had died in the final fight for the spring. It'll be a village of women and children now."

Finding myself quite unable to stomach any more of the major's grisly jubilation, I excused myself on the plea of fatigue and begged permission to retire to my rooms. On the way I stopped by the fort surgeon's quarters and requested him to cover any costs associated with Sikander Khan's funeral out of my monthly pay.

Ali Gul was waiting in my rooms. He begged me to give him two weeks' leave "for urgent personal reasons."

"I don't think that is a very good idea," I told him, but he remained adamant that honor required him to return to his village and defend his people.

"You will die there!"

"I think not," he said, and then, "Someone has to tell the Pir that it is time to do what he must."

He was unable or unwilling to explain this statement, and I could not shake his insane confidence that he would be able somehow to protect his people and himself from the Nur Mast men. And his final argument was one against which I had no reply. "Would *you* stay safely in the fort, Baby Sahib, if it were your mother and sisters awaiting the advance of the foe?"

I threw up my hands. "Very well! I'll speak to Phelps about it at dinner."

"Now," Ali Gul insisted.

"Now," I said, "on one condition." I looked him very severely in the eye. "There is a certain opprobrious nickname, quite unfitting a grown man and an officer in one of Her Majesty's regiments, which I desire you to put completely out of your memory. Are we understood?"

Ali Gul agreed quite gravely that he understood my meaning; but there was a twinkle in his eye that made me rather uneasy.

On the other hand, he did not have at all the air of a man going to his death; and that assuaged my conscience somewhat. The situation seemed desperate to me and hopeless to Major Phelps, but it was just barely possible that Ali Gul knew something we did not know, some clever bargaining trick perhaps by which he hoped to end the feud at the last minute.

I found Major Phelps as adamant against Ali Gul's request for leave as I had first been, and without the understanding of Pathan honor that had swayed me to accede to his request. "Absolutely not," he told me. "Can't have soldiers getting mixed up in local feuds. Don't approve of my people getting killed for no reason."

"But, sir," I explained, "if Ali Gul's village is massacred, he will probably desert from the army and revive the feud on his own account. In fact, his honor demands no less."

Phelps shook his head. "In that case he'll be a damned deserter and none of my problem—unless I catch him, in which case it'll be my duty to hang him. But tonight and until I hear otherwise, he's a soldier of the Queen and he has no right to risk the Queen's property—himself, that is—in a pointless mission."

He was perfectly logical, perfectly English, you might say. And I had, myself, very little heart to persuade him. The longer I stayed talking with Phelps, the less weight I could place on Ali Gul's puzzling confidence. All of logic and reason was on Phelps' side: if we gave Ali Gul leave now, we would be as good as signing his death warrant. I could hardly blame the major for his unwillingness to do that.

I was somewhat surprised to find that, the question of Ali Gul's personal leave settled, Major Phelps seemed eager for me to stay and chat with him awhile. He asked about my theories of the Afridis' Greek descent, listened with every appearance of interest to the etymological evidence which I propounded, but finally pooh-poohed the entire theory.

"You see, my boy," he said, "the Afridis cannot possibly be descended from the Greeks, because *I* have proved that they are really the descendants of the Ten Lost Tribes of Israel. Only look at the names—Ibrahim, Suleiman . . ."

I perceived that I was in the presence of a man whose monomania prevented him from taking a reasoned and logical view of the situation. There was nothing to do but to withdraw.

Once back at my rooms, though, I discovered that I had lingered too long with the major. Ali Gul was nowhere to be found, and when I sent a soldier to look for him, the man reported that he knew nothing about my orderly, but that the guard had seen "a marauding Pathan" jump down from the mud wall of the fort and run away into the hills some fifteen minutes earlier.

Back I went to Major Phelps' office, only to find him inflexible. He would not permit me to follow Ali Gul; he would not grant retroactive personal leave; in fact, he had occupied the minutes since my departure in drawing up an order that anyone found absent without leave "in the present state of tribal unrest" should be subject to the severest penalties prescribed by the army for any such case.

"But that means hanging," I exclaimed, appalled that in pleading Ali Gul's case I had only created a new threat to him where none existed before.

"Or in the case of an officer, cashiering," Major Phelps murmured, staring brightly at me. "I trust a word to the wise will be sufficient, McAusland?"

I excused myself in some confusion and retired—for the third time that day!—to my rooms. Here I have been thinking out my plan of action and inditing this letter, possibly my last, to you, my dear sister.

Ali Gul cannot be permitted to disgrace his uniform in this manner. His years of honorable service demand a better end. Furthermore, if he dies as a deserter, his heirs will not be eligible for the pension he has so richly earned. I have no alternative but to go after him.

There is some possibility that I may be able to negotiate an end to this feud. Surely the two villages can learn to share the watercourse on an equal basis! Major Phelps admits that he has never tried to deal with them directly; perhaps I, speaking something of the language, may persuade the men of Nur Mast and the remaining women of Gul Mast to make peace.

And even if I fail in this objective, I may—I *must*—persuade Ali Gul to return with me, lest his years of service come to naught and his family be left without the pension which was to have supported him and his womenfolk in their old age.

I should be able to leave the fort unchallenged; the guard would hardly question an officer's movements. If I can reach the village of Gul Mast and bring Ali Gul back to the fort with me before daylight tomorrow, we may never be missed and there may be no reason for the major to know of this unauthorized excursion. Should I be caught and cashiered, I hope that you, our sisters, and our dear mother will understand that honor alone forced me into this seemingly dishonorable course. And should I not return— well, this letter should ensure that *one*, at least, knows the truth of my disappearance, and that one the best beloved and most valued sister a man ever had.

> Your devoted brother,
> James Robertson McAusland

Gul Mast village, 19 September 1876

My dear Eliza,

I pen this letter to you from a rude mud-walled hut in Gul Mast village, knowing not whether it will ever reach you. My hopes of a speedy return to Fort Jamrud have been dashed by circumstances impossible to predict, and Ali Gul believes that we shall not even be able to make our way around the scene of the disaster to reach Peshawar. But this can be better explained in the proper place.

I left the fort as planned and rode into the Khyber as far as the place where the first bullets had warned Phelps and myself away on the preceding afternoon. At that time I had marked a small grassy cleft in the rocks where a few stunted trees marked the course of the very stream whose source had been the bone of contention in this feud. I tethered my horse there and proceeded cautiously on foot, hoping to use the cover of the rocks and the rugged terrain to conceal me from the sight of the besiegers. All went well until I was within sight of the high square mud walls of Gul Mast village. There was no sign of life about the place; the twenty-foot walls of yellow mud bricks precluded any view of the interior buildings, the massive gate was shut and barred, and the high mud tower that brooded above the walls appeared to be quite empty. As I approached, the sun struck a flash of light from something at one of the loopholes in the tower; it might have been a rifle barrel gleaming blue-black in the sun, or it might not. The thought did little to ease the creeping sensation at the back of my neck. I had as well the indefinable sensation of being watched by unfriendly eyes.

I was not twenty yards from the locked gate of the village when the shots began. A fusillade of bullets sprinkled the dust about my feet. I ran towards the mud walls of Gul Mast, shouting *"Ashnac! Ashnac!"* which in Pashto signifies "Friend!" Behind me there was the spatter of bullets and the laughter of concealed watchers echoing off the rocky fastnesses of the Khyber; before me, I saw with inexpressible gratitude, the heavy gate slowly opened. A rifle cracked above my head; someone in the tower was firing to keep the besiegers from rushing me. I skidded through the loose pebbles and dust before the walls and fairly hurled myself through the crack.

A thin girl-child in a single dusty, ragged garment laboriously closed the great door again; I put my shoulder to the ponderous boards and together we wrestled it into place. The iron bar which was to fall across the inside was far beyond her strength to lift, and there was a trick to the catch holding it up which I could not at once discover, breathless as I was and with my fingers slippery with sweat. There was a low musical laugh behind me, and a scent of roses; brown fingers slipped over mine and I learned the secret of the catch while distracted by the presence of a female in uncomfortably close proximity.

The bar fell into place with a thunderous clang. Someone shouted in Pashto, "W——! Get back to thy quarters!" and the woman behind me moved away. I turned to see an immensely old man, clad in a turban and robes of snowy white, reclining at his ease on a charpoy (a native string bed) under the shade of a thatched awning. Behind him and to either side of the gate, narrow, dark, malodorous passages led to the inner parts of the village, which I now saw could more properly be termed a single, great, rabbit warren of a fortified house. From one of those passages I sensed the gleam of two large dark eyes and the hint of a smile; then the old man roared again and the mysterious lady vanished into the interior of the house.

While I collected my breath and my wits, the rifleman whose covering fire had saved me descended from his post atop the tower. "You should not have come here, Ba-McAusland Sahib," Ali Gul reproved me gravely.

The hours since his disappearance from Fort Jamrud had been sufficient to complete Ali Gul's transformation from a proud soldier of the Queen into a dirty Pathan. I matched his disapproving look with one of my own as I took in his new character: the uniform he had worn with so much pride replaced by a long loose blue tunic and baggy drawers that had been white a very long time ago; grass sandals in place of his military boots, scented oil greasing his long hair, a wicked curved knife at his side. The only sign of his lifetime of military service was the gleam of the Enfield rifle in his gnarled hands.

"Nor should you have come, Ali Gul," I said at length, after a pause sufficient to satisfy the native penchant for drama. "You have been unfaithful to your salt."

This charge stung Ali Gul; his eyes fell and he heaved a deep sigh. "I know, McAusland Sahib. But these are my people, and I must be with them when we go."

"Go where?" I demanded. "You cannot think that those savages outside will simply let you walk away from the village?"

"We have no intention of leaving our home," Ali Gul replied, confusing me more than ever. Suddenly the brassy rays of the sun, which I had ignored while setting out at midday, seemed to beat down on my head like hammers striking a gong. I put one hand to my forehead.

"We fail in hospitality!" said the old man in his deep, harsh voice. He caught his breath painfully between sentences while he ordered the women who waited in every shadowed doorway to come out and make their guest welcome. A second charpoy was brought out for me, cushions and rugs put round it, and the dark-eyed houri who peeped at me from the doorway was sent to tell the women to prepare food for the guest.

While these preparations were going on, Ali Gul and the mullah of the village—for such was, I deduced, the old man's position—were arguing in low voices that gradually grew louder and shriller.

"I am ready to do it now," the mullah said. He was still gasping between sentences, and there was a blue tinge to his lips that I did not like.

"We will have to wait until after dark," Ali Gul insisted. "My Sahib must not go with us, and he cannot leave the village until night."

"I may not be strong enough by nightfall!"

"If it is a matter of some special prayers which your mullah must offer up," I hazarded, "something which the presence of an unbeliever would spoil—"

"Something like that," Ali Gul agreed gravely.

"Then could I not retire into some other part of the village while he performs his rites?"

Ali Gul was vehement that this would not serve; not at all. "You will leave before moonrise," he said firmly, "and Allah guide your steps back to the fort!"

"I shall have no need of Allah's guidance if you come with me, Ali Gul."

I explained to him about Major Phelps' decree, the fact that if he did not return before daylight he would be accounted a deserter and all would go for naught—his lifetime of honorable service, the pension he had earned a dozen times over, all would be lost for this one night's folly! Ali Gul only shook his head. "I am sorry, Ba-Lieutenant, but these things do not matter where we are going."

"There is nowhere you can go where the Queen's arm cannot reach," I said.

Ali Gul only pressed his lips together and smiled. This was pretentious bombast, and both he and I knew it. Should he lead his depleted tribe into the hills of Afghanistan, we would scarcely risk offending Dost Mohammed by sending our army after a single deserter. I deduced from his obstinate silence that this or something like it must be his plan, and that he did not intend to tell me where his people would seek refuge.

A choking gasp from the other charpoy recalled us to the mullah's side. While we had been arguing, his condition had become much worse; even I, no medical man, could see that his heart was rapidly failing. He could barely draw enough breath to whisper to us, and he clutched his left side like a man in severe pain.

"*Now,*" he whispered to Ali Gul, "by nightfall I may no longer be able to say the words!"

I turned my back and gazed fixedly at the yellow bricks of the wall, in an effort to spare the old man as much as possible of my presence at what must surely be his final prayers. He spoke some words in Arabic and then continued in a tongue I did not recognize, his voice growing louder and firmer with every syllable, as though the very act of praying had brought some relief to his tortured body. The reverberations of his voice increased until it seemed to me that the entire village was trembling with them and that there must be a whole chorus of aged mullahs chanting in unison; the hills outside returned their echoes and for a moment I was well-nigh deafened by the mullah's peremptory shouting, repeated and echoed as it was by the mud walls and the rocky hills.

The ground under my feet gave a sudden jerk and then there was a sickening sliding motion such as I have never experienced. I felt as if I were in the hand of God, being lifted above the earth to be His plaything for a moment; then the world around me steadied.

The mullah fell silent, either exhausted from his effort or shocked into silence by the earthquake. A babbling crowd of women emerged from the dark interior passages of the village and peered through the newly opened cracks in the outer wall.

"It worked," one of the women called out. "The Nur Mastis are gone!"

"They could be hiding," said another one.

"I myself will prove to you that they are gone," Ali Gul announced. Laying down his rifle, he strode to the massive front gate and lifted the bar. With a single powerful pull he swung the iron-studded door inwards and stood full in the open doorway.

I shut my eyes and murmured a brief prayer, expecting at any moment to see him fall, riddled by a dozen bullets.

Nothing happened; no sound but that of birdsong broke the stillness.

Ali Gul stepped out into the barren rocky ground before the village. Still there was no sound of an attack. Solemnly, he made a circuit of the exposed ground, then went down into the ravine and up the other side. Each time he disappeared behind rocks or folds in the hills I wondered if I would ever see him again; each time his blue turban reappeared and he waved to show us that he was unharmed.

"The earthquake must have startled the Nur Mastis away," I exclaimed when he returned unhurt. "Now is your chance to get your people away, Ali Gul! Let the men of the village take their rifles and guard the party. I will take you all to Fort Jamrud—"

I was interrupted by the dark beauty with the rose-scented hands. She left the wall and came towards us, her full skirts swaying with every step, dark eyes sparkling with an expression I was at a loss to interpret.

"These *are* the men of the village, Sahib," she said, waving her hand at Ali Gul and at the mullah, who had fallen back exhausted on the cushions of his charpoy. "Those who did not die in the years of the feud died this morning when the Nur Mastis rushed the spring. Only Sikander got away—"

"Peace, Jamila! Sikander died at the Angrezi fort," Ali Khan said in a low voice.

There was a wail behind us and a woman fell to the ground, clawing her loose hair over her face.

"Silence, fool!" Jamila said over her shoulder. "Now you are without a man, that is all. *I* have been without a man these three years—now we are all without men—now you fools will see how you like it!" She turned back to Ali Gul. Her eyes blazed with anger and her body was braced with a most unfeminine lack of modesty. "What are we to do *now*?" she demanded. "You and the Pir there have saved us from the Nur Mastis—oh, excellently done! Why could your infinite masculine wisdom not have acted a little sooner!"

"I had hoped that we could wait until the Pir was a little stronger," Ali Gul excused himself. "See for yourself how much this effort has tired him."

Indeed, the old man lay like one near death, his cheeks fallen inward and his skin already covered with a waxy pallor, and I feared that the shock of the earthquake might have been sufficient to kill him. But his eyelids still fluttered and the faint rise and fall of his chest reassured me that he still breathed.

Jamila spared the old mullah just one look. "I care not if it *killed* him," she berated Ali Gul. "You have just killed us all. What are we to do now, a village of women in a land without men? Who is to till the land? Who will give us sons? Do you and this Sahib here think you can service the lot of us, like two stallions put to a herd of mares, and then go out in the day to work the fields for the whole village?"

The look of withering scorn with which she accompanied these words ended my dreams of dark eyes and tremulous lips forever. The woman was possessed of a devil!

How long her tirade would have gone on I do not know; fortunately she was interrupted just then by a chorus of shrieks and wails from the far side of the village. Ali Gul and I, thinking someone had been injured and just now discovered, ran to the spot, only to find a group of women staring disconsolately at an empty ditch.

"The spring has dried up!" one of them said accusingly.

"Or the Nur Mastis have blocked it!" hazarded another.

"What shall we do without water?"

"Peace, women!" roared Ali Gul in the parade-ground voice that had trained so many generations of raw new Pathan recruits. "The Nur Mastis are not here."

"As for the spring," I interposed, "may it not be that the earthquake which shook the village may also have changed its course slightly?"

"An excellent suggestion," said Ali Gul. "You and I shall go and investigate, Baby Sahib."

As we left the village I noticed that Ali Gul's forehead was beaded with sweat. He wiped his face and exclaimed with feeling, "Truly is it written that one woman may be the light of a house, but two or more together are the devil! I had not considered what it would be like to live in a village of nearly twoscore she-devils without men to keep them in order!"

"You have always the option of returning to your duty at Fort Jamrud," I pointed out.

He shook his head. "There is no going back now, Baby Sahib, for either of us."

"*You* may choose to be a deserter if you like," I said, rather sharply, "*I* intend to honor my oath to the Queen!"

We climbed in silence to the promontory whence the spring issued from the rock. Here my hypothesis was verified. Instead of running along the old *nullah,* the spring rose into a bubbling pool in the limestone rock, then vanished underground again. Curious to relate, the earthquake had left no visible scars on the ground; yet there was no trace of the old watercourse. It must have been swallowed up in a single convulsive opening of the earth; but why were there no other signs of the earthquake—freshly tumbled earth, broken rocks or trees uprooted?

I was at a loss to explain this, but the mystery of the vanishing *nullah* soon became insignificant compared to the other disappearances which I discovered. Ali Gul's continued gloomy insistence that I could not return to the fort had annoyed me beyond all reason. Once we had located the spring, I bade him a curt farewell and announced my intention of returning to Jamrud immediately.

"If you have any desire to save your name and your pension, you will come with me," I told him.

Ali Gul gave me a sad smile but said nothing. I turned away from him and went down the hill on the east side, aiming for the spot where I had tied my mare earlier.

The horse was no longer there. I was not overly surprised. No doubt the convulsion of the earth had terrified her so that she broke the reins tethering her and ran away. It did seem strange that there were no broken strips of leather dangling from the little tree where I had tied her, but I had not leisure to consider this minor mystery in detail; I was too preoccupied with other, more pressing questions. Such as, could I walk from here to the fort without severely blistering my feet? And, if the mare had run into the hills, how could I conceal her loss?

I would, I decided, have to claim that I had been thrown when a *chikor* rose from behind a rock and startled the mare; a story which, while reflecting no credit on my horsemanship, at least saved me from admitting that I had ridden out with the intention of disobeying Major Phelps' express orders. Still pondering this story, and brooding over my loss of Ali Gul, I topped the rise of a low hill and surveyed the bare plain before me without comprehension.

From where I stood, the rolling hills of the Khyber smoothed out into a long, rocky slope that should have presented no barrier to a view of Fort Jamrud. But nowhere did I see the square mud-colored walls and stubby guard towers of the old fort. Like the *nullah* through which the Gul Mast spring formerly ran, it had vanished without a trace. Not even a pile of rubble marked the former site of the fort.

I could scarcely credit that the minor tremor I had felt in the village could, in the open plain, have become an earthquake of such power that it could engulf an entire fort and all the horses, men, officers, and followers housed within its walls. The magnitude of the calamity was then, and still is now, too great for me to comprehend. Stumbling like a man half bereft of his senses, I made my way back to the only refuge known to me in this wilderness—the Afridi village of Gul Mast. As I walked, it occurred to me to wonder whether Ali Gul had known of the fort's disappearance, and if that had been why he felt so sure that neither he nor I could return thither. But how *could* he have known? No human being can predict the course of an earthquake. Ali Gul had not left the village until I myself did.

Could it have been, not an earthquake that I felt, but the after-shock of some devilish explosion engineered by Moslem fanatics? Impossible. Such a quantity of blasting powder could hardly have been brought secretly into the fort, nor would such an explosion have caused the debris of a mud-walled fort to vanish without a trace. With some relief I exculpated Ali Gul from the fiendish plot I had begun to imagine; but I was left without explanation, without plans. All I could think was that I must borrow a horse in the village so that I might ride to Peshawar with the news of this disaster.

I returned to find that the women had, thankfully, somewhat calmed down since my departure. The mullah had sent several of the younger women, including the contentious Jamila and his own daughter, to fetch water from the spring; the rest were engaged in preparation of the evening meal.

When I broached my plan to Ali Gul, he said only: "And what makes the Sahib suppose that Peshawar is still there?" But seeing, I suppose, the determination in my countenance, he sighed and agreed that I might have the loan of a horse from the village stables in the morning; it was clearly too late now for us to set forth.

"Us?"

He would, he said firmly, accompany me; he left unspoken

what he might as well have put into words, that I would need
someone to turn to when I discovered that Peshawar had met the
same fate as Fort Jamrud.

I cannot credit that such a thing could be, that a city of over
fifty thousand souls could vanish without a trace. But then, an
hour earlier I would have said the same thing of Fort Jamrud
and the seven hundred men quartered there. Ali Gul's persistent
pessimism begins to infect my spirits, Eliza, and now as the
shadows sink over the hills and night covers the Khyber Pass I
feel as though my whole world had disappeared in the twinkling
of an eye, leaving me and the people of Gul Mast alone in a
new-made universe.

Such melancholy speculations make a poor close to a letter,
but the light fails now and—

Someone is shouting outside the walls; I must go and see what
has happened. Can the men of Nur Mast have recovered from the
shock of the earthquake and returned to wreak what damage they
may? The women should have been back with water by now. In
haste and grave concern, Eliza, I remain—

> Your loving brother,
> James Robertson McAusland

20 September 1876

My dear Eliza,

I hasten to reassure you that all has ended happily, thanks to
your brother's quick wits and ready application of his classical
studies to everyday life. Those shouts which caused me to close
my previous letter so rapidly did indeed represent a potential
danger to the villagers and to myself, but by quick thinking
and superb negotiating skills I have turned a near tragedy into
triumph.

To revert to the events of last night:

Immediately after sealing my letter to you I went out to find
what I begin to think of as the archetypical Gul Mast scene: a
group of women wailing and howling imprecations round the
charpoy from which the aged mullah held court. Ali Gul shouted
to me to come up into the watchtower where he stood. I mounted
the stairs and saw, standing boldly less than a musket shot from
the walls, a group of emaciated, ragged fellows whose antiquated
arms of short swords and curved leather shields might as well

have come from the days of Homer as from the hills of modern Afghanistan. (This comparison did not come to me without reason, as you shall see, dear sister.) At first I wondered why Ali Gul did not shoot at the men to warn them away from the village bounds in the traditional Afridi manner, but then the spokesman for the group moved to one side and I understood the reason for Ali Gul's agonized indecision. The widow Jamila stood in the midst of the group, her arms tightly held, a knife at her throat. Her black eyes flashed defiance at her captors and her fine high bosom heaved in a manner which—well, Eliza, you are far too pure and delicate to understand the effect which certain sights can have upon a man's animal nature. Suffice it to say that although I scarcely knew Jamila and did not like what little I knew of her, my whole being was afire with the necessity to rescue her from the brutes who held her.

The intruders shouted something which sounded not at all like any dialect of Pashto. Apparently their words were also unintelligible to Ali Gul, for he called back, "What are you saying? Who are you?"

This exchange of mutually incomprehensible shouts went on for a few minutes more. The only word which came out clearly was something like *"ksandros,"* repeated over and over again with emphatic gestures to the north. Could this, I wondered, be another dialect's version of "Sikander," the name by which Alexander the Great had been remembered in these hills? For a moment my mind wandered to my etymological researches concerning the affinity of the Pashto to the Greek, and in that moment, when I was no longer trying to understand the strangers' speech *as Pashto,* their words seemed to make sense to me—*as Greek!*

Deciding to test my theory, I shouted forth, *"Chairete!"*

The tribesmen started and muttered among themselves, then one who seemed to be their leader advanced and called, "Speak, barbarian!"

For a few minutes longer we called back and forth across the space of ground which separated us. I had the greatest difficulty in understanding the man, for his use of accents was entirely wrong and he mispronounced the words barbarously, half swallowing every third or fourth syllable; still, I could follow enough to establish some communication. And the *manner* of that communication excited me beyond words, proving as it did without any doubt the validity of my hypothesis concerning the origins of the Afridi Pathans.

I turned to Ali Gul. "They have captured all the women who were sent to fetch water," I announced, perhaps a shade too cheerfully considering the gravity of our situation. "They wish to barter for them, but what they want to trade I cannot quite understand. They want me to go down and talk with them outside the fort."

"Impossible," Ali Gul growled. "You are our guest. Our honor will be violated if you are harmed while under our protection."

"And what if the women are hurt?" I demanded. "What does your precious honor have to say about that?"

He shrugged. "They are only women. We have too many females now anyway."

"Let him go," said a wavering voice behind us. I turned and saw that the ancient mullah had somehow summoned up the energy to haul himself up the steps of the watchtower. He looked on the point of death; I hurried to support the old man and eased him gently down upon the floor where he could lean his back against a wall.

"For an unbeliever and an eater of pigs, my son, you are not entirely a bad man," the mullah sighed. He looked at Ali Gul again. "My daughter is one of the prisoners. If this Sahib can persuade the strangers to let her go, I say he should be allowed to try."

A few minutes later I crossed the rock-strewn flat ground before the fort until I stood within speaking distance of the tribesmen who had captured our women—for so I felt now; Gul Mast was *my* village, and the women who had been taken were *my* responsibility.

I was greatly relieved to see that they had not yet been harmed. Indeed, they seemed, if anything, happier than they had been in the village. Jamila was flashing her eyes at the man who'd dared hold a knife to her throat while he stammered words of apology. The thin ragged girl whom I took to be the mullah's daughter was seated on a grassy bank just out of sight of the fort and admiring her face in the polished brass of another man's shield. And the other two girls were laughing in a most improper manner while three more sunburnt tribesmen petted them.

If these tribesmen had not been so gaunt and hungry-eyed, with skin stretched tight over their bones and teeth bared like wolves come down from the mountains, the scene might almost have been a pleasant one.

I do not know whether the idea came to me just then, or whether it was a few minutes later, while the leader was setting forth in atrocious Greek his demands for food, horses, and weapons.

"You should be ashamed of yourselves," I said sternly, "strong men like you turning to brigandage instead of working honestly on the land."

I spoke with the pure classical accent inculcated at the Academy, of course, and so several repetitions were required before my statement could be understood in the degenerated semi-Greek jargon spoken by these men; but when they did take my meaning, they responded immediately with a babble of indignant protests that I, in my turn, took some time to sort out.

They had no wish to be brigands, they claimed, but what choice did they have? Their leader, the "Ksandros" mentioned before, had taken them far, far from their homeland and then had divided his army, he himself going to the north while he ordered them to the south. Without "Ksandros" to inspire them they had lost faith and run away from their fellows, hoping to walk back to their home; but the way was too hard, they were hungry, they had been wandering in these hills for weeks without seeing a friendly face. The natives of these parts hated them and tried to kill them. What were a group of poor soldiers to do?

I suffered the most intense curiosity concerning the location of their home, which to judge from their primitive clothes and equipment must have been somewhere very far back in the hills indeed. They carried only short swords and a few round shields—no rifles; not even matchlocks! And although their manner of speech was crude and ungrammatical and interlarded with incomprehensible obscenities, I felt sure that at least one-half their vocabulary— quite possibly more—was quite recognizable as a degenerate form of the very classical Greek which I had learned at school.

Somewhere in the remote fastnesses of Afghanistan there must be tribes which had remained hidden since the time of Alexander, almost uncorrupted by contact with the outside world. These pitiful, ragged representatives of the tribe, sorry specimens though they were, were the lineal descendants of Alexander's soldiers.

Excitement all but distracted me from my task as negotiator. But I put aside the question of locating their homeland for a later time, thinking—fool that I was—that if my suggestion succeeded,

there would be more than enough time to make detailed ethnographical notes, collect vocabulary samples, get a description of
their home valley—in short, to learn all I needed to know in order
to substantiate my case. And so I let all that wait while I proposed
a solution that would benefit these hungry men and the villagers
of Gul Mast equally.

They must have been very tired of wandering, for they acceded
to my suggestion almost at once. Now it remained only to convince the people of Gul Mast. Jamila volunteered to return with
me to speak for the newcomers, but the soldier who had captured
her objected somewhat vociferously; so, much to my relief, one
of the quieter women came with me instead.

"They are good boys," she told the assembled women after I
had explained my plan. "Confused, yes. But mostly they are tired
and hungry and they have not had women to care for them for a
long time."

The women of the village nodded and crowded to the cracks
in the wall so that they could peep out at the tribesmen.

"That one has rather a look of my Ibrahim, Allah keep him,"
exclaimed one of the new-made widows.

"What a fine, strapping fellow the one with the helmet will be,
after I feed him some good pilaf!"

"I like the one with blue eyes."

"I saw him first!"

Well, women will squabble; I see no reason to repeat all their
babble to weary you. Suffice it to say that they accepted my plan
with immodest enthusiasm; indeed (and this I can only put down
to the pernicious influence of that sharp-spoken Jamila) they did
not even pause to consult Ali Gul and the mullah, who as the only
remaining men of the village should have been the ones to make
the decision. By the time Ali Gul had helped the mullah down
from the watchtower, half the women were busy cooking a feast
of welcome for the newcomers while the other half had pushed the
outer doors of the village wide open and were advancing shame-
lessly to take their pick of the husbands I had found for them.

My memory of the next few hours is, I regret to say, somewhat
confused. The women of Gul Mast had gotten completely out of
hand! They produced skins of some fermented drink which they
had, it seems, been in the habit of making and concealing in
direct contravention of the Prophet's law. They and the brigands
proceeded to get uproariously drunk in the name of what they

termed a "wedding feast," though the mullah refused to bless a
ceremony in which all the participants were blatantly violating
the laws of Islam. The lack of a common language did not seem
to hamper either the women or the brigands; they quickly found
their own means of communication.

Even I was not safe from the importunities of those shameless
females. They began by suggesting that I should join the brigands
in choosing a bride from among their number "since you cannot
now return to your own people"; continued by making increasingly lewd suggestions as to the tests I might employ to select my
woman; and finally began an actual assault on my own person—
on my nether garments, that is. "Let us see if the Angrez are made
like our men!" shrilled Jamila.

I removed myself somewhat unceremoniously from her grasp
and fled to the watchtower, where Ali Gul and the mullah greeted
me with long faces and dour looks.

"Women need men to rule them," Ali Gul said sourly.

"These particular men are as bad as the women," I said, indicating a bridegroom who was dancing under a woman's veil while he
gnawed on a leg of roast mutton. And I sighed for the ethnograph-
ic opportunities going to waste. I had hoped that the brigands'
marriage customs would demonstrate some unquestionable cultural survivals from the chaste, dignified ceremonies recorded by
their ancestors of classical times. Instead, they seemed to have
nothing more in mind than drinking and enjoying themselves. It
was a most unedifying spectacle.

"What can you expect? They are all *Kafirs*," unbelievers, said
the mullah most gloomily of all. Before the festivities grew so
wild he had asked me to pose a few questions to the brigands, and had grown very long-faced on discovering that not
only could they not tell him whether they belonged to the Shia
or the Sunni sect of Islam, they had never even heard of the
Prophet.

"You will teach them better," I suggested.

He shook his head. "No. It is too soon for that. The Prophet
has not yet come."

This statement made no sense at all to me, but then it is possible
that my grasp of Pashto tenses is not quite perfect. In any case,
I did not conceive it my place to enter into metaphysical or
theological arguments with an uneducated Pathan, so I made
myself as comfortable as might be in a corner and went to sleep

while Ali Gul and the mullah complained in low tones about the wild behavior of their women.

"This is no place for a good Moslem," was the last thing I could remember the mullah saying. "I had rather return to die as a Moslem than live here as a *Kafir*. Besides, I owe this young unbeliever here a debt for the safe return of my daughter—even if she has chosen to follow the pagans into debauchery."

"If you return, then so shall I," said Ali Gul. "You are right, my grandfather. This is no place for decent Moslem men."

At that point I fell into a confused sleep interrupted sometimes by the sounds of revelry below, sometimes by the mullah's sonorous chanting. In my dreams I fancied that the sunburnt, ragged barbarians below shouted *"Euoi! Euoi!"* to Bacchus and bound garlands of leafy vines round their heads. And in my dreams I took painstaking notes of this and other customs that could only have been handed down from their Greek ancestors in antiquity.

I woke chilled and stiff, bruised and tumbled as if I had just fallen out of bed. I must indeed have fallen from a considerable height, for I lay now on the bare ground, rather than on the floor of the topmost chamber in the watchtower. The ground was slightly softer.

Sitting up, I looked about me in confusion. This was clearly the ravine where the village of Gul Mast had stood; but the village itself was nowhere to be seen! Could a second earth tremor have swallowed up the village, just as the first had engulfed Fort Jamrud?

I looked to Ali Gul for enlightenment. He was holding the mullah in his arms. The old man's face was waxen and his cheeks had fallen in; the bright dark eyes stared unblinking at the dawn sky.

"Ali Gul, do you know what has happened?"

"He has come home," Ali Gul said softly. He lowered the mullah's emaciated body to the earth and gently closed the staring eyes. "The effort was too much for him, but he lived to see the dawn rise in a world that knows the Prophet and Allah. And with the last of his strength he brought us home also."

And that was very nearly the last word Ali Gul has ever said upon the subject. He does not grieve for his people, and seems sure that they have escaped the earthquake; but whither they have fled, or where they may have settled in the hills of Afghanistan, he will not or cannot say.

I had no leisure to question him at this time, for we were

approached by two separate groups of men. From the ridges of
the Khyber Pass to the west came the men of Nur Mast, jezails
at the ready, calling to one another to witness the miraculous
disappearance of the enemy village. And up the long slope to
the eastern plain came a troop of men from Fort Jamrud, headed
by none other than Major Phelps, whom I had thought dead and
buried in the disaster that overtook the fort.

Explanations were confusing and misunderstandings were rife
in the minutes that followed, and I can only account it a miracle
that the two groups did not shoot at one another but instead
gathered around Ali Gul and myself to satisfy their curiosity. Not
that I could say very much to any of their questions. Fortunately,
both Major Phelps and the Afridis of Nur Mast behaved much
as men usually do; that is to say, they asked questions without
waiting for the answers, then answered themselves according to
what seemed most probable by their lights.

Thus, the men of Nur Mast decided that I, the stranger whose
arrival had preceded the disaster, must be a mighty wizard who
had ended the feud by destroying an entire village. I had com-
pounded my favor to them by rescuing from the wreck the body
of the mullah, whom they now proposed to venerate as a saint.
"We have long needed a saint's bones so that we could set up
a shrine of our own," their spokesman informed me cheerfully,
"and I suppose the old man was as holy as any, though his magic
was not as strong as yours, Sahib."

"No magic is so strong as that of the Sahib's," murmured the
men behind him. "Allah! an entire village is gone as though it had
never been." They shuffled about nervously, each one trying to
get behind the other, and their eyes showed white as they glanced
sidewise at me, trying to judge the danger that I would destroy
Nur Mast as I had done Gul Mast.

The moment seemed propitious to obtain their agreement to
the project which had originally brought me into these hills. I
drew out the small writing case which I have always with me
and, after some discussion with the headman, wrote out the text
of an agreement by which the Afridis of Nur Mast promised to
allow into their hills and to guard with their lives any surveying
party led by the British officer McAusland. The headman of Nur
Mast stamped the impression of his silver ring on the paper just
as Major Phelps brought his troop of cavalry to a stop in a cloud
of dust. For good measure, he offered to send back with us one

of his own sons to act as escort through the secret ways of the hills and to serve as a sign of his protection over us.

Since the agreement names me specifically, Major Phelps has decided to officially overlook my night's absence without leave. And since I am not to be cashiered, he agrees that it would hardly be fair to hang Ali Gul.

We rode back with the major's men, mounted double behind two of the lighter soldiers. My relief at seeing Fort Jamrud in its accustomed position in the plain was inexpressible; I was only heartily glad that I had not already expressed my belief that the fort had somehow mysteriously disappeared. A village gone without a trace is bad enough; were I to begin babbling of forts that pop in and out of existence like part of a conjuror's sideshow, Major Phelps would very likely confine me to quarters until I had recovered from the sunstroke.

I must have lost my direction the first time I attempted to return to the fort, and wandered until I came to a place where mountain ridges blocked my view of Jamrud. No other explanation for the fort's seeming disappearance is tenable.

So, my dear Eliza, all has ended much better than I had any right to expect; except that it is a very great pity that I neglected to take notes on the customs and language of those hill barbarians while I had the opportunity. I may never again come across so convincing a proof of my thesis that the Afridis are descended from men out of Alexander's army. It is too late now; the hill barbarians and the women of Gul Mast have vanished, doubtless to settle somewhere back in the secret valleys and unmapped passages of Afghanistan. Ali Gul assures me that his kinswomen are well but absolutely refuses to say whither they may have fled; when I press him, all he will say is, "If I told you, McAusland Sahib, you would not believe me."

Once, indeed, he vouchsafed one further hint on the subject, but even I have been unable to decipher it. He told me that in the course of thirty years' service he had heard a great many preachings from the Angrez chaplain, and that there was a text in our Holy Book which might give me some enlightenment on the subject. I immediately consulted my Bible; but I cannot for the life of me see what Mark 8:18 has to do with the matter.

I remain, my dear Eliza, as always,

Your loving brother,
James Robertson McAusland

Betcha Can't Eat Just One

by
Alan Dean Foster

To a writer of humorous bent (or perhaps one who is simply bent), everything that surrounds us, from the starry firmament to the sands on a crowded shore, is source for amusement. Contemporary American society is an especially prodigal reservoir of humor, most of it unintentional. Nothing's funnier than somebody or something who takes themselves deadly serious.

It's hard not to smile, for example, when you envision a dozen or so handsomely paid men and women spending the bulk of their lives in eternal torment occasioned by a desperate quest for a new way to describe a fragment of fried potato ("Tingly tart? Crunchy sweet? Lightly salted with a hint of Idaho's rolling hills? God help me, where's the Valium?")

That's American society, though. Prodigious energy expended in deification of the trivial. Those of us not intimately involved with such can recognize it for the absurdity it is, but rest assured those whose lives and careers depend on these matters of infinite inconsequence treat it with deadly seriousness.

"Can I help you find something, sir?"

Moke glanced sharply at the clerk. He was more nervous than usual these days, with the Study so near completion. Always having to watch his step. Never knew when *they* might be watching.

"You cannot. I can find everything by myself, when I want to. I simply choose to proceed at my own pace." He smiled. "I've found a great deal already, and am in the process of finding more all the time."

She eyed him uncertainly. Usually the people she found wandering in this aisle all wanted to know the location of the new Adolescent Altered Killer Gerbil cookies, the latest kid-food and comic sensation. This customer was different. For one thing, he was bigger. And he seemed not so much lost as preoccupied.

That's when she noted the microcassette recorder he was carrying in lieu of a shopping bag. "You from the Health Department or sump'in? You want I should get the night manager?"

"No. If I was from the Health Department I'd already have shut down this establishment . . . and every one like it, until they changed their policies. I'm not in a position to do that . . . yet." The widening of his humorless grin failed to enlighten the baffled clerk.

It was one in the morning; near closing time for this particular market. A few amnesiac shoppers remorselessly cruised the aisles, dumping toilet tissue, canned dog food, cereals and breads and hopefully dolphin-safe tuna into their carts. Their expressions were resigned, their posture lethargic. Except when they passed through *this* aisle. Then cheerful gossip freshened the air like verbal Muzak.

Everyone took something from Aisle Six, and luxuriated in the process.

The clerk was reluctant to abandon her angular stray. "So if you don't mind my askin', mister . . . what's to shut down? We're as clean as anyplace in town, an' our inventory's just as fresh. We ain't violating no ordinances. We ain't guilty of nothin'."

"No?" Moke's sweeping gesture encompassed the entire aisle. "You're like everyone else. You don't see what's going on here. You really don't see it."

The clerk blinked at the shelves, seeking enlightenment and finding only cellophane and plastic.

"This is all *garbage,* young lady. Offal, swill: the insidious poisoning of a people who have forgotten the nature of real food."

Until now emotionally becalmed, the clerk straightened. "Our stock is checked and replaced every day, *sir.* Everything on our shelves is fresh. If you don't like it here, why don't you shop someplace else?"

"It wouldn't make any difference. It's the same everywhere," Moke informed her sorrowfully. "Do not think that in my ire I have singled out your place of work for especial condemnation. The entire supermarket industry in which you are but an insignificant cog is equally culpable. All participate in the conspiracy." He peered intently at her.

"Are you aware that today's junk food contains more than a hundred times the volume and variety of chemical additives than the junk food of just twenty years ago? That the very companies which disgorge this mountain of hyena chow on an innocent unsuspecting public have little or no idea of how the human body will react to increased consumption of same over a decent period of time?"

The clerk relaxed. Everything was clear enough to her now for her even to forget that she'd been called an insignificant cog. She even managed a sly smile.

"You're a health-food nut."

"And proud of it. Do you know that ever since I first unearthed the conspiracy and swore to expose it I haven't touched any of this stuff?" He indicated the marshaled ranks of sugar-stuffed cakes, of candy-coated marshmallow, of puffed imitation cheese and fried air. "And that since then I haven't been sick a day? Not a day! Not a cold, no flu: nothing. There *has* to be a connection. And I'm going to reveal it."

"Uh-huh." The clerk was retreating slowly.

Moke noticed the look in her eyes. "You're the one who should be afraid of these remasticated additives; not me. My system is clean. I'm a trained scientist, young lady. My specialty is nutrition chemistry. I have devoted all of my adult life to this Study, and next week I shall at last begin to publish. What I will reveal will rock the American junk-food industry to its grotesquely profitable core."

She halted, grinning insouciantly. "I ain't afraid of no potato chips."

"You should be, because I have discovered that they, in common with most other popular junk foods, contain hidden within their artificial flavorings and artificial colors and preservatives and pseudoingredients newly developed complex amino acids of extraordinary vitality and volatility. Either the food companies have been far ahead of the pharmaceutical and pesticide industries in genetic engineering or else we are witnessing an organic mutation on an undreamt-of scale.

"To what nefarious end the food companies are striving I have yet to discover, but rest assure that I will. Some of the molecules I have isolated within Shoo-pie Bunny Cakes, for example, are positively Byzantine. Something sinister is taking place within our stores, and whatever it is, it's finding its way into our children's lunch pails." He turned wistful.

"Thirty years ago I would've said it was all a Russian plot, but I think the poor Russians are likewise on the verge of succumbing to the same sort of global gut-busting infiltration."

"Right." She made a production of checking her watch. "Well, you'd better finish up your studies here fast, professor. We close in thirty minutes."

"I need more time than that."

"Thirty minutes." She turned and headed north, in the direction of the checkout registers.

Idiots, Moke thought. Blind fools. *He* was going to save the country, save the world, in spite of its slavish ingrained genuflection to oversweetened dreck. Considering current dietary habits it was a wonder the species continued to survive at all.

Facts were undeniable. When his paper finally exploded on the world convenience-food scene, specialists would rush to confirm his findings. Too late then for the bloated minions of a bilious multibillion-dollar industry to conceal the truth any longer from a hitherto duped market-going public.

Emerging from beneath the concealing pile of uncrushed cartons, he climbed out of the compactor and surveyed the storage room at the rear of the market. It was dark and deserted. He had a couple of hours before the store reopened.

Using his key-chain flashlight, he returned to the aisle where he'd had the encounter with the young clerk. Going to save her too, he thought determinedly, before her body was unalterably poisoned. It was his crusade, and his alone. The big health-food groups didn't have a clue. Or his analytical expertise.

A few final notes and his research would be complete. Then to the computer, to integrate final thoughts with the rough manuscript. Polish and publish.

This was the last store on his list, the final line of the last page of statistics in a study that had taken decades and encompassed more than fifty cities and towns. All visited personally by him. He couldn't trust graduate students to carry out the fieldwork. They were all contaminated by the very products he was sworn to eradicate from the shelves of the world's supermarkets. He'd been forced to do all the research on his own.

It was the same wherever he went. Identical strange molecules and peptide chains in dozens of products, regardless of brand name. Clever *they* were, but Moke had stumbled on their secret. Soon he would expose the nature of their callous perfidy to a shocked public.

Aisle Six stretched on ahead of him; shelves crammed full of brightly colored air-puffed victuals utterly devoid of nutritional value and inherently antithetical to the digestive system of the human body. They all but glowed behind their chromatic wrappings; tantalizingly easy to consume, irresistibly crammed full of false flavor, quisling comestibles capable of rapidly weakening both mental and physical resolve. He knew them for what they were. Nurturance for the brain-damaged.

Something quivered slightly on the shelf just behind his left shoulder.

He whirled, saw nothing. Chuckling uneasily, he sauntered on. And froze.

They were moving. The packages on the shelves ahead. Twitching slightly, jerking against their containers and restraints. Huge bags of intimidating chips, densely packed containers of tightly bound pretzels, stacks of creme-filled non-cakes. All gyrating and weaving and rustling invitingly. And he could hear the sound now: a low, insinuating moan. The tempting murmur of empty calories, of empires of gluttony built on salt and refined white sugar.

"Eat us," the enticing susurration whispered coaxingly. "You have deprived yourself for too long, have put yourself outside pleasure for no reason. Devour; and delight."

He blinked, clapping his hands over his ears. The micro-cassette recorder slipped from his fingers to strike the unyielding, Hawaiian-punch-stained floor. Its cover popped open and the tape flew out. Pained, he knelt to recover it.

Something landed on his back.

Forgetting the recorder, he reached around wildly. Something soft and sticky filled his fingers. Terrified, he found himself staring down at a handful of squished, blood-red lunchbox cherry pie which contained no cherries and no pie. It oozed between his fingers, the unctuous crimson gunk crowding beneath his fingernails.

"Eat me," the glutinous mass urged him. "Suck me up. You'll like it."

With a cry he rose and flung the fragments of pseudo pie as far as he could, but some of it stuck to his fingers anyway. Stumbling backwards, he crashed into the nearest shelves. Flailing wildly, he brought down on top of himself piles of chips, stacks of cheetos, heavy lumps of sponge cake and devil's food cake and white cake and lemon cake differentiated solely by the type of artificial coloring they contained.

They were all over him now, moving; those strange molecules he'd discovered boldly asserting themselves. They wanted, cried out to, demanded to be consumed. He struggled beneath their empty weight and tried to yell for help, but the eight-year-olds who could have rescued him were tucked snug in their beds far from the shuttered market.

Looking down, he saw bags of pretzels and honey-roasted corn-nuts splitting open; their overbaked, oversaturated, over-salted entrails spilling across his chest and legs. He kicked wildly, sending crumbs flying but unable to get to his feet. His arms and chest were slowly disappearing beneath thick cords of plaster-white creme and dark imitation-fudge filling.

His eyes widened as he saw them humping sinuously towards his face; death reduced to spongy sweet blandness. They crammed themselves into his mouth, shoving his lips apart, forcing themselves down his throat. He continued to struggle, to fight, but it was useless. They overwhelmed him, relentless and unyielding in their desire to please, to slavishly gratify the basest of human desires.

The light began to fade from his eyes. He'd been careless, he realized. Unwilling to envision what *they* were capable of. But who could have imagined? Did even the bioengineers who'd given impetus to such mutations imagine what the ultimate result of their work might be? He doubted it. Surely the lethal reality he was experiencing exceeded even their capacious greed.

He was going, but at least he wouldn't die hungry.

"Gawddamn! What a mess."

The officer wrinkled his nose at the sight and its attending smell. Forensics was finishing up, making way for the coroner. Their jobs were relatively straightforward.

It was the mortician he didn't envy.

The coroner's assistant was writing on a pad. The officer nodded to him. They knew each other.

"Kerwin."

"Hey, man." The assistant looked up. "Ever see anything like this before?"

The cop shook his head. "What do you think happened?"

The coroner glanced up the aisle. "Off what I'm used to seeing on the street, my first guess is that he swallowed a twelve-gauge shell that let go inside him, but there's no sign of powder or shell fragments. I'm beginning to think he just overbinged and self-destructed."

"The hell you say. Look at him."

"I'd rather not. At least, no more than I have to." The coroner's reluctance was understandable. Most of what had once reposed in the cavity between the dead man's sternum and crotch lay scattered across the supermarket floor and shelves, shockingly bright amidst the frozen, undulating sea of partly digested cakes and cookies, snack foods and fruit chewies.

"As near as we've been able to figure it, the guy went on a junk-food binge to end all junk-food binges. It was like he couldn't control himself. As if he had no resistance to the stuff, no resistance at all. Like the Polynesians who were suddenly exposed to European diseases to which they had no built-up immunity.

"You know how much air they cram into this junk. Ordinarily it doesn't give you anything except maybe a little gas now and then. But he was downing the stuff so fast it must've blocked his colon. Then he choked on it, and with no escape valve, as it were, the pent-up gas, well . . . he just blew up. Damnedest thing I ever saw."

"You ain't alone, ol' buddy. Wonder what made him do it?"

"Beats me." The coroner shrugged, finishing his notes. "He's got all the signs of someone who's been force-fed, except that he obviously did it to himself. Like a French goose on the pâté line. And I thought I knew every way a person could commit suicide." He shook his head ruefully. "This is one business where you don't get a kick out of learning something new." He put his pen to his lips. "What the hell am I going to list as 'reason for demise'?"

The cop looked thoughtful. "If it was up to me I'd put down

'Accidental' and leave it at that. It'll get you off the hook until something better turns up."

The assistant coroner looked resigned. Then the corners of his mouth turned up slightly. He scribbled on the pad, showed it to his friend.

"I can't turn it in this way, of course. The boss'd have my ass."

The officer looked down, similarly smiling in spite of himself.

(17)—CAUSE: Death by Twinkie.

They shared a chuckle. The coroner pocketed his pad. As he turned to leave he noticed a broken but otherwise undisturbed package on the floor. Reaching down, he rescued a couple of orphaned creme-filled cupcakes with garish orange icing, passing one to his friend. With a wink the cop bit deeply into his own.

The sensation as the thick-cremed, sugar-saturated, calorie-rich crumbly mass slid down his throat was indescribable.

The (*burp*) End

New Hope for
Denture Wearers

✧

by
Ron Goulart

We'd all like to be better than what we are. Oh, I don't mean necessarily better morally, or intellectually, or emotionally. Those qualities don't really matter in today's America.

No, what we want is to have flatter tummies, more hair, prettier visages, more money, sleeker cars, sharper clothes, a bigger house, tons of sophisticated electronic equipment we have no time to use, a minimum of twelve hundred kitchen gadgets that will enable us to carbonize half a dead chicken in the absolute minimum amount of time, and most critical, most vital of all, something that will make us smell better.

According to what, I always wondered?

Nobody actually acquires all these things, of course. They belong only to the world of television commercials, a universe unto itself inhabited solely by ephemeral homunculi.

They can be sampled, however, through the magic of story as helmed by that consummate steersman of fantastical humor, Ron Goulart.

In fantasy even as in real life, things ofttimes get royally screwed-up.

It's safe to say that few if any readers of the *New York Times* realized there was any connection between two small items that appeared there on a recent Tuesday. One story, buried deep in the business pages, stated that the longtime editor of the satirical monthly *Screwy* had suddenly and unexpectedly retired. The other, taking up only a few inches in the metropolitan news section, reported that a young cartoonist, a brand-new contributor to the satirical monthly *Nutz,* had seemingly disappeared. What the venerable *Times* and most all of its readers weren't aware of was that both stories were about the same person.

That person was Les McDermott and on the bleak January morning that his life began to veer off on a peculiar new tangent he was holed up in his Gramercy Park apartment. Wearing a baggy sweater his second wife had knitted for him just prior to running off with a much younger man, he was trying to put together the May issue of *Screwy* and, as was his habit when doing editorial work at home, he wasn't answering his telephone.

McDermott had recently turned forty-nine, an event that had caused him considerable anguish and infected him with a severe and ongoing case of a once popular malady known as the heebie-jeebies. One of his basic problems was that he simply wasn't aging well. Three years ago, for instance, most of his curly and bushy blond hair—"a golden mane," his first wife had once called it—had departed his head. Next, most of the teeth remaining in his upper jaw had died simultaneously and been extracted. His once lean and distinguished face developed numerous crinkly little wrinkles, especially under the eyes, which, virtually overnight, had lost their old sparkle.

His spine let him down next, two fairly important disks having virtually wasted away. This caused him considerable pain from time to time, as well as screwing up his long-held plan to take up weight lifting later in life so that, if need be, he could get back into the tip-top physical shape he'd enjoyed earlier in life.

Enjoyed, in fact, up until three years ago. He'd also met Wendy Mintz three years ago, but the fact that he'd gone into a steep physical and psychological decline during the period he'd courted her was probably coincidental.

As he looked again at the finished pages of the May movie parody for *Screwy,* he wondered if he could liven it up by drawing in a few glimpses of the Simpsons.

His phone rang. He ignored it.

After four rings his answering machine message kicked on. "You've reached the McDermott residence . . ."

"My voice used to be deeper, too," he observed aloud, glancing over at the small table that held the machine. "Now I'm sounding like Sam Jaffe in *Lost Horizon*."

" . . . after the beep."

"Pick up the damn phone, asshole!" ordered the bellowing voice of Jock Wurbling, forty-five-year-old publisher of *Screwy*. "I know you're there."

"You're forgetting our deal," McDermott said in the direction of the phone. "I get to work undisturbed at home every Thursday and Friday."

"Listen to me, Lester. We are sinking ever deeper into a pit of trouble. The very future of *Screwy* is at stake. More importantly, your job is at stake and your butt is perilously close to being in a sling once again. Speak to me!"

McDermott studied the beamed ceiling of his small study, then looked out the small window. He hadn't noticed it until now, but there was a dead pigeon sprawled out on the sill.

Wurbling's time ran out.

McDermott turned to the artwork for this issue's comic book parody—Batman again. Picking up his yellow pad, he made a few quick sketches for possible last-minute changes to suggest to the artist.

"My hand's not as steady as it once was either," he noticed.

The phone rang again.

"You've reached the . . ."

"Yep, there's a distinct quaver in my voice. You can tell that I wear a partial plate, too." He slumped slightly in his chair.

" . . . beep."

"Answer or die!" yelled his publisher.

Sighing again, McDermott got up, walked to the little table and grabbed up the receiver. "There's something in my contract someplace about your not being able to howl at me like a banshee, especially before noon."

"Listen, asshole, I've been trying to—"

"And you agreed not to call me asshole anymore," he reminded the publisher. "A man whose first name, by the way, is a synonym for an intimate piece of athletic equipment isn't exactly in a position to—"

"Attend to me, schmuck! Sales dropped another 56,000 copies on the last issue of *Screwy*. The figures just came in and—"

"It's seasonal, Jock."

"How long have you been with us, Leslie?"

"Twenty years. And my whole and entire first name is Les."

"Twenty years of trying to produce material that will amuse the underage half-wits who comprise our readership is a long time. Perhaps too long."

"Perhaps."

"But if I toss you out on your can, what would you do?"

"Starve."

"Exactly. So now, then, Lester, here's what we need, exactly what we need to pep up the old mag."

"Can't this wait until Monday?"

"Do you happen to know how much the circulation of our rival periodical, *Nutz,* climbed last month?"

"I hope the answer isn't 56,000."

"No, nay, it isn't. They went up a whole bloody 100,000. We drop, they rise. And why is that, Leslie? We both make fun of the same currently hot TV shows, the same dumb commercials, the same movies, the same ephemeral fads. Why, then, does *Nutz* outsell us?"

"Actually, Jock, if you adjust the figures, it—"

"I'll tell you why," cut in Wurbling. "The answer, my friends, is Wendy Mintz."

"Oh, shit."

"Yes, Wendy Mintz, a cartoon phenomenon. The idol of prepubescent lads and lasses across the land. Her dismal scribbles cause hundreds of thousands of moronic youths to snicker, chortle and plunk down the money they've wheedled out of their benighted parents. She is the reason for *Nutz'* increasing success. And you, Leslie, let them hire her over there."

"When I showed you her samples, three years ago, you said she drew like a chimpanzee."

"You should have told me that our dim-bulb readers like the work of chimps," said Wurbling. "Now, as I recall, you carried on a passionate affair with Wendy Mintz, despite the great gap in your ages."

"Twenty years."

"That's a great gap, yes."

"What exactly is the purpose of this harangue?"

"Wendy Mintz' contract is coming up for renewal at *Nutz,*" explained Wurbling. "We need her here at *Screwy*. Her wretched scrawls will get us 100,000 new readers at the very least."

"Obviously Sonny Blewton over at Nutz will simply top any offer you make."

"Maybe, but I know Blewton. He won't offer her a percentage on all reprint rights or the return of her original artwork."

"A percentage? You've never even offered me that."

"You don't happen to be the idol of millions of half-wits."

"True, yet—"

"Hire me that bimbo."

"Wendy and I haven't even spoken for nearly three years, Jock. I haven't seen her for over two," he said into the phone. "I'm not the right person for this job."

"Since she was fond of you once, you should still have an inside track," his publisher told him. "If you don't succeed in hiring her for us by next week—your long tenure is at an end." Wurbling hung up.

McDermott sat forlornly in his chair for several minutes, absently doodling dead pigeons on his yellow pad. Finally he rose up and put on a warm coat and the knit cap his second wife had once made for him. He went out into the wintry streets of Manhattan.

The early afternoon sky turned black as night while McDermott was explaining his current dilemma to his closest friend. A great wind started blowing through Greenwich Village and something that was a vicious mix of rain, sleet and snow suddenly began pelting the street outside the Great Oblivion Cafe.

He probably should have interpreted these signs as omens of trouble to come, but McDermott ignored them and, after taking a thoughtful sip of his herb tea, asked, "Are you serious, Jim?"

Sitting across the little table was Jimson Neely, a small pudgy man in his late forties. His greying hair was close-cropped, his tweedy sport coat had leathery patches on the elbows. Neely, a friend of McDermott's since their long-ago youth in Philadelphia, was a professor of Arcane Folklore at Manhattan College. "I am always completely serious, old buddy," he answered, picking up his glass of alcohol-free wine. "I'm serious because I see the tragic side of life. Besides making me somewhat of a grouch, that's kept me from becoming a regular contributor to *Screwy*."

McDermott rubbed at his nearly hairless scalp. "Then you really know of something that can solve my problem?"

"I do. It's an elixir, matter of fact."

"What do I do? Slip it into Wendy's coffee or—"

"No, no, you have to swig it yourself."

"Just how does this persuade her to sign a contract with our magazine?"

Neely was gazing out the cafe's small, dingy window, watching whatever it was that was falling out of the blackened sky hit a sweet little old lady and knock her to the pavement. "First tell me what the major problem was between you and Wendy back when you were dating her."

"Well, initially we hit it off fine. Then, though, as I started to lose my hair and so forth, Wendy decided I was an old coot. She even alluded to me as Gramps on more than one occasion and mentioned that I'd soon be too old to cut the mustard," recalled McDermott ruefully.

"Here's how life goes." Neely held up a plump forefinger at chest level and then, making a raspberry sound, sent it diving swiftly down to the tabletop. "Youth, middle age, death. With sometimes a short stop on the way downward for the old coot stage."

"Jim, I'm feeling gloomy enough without a lecture on the briefness of life."

"However," continued the pudgy professor, "there are ways to outwit—briefly, unfortunately—the inevitable slide to the boneyard." He allowed his forefinger to rise a few inches above the tabletop.

"I know, Jim, I know. Wendy suggested all that—exercise, sensible diet. The thing is, I have to sign her up for *Screwy* by no later than next week. Otherwise I'm out. Even a crash program at a spa isn't—"

"Suppose," cut in Neely, lifting his finger another few inches higher, "suppose, old buddy, that for ten or twelve hours tonight you could look exactly as you did when you were, say, thirty-nine?"

"You mean with hair and without dentures?"

"Exactly, precisely." Neely nodded. Out in the street several people were gathered around the fallen woman. "You'd be able to approach Wendy glowing with youth and vigor, smiling handsomely with all your very own teeth. Your full head of hair will glimmer in the moonlight, if the moon ever breaks through this gunk, and when Wendy views your locks, she'll no doubt compare them to a golden mane or a—"

"I'm truly sorry I ever confided in you that Wendy once—"

"Pay attention, old buddy. Sit up straight in your chair and just listen," urged his friend. "If you were to look better than you have in over a decade, might the lady then react cordially to you?"

"She might, Jim. But how do I suddenly become younger?"

"That's where the elixir comes in."

"C'mon, no elixir is going to knock ten years off my age."

"Old buddy, this stuff can. I know, because I am a satisfied user myself." Leaning forward, Neely rested both leather-covered elbows on the table. "I discovered the ancient formula three years ago while researching some of the more obscure sorcerers of sixteenth-century Europe for a paper. Trust me, this liquid really works."

"How come you never told me about it before?"

"I had, by chance, unearthed a long-lost magical secret. I wasn't particularly anxious to share my knowledge with anyone, even my oldest buddies," explained Neely, shoulders hunching and voice lowering. "Selfishly, I determined to use the stuff exclusively for myself. So most weekends I'd swig some and be miraculously transformed into a lad in his thirties. I'd drop into one of the many singles bars that this fair metropolis was then blessed with. It was my practice to pick up a different young lady each time. None of them over thirty, I assure you. I'd spend the night with her, performing as I hadn't for many a year. By the grim light of dawn, before the potion wore off, I'd slip away. It was, I assure you, old buddy, perfect for one-night stands."

"What did Margo think about your—"

"I didn't tell you, Les, and I sure as hell didn't tell my wife."

McDermott studied his friend's face for a few seconds. "Why are you telling me now?"

"The times have changed. New plagues and blights are afoot in the world," answered Neely sadly. "Until someone comes up with an antidote for some of our latest popular social diseases, I'm abstaining from pursuing my career as a youthful man about town."

"This stuff only lasts a few hours?"

"It'll rejuvenate you for no more than twelve hours. That was my experience anyway—and that's what the old manuscript promised."

"Okay, suppose it does work for me? How do I explain my new youthful look to Wendy?"

"That's simple, since you haven't seen her for a long time."

"About two years."

"Fine. When she comments on your golden mane, your unwrinkled flesh, your sparkling choppers, you have merely to explain that you took her helpful criticisms to heart and have been devoting the past two years to—"

"Helpful criticisms? Calling me a senile old turkey isn't my idea of—"

"Since you're anxious to hire her, old buddy, some bullshit is needed along with the magic," advised Neely. "You tell her you took her helpful criticisms to heart. You've been eagerly attending fitness centers, health spas, vegetarian bistros. You've given up drinking, smoking and most other social ventures. And now, a better and younger looking fellow, you've returned to throw yourself at her feet."

"I don't know if we need quite that much bullshit."

"It'll work, trust me."

"I suppose I could try this. I have to do something so I can get close enough to Wendy to persuade her to work for us."

"Of course, old buddy, you could simply quit *Screwy*," suggested his friend. "Tell Wurbling to shove it and get back to writing and drawing that brilliant comic strip you've been planning for years."

"No, I don't draw much anymore. I'll go with the elixir," said McDermott. "How do I get some?"

"I happen to have a supply right here in my attaché case, indicating that fate is on your side," said Neely. "I was cleaning out my office today and came across my spare bottle." He reached under the table. "The stuff, by the way, is called Count Monstrodamus' Youth Elixir."

"That's not an especially catchy name."

"Everything can't be named Nyquil and Tylenol." He lifted up a battered tan attaché case, plumped it on his lap. "What you do, old buddy, is take a full tablespoon a half hour before you want to be transformed. The changeover usually requires between twenty and thirty minutes."

"Any side effects?"

Neely was again studying the storm-tossed street. Two passersby were starting to carry the fallen woman away. "No, not really."

"Jim?"

"Well, you may feel sort of woozy the first time you take a

swallow," he admitted, snapping open the case and reaching inside. "Oh, and your palms will start itching just before it's about to wear off."

"Can I just take another dose then, and add another twelve hours?"

Neely shook his head. "Nope, not according to what old Count Monstrodamus warned. Actually, you can only use the stuff once every forty-eight hours. Otherwise . . ."

"Otherwise what?"

"There was a page missing from the old manuscript I was consulting when I stumbled onto this recipe. So I missed some of the sorcerer's warnings and cautionary advice. But, hey, I used it for well over two years without any serious trouble."

"Well, I'm probably not going to need more than one dose anyway. Only enough for one encounter with Wendy."

From out of the case the professor produced a brown plastic bottle. After glancing around the nearly empty cafe, he slid the bottle across the table. "Here, good luck."

"This is an old Granny Sweetcakes pancake and waffle syrup bottle."

"I didn't have any empty youth elixir bottles, old buddy," said his friend. "Trust me, the bottle is full of what you need."

Cautiously, McDermott twisted the cap off to sniff at the bottle's contents. "Geeze, it smells awful."

"The worse it smells, the better it is for you," said Neely. "Just like medicine."

The stuff that was falling out of the bleak wintry sky turned into snow at sundown. McDermott was sitting in his small living room, watching the oncoming night fill the street below. The Granny Sweetcakes bottle containing the allegedly magical elixir was sitting on his coffee table atop a scattered pile of back issues of *Screwy* and *Nutz*.

The phone rang.

McDermott remained where he was. The *Nutz* cover that topped the stack was one Wendy had drawn. She really was a god-awful artist, especially when it came to things like layout, perspective, anatomy and rendering.

After his tape had spoken, the voice of Wurbling came roaring out of the answering machine. "Eight o'clock tonight," he boomed. "Wellington Room, Hotel Waterloo. Cocktail party given by the

Satirical Cartoonists Guild. Wendy will be there. Blewton will be there. *You* will be there."

After a few moments McDermott muttered, "Maybe I could quit."

Nope, he was afraid to try that. Free-lancing at his age, especially for a man with so little hair and so few teeth of his own, was a terrifying prospect. So was looking for a new editorial job.

Sighing a sigh that was close to a wheeze, he left the armchair. Going into his small bedroom, he changed into a fresh shirt, put on his newest tie and his favorite sport coat.

Then, feet dragging some, he went back to the living room. He stood, slightly hunched, beside the coffee table and contemplated the syrup bottle.

"I'd feel more confident if the damn bottle wasn't shaped like Granny Sweetcakes."

Still, if Neely was to be believed, this elixir just might solve his immediate problems. Wendy had been fond of him originally and it was mainly his rapid physical decline that had caused her to dump him. With a more youthful appearance, he ought to be able to charm her into signing an exclusive contract with *Screwy*.

He also might, timing it just right and only courting her when he was in an elixir phase, start up a romance again.

"Whoa, your job is more important than romance," he reminded himself. "Let's concentrate on getting Wendy to draw for *Screwy*. Draw? Well, scrawl."

Snatching up the bottle, he unscrewed the cap. The elixir's foul odor came wafting up to him, causing his nose to wrinkle and his eyes to water.

He shut his eyes and took a gulp of Count Monstrodamus' magic potion. The liquid tasted even worse than it smelled, reminding him of the worst cough medicine he'd ever had to swallow as a kid.

After he'd drunk down what he estimated was the required tablespoon, he capped the bottle and started to replace it on the table.

Instead he fell over.

He landed hard on both knees, banged his head against the chair. The chair went nudging into the coffee table and the magazines cascaded to the floor, displaying several more of Wendy's dreadful covers.

He was suddenly visited with several flulike symptoms. Upset stomach, cramps, chills, headache among them.

Then, against his will, he went sprawling flat out on the rug, feeling as though he were melting.

Lying there, woozy, he became aware of a growing pain in his jaw. McDermott managed to reach up, tug out his dental plate. Then, cautiously, he poked at his gums.

"Teeth," he murmured.

His front teeth had come back.

Aware of an uncomfortable feeling all across his scalp, he twisted further and got his hand up to the top of his head.

"Hair."

Setting his denture carefully on the rug, he began working on getting himself upright again.

An interesting variety of flashes of intense color began blossoming all around him for the next sixty seconds or so.

Then the room resumed its normal aspect.

Walking in jerking steps, he made his way to his small bathroom.

He hesitated before clicking on the lights.

"Holy shit," he remarked on first viewing himself in the mirror.

He did indeed have his blond hair back.

"And, even though Neely kids me about this, my hair is sort of a golden mane."

He smiled, pulling his lips far back from his teeth.

The smile was impressive, sparkling even, and it made use of teeth that were obviously entirely his own.

McDermott noticed that his skin had changed as well. It looked fresher, contained very few wrinkles, and all those odd little splotches he'd been noticing lately had vanished.

"Count Monstrodamus was a very bright guy."

Returning to the living room, he collected his denture and the bottle of elixir. He stored both in the lowest drawer of his desk.

From the hall closet he took his only overcoat. He decided he wouldn't need any sort of hat, not with all this great new hair.

A block from his place, walking toward the nearby Hotel Waterloo, he felt suddenly dizzy again. He stepped into the doorway of a closed deli. He saw splatters of light once more, suffered stomach cramps for almost a minute.

Then, realizing he felt fine again, McDermott went strolling on toward the cocktail party. His back felt better than it had in some time.

There were about a hundred people in the Wellington Room, most of them standing in small clusters. A bar had been set up at the far end of the medium-sized ballroom, just in front of the mirror-paneled wall.

Near the doorway as he was walking in McDermott noticed a cartoonist who occasionally contributed to *Screwy*. He nodded at him.

The cartoonist, who was holding two glasses of white wine, frowned at McDermott but didn't return the greeting.

Shrugging, he continued on his way to the bar. Two other sometime contributors failed to return his greetings.

He slowed when he spotted Wendy Mintz. She was sitting at a small table near the bar. Sonny Blewton, the editor and publisher of *Nutz,* was slumped in a chair opposite her.

McDermott squared his shoulders, went striding right up to the table.

Wendy, whose hair was worn longer these days and was a lighter shade of auburn, had on a simple black cocktail dress. She was quite pretty.

"Well, I didn't expect to . . . Oh, excuse me," she said, smiling up at him and shaking her head. "I mistook you for someone I used to know."

He halted beside her table. "No, as a matter of fact, I am . . ." Then McDermott happened to glance beyond her and toward the mirrored wall.

He took a step back, then two ahead, squinting. He'd just seen his current image in the bright panels. Somehow, since he'd inspected himself back at his apartment, he'd lost another dozen years and appeared at the moment to be in his middle twenties. His blond hair was now shoulder length and there was nary a trace of a wrinkle on his boyish face. He wasn't going to be able to pass himself off as a spruced-up version of himself.

"As a matter of fact," he explained amiably in his young man's voice, "I think I know who you've mistaken me for."

"Are you, maybe, related to that pinhead Les McDermott?"

"I am, and you're Wendy Mintz. Yes, Cousin Les has told me a lot about you."

"I can imagine what that old coot has had to say about me."

"I'm his Cousin Phil from Boston," he informed her. "Down here staying with him for a couple weeks."

"Is he still living in that rancid rathole?"

"His apartment is quite charming actually."

"Um," said Blewton, who'd noticed McDermott.

"Hush," advised Wendy. "He always gets very sappy after a few drinks."

"Um."

Wendy stood up. "You're much better looking than your numbskull cousin, Phil." She took hold of his arm. "Let me buy you a drink."

"Oh, no, I'll buy you one. I mean, you're one of the great cartoonists—as well as one of the great loves of my cousin's life," he said, smiling with his youthful teeth. "He's often told me he was fonder of you than either of his wives."

"I saw pictures of both of those bimbos and that's not much of a compliment." She guided him to the bar. "I imagine the old poop is in even worse shape now than when I dumped him."

"No, Cousin Les happens to be in tip-top shape. Been working out at a fitness center," said McDermott. "And, you know, I'm sorry to hear you speaking so negatively about him, Wendy, because the guy still mentions you very fondly. And, of course, he's in awe of your artwork and cartooning."

"Awe, huh?"

"His two biggest regrets, he was telling me just tonight, are that you two broke up and that you didn't come to work for *Screwy*."

"I don't know which is the more repulsive—your doddering old cousin or that putrid excuse for a magazine," she said. "I'm drinking vodka on the rocks. You?"

"Same."

Wendy rested a pretty, bare elbow on the counter. "Sounds like your senile old pinhead of a cousin still has a yen for me."

"Oh, his feelings for you are more tender than that."

"Right, at his advanced age he probably can't even work up a good yen anymore."

"Well, forty-nine isn't exactly ancient."

"Is that what the old coot told you he is? Sheesh, he's got to be, judging by all the wrinkles he's carrying around, at least fifty-five. Maybe older."

"I'm no more than . . . He's no more than forty-nine. I've looked at the family archives, Wendy."

"Then the poor pinhead got a bum deal when the genetic codes got passed around," she said. "What do you do, Phil?"

"I'm . . . I'm a cartoonist," he told her.

"That's great. Most men cartoonists are pinheads, but you look like the exception."

"I am. I have few if any pinhead characteristics." He touched his glass to hers. "Cheers."

"Ugh." She shuddered. "Wow, for a second there you sounded exactly like Granpappy McDermott. He was always clicking glasses, smiling at me with his rancid dentures and babbling, 'Cheers.' "

Gradually McDermott was able to ignore her slurs about him, about the man she thought was his Cousin Les. Concentrating on the task at hand, he forced himself to get along with the pretty cartoonist.

He intended to bring up the possibility of her moving over to *Screwy*. But, somehow, after a half hour he found his thinking was getting blurred. In fact, he was feeling as though he were standing outside his body and watching someone else chat with Wendy.

After another half hour he lost track of himself entirely.

•

The first thing he noticed on awakening was his hands. They were both stained with black ink. And one of them was resting lightly on the naked back of Wendy Mintz.

Very slowly and carefully, as though he were dealing with a potential bomb, he lifted his hand off the sleeping cartoonist's flesh.

McDermott found himself on the left side of a large four-poster bed. Out the curtained window on his left a pale wintry sunlight showed.

He'd apparently spent the night with Wendy, though he had no recollection of what had happened.

Well, that was okay. If they were close now, he ought to be able to persuade her to leave *Nutz* for *Screwy*.

Quietly, he sat up, stretching and yawning.

The air he sucked in came rushing into his mouth in an odd way.

He reached up with an ink-stained forefinger to poke gingerly at his upper gums.

"Shit," he whispered.

All his front teeth were gone.

Very cautiously he inched his hand up the side of his face toward the top of his head.

"Wrinkles," he said.

And he was bald again, too.

Moving with infinite care, McDermott started to remove himself from the bed. His spine had returned to its former state and produced a series of creaking noises.

Wendy stirred, murmured, "Darling?" in a half-asleep voice.

Reaching out, he patted her reassuringly on her bare backside. He hoped his hand wouldn't feel too old and cause her to awaken.

She wasn't the sort of woman who'd accept any explanation that involved Count Monstrodamus and a magic elixir in a syrup bottle.

As he held his breath, Wendy dropped slowly back into slumber. Very gingerly, he gathered up his clothes and went into the living room to dress.

Wendy's drawing board stood near a tall window. A portfolio rested on the chair.

McDermott found a memo pad on the taboret next to the table. He wrote, in what he hoped would pass for a handwriting other than his, a short message.

Wendy—Had to leave in a hurry. Will call you soon. Love, Phil.

After he pushpinned that to the board, he quietly slipped free of her third-floor apartment.

A chill wind came rushing along the midday street, brushing harshly at his hairless head.

The Les McDermott who came tottering into the Great Oblivion Cafe at twilight six days later was bundled up in a storm-tossed trench coat and had a shaggy knit cap pulled down over his ears. He wore a pair of misted dark glasses and his mittened hands were shaking.

When he started to sit down at Neely's table, the professor looked up and said, "I'm sorry, I'm expecting . . . Say, is that you, Les?"

Sinking into the chair, McDermott whispered, "Things aren't working exactly right, Jim."

"So you implied over the phone." The pudgy professor rested both elbows on the table, eyeing his friend. "Have you been guzzling that stuff more than once every other day?"

"I don't know. Maybe. Hard to tell."

"Count Monstrodamus was very explicit about not using the stuff too frequently or—"

"Take a look at this." After glancing furtively around the nearly empty little restaurant, he lifted up one side of his knit cap. Blond curly hair came tumbling free out over his ear. Quickly he stuffed the hair away out of sight again. "And look here." He whipped off the glasses briefly and stared directly at his friend. "My eyes are bright. No bags under them."

"You've got lots of hair again and no wrinkles, granted. Why does that make you unhappy?"

"Jim, I'm twenty-five."

"That's what the elixir is supposed to do."

"All the time, I mean."

The professor frowned. "It doesn't wear off?"

"Not since three days ago."

"Well, being young—is that really so awful, old buddy?"

"Nobody recognizes me anymore. Even you didn't at first. I haven't been able to go near the office looking like this. This morning they wouldn't even cash a check for me at my bank."

"Keep calm," advised Neely. "Let's review the situation. Initially you wanted to look a few years younger so that you could charm Wendy Mintz into working for *Screwy*."

"That hasn't worked out right either."

"She doesn't like you even though you appear so much younger?"

"No, she loves me. We're sleeping together."

"Is that wise these days? With all the social—"

"But Wendy thinks she's sleeping with my Cousin Phil."

"I didn't know you had a Cousin Phil."

"I don't. I'm Cousin Phil." He gestured at his now youthful face.

"Still, it's really you who's having the affair, Les."

"This bastard Phil wants to be a pro cartoonist. Every time he goes up to Wendy's, when he isn't in the sack with her, he's batting out cartoons and caricatures," McDermott told him. "He's been drawing all sorts of spot cartoons and Wendy is buying them to use in the margins of the magazine. Phil will make his debut in the next issue of *Nutz*. And the month after that he's going to be drawing the parody of the new Stallone movie."

"Easy now, old buddy. Since you are actually this Phil, you can prevent the work from appearing in a rival magazine."

"Phil's already signed a long-term contract with Blewton."

"Why the hell did you do that?"

"I didn't. Phil did."

"But you're Phil."

"Not all the time," confided McDermott. "See, he seems to be carrying on a life of his own. I doze off, the guy takes a swig of the elixir and appears. I wake up—sometimes a whole day later—and I find out I've been dining out at some expensive bistro with Wendy and it's all been charged to my American Express card. Besides having dinner, he's slept with her and drawn another batch of spots."

Drumming his fingers slowly on the table, the professor said, "This is very odd, old buddy. Not once in the manuscript did Count Monstrodamus mention any of these side effects."

"They didn't have cartooning in his day. They didn't have satirical humor magazines or credit cards."

"Even so, Les, the basic notions of magic ought to remain the same."

"You're starting to look at me as though I were a guinea pig, or a mouse in some maze," McDermott complained. "Listen, Jim, I've got to stop being Phil all the time. What's going to happen to my job? What's Wurbling going to do when he learns that not only haven't I signed Wendy but now I'm a contributor to *Nutz*?"

"You haven't mentioned any of this to your boss?"

"Of course not. I put a new message on my machine, explaining that I'm felled with the latest flu and have lost the power of speech. I've succeeded in stalling him, but his messages to me are growing increasingly hostile."

"First thing, you have to give me back what's left of the elixir. That way you won't be tempted to guzzle any more."

"Jim, I flushed the entire contents of the syrup bottle down the toilet yesterday. But it doesn't seem to matter. I remain young. I'm afraid that I'll just become Phil permanently." He rubbed his mittened hands together. "I keep blacking out every so often, then go out on Phil binges. I'm having, apparently, an impressive sex life and making gratifying career moves. Thing is, I don't remember a damn thing about any of it."

"I'll have to make use of the Monstrodamus codicil."

"The what?"

"It's a manuscript I came across about a year ago," explained the professor. "Supposedly it contains an antidote to the youth elixir."

"Antidote? Why didn't you mention prior to this that the stuff required an antidote? No, instead you gave me a glowing testimonial that implied there were no risks at all."

"I swear to you, Les, I never experienced any of the problems you're having."

"Will this antidote help me?"

"It should, yeah. I'll mix up a batch tonight. Then we'll test it on some mice to—"

"We don't have time for mice."

"Nobody's used this antidote for several hundred years. It, too, may have side effects we don't know about."

"Will it age me back to my proper age again?"

Neely nodded. "Sure, that's the chief thing it's supposed to do. At least according to the dubious Count Monstrodamus."

"We're not dealing with the same Count Monstrodamus who invented this in the first place?"

"Scholars disagree. Myself, I'm inclined to think it was a protégé of his who penned this particular manuscript," replied his friend. "If you'd rather not try this particular antidote, I may be able to track down something else eventually."

"No, we'll try this. Mix me up a batch." Pulling his cap down lower, he stood. "I'll drop over to pick it up late tonight."

McDermott spent the entire next day mostly sitting in the armchair in his living room. He felt incredibly weary and dozed a good deal. A light snow fell throughout the day.

The phone rang several times in the late afternoon. His answering machine took all the calls.

Wurbling warned him, "Okay, asshole! Either Wendy Mintz is an employee of *Screwy* by noon tomorrow or you aren't."

Neely called to say, "Listen, old buddy, if you haven't tried that aging potion yet, maybe you'd better not. I've just come across some new background material that makes me uneasy. Right after my seminar tonight I'll drop over and explain. Be good."

Then Wendy called. "This is for Phil. I'm very worried about you, dear. Please get in touch with me and tell me where you are. I was so desperate and worried—well, I actually used that spare key you gave me and came over to the apartment to see if I could find some trace of you. Even though that meant I might bump into your odious Cousin Les. But Les wasn't there, though neither were you, sweetheart. Please do let me know if anything's wrong. Oh, and apologize to the old gentleman who was dozing in the living room. I don't think I woke him up, but if I did, I'm sorry. I'd guess, judging from the family resemblance, that he's your grandfather."

Small Miracles, Part II:
That's the Way
the Golem Crumbles

by
Mel Gilden

*Readers often ask if writers are inspired by other writers.
This is as true of writing as of painting, or sculpture, or any
other field of creative endeavor. Sometimes the inspiration can
serve as a takeoff for an entire new work, one that rushes off
in a wholly different direction. In music, for example, witness
Rachmaninoff's Rhapsody on a Theme of Paganini, or Brahms's
Academic Festival Overture (original work centered on variations
of a student drinking song). Sometimes an artist's reworking of
another artist's efforts transforms the original in ways you never
imagined, like the Kronos Quartet's version of Jimi Hendrix's
"Purple Haze."*

*Writers frequently produce sequels to earlier works, but they
usually take the form of straightforward follow-ups to the original.
More unusual is for the first effort to inspire a second which flies
off in a different direction. Mel Gilden has been flying off for
years, as witness the following.*

The room is dark but for the alien green glow of my computer screen. The only thing typed there so far, in—you should
pardon the expression—letters of fire, is the words "An Essay
on the Romance of Jewish Fantasy and Mysticism." The title is
optimistic. It has been alone on the screen for hours.

My editor thinks that I know more about the subject than I do,
in fact, know. I am no expert. I need help. I rack my mind for

something to say. I know. I'll tell a brace of jokes about *tzaddiks*, or wonder-working rabbis, that will illuminate not only wonders but the nature of Jewish thought.

(I am barely successful ignoring the impulse to say, "Yeah, yeah, that's the ticket!")

I take the keyboard across my knees and type:

A village in Poland wanted to hire a tzaddik. When their prospective wonder-worker arrived, he was asked to perform a miracle. Just a small one, nothing fancy, he was probably tired from his journey.

The tzaddik agreed and promised that if he were taken to the grave of the person most recently dead, he would revive that person to perfect health. The townspeople did as requested and the tzaddik was taken to the final resting place of a certain Mrs. Blatstein.

The widower Blatstein looked nervous as the tzaddik began to pray over the deceased. He fervently rocked up and back, his side locks swinging like pendulums. Nothing happened. The mayor of the village encouraged him to try again. The tzaddik began to pray more loudly. He did little dance steps at the head of the grave and made mystic signs in the air. Still nothing happened.

The villagers stared silently at the back of the tzaddik, who now stood motionless and made soft smacking sounds with his lips. At last the tzaddik shook his head, and without turning around, he pronounced, "That's what I call dead!"

Remember that punch line. It will be important. Now, the companion joke.

Two men were walking through a cemetery where they'd heard a Rothschild was buried. They finally came to the grave marker, a huge marble edifice covered with classical statuary and words of wisdom. It was definitely a finer building than the one in which either of them lived.

At last one of them shook his head and said, "That's what I call living!"

Two jokes about death, which is, after being born, certainly the most mysterious thing that happens to us. And the first joke, at any rate, begs us to ask the question, Is the tzaddik a true wonder-worker, or just a con man like Harold Hill in *The Music Man*? It also illustrates a point, that being—

I hear a voice coming from a thick lump of shadow on the other side of my desk. In a sarcastic tone, the voice says, "You really do need help if you are running to the *goyim* for examples. Boring examples."

I jump in my chair when I hear this. As far as I know, I'm alone in my apartment. "Who's there?" I cry.

"It's me. Rabinowitz," the voice says.

"Rabinowitz who?"

"*Schlemiel!* Rabinowitz, the *batlan* angel from your own story, 'Small Miracles.' "

I had, in fact, written a story called "Small Miracles." It was about batlan angels, second-class angels who don't lack the will to do good, but only the talent. One of the characters says that the miracle of a batlan angel is like week old seltzer. A nifty turn of phrase, if I do say so myself.

The story had enjoyed a vogue among the more Jewish element of the science fiction world, and had even been reprinted. It wouldn't take a genius to know about it. Still, if the voice comes from a burglar, he is obviously not one of your average second-story men. I decide that I've been living inside my own head too long. This guy is a figment of my feverish and desperate imagination.

As if answering a question I'd spoken out loud, the voice says, "Don't put on airs. Only the Almighty could imagine me as I am. As only He could imagine you as *you* are."

"How did you get in here?" Not even a Talmudic second-story man is welcome in my apartment. Already, I'm wondering how I could convince the landlord to install bars over the windows. Not by telling him the truth, certainly.

"The usual way," the voice says. The batlan, if that's what it is, sounds surprised that I'd asked.

"What do you want?" I say as I peer into the darkness. I can see the general shape of a man embedded in shadow across the desk from me. A bar of pale streetlight from outside falls across one of his black thick-soled shoes, and glints on the tiny silver wings attached to it.

"It's what *you* want that's important, *kinder*. I'm here to work a small, batlan-size miracle."

"You'll help me with my essay?"

"I thought I said that."

"All right." I poise my fingers over the keyboard of my computer and say, "Go ahead."

There is a long silence, then the sound of someone trying to get comfortable in a chair. (There is no chair—no room for a chair—on that side of my desk.) The shoe disappears from the bar of light, then reappears.

"So, *nu,* already?" I say.

"You know," Rabinowitz says, "in *Raiders of the Lost Ark,* there were Jewish demons guarding the Ark of the Covenant."

"Terrific," I say. "That ought to take twenty or thirty words to say. What do I talk about for the other two thousand words?"

"You could talk about television," he says. "Have you watched it lately? Refugees from Chelm are everywhere. And," he concludes darkly, "not all of them are Jewish."

I realize he's right. With all the silliness on TV, any number of actors, writers, and members of the production staff could be from the little town that logic forgot. I type a note to remind myself what Rabinowitz has just said.

Eagerly, I say, "What else?"

Suddenly the room is filled with strange heavy perfume, the way I imagine a garden in the Mysterious East might smell. Someone lays gentle hands on my shoulders and I jump again.

The hands are long, and at the end of the fingers are well-manicured nails painted with black glittery polish. Looking over my shoulder, I see a dark beautiful woman dressed in wisps of nothing-at-all. She takes a few steps back and looks at me up from under, like Lauren Bacall in *To Have and Have Not.*

I stand and turn, my back to the computer. Rabinowitz announces, "Lilith. Adam's first wife. Also a murderer of babies and a professional succubus."

Lilith smiles at me coyly. I can see that her canines are enlarged, reminded me of late-show vampires. As she steps toward me, her hips moving provocatively, she speaks in a breathy voice, heavy with musk. "Don't worry about a thing, *kline mensch.* I've had a lot of bad press. Come to momma." She wiggles her fingers as she reaches for me.

"This, by you, is help?" I cry. "I have an essay to finish. If I should live through what she has in mind, my editor will kill me for missing a deadline!"

"You need coins," Rabinowitz says, unperturbed. "Each one inscribed with the words 'Lilith, be gone!'"

I madly pull things from my pockets—ancient Kleenex, a pen, and a credit card.

"No change," I mourn. Lilith presses herself against my back and folds her arms around me; her hands are rubbing my chest and moving south.

Frantically, I turn the credit card over, and on the tape where I have neglected to sign my name, I scrawl the magic formula. I shake the card in her face and cry, "Lilith, be gone!"

Suddenly Lilith disappears in a spout of flame, and I am back in my chair as if the preceding two minutes had never happened. The perfume is gone too. About that, I'm sorry.

"Excuse me, mister." That isn't Rabinowitz's voice. I look around. Behind me now stands a thin man, dressed in rags, and bent over with age or disease or both. I can imagine hungry germs crossing the room between us and I try, without success, not to breathe.

Rabinowitz says, "Gosnik, the lahmed wufnik. He's one of the thirty-six virtuous men who justify the continued existence of humanity to the Lord."

"Who, me?" says Gosnik, clawing at his sunken chest.

"Absolutely," says Rabinowitz.

Gosnik smiles beatifically and disappears, leaving behind a tiny tornado of dry leaves that settle and evaporate.

"What happened?" I say.

Rabinowitz shrugs and says, "It is written that if one of the thirty-six learns of his place in the universe, he dies."

"You killed him."

Rabinowitz shrugs again and says, "Who knows? It's only folklore. Do you want to see any more?"

I do. I'm not sure that I have enough information to finish my essay. Still, I'll have to be careful, and so will Rabinowitz. My downstairs neighbor won't stand for anything that makes noise or interferes with his TV reception. I try to remember if, anywhere in the annals of Jewish fantasy, there is a creature that would do either of those things.

Feigning nonchalance, I throw an arm over the back of my swivel chair and say, "Sure. Fascinate me."

"Fascinate? Hmm."

Suddenly words begin to appear on my computer screen. I am—you should pardon the expression—fascinated as they spell out:

GOOD EVENING. I AM THE DYBBUK OF MARVIN FLEISHMAN. GEE, THIS IS GREAT. I ALWAYS WANTED

TO BE A WRITER. LIVE LONG AND PROSPER! CALL
ME ISHMAEL! HERE'S LOOKING AT *YOU*, KID!

"I thought dybbuks were spirits that possessed *people,* not
computers," I say as Fleishman continues to fill the screen with
famous quotes.

"It's an age of miracles," Rabinowitz says.

It's interesting that Fleishman should lead off with "Live long
and prosper," the famous Vulcan salute from *Star Trek.* When
Mr. Spock said it, he made the same hand sign a rabbi makes
when he blesses somebody. I can use that in my essay—good
pop cult stuff.

IT WAS THE BEST OF TIMES. IT WAS THE WORST OF
TIMES.

"This dybbuk is terrific," I say. "I can actually interview him."
I begin to type, SO TELL ME, MR. FLEISHMAN, but I see that
none of it is appearing on the screen.

Fleishman finishes the screen with COGITO ERGO SUM and
the text obligingly scrolls upward. FOR THE LOVE OF GOD,
MONTRESOR!

"I can't get a word in edgewise," I say. "Can you make him
stop quoting long enough to answer my questions?"

"To tell the truth," Rabinowitz says, "I don't even know how
he got in there."

I "harrumph," letting out a breath. I type a few more words, to
no effect. A moment later, I say, "How do we get rid of him?"

"Do you know the Ninety-first Psalm?"

"Well, no."

"Neither do I. We're in trouble."

Quotes continue to roll up the screen. FRIENDS, ROMANS,
COUNTRYMEN. BEWARE THE JABBERWOCK, MY SON.
SHE CAME IN THROUGH THE BATHROOM WINDOW.
On and on.

I lean forward, study the keyboard, then push three particular
keys all at once. Fleishman has enough time to type H-E-E-E-E-
Y! before the screen goes blank. Seconds later, the screen asks
me to restart my system.

I lean back in my chair and sigh. I say, "How about someone
not quite so talkative?"

"You got it, boychik," says Rabinowitz.

Seconds later I smell damp earth. I swivel around and see a

man-shaped creature, his head brushing the ceiling, a Hebrew word carved into his forehead above eyes that stare without comprehension across the room. He is not moving, not even breathing. Just standing there, the thing has an aura of tremendous power. And like many statues, it always seems about to move.

"The golem of Prague," Rabinowitz whispers. "Created by the rabbi to protect the Jews and to help him in the synagogue."

"Why are you whispering?" I whisper.

"I don't know. Why do people whisper at the Grand Canyon?"

I glance at the golem. I can see Rabinowitz's point. Not only is the thing huge, but it is the ancestor of every artificial creature from Frankenstein's monster to C3PO in *Star Wars,* the Terminator and Robocop.

I say, "What's its name?"

"Call me Golem," the golem says in a harsh lugubrious voice that raises the hackles on the back of my neck. Makes sense. When you're the only one there is, names are easy.

"Tell me about yourself," I say.

"I am the golem," the creature says. "I was built by Rabbi Yehuda Loew to protect the Jews."

"I could use some protection myself," I say. "That guy downstairs is crazy."

"I hear and obey," the golem says. With a squeak and a gritty slide, the golem turns and heads for the door.

"Hey, wait a minute!" I cry after the thing as it smashes through the front door and lumbers down the stairs.

"Single-minded, isn't it?" Rabinowitz says calmly.

I run back into my office and shout, "Make it go away! He'll destroy the building. He'll murder the guy downstairs!"

"Here," says Rabinowitz. A sheet of paper floats onto my desk. On it is one short word written in Hebrew. I can hear the sounds of splintering wood coming from below. The man downstairs shouts hysterically.

"Do something," I cry.

"Erase the first letter in the word," Rabinowitz says.

I take a pencil and hastily scratch out the first letter. The hullabaloo downstairs continues. I remember that Hebrew is written the other way and that I've scratched out the wrong letter. I scratch out the first letter at the other end of the word. Suddenly, there is silence.

"Why didn't *you* do something?"

"I'm only a batlan angel, remember."

"Yeah."

"Heaven helps those who help themselves."

"You sound like Fleishman," I say.

A moment later, someone knocks on the door. It is the man downstairs, looking a little bewildered, but otherwise unharmed. He has a small figure in his hand. It is the golem. "This yours?" he says. I take it from him, and when he is gone, I crumble the dry earth from which the figure is made into the trash, hoping it will not magically reconstitute itself.

I go back into the dark office and say, "Are you still here?"

"Where else would I be? You want more?"

"No. I've had enough." I'm still trying to catch my breath. I sit in my swivel chair and take the keyboard into my lap. "That's plenty." As I study the alien green glow of the letters on the screen, my mind races with ideas and literary possibilities. I poise my fingers over the keys.

"So, *nu*, already?" Rabinowitz says.

I delete the old name of the essay—I see now it is a boring thing of dead academic wood—and start again: "My Date with Lilith, and Other Miraculous Encounters I Barely Lived Through."

"Very nice," Rabinowitz assures me, and suddenly I am quite positive that I am alone again. I shudder. A man is not visited every day by an angel, not even by a batlan angel.

I go get a glass of water, which I sip slowly while sitting in my chair and pondering the theological implications of the visitation. I decide to worry about them later. Right now, I have a deadline. I take a deep ragged breath and continue to type. I will tell the story exactly as it happened. Truth, while frequently stranger than fiction, can sometimes be substituted for it, and no one the wiser.

The Smart Sword

✧

by
Edward Wellen

Parody might be defined as the Emily Post version of sarcasm. A kinder, gentler bashing, as it were.

There are some who believe that any deliberate attempted parody of the fantasy sub-genre known as Sword and Sorcery is an oxymoron. This depends on the reader's point of view, not to mention his or her degree of cynicism. Certainly the fans of Robert E. Howard take his Conan tales (take my Conan, please) as seriously as did the author himself. Others are, shall we say, less respectful.

To produce a work which treats the genre with affection while simultaneously parodying it requires a literary balancing act of some skill. That is to say, it leaves it to the reader to decide whether to take the telling with seriousness or a smirk. Or it can be read both ways, thereby giving you a bonus.

Herewith a twofer from Edward Wellen.

> I would tell the tale of Khur,
> How the hero bold and pure
> Came to win the wonder sword,
> Warred upon the wicked lord,
> Cut in two the airy cord,
> Then dragooned the dragon horde.
> —Wythu, *Lay of Khur*

1. The Coming of the Sword

Had Khur been in his right mind this night, he would not have cut across free-farmer Snezre's zlok field. Khur still bore weals to remind him the small spry Snezre could pitchfork-jab the massive muscle-bound Khur all over the lot.

Sober, Khur steered wide of Snezre's boundary stones, and whenever Khur encountered Snezre in Wodby Vuroy on market day he took care to express his open scorn from a distance and by ambiguous gesture.

This night, though, Khur had drunk too well, seeking to wash his brain of impotent rage. Because this night the Grand Duke Borrgot of Jusgot would be preempting Khur's bride of this afternoon, the maiden Laxtma.

"Laxtma, O Laxtma!" Khur moaned. "I know it ain't right to think this way, but it just don't seem fair he should have dibs on you!"

He looked for comfort to the moon.

But Zhalsspal, who had lit his way, now drew a veil across her face in cold rebuke for questioning the ways of Cynarg.

Khur heaved a beery sigh. He could only hope Borrgot's use of Laxtma would not last excruciatingly long or end humiliatingly soon.

The sniggerings behind Khur's back and the smirkings to his face—and he having to stand treat!—had made him drink up with nose-spurting haste, shake the green sawdust of the Green Dragon off his newly patched boots, and seek the small comfort of limitless night.

And so it was that these same boots trampled the proud young stalks that fate placed in Khur's wavering way home under the sarcastically romantic light of Zhalsspal (reflecting the class G glory of Abiz Wyr) at this fateful hour.

As he lumbered through Snezre's zlok field, his weavings making the shortcut as long as the long way around, Khur muttered to himself and swung heavy fists at forms his mind shadowed forth.

"Take *that,* you splat of dragon dung. And *that*."

Saying and doing now what he should have said and done back there at the tavern, he drew a measure of satisfaction from these belated comebacks. Deep down, though, he knew he would have made an even bigger fool of himself had he taken on the tavern

regulars when they wondered back and forth what Borrgot would
be up to at this point and that in the course of the evening. His
lighter and livelier tormentors would have danced beyond his
physical and mental reach.

Of course as far as had to do with Borrgot's name they dared
not overstep the boundary stones of prudence—the Duke's ears
reached everywhere. On the other hand, the lawful facts were
fair game.

Borrgot had gone a-hunting last fall in the game park hard by
Wodby Vuroy. Good hunting for Borrgot, lean pickings for Khur.
Borrgot bagged a brace of grosshorned sryvar, then his unsated
eyes lighted on lissome Laxtma out berrying against all season
and reason.

Borrgot marked her then for his future pleasure. Some held that
was how Khur had come by the means to wed Laxtma: that, to
hasten the honeymoon, Borrgot's hidden hand had helped Khur's
widowed mother unload a hardscrabble patch to raise bride-buy.
Whatever, all knew that Borrgot's henchmen had swept Laxtma
from the chapel at Wodby Vuroy to the castle at Lisre Urtcyn
hard upon the exchange of vows.

And now, stale from celebrating the occasion as tradition called
for, Khur breathed out the fumes of zlok liquor and breathed in
the smell of zlok ripening on the stalk and crushed underfoot.

And *now* now, the senses he had sought to deaden came lethally
alive. The air hummed loudly, a rumble like as though some
great engine, a thousand thousand times more powerful than any
waterwheel, were grinding behind the airy fabric of the world.

A crackle like you wouldn't believe, then the air split open.

An oval floated upright and in its frame a being unlike any Khur
had ever heard of stood staring at him. It looked just as startled
and dismayed at sight of him.

Two ovals, the same figure in each. The ovals linked and
unlinked like a magician's rings, and the figures faded in and
out of oneness and doubleness.

He closed one eye but the two spitting images remained. Didn't
surprise him. Went with having a load on.

*Your blood alcohol level has nothing to do with your seeing
double.*

Seeing double was nothing to hearing double, to having two
overlapping voices sound in his head without going through his
ears.

There are two of me, caught in a time paradox. Instead of forking at a significant point, I remain in tight tandem with myself. I can't maintain this anomaly—I can hardly call it a singularity—much longer. Help me, or I'll cancel out, with unfortunate consequences to your own continuum. Quick, the Like-him maneuver!

Before Khur could think to ask what a Like-him maneuver was he saw in his head what the Like-him maneuver called on him to do.

He grinned savagely. In his present state of mind it would be his pleasure. But which one should he perform it on?

It doesn't matter. Just do it. Now!

Khur closed his eyes and his fist, wound up with such force that he whirled around twice, and swung.

He felt a powerful tingling as he connected. The background hum downsized by half. He opened his eyes. Only one spitting image remained.

Now he could see it more clearly, and wished he couldn't. It was blue-skinned and naked and fleshy pouches grew on chest and belly.

It drew a cloth from a pouch and gingerly touched the cloth to its nose. A green stain spread on the cloth. The creature gestured comfortingly. *Don't blame yourself. You never laid a finger on this me. Purely psychosomatic. Thank you, thank you, thank you.*

Khur waved the thanks away. "It wasn't nothing." But his hand hurt and when he looked at it he saw his knuckles were scraped raw. He felt faint at the sight of his own blood. So it was something.

The creature took a wand out of another pouch and pointed it at Khur's bruised hand. The skin healed at once.

Sorry for your scraped knuckles, but the added mass of your matter, minimal though it was, made the other I implode. Now the other I never was.

The nose still dripped, and the creature employed the cloth again.

"Why don't you use the wand on your nose?"

The creature froze, then smacked one of its hands against the side of its head. *Never occurred to me. My mind-set kept me from seeing a psychosomatic symptom as a treatable reality.* It pointed the wand at its nose and the dripping stopped. *Thank you, thank you, thank you.*

"Don't mention it."

Too late, I already have. But now that I've split I must be going. I can't go forth to encounter the reality of experience, however, without leaving behind a concrete expression of my gratitude— please don't ask me not to mention reward.

Of all that, Khur grasped the last concept. Oh, boy. "I won't."

Thank you, thank you, thank you.

Khur waited. And waited. Was that it? What kind of reward was thanks? Pretty cheap, if you asked him. What could you buy with empty words? He felt like giving the creature another poke in the snoot, only the creature would take it as another favor. Khur set his jaw. No more pokes for free, buddy.

But the creature was digging deep in a pouch and—by the creature's slow care—working something precious and substantial out of it. One last finicky tug brought the reward to light.

The creature handed it to Khur with such reverence that Khur took it with equal reverence though it looked to be only a lump of lead.

You have but to visualize your dearest wish—and the adaptive artifact, with its smart miniaturized cosmos-powered servomechanisms, will conform to serve you.

Khur stood staring at the lump in his hands.

After a minute, *No need to thank me. We are quits. I go momentarily. As I'm now totally probable, there'll be a sizable displacement reaction. So, if you'll kindly take a step backward . . .*

"Uh, sure." Khur took three quick giant steps backward.

No fear, the artifact's force field will protect you from the special effects as my oval gate attains infra-zero value, ultra-zero volume, and relative-zero velocity. And now, farewell!

The oval closed in upon itself in nothing flat. Simultaneously, the artifact formed a protective shell of air around Khur, dulling for him the flash and muffling for him the bang as the ex-oval shot from this universe.

Even so, the whooshing away packed the wallop of an honest quart of zlok liquor chugalugged, staggering him. The artifact lump in Khur's hands pulled this way and that to help Khur keep his drunken balance.

Already the creature was a thing of delirium tremens heroically cast out of his mind. But the lump was real. Khur blinked at it. Now that he had it, what was it he had?

He eyed it hopefully. It stared back blankly.

·

Was it worth anything?

It changed in his hands to an ingot of gold.

He had only heard talk of gold ingots, never seen one, so it was quite unlike the real thing. But with its shimmering yellow aura it more than matched his image of what one should look like. Oh, boy.

His delight gave way to dismay.

He knew what his ma would say when she saw it. She would say only a Borrgot could possess such a thing. She would shake her head and say it was worse than useless, like him. She would hide it in the hollow place under the hearthstone while she tried to figure out what to do with it.

Ma was right. How long would it be before the gold found itself from Khur's hands to Borrgot's? In between, there were many shrewder minds than Khur's. Once others knew Khur had it they would scheme to trick or steal it from him before he could buy anything with it.

A rare thought, almost as if it came from the ingot itself, entered Khur's mind. Why not take the ingot straight to Borrgot and offer it to him as a kind of bride-buy for Laxtma before too much moon honey was spilled?

No. On the way to the castle he would run into thieves and tricksters. If he got by them, in the castle itself were officers between Borrgot and the people. They would seize the ingot, say he had stolen it, and throw him into Borrgot's dungeon. In the end, whatever Khur tried, Borrgot would have the ingot and Khur would have nothing.

Khur had a mind to cast the ingot after the creature into nowhere, but he didn't know where nowhere was.

The ingot instantly resumed its default mode, a lump.

> Now is when the far-eyed sage
> Turns to scan the star-writ page
> Whereon by his art he reads
> Signs of Khur's predestined deeds.
>   —Wythu, *Lay of Khur*

Checyr, court astrologer to the Grand Duke of Jusgot, swiveled his telescope 180 degrees to peer at the wrong end. He satisfied himself that he had observed a phenomenon in the heavens, not a sparkbug disporting on the object glass.

He had spotted a shooting star with a difference. All other shooting stars fell to earth from space. This one rose from the earth. He unstuck his pointing pin from his lapel and touched it to the lens.

The pin picked up the ghostly memory of the shooting star's trajectory and traced back along it without scratching. He took a reading. Lift-off was from a point near Wodby Vuroy.

His hand trembled as he stuck the pin back in his lapel. "Ouch."

He raised the skirt of his cloak, raced down the western tower's winding stairs, spun dizzily along the corridor to Borrgot's chambers, and caromed off the guard's rump.

The guard whirled, straightened, and held his pike at port arms.

"Who goes there?"

"You know me, damn it," Checyr wheezed. "I must see the Grand Duke."

"You must not. I got strict orders not to disturb."

"Now, damn it, or I'll tell him I caught you peeking through the keyhole."

Ulp. "If you swear it's an emergency . . ."

"I swear, damn it."

The guard brushed the door panel lightly with a knuckle.

Checyr made a face and gave three loud knocks of his own.

Heavy padding across carpeted floor. The panel unlatched from within and swung open. The face of Borrgot glowered in its most unfavorable aspect. "This had better be good."

Ulp. "Sire, Checyr swears this is an emergency."

The glower swung from the guard to Checyr.

Ulp. "Sire, I know not whether you saw the flash and felt the rumble, but—"

Borrgot's eyes rolled heavenward. "He brings us a weather report."

Checyr put his hand to his heart. " 'Tis my grave duty to forewarn you a new star arises from Wodby Vuroy."

Borgott's eyes lidded dreamily. "True, the wench hails from Wodby Vuroy, but if the earth trembled, look nearer home for your influences."

"Sire—"

"Toddle back to your pinpricks in the sky, old star-starer, and leave me to matters of more moment down here."

"Sire—"

"Beat it before I have my guard spit you on his pike."

The panel slammed shut. Heavy padding faded away.

Checyr burned from scalp to sole thinking how he had given himself to serving this boorish and unworthy usurper.

"You heard the Man." The guard touched the point of his pike to Checyr's rump.

Skirt of his cloak dragging, hands clasped behind in fore-thought, Checyr plodded back to his tower room.

So be it. Let the usurper learn the hard way, without benefit of omens to minimize disaster, without guidance during conjunctions to reshape the future. It seemed auspicious to hook up with the coming barbarian conqueror. Such a one's mind Checyr should find simple to sway.

> Meanwhile, in her heir-tight cell,
> Fair Dankeja breaks the spell:
> Dreams of rescue from the keep
> Keep her smiling in her sleep.
> —Wythu, *Lay of Khur*

In another part of the castle, the lovely young Dankeja revised her running dream.

Till now, her champion merely leapt the moat, caught hold of the clinging vine on the castle wall, climbed to her window, tore out the bars, and . . .

Tonight, the bold young hero more flashily flew to her rescue on the wings of his dragon mount, alighted on the parapet, took out the sentries on the roof, blazed a bloody trail to her cell door, and . . .

As ever, however, he momentarily broke their clinch to slay with his magic sword her wicked uncle, the usurper Borrgot.

A flash penetrated her eyelids. A distant rumble sat her up.

She looked and listened, but it didn't repeat itself.

Whatever had wakened her from her warm dream, it had brought her back to cold reality. Wait for a dream hero to rescue her and she would wait still in her coffin, past dreaming. She shivered though the night assayed mild.

Whatever had wakened her had stirred others. She heard the sentries overhead. Most nights the two on watch took turns snoring. This night both were up, murmuring about a flash and a rumble.

She heard too the prowling and growling of Borrgot's hounds on the grounds below.

And a bird that nested in a nearby crevice of the keep seemed shaken restless. It hopped onto Dankeja's sill, in a space between tendrils of the clinging vine that graced the bars in passing, and preened its ruffled feathers.

Dankeja wondered idly, as she often had before, that the bird knew not to sink its beak into the vine's poisonous berries.

She rose from her straw bed and moved to the barred window. A full Zhalsspal gilded the bird and the vine. She crooned to the bird and the bird cocked its head and fell still. Slowly she reached through the bars to stroke the bird. Just before her touch the bird exploded away.

After a moment Dankeja filled her empty hand with berries she painfully plucked.

She looked at them. How deadly were they? She sat cross-legged on her pallet, lifted her cracked plate onto her lap, gouged holes with the handle of her wooden spoon in the scrap of gray meat left over from supper, and buried the fruit of the vine in the holes.

This done, she returned to the window, dropped the meat to the hounds below.

She heard the hounds fight over the meat. From the sounds, one won. Then she heard an agonizing howl that ended abruptly.

Dankeja smiled bitterly. She had found one way out.

> While my pen doth well imbibe,
> Let me muse ere I inscribe
> (Ere I scratch quick as a flea),
> That the gall may honey be.
> —Wythu, *Lay of Khur*

A distant rumble, following a subliminal flash, roused Wythu from the doze he at once rationalized as meditation. He rose, stretched, and stepped over crumples of paper to the window. A wearying business, this delving soul-deep for inspiration.

He gazed out over moon-glazed tiled roofs to the castle on its height overlooking Lisre Urtcyn. A light burned in the western tower.

That would be Checyr, the Grand Duke's astrologer, dipping into the well of night.

Wythu envied Checyr, not that Checyr ate Borrgot's bread—
better a stale crust here in this garret than a feast at the usurper's
board!—but that Checyr had the means, at whatever expense of
spirit, to render the unirhymes of the universe. Wythu envied
Checyr, who saw what Wythu only dreamed.

Yet, what earthly good the getting the lay of other worlds?
Checyr, like Wythu, was stuck on this forsaken world, in this
rotten land.

The land needed a hero, a hero Wythu might sing of. Ah, that
such a hero come, and swiftly! And that Wythu's song sound,
and widely!

Then would Checyr envy Wythu, who dreamed what Checyr
only saw.

> Lightning-spawned, the sword alarmed
> Fearsome gnomes, who came forth armed,
> Magnet-drawn, as though becharmed.
> —Wythu, *Lay of Khur*

Free-farmer Snezre had hit the hay at his usual hour, but instead
of lying fallow, renewing himself for fruitful work, he lay awake
brooding till light and sound woke him from that barren wake-
fulness. Something had burst upward from his rows of zlok.

He sprang out of bed, raced to the window. Dimly he made
out a figure overtopping his zlok. It looked ungainly enough to
be that oversized oaf Khur. Snezre's small tight face grew tighter.
Was Khur trying to set the crop afire?

Snezre threw on his robe, rushed out, grabbed his pitchfork
without breaking stride.

> Shining bright, though unadorned,
> Darkly then the weird sword warned,
> "I'm the get of thunderburst!"
> Risking to be blessed or curst,
> Khur now dared it do its worst,
> Grasped the blade none other durst,
> Mastered swordplay from the first,
> Gave the sword its unslaked thirst.
> —Wythu, *Lay of Khur*

The lump weighed heavy on Khur's hands and in his mind.
It wanted to *be*.

It wanted him to tell it *what* to be.

"How should I know?" he asked it plaintively.

Snezre's voice behind him, reinforced by sharp prongs of pitchfork, made him jump. "You answer before I ask. But I want a better answer. Why . . . are . . . you . . . here?" The pitchfork punctuated the question and punctured Khur.

Now the artifact felt Khur's need. It warmed in his hands to the task.

Khur's hair raised, his skin tingled, his bones vibrated. All the zlok liquor fumes sucked from his brain and he filled with a new intoxication. A questing strength flowed from the lump, in readiness to shape to his will.

Vaguely, a sword took form in his mind.

The artifact's sensors determined that he was a lefty, and the lump quickly worked its way swordward. The sheer speed of the happening almost surprised it from his hand. But the hilt fitted to his grip with a grip of its own.

So, blankly, he beheld himself holding a finished sword in his left hand.

2. The Flashing of the Sword

> Hard-pressed, Khur came through unharmed
> While the gnomes bought what they farmed
> Clashing with him for the right,
> Trading sword strokes in the night.
> —Wythu, *Lay of Khur*

Another jab of the pitchfork sent Khur stumbling forward. He felt the sword help him keep his balance. He turned halfway, right side toward Snezre, sword at his left side. The sword tugged as though strongly advising against this tactic, but he did not feel ready to let Snezre see him with a sword he did not know how to use.

Snezre's nose wrinkled. "Phew! You reek of zlok liquor. Been celebrating a tad overmuch? Your wedding night, ain't it?"

Khur grinned foolishly.

Snezre's eyes shone with hate. "For years I slaved and scrimped till I raised bride-buy. Hadn't been for a chance to lay in seed real cheap, Laxtma'd be mine tonight—saving the Grand Duke. I felt sure I had a clear field. How could I know your ma'd step in and beat me out?"

He looked Khur up and down, then laughed with great lack of humor. "For her son the blockhead. Have to hand it to the old bag. She's the man in your family."

Khur's face flamed. He felt his hand tighten on the hilt. Snezre shouldn't oughta mouth off that way about Ma.

Snezre's eyes sharpened. "What you hiding behind your back?" The pitchfork jabbed at Khur's groin. "You been stealing something from me?"

Before Khur could back away the sword swung him around and parried the pitchfork with a force that sent Snezre spinning.

Snezre faced around to square off again. He got Khur and the sword in focus. "A sword! Where'd a clod like you get a sword?" His eyes slitted. "You been digging up treasure on my land. Always knew there was truth in the old tales. Well, anything you find on my land is mine. That's the law—not that I need the law to make you fork it over."

Khur stiffened. "I didn't dig it up. I got it from a—a guy. I done the guy a favor and he give it to me. It's mine."

Snezre shook his head. "Can't even come up with a manure-quality lie." He braced himself and his pitchfork. "You caught me off guard with a lucky stroke, but I'm ready for you now. You're on my land, with a sword you can't prove belongs to you, so it's forfeit. Drop it and get off my land. Last warning."

Khur sagged. Snezre had him on all counts. He couldn't prove he owned the sword. He had no business on Snezre's land. It had been a lucky stroke. Khur's arm lowered the sword and his hand began to loosen its grip.

Snezre laughed with great good humor. "That's the way, you big lump." With one-handed disdain he jabbed the pitchfork at Khur.

The sword jerked Khur out of his cringe. Khur followed openmouthed the dexterity of his sword hand as it leapt to engage the foe. It slashed rapidly and repeatedly at the goading pitchfork. Blurs of blade lopped off the tines and moved up the handle slicing. In a trice, Snezre held out a baton.

The next stroke would cut through Snezre's wrist. Snezre seemed too frozen to yank his hand away. But the sword forbore.

Khur recovered first. He wrinkled his nose. "Phew! You done soiled yourself. But I misdoubt it's manure quality."

Never before had Khur stretched and swelled to his full size. Always large for his age, he habitually scrunched up to minimize himself so folks who did not know him better would not look for him to be wise beyond his years.

Now, looming over a helpless and powerless Snezre, he strained his skin's bounds.

The sword was an extension of himself; what it touched he felt. He put its point to Snezre's chest and felt the pounding of Snezre's heart.

"Still want the sword?" For the first time Khur's voice had resonance, coming from an uncramped voice box.

It was Snezre who squeaked. "Who said anything about wanting the sword? Keep it! It's yours!" Snezre backpedaled out of reach, then turned and trampled zlok in his haste to leave the field of battle.

Khur raised the sword high in triumph and continued homeward.

> Blessings of the worthy dame,
> Who in dearth but not in shame
> Gave him birth and eke his name,
> Sped him on the path to fame.
> —Wythu, *Lay of Khur*

Khur quickened his step, bursting to boast of his feat. *Ma, you shoulda seen me make Snezre haul ass!*

Then he slowed, bethinking him of Ma's likely comeback. *Fool! Must you rub a somebody like Snezre the wrong way? Now you've done it. He'll ruin us.*

The sword hilt's wicking action dried the sweat of his palm and slapped rosin into his grip, restoring his sense of sureness and power.

Khur conjured up Snezre's image and savagely dealt it the deathblow he should have dealt the solid Snezre. The sword flashed, dripping moonlight, struck head from body, and the image dissolved in a liquid glitter.

His savagery satisfied, Khur would have let fall his sword arm. But, as if Khur had loosed unsatisfied lust in the sword, the sword still sought the foe.

He held tight to the hilt, his sinews knotting as he fought to control the slashing sword. "Hold on! There ain't nobody there!"

The sword subsided.

He hurried homeward. A scary feeling came over him. This thing had already changed his life. What more would it get him into, good and bad?

Home, with its shaky sides and swaybacked roof, looked suddenly unfamiliar. Would Ma look different too?

Weeds choked the vegetable garden astride the crooked walk, but he watched his step. Ma was just as protective of her miserable patch as Snezre was of his rich spread.

Khur ducked under the lintel and remained bowed under the low-pitched roof. Trimming his eyes to the dimness, he made out in one corner the bundle of rags that was Ma.

His hand convulsed on the hilt. The sword gathered for the thrust.

"No, no," he whispered in horror, and twisted himself and the sword away. "You got me wrong. It just hit me Ma might take you away. She always warned me to watch out for sharp things."

The bundle of rags stirred. Amhsa poked her head out. "Sir Twoleftfeet stumbling home at last. Thought that was you before but it was only thunder and lightning." She got to her feet and stood scratching herself and looking up at her son. "I guess you pissed away every bit of the silver I handed you."

Khur hung his head.

But Amhsa laughed. "Well, it's once in a lifetime. The world had to know we have something to celebrate. Laxtma should make you a fine strong mate after a litter licks her into shape." She cocked her head. "I only hope you can do your part. I done your thinking for you, raised your bride-buy for you, but you have to do your own bedding—once Borrgot's broken her in for you." She ended on a bitter note.

The disloyal thought struck Khur that the Grand Duke of her day had not taken his right of her, something Khur had not from Ma but from jeers of playmates.

Amhsa cocked her head the other way. "What you got there? An ax?"

"Hell, no, Ma. It's a sword."

She stretched to slap his face smartly. "Don't you never dare 'Hell, no, Ma' me again. A sword! What good's a sword to the likes of us? An ax, on the other hand . . ." Still, she raked the coals on the hearth to life and beckoned him near the glow for scrutiny of the sword. "I won't ask you how you come by it."

Khur made eagerly to tell her, but she shushed him.

She toed a stool toward Khur. "Sit down and shut up with some hot soup while I think what's best to do with this thing."

"But it's mine," Khur whined. "Even Snezre says it's mine."

She waved his words away. He tightened his mouth but sat down, sword on the side away from Ma. She ladled him a bowl of soupy water from the crusted pot hanging over the coals.

"Don't matter how you come by it. Point is, a sword like that's too good for the likes of us. But that don't mean we shouldn't gain by it." She sucked absently at an absent tooth. "Come morning, you'll take it to Lomn the Smith and bring back however much he gives you for it." She raised a finger to second-think herself. "Nope. There's no call for swords in these parts. Lomn would only treat the sword as scrap for beating into a plowshare, and pay according. The city's where the call for swords is, and where the money is. Are you listening?"

He nodded with his mouth full and his heart empty.

"Wipe your chin and go to bed. You'll set out for Lisre Urtcyn at dawn."

3. The Wearing of the Sword

> Bound from home, our hero found
> Ties to home still held him bound.
> But the sword, with sigh profound,
> Cut the cord and broke the spell.
> Bidding home a fond farewell,
> Khur set forth, his heart aswell,
> His sword keen his foes to quell.
> —Wythu, *Lay of Khur*

Fear shook him awake. The sword!

Ah, the sword lay at his side.

Yet fear remained. The sword seemed diminished, melted by daylight.

Ah, but diminished only because half sunk in the straw. (That it was new straw in anticipation of Laxtma brought a pang.)

Yet fear remained. Was the sword real?

He reached for the sword, then snatched his hand back. He would hold on to the dream or illusion a spell longer.

Amhsa, muttering about great lazy louts, stirred her bones and her rags. "Now, where's me pail of cold water? Ah, here 'tis."

Khur leapt out of bed, sword forgotten in his zeal to forfend a splash.

Breakfast's wordlessness was more pronounced than usual.

"Time to set out," Amhsa said. She took a good look at the sword. "Seems brand-new. I only wish I knew what it ought to fetch. I only hope you bring back a tenth of what it's worth. I only expect you to find your way there and back."

"Yes, Ma. But—"

Amhsa pressed into his palm—hard, to impress on him its value—just enough brass to see him to Lisre Urtcyn with a night's stay at an inn.

She handed him a worn leather knapsack that held a crust of zlokmeal bread and a flask of ill-souped well-water. Her mouth up at one corner and down at the other, she watched him tie a loop of cord to the hilt and so sling the sword.

"Now, don't jump at the first offer and don't drag it out waiting for the best offer. Get rid of the sword and out of town before anyone can ask you too many questions about it. The knapsack was your father's, so you may as well say the sword was his too. Lord knows he got out of everything, so you can put the sword's like-new condition to his getting out of battle too. Think you can remember all that?"

He nodded impatiently.

She shook her head but said nothing more.

He set out on the road and did not look back till time to top the rise.

Ma stood with one fist on hip, elbow pointing like a signpost in the direction of Lisre Urtcyn.

Neither Amhsa nor Khur waved goodbye.

4. The Blooding of the Sword

"Ere you offer to stand treat,
Know the proof my sword drinks neat."
Thus spake Khur, plus this I quote,
"Bloody smile, worn at your throat—
That consider, ere you gloat."
Still the landlord took small note.
Mine host never knew what smote.
                    —Wythu, *Lay of Khur*

Rising ground mist swirled like foam; the first wave of dawn broke over the hills. In this cold light it seemed a fluke that he had bested Snezre.

With chill air pebbling his skin, he felt scant warmth for another encounter. He took the long way around Snezre's field.

He would have skirted Wodby Vuroy if he could, but that would have taken him through the fields of others almost as unfriendly; Dame Amhsa had not endeared self and son to the neighbors. Trying to shrink inside himself, he hurried through the village. He wished himself a pale ghost in the pale ghostly light, but he knew his ungainly frame and heavy-footed walk made him manifest to all.

But Wodby Vuroy had just begun to rub the sleep from its eyes, yawn the dream out, and scratch the day in. Only once did a fit of giggling, from a girl feeding fowl in her yard, mar his passage.

The Green Dragon, at the other end of the village, marked the farthest he had ever gone from home.

He licked dry lips. He stopped. The sword swung to rest. Landlord Ogejgan, a man of the world, would know roughly what such a sword should fetch in Lisre Urtcyn. Khur might not haggle the better but at least would know someone had cheated him.

Ma would want him to keep moving.

Khur pushed his lips out and turned in at the tavern. A sign hung from a nail on the door. It fell as Khur swung the door inward. Ogejgan was busy behind the counter, back to the door. Khur bent to pick the sign up.

He heard Ogejgan's startled voice. "Who the—" Then a sigh of relief. "Nobody. Only the wind."

Khur straightened with the sign. He watched Ogejgan funnel fluid from a pail into a keg of beer. His eyes widened as Ogejgan paused to draw a fish from the pail and toss it over his shoulder to flop on the green sawdust. He coughed.

Ogejgan quickly lowered the pail out of sight, then turned. His face had reddened to match his nose. "If it ain't the bridegroom. Can't you read?"

Khur hung his head.

Ogejgan lowered his brows at Khur. "You ought to know anyway I'm closed at this hour."

"I didn't think."

Ogejgan put on a smile, picked up a glass, breathed on it, wiped it with his dirty apron. "I can see what you need, my friend."

Khur brightened, then shamefacedly shook his head.

Ogejgan frowned. "No brass left?" Then he shrugged and grinned. "That's all right. You lined my pockets last night. Have a mug of dragon's piss on the house."

He brimmed the mug under a spout and sailed it along the counter to Khur.

Khur's hands closed around it. He knew in shuddering foretaste that the stuff would burn straight down to his belly button. It lived down to its promise and below.

Ogejgan took in Khur's knapsack. "One for the road, looks like. Off to the Big Jiggy?"

Khur nodded. The burning took away speech.

Ogejgan's gaze widened to encompass the sword. "Since when did you take to wearing a sword?" He choked on a laugh. "Can't wait to escort your bride home? Let me give you a tip. Don't hang the sword so near the family jewels. Remember the old saw, 'No heirlooms, no heirs.' "

Khur felt the teeth of the saw and remembered something else. Here was last night's sneering voice that had egged the others on, the jeering laugh that had infected the others.

The voice sounded across a drumbeat of blood in Khur's ears. "True, there's Borrgot to prolong your line."

The heat that filled Khur now came not from dragon's piss but from an awakening volcano in his guts. He had a skinful of Ogejgan's needle, a bellyful of Ogejgan's laugh. He smashed the mug on the counter.

"Hey! You break it, you pay for it."

Khur felt the sword feel his fury as he and the sword grabbed hold.

Ogejgan backed away. "Watch out how you wave that around. Forget the mug. Could happen to anyone. I won't bill you for it. I figure breakage in."

The blade shore through the bar at midspan. The counter collapsed. Khur gaped at his deed and smarted from his mighty stroke. But he heard himself say calmly, "Figure that in."

Ogejgan roared and reached for a bungstarter.

The sword pinned his arm to the wall. The yell of rage turned to a cry of pain. He waved his free hand in frantic surrender.

Khur savored the transfixion a few beats before thinking at the sword that it could unstick Ogejgan now. He felt the sword feel the withdrawal and tasted the sword taste the blood dripping from its nonstick coating.

He watched Ogejgan slide down the wall. He felt the man's faintness. The blood flow dizzied him.

Swiftly the sword pulled him below the black cloud settling on his brain.

His mind cleared. He picked up the bar rag, shook off most of the sawdust, and knotted it clumsily around Ogejgan's arm.

He left, aware of Ogejgan's glazed glare stabbing at his back.

Not too many dusty paces along, Khur remembered he had forgotten to ask Ogejgan how much the sword should fetch. He started to turn back, then laughed the first full-throated, whole-hearted laugh of his life.

Sell the sword? They made an unbeatable pair—his sword and the sword's him. Sell the sword? Never.

5. The Testing of the Sword

When as yet its spires were dim
Lisre Urtcyn summoned him.
When he stood within its wall
Hard it was to heed its call.
    —Wythu, *Lay of Khur*

It came on rain, one of your wetter rains, and, by the time Khur reached the fork, one of your darker rains.

Khur huddled deeper inside his collar, trying to make out from the signpost the way to Lisre Urtcyn. The pointer told him to head straight down.

He was too shrewd to let that fool him. What must've happened, wind shook the pointer loose so it dangled by one nail.

If he swung the pointer so it pointed left, the lettering on it would be right side up—he knew that much—and that would point you the right way. If he swung the pointer so it pointed right, the lettering would be upside down, and that would point you the wrong way. Showed what you could do if you stopped and reasoned a problem out. He had his finger to the pointer, about to put theory into practice, when he heard hoofbeats and wheelsqueaks.

Khur waited, hand on hilt, blocking the road.

A droop-headed nag and a laden farm cart formed out of the mist. The driver, hunched under a streaming slicker, muttered beneath his breath but reined in.

He gave Khur a sour look. "Unofficial tariffman, eh?" He reached inside his slicker and tossed Khur a coin.

The sword intercepted it. Met it, juggled it, balanced it on the point of the blade.

The driver sat up straight. "I never saw the like of that."

Neither had Khur seen its like. But it suddenly seemed natural. After all, he had been taken for a bold road agent, and everyone knew road agents were daring and deft. He nonchalantly caught the coin as the sword tipped it into his free hand. He had the manners to bite it appreciatively before stowing it away. "Thanks."

The soft touch made the lift he had hoped for look a cinch.

He opened his mouth to ask for a ride but the driver spoke first. "How come a master swordsman like you isn't in Borrgot's service?"

"Well," Khur confessed, "I was on my way to sell my sword." His brow creased. Out of curiosity, "Do you think Borrgot would pay well?"

The driver's face hardened. He slapped the reins against the nag's flank. The nag lurched into the traces and the cart rumbled forward.

The sword yanked Khur out of harm's way.

The cart headed toward Lisre Urtcyn.

"Wait," Khur hollered, "how's about a hitch?"

The carter's voice drifted back. "Have a heart, tariffman. Poor old Knoxan has all she can do to pull this load of jervs. Your weight would be the last ruva tree in the forest."

The cart diminished into the mist. Khur stood watching nothingness, then hunched inside his soggy clothing and trudged after his memory of the cart.

An eternity later he caught up with the cart. It had mired axle-deep.

Khur squidged by. He nodded to the carter, who stood planted slipperily out front tugging at Knoxan's bridle. The carter gave him a silly grin. Once past, Khur hovered near to see how the carter would get out of the fix. All that the tugging did was stretch poor old Knoxan's neck.

A voice came from the sacks of jervs. "Well?"

The carter froze and Khur gaped.

The voice came again. "Well?"

The carter spoke to Khur more loudly than necessary; they stood almost nose-to-chest. "Shook me too at first, but it's a natural phenomenon with a perfectly logical explanation. You've heard folks say jervs repeat themselves."

Khur blinked with the effort of thinking it out. "Sure, but I always thought that was after you eat them."

"Normally, yes. But when you factor in soil, manure, weather, mutations, and so on, you can understand the likelihood of an odd before-the-fact jerv."

Khur's blinking stepped up into a steady blur.

The carter sighed. "But this gets us no nearer Lisre Urtcyn."

"Us?"

"Help me and I'll give you a hitch."

"But what about poor old Knoxan?"

"She'll be that grateful she won't mind."

So, Khur in Knoxan's place and harness, they wrenched the cart free.

And so, Khur crowding Vitrik on the driver's seat, they with an occasional groan from the sacks of jervs rattled toward Lisre Urtcyn.

If Knoxan felt gratitude, she did not show it in the glances she cast Khur over her withers.

Vitrik was the carter's name. In return he got Khur's name and life story. And he sounded out Khur's thoughts on Borrgot.

"So when you say you journey to sell your sword you don't mean as a mercenary, you mean as a merchant?"

Khur guessed that was what he meant, so he nodded.

"But you don't hate Borrgot for deflowering Laxtma?"

Khur slid his eyes at Vitrik. "Ain't he just doing what dukes always do?"

"Does that make it just?"

Khur hung his head. "It just don't seem fair."

Vitrik slapped him on the back. "The sense of inequity is the beginning of justice. We'll talk more of this, but here's the gate of the city."

A line of carts sought entry. While waiting his turn, the carter busied himself adjusting the sacks in back and murmuring soothingly to them. Khur guessed it would be embarrassing if they repeated while passing through.

The nearer they drew, the less ethereal and the more squalid

Khur found the city. Almost like home, though home piled high and packed tight. Still, the castle on its height held promise of enchantment.

The sun had come out. Khur raised his wondering eyes from the tiled roofs of the great city to the gilded spires of the castle. An uplifting sight.

Khur fought his sense of awe, and the sword stirred at his side. Enchantment, nothing. There Borrgot enjoyed Laxtma. Khur groaned.

Vitrik, back beside him on the seat, patted Khur's knee. "Say nothing, do nothing, look nothing to excite the garrison's suspicions."

Last thing Khur wanted, to excite the dozen armed guardsmen screening inbound traffic. The sword was good, but the odds were bad.

"Maybe," Vitrik whispered in his ear, "you should hide your sword; the front board of the seat has hidden hinges."

Just what Khur had been thinking, hide the sword. Khur reached for it.

It was gone. In its stead a lump of metal hung from the cord.

Unless he had dreamed the whole thing, and unless Vitrik had dreamed the last few hours with him, the sword had transformed itself back to the lump. "What sword?" he asked. Let Vitrik explain it to him.

Vitrik looked from Khur to the lump a few times. "A magician as well! Khur, we have a good deal to talk about—when we're free to talk."

A good deal sounded fine, that was what Ma had sent him in search of, but Khur was not even free to think, for they were now up with the guardsmen.

The lump of metal at once excited suspicion.

"What the hell kind of charm necklace is that?"

Vitrik answered quickly for Khur. "A cure for goiters. The metal draws the poison into itself."

"Must've been some goiter."

"It was. You should've seen him only a month ago."

"I don't even want to see him now. Big hick too dumb to speak for himself."

Khur's ears burned. He felt stirrings of shared resentment in the lump and strove to chill out.

The one with a sergeant's tattoo on his brow said, "Cut the

chatter, Corporal. Let's get on with business."

Vitrik smooth-talked and palm-greased the guardsmen into lowering the tally of taxable sacks of jervs, paid the tax, and made to get Knoxan going.

The sergeant had gone into the guardhouse with his take. The corporal said, "Hold on." He stepped up onto the hub of a wheel, drew his dagger, and slit an opening in a sack. "It's still an hour till lunch and I could use a nosh." He reached inside the sack. He stiffened, then felt around, made a grab, and tugged something out.

Khur had seen strange-looking jervs in his time but never one in the shape of a human foot. Much less one attached to the rest of a body.

While Khur gaped, the full human sliced the sack open from within, sat up, and plunged his own dagger into the corporal's breast.

Vitrik snatched a sword from under the seat and shouted, "We're spotted! All out and into the fray!"

Two other sacks heaved and split open.

In a trice, the three ex-jervs and Vitrik were engaging the guards.

The four fought well, but numbers told. The guards drove them into a corner.

Vitrik looked over at Khur. "Khur, are you with us?"

Even if he really wanted to be with Vitrik, Khur lacked a sword. The lump remained a lump. Did that mean he didn't really want to be with Vitrik? Who knew what Vitrik and his friends had been up to? He smelled his own fear and slumped miserably on the seat of the cart.

Harder pressed now, Vitrik smiled a sweaty, bloody smile. "Do you think . . . they'll spare you . . . even if it's not . . . your fight? . . . Drive off . . . and save yourself."

Khur stared at the reins. Should he pick them up and slap Knoxan into motion?

The sergeant settled that for him. The man stepped up to Knoxan and with a mighty two-handed stroke of his sword lopped off her head.

Khur saw red.

When the red flood receded he had the dripping sword in his hand and he stood staring around at the corpses of the guards and Vitrik was pulling at him to follow the other three outlaws pelting into a twisty alley.

6. The Bruiting of the Sword

Far is near and near is far,
Whether brain synapse or star.
Bright as starfall streaks the sky,
Gleam of steel matched glint of eye.
Grim as Death Himself might reap,
So the magic blade etched deep.
                    —Wythu, *Lay of Khur*

Everyone from Borrgot down believed Checyr spent his nights deciphering the sky and his days dozing. Checyr propagated this with a Bug Me Not sign outside the door and propped it with a bar inside. But he was never more awake than during daylight hours and his telescope never more busy.

This day he had early brightened with a peep across into Dankeja's cell; she had been all aglisten from her weekly dip in a laboriously filled wooden tub. Then he had lowered his sights to watch Borrgot's steward pocket a payoff from a provisioner, the steward's wife play the steward false with the gardener, the gardener's daughter flirt with the provisioner's helper.

Now he tilted his telescope farther afield, to observe what went down in town. He thought to pick out the home of the head of the Leatherworkers Guild; the man had a lot to hide.

The fracas at the Market Gate stopped him short.

He had a clear line of sight. He focused for detail. It appeared he had come upon the battle near its end.

Ten or so guardsmen cornered four civilian swordsmen. One guardsman lay on the cobblestones among jervs spilled from a nag-drawn cart. A sergeant senselessly beheaded the nag.

A shower of blood. It seemed to Checyr that a sword leapt to the left hand of an outsized youth on the driver's seat and hurtled the youth to a wobbly stance on the cobblestones. The youth looked to be half-choked by the cord around his neck tied to the sword and only cat's-cradled himself tighter trying to get out of it. It seemed to Checyr that the flat of the blade rapped the knuckles of the youth's right hand to stop him, then the sword untangled itself.

The youth appeared in a daze, the sword appeared in a fury of its own. Quicker than the onlooker could follow, or the youth himself without stumbling, the sword beheaded the sergeant, then cut the guardsmen down. The four civilians fled. The youth stood looking around as though daring the world to do its worst, till one of his fellows came back and drew him away and together they took to their heels after the others.

Checyr closed the eye at the telescope and opened the other. Someone had raised the alarm; patrols converged on the Market Gate.

"Can't you see, you fools?" Checyr muttered to himself. "There they go, down Pearl Alley, up Cockle Lane."

Not that he wanted the patrols to catch the fugitives. That was for his eyes only.

Eye again at the eyepiece, he swore at buildings for standing in the way, but he tracked the fugitives all the same. They dodged in and out of sight but in the end he caught them slipping into a lodging house the back way. He fixed the place by its neighboring cross streets. The patrols kept rushing this way and that. His eyes were weary but it was his hands he rubbed.

Checyr engaged in epistemological dispute with himself. Checyr devoutly held that things happen on purpose by accident. Checyr just as devoutly held that things happen by accident on purpose. He sidestepped the impasse.

In either event, to what purpose should he put this juicy bit?

He drew forth a newly minted coin whose obverse featured the usurper and whose reverse bore the legend "I serve, therefore I deserve." He flipped it. It came up Borrgot. That settled Borrgot's hash. Borrgot had put his own head upon his own price.

7. The Glorifying of the Sword

> Water-bagger and her nurse,
> Taker-under and his hearse,
> Know one way of life and death.
> Thread of ink keeps thread of breath.
> —Wythu, *Lay of Khur*

Vitrik and the ex-jerv-sacks spoke warmly of Khur's coolness in combat.

Two dozen men and women had joined them in a hidden basement room.

Khur listened with these as intently and marveled as greatly. The trick sword had so taken over that in the thick of the fray he had thought himself in a dream; only after cessation woke him were the strewn bodies bloody reality.

"Ah!" said a scrawny fellow. From a bag tied to his belt he whipped out a vial of ink, a scrap of paper, and a quill. He unstoppered the vial, dipped the quill, and scribbled on the paper. " 'Battle-trance.' "

"That," Vitrik told Khur, "is Wythu, our public relations man."

Wythu looked up with a gap-toothed smile. "Our baron of broadsides, our graf of graffiti, our sultan of insult. And now our herald of heroes." He pointed the top of his quill at Khur. "I feel inspired to write the epic of our overthrow of Borrgot."

Khur blinked at the news. "I didn't know Borrgot was overthrown."

"He's as good as, now that you're with us."

Khur blinked at *this* news. "I—"

A coded rapping at the partition brought a total hush and a general reaching for weapons.

Vitrik looked around as if to gauge readiness, then rapped back.

Khur recognized the voice of the landlady who had let them in. "It's a stranger who doesn't want to show his face. He says he knows you're all here and what you're up to."

"And wants to help," said a muffled voice. "Ow!"

"I warned you to keep your mouth buttoned. I blindfolded him and Weed has a knife to his throat. Want to see him or do we cut him up and get rid of the pieces?"

Vitrik looked around and counted shrugs. "Shove him in."

The partition slid open, a man stumbled in, the partition slid shut. A mask under the blindfold, a floor-length cloak.

"You can unbutton your mouth," Vitrik said.

"First, the inauspicious news. Borrgot has ordered a house-to-house search starting at dawn. So you must strike this very night."

Vitrik silenced the group murmur with a gesture. "And the auspicious news?"

"I can show you a secret way into the castle."

Vitrik cut the group murmur again. "What's your price—other than your life?"

"Merely that I keep my post."

"Which is?"

"If you succeed, I'll unmask myself. I don't want you fingering me to Borrgot's thumbscrewers if you fail."

Vitrik smiled. "Fair enough. Now, the secret way in?"

"The late High Duke kept a mistress hard by the castle. He ran a tunnel from the sub-dungeon level to the cottage he built her. I wedged open the door at the castle end when I came out; I'll leave it so when I go back in."

Vitrik patted a murmur down. "Where's the cottage?"

"Not so fast. I need a token I can flash to save me from your blades."

"What sort of token?"

The stranger reached inside his cloak and brought forth a shiny coin. "Scratch some sign on this that you will all recognize."

Vitrik took it. After a moment, he scratched on it with the point of his dagger. Then he passed the coin around.

Khur saw, when it reached him, that Vitrik had added horns to Borrgot's likeness.

Vitrik, when it came back to him, pressed it into the stranger's palm. "We've all seen it; we'll all know it again."

The stranger put it carefully away. "One of you will come with me to the cottage, where I'll show him or her the hidden egress. Then that one will come back here, give you the directions, and the rest of you can go there singly or in twos or threes. You can all be in place before dark. From what I've seen, there are twenty of you. Borrgot has thrice that. But surprise and your master swordsman, the big fellow, may just even the odds."

"You know a lot more about us than we know about you. I'm tempted to tear off your mask."

"Do so and I'll keep the secret." The stranger put up a hand. "You may have thumbscrewers to equal Borrgot's best but you'll never know what trick I'm holding back about the way."

Vitrik grimaced. "Sorry. I misspoke."

"We all face temptation. Shouldn't I be going now?"

"Of course. I'm sending a good man with you." Vitrik pointed an Uncle-Urtcyn-Wants-You finger at Lirgl, one of the ex-jerv-sacks.

8. The Whetting of the Sword

Not the singer but the song
Knows the words that best belong.
Not the songsheet but the word

Knows the listener has heard.
Not the word but space jejune
Knows that silence calls the tune.
Thus the rebels made their choice—
"Khur shall lead us!"—with one voice.
Khur forthrightly swelled with pride,
Shaming those hot-aired inside.
                              —Wythu, *Lay of Khur*

Silence fell as the stranger and Lirgl left, then all spoke at once.

Vitrik rapped them to order; two or three heads was all it took. "Everyone sharpen weapons, eat a light meal, rest up. Urapu, come here and update the plans of the castle."

Urapu, a stripling in a provisioner's apron, sketched in what he had learned of the layout from the gardener's daughter.

Just as they began to worry about Lirgl, here Lirgl came.

"The guy's on the level. What took so long, the town's lousy with patrols. I untied his blindfold and he led me crooked to the cottage. He unlocked the door and we went in. He lifted a trapdoor. Never find it ourselves without we tore the place apart. He lit a torch, dropped down into the tunnel. I followed. At the castle end he showed me the door was wedged open, handed me the torch, waved so long, and split. I made my way back through the tunnel, climbed out, lowered the trapdoor, put out the torch, locked up, and came crooked home. Here's the key."

"Where's the cottage?"

"Northwest corner of Zosk and Urceg. You can't miss it."

Vitrik huddled with his lieutenants.

Khur caught only an occasional word (*cake*) or phrase (*It could be a trap*).

Their murmuring and the candle flame shining out as a six-rayed star through the mica pane of the lantern mesmerized him. With a start he found everyone eyeing him.

Vitrik broke the silence. "Khur, we've just voted you the honor of leading us into battle."

Before Khur could take that in, Wythu made a grab at him. Wythu froze as the sword came up.

"Only wanted to shake your hand. We're in business."

Khur creased his brow.

Wythu waved a sheet of paper with pen scratches on it. "Let

me read the lines I was just inspired to write. 'In smithereens the smithy stands;/Decay's the work of idle hands—' Sorry, wrong side." Wythu reversed the paper and read again. " 'I would tell the tale of Khur,/How the hero bold and pure/Came to win the wonder sword,/Warred upon the wicked lord . . . ' "

Khur got chills. "Go on."

"I can't, till you go on and do the deeds I'll sing," Wythu said.

Khur got chills.

9. The Ramifying of the Sword

"Mirror, take yourself to task,"
Says the face behind the mask.
        —Wythu, *Lay of Khur*

Checyr removed his mask to make breathing easier. The climb from the sub-dungeon level to the first floor really took it out of one.

He paused often before he reached the arras hung across the opening at the head of the stairs leading to and from the tunnel. He stopped gratefully behind the arras and peered through the piercing gauze gaze of the first High Duke on the face of the tapestry.

The High Duke's library looked unused as usual. The usurper paid only lip service to learning. But that did not mean Borrgot would not have noticed a volume missing or out of place. Color-coded bindings made a pleasing design.

Checyr slipped out from under the tapestry, straightened his cloak, and made for the door to the corridor.

He heard a measured tread and stopped. His heart beat double-time. The changing of the guard.

As soon as the corridor cleared he made for the stairs leading to his tower rooms and started up. He halted halfway.

The event was in motion. To change now would be like asking Abiz Wyr to go backwards and unmake day. Checyr's course was set. But it would not hurt to hedge his bet. If in a few hours from now Borrgot prevailed, would not it be prudent to have on record a warning, however ambiguously phrased?

Checyr started back down.

Pain seized him by the arm, squeezed his chest. He clutched at himself, lost his balance, fell headlong to the foot of the stairs.

A guardsman posted just around the bend of the corridor came running.

Checyr, with a drool of blood.

The guardsman felt for a pulse, found none. He looked around, then rolled Checyr to get at the inside pockets of Checyr's cloak. They yielded a cloth mask and a newly minted gold coin. The guardsman looked around again, then slipped the coin into his own pocket. He straightened and let out a shout for the corporal of the guard that passed along to the corporal of the guard.

10. The Trailblazing of the Sword

> Green (though of heroic mold),
> Khur (as ever overbold)
> Did increasingly unfold
> All that Checyr had foretold.
> —Wythu, *Lay of Khur*

Though Lirgl held high the torch to shine ahead over Khur's shoulder, it seemed to Khur that the sword felt the way without the aid of light. Well that was, for the resiny torch burned fitfully, putting forth more smoke than light.

The others followed in single file. Damp and close the tunnel. Dry and coppery Khur's mouth. Sweating, he felt the icicle stab of fear.

This though he and the sword had done themselves proud on the way to the cottage. Khur and Vitrik had run into a patrol and the sword had answered the challenge with a smear of motion, with merciful ruthlessness. Six more of Borrgot's best men dead, Khur and Vitrik without a scratch.

Khur had outgrown the closet Ma locked him in for punishment growing up, but not the dread of confinement.

And now he had a new thing to deal with, the breaths of many keyed-up outlaws blowing at his back.

The tunnel at last had an end, the beginning of steps going up.

Many steps.

Far up, like a guiding star, a faint glow. That and the breathing behind him moved him on.

At the top a thick cloth across the opening blocked the way.

The glow was a thin spot where light came through from the other side. He peered through the spot. Walls of prettily patterned upright bricks broken by a window that let moonlight in.

"Well?" A whisper from Vitrik.

Khur jumped.

The sword sliced through the cloth, cut a flap for Khur to step through.

Lirgl nudged him aside, followed him in, and the room quickly filled.

Vitrik padded to the door at the far end of the room and listened at it.

"Ah!"

Khur turned to see Wythu, eyes shining, step to the nearest wall and pull out a brick.

"Song of Miham!" Wythu opened the brick.

Khur gaped. It was a book. The place was full of books! Think of the power locked up in them! What if they all exploded at once?

Wythu shook his head, slammed the book shut, shoved it back in place. "Uncut. No one's ever read it."

If all that kept folks from reading was the need to cut, then the sword was an even handier thing to have!

But right now, as Vitrik's hiss of impatience said, the sword had more pressing work.

11. The Plowing of the Sword

> Make the matter manifest
> Who does what at whose behest;
> Let the wherewith know it, lest
> Its possessor be possessed.
> Khur the uninvited guest
> Did in earnest, not in jest,
> From the host the power wrest.
> —Wythu, *Lay of Khur*

"Remember," Vitrik said softly right before he opened the door and motioned Khur out into the corridor, "the wise warrior meets the crafty stroke but fears the lucky stroke."

Khur saw Wythu scribble and assumed Wythu was taking it down, so it had to mean something. But Khur left it for the sword to grasp and apply to the work at hand. Khur himself was all too busy holding onto the sword as it thrust into the surprised throat of a guardsman walking his post.

"Great," said Vitrik. "Now keep going down this corridor, make a hard right, and take out the guardsman in front of the first door you come to. That'll be Borrgot's bedchamber. After you deal with the guard, go in and deal with Borrgot. I'll stand outside to cover your back."

Khur found Borrgot in bed with Laxtma.

Borrgot and Laxtma broke apart with equal anger for the intruder.

Battle now raged throughout the castle, and Borrgot was quick to catch on. He wasted no time calling for help but reached for his sword, and leapt naked from bed.

Laxtma found her voice. "It's only Khur, your dukeship. Khur, what do you mean breaking in?"

"Khur? Is this clod your groom?"

"Yes, your dukeship." She climbed out of bed and stood with her hands on her naked hips.

"Do you wish me to make you a widow?"

Laxtma shrugged. "As you wish, your dukeship."

Borrgot looked Khur up and down, and laughed with the cruel vindictiveness of the bully toward a victim. He slashed viciously at Khur.

Khur's sword twisted Borrgot's sword from Borrgot's grip. Khur laughed with the good-natured scorn of the expert for the bumbler.

Swordpoint at his chest, Borrgot stood stock-still. Then he buried his face in his hands. Hollow grief sounded from that shallow grave. "All is lost. And all I ever wanted was to serve my people."

Laxtma stamped her foot. "Khur, you stop it right now."

"I won't listen," Khur said, his voice thin in his own ears.

"You're spoiling everything, you oaf. The High Duke promised to set me up as his mistress in a swell cottage nearby. He said he'd pay you off to stay down on the farm."

Borrgot peeped through his fingers.

"I'm not listening," Khur said. He scuffed his feet.

"So you just lay down your silly sword and say you're sorry, and the High Duke will forgive you."

Borrgot nodded.

"I didn't listen," Khur said.

Laxtma came at Khur with her fingers ready to rake.

The sword leveled itself at her navel.

"No, no!" Khur said in horror.

The sword wavered. Khur struggled with the sword. Who was boss? The sword lowered.

Laxtma showed her teeth. She clawed at Khur's face.

The sword smacked Laxtma across one hip with the flat of its blade. This shunted her aside and gave the sword a clear run at Borrgot.

But before the sword found its slot, Vitrik looked in. Vitrik, bloody from dealing with a guardsman, sized up the scene. He laughed. "Need help?"

Khur turned with a smile. "Who, me?"

Borrgot dashed past Khur—knocked Vitrik over—snatched up Vitrik's sword—resumed his dash.

Khur made to help Vitrik up.

Vitrik, angry with himself, waved Khur's hand away. "Never mind me. Get Borrgot."

Khur lumbered after Borrgot. The sword strained at the hilt to help Khur narrow the lead.

Borrgot raced to the cell at the top of the tower keep. Borrgot had just time to take a key from a hook in the wall, unlock the cell, and leap inside.

Khur heard a woman scream.

"Uncle Borrgot! Does your naked aggression have no limit?"

Khur came in sight of the cell. Borrgot held Vitrik's sword to a maiden's breast. As Khur stumbled inside, Borrgot put the maiden between them.

"Stop right there," Borrgot said, one arm around her neck, the other holding the sword to her spine.

But it was sight of the maiden that halted Khur in his tracks. She had less meat on her bones than Laxtma, but the bones were better proportioned.

"Allow me to introduce you two," said Borrgot. "Dankeja, this desperate brute is Khur. Khur, this shrill beauty is Dankeja."

Khur stared. Was this the dull sickly child Borrgot served Jusgot by ruling for? She looked thin but not dull.

He had heard Vitrik and the others speak of overthrowing Borrgot and ruling Jusgot in the name of the rightful heiress to the duchy.

Khur made an awkward bow to Dankeja.

She smiled wanly back.

"Think well, Khur," said Borrgot. "You don't want to endanger her life. Put down your sword or I run her through."

Khur struggled with himself and the sword.

Borrgot was a monster and deserved death. But Dankeja was more than the rightful heiress, a swell-looking dame, and deserved life.

Khur's hand opened. The sword struck a spark from the stone floor.

A spark answered in Dankeja's eye. "Brave Khur, foolish Khur."

The wind moaned through the crenellations overhead.

12. The Weighing of the Sword

> Drink it down or drink it up,
> Bitter is the borrowed cup.
> —Wythu, *Lay of Khur*

"Now back away, Khur," said Borrgot.

"Wait, Khur," said Dankeja.

Borrgot's arm tightened around her throat.

She bit the arm.

Borrgot howled and loosened her.

She snatched from her pocket a vial, unstopped it, lifted it to her lips. "Poison from vineberries. If I die, bold Khur, Borrgot has nothing to bargain with. When I fall, seize the sword and run him through." She tilted the cup, worked her throat, rolled up her eyes, fell.

The sword leapt to Khur's hand.

13. The Plighting of the Sword

> Last gasp Borrgot might just mime,
> Khur's sword stroke the death knell chime.
> Bathed in blood and caked with grime,
> Thus did Khur undo the crime,
> Spring Dankeja in her prime.
> His own heart from thence did time.

. . .

Never did the True Sword break,
Neither did it rust away.
Night it had its right to take
Just as it had had its day.
                    —Wythu, *Lay of Khur*

Vitrik and several others clustered at the door.

"Good, you got the bastard," said Vitrik. "Too bad about the girl. Dankeja?"

Khur could not find his voice. He started to nod.

But Dankeja answered for herself. She opened one eye, sat up, and spat. "Ugh. Yes, I'm Dankeja." She smiled at the look on Khur's face. "I wasn't stupid enough to swallow the stuff." She raised a hand for him to lift her up.

Khur stood by, happily confused, while Dankeja and Vitrik talked about the new regime. Then, with a bow to Dankeja and a backslap and a wink for Khur, Vitrik left with the others.

Dankeja looked Khur up and down. "Have you given thought to marriage?"

Khur stammered out about Laxtma.

She gave him a thin smile and a narrow stare. Then her eyes softened and her smile broadened.

"No problem. As Grand Duchess, I can claim first night of *you*." She started to rest a hand on his sword arm, then swiftly transferred it to his free arm as the sword moved to fend. "If it works out, I'll dissolve your marriage and take you as consort."

And so it went down.

Khur wed Dankeja. (Dankeja paid Amhsa an annuity on the understanding that Amhsa remain at Wodby Vuroy and away from court.)

Laxtma wed Snezre. (Laxtma was heavy with Borrgot's child. Snezre raised the boy as his own. Both instilled in the youth the design to take vengeance on Khur. But that's another tale.)

But on this first night, while Khur and Dankeja were otherwise engaged, Vitrik set up his temporary headquarters in the library. Here his victorious forces brought their prisoners, the few guardsmen who survived to surrender, for interrogation and disposition.

The talisman, the masked stranger's safe-conduct, the marked coin, turned up in the pocket of a prisoner Lirgl had taken.

Lirgl clapped the guardsman on the back.

"No wonder you fought so poorly and surrendered so quickly."

The guardsman looked around. All the stern faces were now smiling faces.

"We stick to our bargain," Vitrik said. "You keep your post."

Glory to Abiz Wyr! the guardsman thought. If these guys are bought so cheap, I'll do great under the new regime!

Meanwhile, a weary Khur stretched out beside a sleeping Dankeja and lit the dark with bright thoughts of the coming day—as they said Abiz Wyr did in the real world, of which this world is the shadow.

In his dream he had faint foreshadowings of deeds Wythu would sing of: doing battle with dragons, wizards, specters, and Death Himself.

Always with the sword at his side. But for the sword, he would be doomed to live out his days stuck in Wodby Vuroy, doomed to shrink at sight of Snezre, doomed to pine for an unworthy Laxtma. Ah, the sword, the sword, the sword . . .

> Each sphere is an undying note,
> Dead stars still beam from times remote,
> In prologues dim the end is bright.
> Where are the whences of tonight?
> —Wythu, *Son of Lay of Khur*

Yeti

by
Wolfgang Jeschke

Sometimes it seems like the only thing regular readers of fantasy and science fiction enjoy more than their favorite reading matter is debating the distinctions between them. Depends on your personal perspective. Humor is much the same. What sends one individual into gales of laughter often leaves the other cold.

Those of you who read the German edition of Playboy *or happened to peruse the anthology* Die Gebeine des Bertrand Russell *will already be familiar with this borderline tale. For those one or two of you who haven't encountered it in the above versions, it is presented here.*

Dedicated to Reinhold Messner
and Frank Herbert, who is going to go

Events which are destined to become milestones in history do not always stand out immediately. Their origins sometimes develop unexpectedly from everyday occurrences. One of these events was the sixtieth birthday of Lipps, which we mountaineers celebrated in the Hook and the Rope. Lipps had sent out thousands of invitations and when I arrived at the club on that rainy November evening, a lot of members had gathered.

Rich Wolsley was standing in the foyer distributing hot-off-the-press copies of *Mountain*, a special number on Lipps. On the title page was the picture of Lipps that had made the rounds of the world press at the time of his fame. Lipps straddling the summit of the K2 after successfully climbing it alone.

Wolsley made a beeline for me, as always dressed in a dark blue blazer, his well-groomed red moustache hiding his impeccably crowned teeth.

"You and Bob have received the permit for Mount Eve, eh?" he greeted me triumphantly, and shook my hand.

I nodded and fumbled involuntarily in the pocket of my jacket for the official letter. It was a letter with the splendid coat of arms of the Nepal government and an imposing list of government officials, secretaries of state, civil servants in charge of international mountaineering right down to the Sherpa guide. All this took up so much room that there was only enough space left for two words—"see enclosed." The enclosed was a crumpled, ripped-off and hardly legible computer printout on which the date and time of the authorized ascent was registered.

"You can count me in on it!" Rich assured us, and scrutinized me with a meaningful look over his rimless glasses. "I've got a brilliant idea," he said, and stretched his hand with the thumbs-up sign under my nose. "Mountaineering is gaining in importance! I've got to talk it over with you and Bob."

He grabbed me by the shoulder and pushed me into the back room. Things were pretty lively and a lot of empty bottles were already lying around.

"Zere are some, who after a fight with zere vater, vere drifen up zose stone tits and at ze top, zey could survey the whole valley and say, 'Look here, Vater, I'm bigger zan you and Mami belonks to me,' " Seifeneder said philosophically to a fellow countryman. Dr. Alois Seifeneder, an experienced mountaineering medical specialist from Meran, had already accompanied many British expeditions. However, he still tried to combine English with his native South Tyrolean dialect. A lot of unsuspecting Englishmen pitied him because of what they thought was a stubborn throat ailment.

Lipps was sitting in a large, shabby red leather armchair in the place of honor under Hilary's portrait. An imposing row of gift-wrapped bottles was lined up in front of him and he was sucking on a huge cigar, his eyes slightly glassy. I cordially shook his hand and drank to his health.

Mountain had spared no expenses and had interviewed mountaineering veterans the world over for this special edition. Harry

Findlay, who had drunk at least five or six glasses of champagne, read parts of the texts out loud and crowed with delight.

"Those old boys," he cried. "Not only were they excellent mountaineers, their hearts were in the right place. Listen to this: 'The mountains are such a primeval force that it is neither man's duty nor his right to conquer them with the trappings of technology. Only those who approach mountaineering with humble and modest means can experience the harmony of the world . . .' "

"Hey, dat kills me!" Seifeneder cried, and slapped his knee. Tears ran down Bobby Crook's cheeks. "Reinhold Messner!" he tittered again and again. "The greatest living mountaineer in the world!"

" 'The oxygen mask is like a wall between man and nature,' " Harry continued reading aloud. " 'It is a filter which prevents visionary experiences.' "

"Hey, strictly speaking, long johns are, too," shouted Tim Gerrington.

"You're killink me!" Seifeneder cried.

"The critics were right after all, eh?" Henry Mudden cried excitedly. "The real sportsman is the one that succeeds without any artificial aid. By fair means," he said mischievously. "The trend is perfectly logical, the final ascent without oxygen equipment, then without ladder, without rucksack, without a rope, without snow goggles, without headgear, without gloves, without shoes, without undershirt, without underpants, without shirt and pants . . .

"Where does it all lead to?"

"Aha," Rich Wolsley said, and nodded meaningfully in my direction. "We are living," he assured me, and emptied my glass, "in the era of biotechnology, fashion mutants and hormone corrections."

"What's all that supposed to mean?" Mudden said grumpily.

"Just a minute," Rich interrupted him. "Biotechnology is the absolute science of the future. It is already capable of manipulating congenital factors at will. Think of the Sphinx, of dwarf elephants, of poodles with their individual scents and multicolored ruffs or think of the endless number of diminutive Pegasuses lolling about in the editorial staff quarters, the mini-sharks for the weekly bloodbath in the living room aquarium. Endless possibilities. Scientists now build their creatures according to specifications. Of course, such experiments are not allowed on humans, but the use of hormones alone can do wonders. There are unfathomed possibilities. They just have to be awoken."

"Dopching," Seifeneder interrupted contemptuously.

"All that has nothing to do with doping," Rich said, and drank from Henry Mudden's glass. "It's simply adapting the human body to specific circumstances. Resources are tapped using natural means, those not available to traditional medicine."

"They're supposed to be able to swim, not sing," Bobby Crook insisted with a voice that sounded as if he had just risen from his grave.

"Those swimmers from East Germany were just the beginning," Rich dismissed the subject. "Today, Bob, one could make seals out of them in just a few months with webbed fingers and toes. No problem!"

"Dopching," Seifeneder grumbled contemptuously, and stared at his glass in disgust.

"And what's all that got to do with us?" Bob wanted to know. "I mean with Chris and myself and the permit for Mount Eve?"

"Listen! We'll make a great story out of this, the greatest story ever told in the history of mountaineering. You'll be millionaires overnight! If you give me the exclusive rights to the story, I'll take care of the rest and make a real big splash."

"Yes . . . ? And what does that mean for us? Energy pills or something?"

Seifeneder cleared his throat with a disparaging sound. "Don't you guys understand? Dey are making mountain goats out of you!"

Rich Wolsley held out the bait until we swallowed it. What finally convinced us was the fact that he agreed to completely foot the bill for the whole expedition. We had no idea at the time just how little it would cost.

Our Everest permit was not valid until next July. However, it was already before Christmas when Rich dragged us to Professor Brian McKillipson at the London Hospital, who according to Rich was "absolutely top in his field and a candidate for the Nobel Prize." McKillipson, a fat little man with a hunted look and nervous movements carried out the preliminary examinations assisted personally by Dr. George Dearslay, Jr., an elderly quiet man almost six feet tall in a stained laboratory coat, which completely buttoned down looked rather like an exoskeleton and gave the impression that Dearslay would slump together like a wet sock if one unbuttoned his coat. Professor McKillipson and Rich waived aside all our arguments and convinced us that any objections to doping were unfounded and ridiculous. It was like a visit to a health officer, who wanted to pocket his bonus for the fit-to-work certificate at all costs. A doctor who encourages and at the same reprimands and otherwise pretends he is deaf.

Medical treatment was to begin at once at the beginning of January and was to be completed by the start of the expedition.

"And what kind of treatment will that be?" Bob wanted to know. He still hadn't fully understood.

Rich folded his hands and explained his idea in detail. "We'll succeed without any artificial aid," he decided. "Without silk underwear, without a flannel suit, without a down jacket or sleeping bag, without special footwear, without a tent, without pitons, and without any mechanical tricks, without anything . . . by fair means! This time round really genuinely honest. Only man himself with his natural resources. These, nevertheless, will certainly have to be stimulated during the next six months."

"And you're sure this will work, Richy?" Bob asked.

Rich dismissed the question scornfully. "One hundred percent sure! You'll be prepared biologically and ideally adapted to the requirements."

"And afterwards . . . ?" I asked with the disastrously pregnant words of Seifeneder still ringing in my ears. "Will it be possible to reverse the process completely?"

"Of course! This is just a temporary modification. It's recessive, the moment the hormone shots are stopped. Absolutely no problem. Dr. Dearslay and Professor McKillipson get their Nobel Prize, you'll become world-famous, and I have my story. No more money worries for the rest of our lives! I have already made important contacts. As industry is not involved in this at all, we'll really need the help of the advertising world. This will be the biggest sensation ever—a complete success!"

He clapped his hands in excitement.

"And another thing," he said. "We are starting earlier. We are not going to let any swaggering mountaineer say that we flew to Pangboche and just had a seven-thousander in front of us. Mount Everest—by fair means. Our ascent starts at the Bay of Bengal, at sea level and at low tide."

The evening before the start of our ascent, we celebrated on the beach at Digha, a tiny village near Balasore. Bob and I had been flown in by helicopter from Calcutta.

It was a pleasant May evening, warm and moist like all pleasant

May evenings on the Bay of Bengal. The natives who had been standing around inquisitively all afternoon had been driven off to make way for the hundreds of cameras. Rich Wolsley directed them as an admiral would his fleet.

"Don't fool around!" he shouted, waving his arms. "You must get them with the sea behind. That's the whole point! That's why we're here. And get the sunset in the picture at the same time! It doesn't cost a penny extra!"

Bob and I stood obediently at the water's edge, wearing our track suits in spite of the heat. Wolsley was making a great secret of our physical condition and would have torn to pieces anyone who tried to touch us.

Lipps had come with Henry Mudden and Findlay, who had buried several bottles of champagne in the sand and, after digging out the second one, had trouble finding the others. And Professor McKillipson was there, of course, inspecting us proudly and affectionately as a researcher does his prize guinea pigs, continually wiping the sweat from his brow. Dr. Dearslay, Jr., on the other hand, didn't seem to mind the heat; he was buttoned up as ever.

The two doctors kept a check on our health. We had been having our injections twice a week for the last five months, but not a great deal had changed. The first thing I noticed was an increase in appetite and I put on weight at an alarming rate. It was the same with Bob. I soon had to shave twice a day and the hair on my chest grew thicker. On my back and shoulders and places where I had previously had a light down, I discovered dark clumps of hair beginning to sprout. I sometimes awoke at night with muscular pains and a slight feeling of dizziness as if I had a high temperature. And after three months, I could only cut my finger- and toenails with a pair of scissors.

McKillipson noted these symptoms with obvious satisfaction and prescribed a program of physical training for us that became more and more strenuous. These efforts soon bore fruit—I got into the habit of asking the barman to open cans of beer for me because I was always breaking the ring off the tab and I constantly had to remind myself to pick up glasses more carefully. But, externally, at least, the change was no more than that of a woman in her fifth month of pregnancy. We just looked— well—a little plumper. The seams had burst on my jackets, but

Wolsley assured us that soon we wouldn't need to wear them anymore.

We meandered along the holy river and mingled with the crowds of pilgrims making their way to Benares. They inspected us with interest because white men—even hippies—rarely travel on foot in India.

Rich and his cohorts took care of us solicitously. Wherever we stopped to rest, his van was there with food and a fridge full of drinks.

In Patna, we left the Ganges and turned north. After Motihari and Sagauli, the country became gradually hillier. We were climbing slowly, and one day we had actually accomplished our first thousand-meter ascent.

We were thankful to be on higher ground at last, because we were now able to do without most of our clothes. Even so, the heat in the fur sprouting all over us became unbearable. Bob and I began to resemble a pair of shaggy gorillas. The natives fled with shrieks of terror whenever they caught sight of us. I thanked God that in the high valleys of Darjeeling there were no more of those shortsighted English colonial officers with loaded firearms out for a day's hunting.

In Katmandu, the journalists and TV crews discovered us again. We gave interviews and let ourselves be photographed. The cameramen showed particular interest in our thick beards and facial hair and zoomed in without any inhibitions at all on our great clawed, pawlike hands which would have done credit to the Abominable Snowman.

After a short rest, we continued to the Dudh Kosi Valley and along the trail taken by international trekkers, past Lukla and Namche Bazar to Pangboche, where we had to wait our turn. On July 10 we were allowed to move into our base camp quarters. The valley below the Khumbu Ice Fall is a hideous place. For the past hundred years, it has been the starting point for expeditions and looks like an international rubbish heap.

A group of mountaineers from Togo and a female team from the Fiji Islands were just returning from the summit. They resented the fact that the swarms of pressmen took no notice of them and that we stole the whole show. Professor McKillipson gave us a final checkup and Dr. Dearslay, Jr., assisted him. They both appeared to be satisfied and we were put on a diet consisting solely of concentrated food. The thick fur on my rear mercifully hid the needle marks of their last injections. Then, on the morning of July 13—it promised to be a day of brilliant sunshine—we were finally ready. We discarded the last of our clothes (Wolsley made sure that the cameras only saw our furry backs), breathed in the cool, fragrant mountain air, and when our names appeared on the board, set off for our assault on the summit.

Mount Everest is not a beautiful mountain—it's rather unsightly, in fact. But it's the highest mountain. We hadn't chosen any special route (that would have been too much for the Nepalese mountain authorities), but decided to use the traditional route up through the Ice Fall into the Valley of Silence and then along the Geneva Spur to the South Col. We had no problems. We surmounted steep, icy slopes easily by melting handholds and footholds into them. McKillipson had raised our body temperature so much that we were impervious to the harsh mountain climate. It only had one disadvantage—we couldn't rest too long in one place and often had to move and sleep elsewhere during the night. Bob ignored this warning during our night on the South Col. This almost proved fatal. When I awoke at dawn, he had disappeared without a trace. I looked for him desperately, but, at first, without success. Then I heard a familiar noise nearby and found him snoring peacefully at the bottom of an eight-meter shaft, which, in his carelessness, he had melted into the ice. If several hundred thousand pounds' worth of rope, camping equipment, tin cans, oxygen flasks, canvas covers, dirty silk underwear, and aluminum ladders of the last four decades had not been lying around there to prevent him from sinking even further, he would have melted through to the rocks and perhaps never seen the light of day again.

I woke him with a couple of snowballs and he clambered out in a daze.

Three hours later, we had conquered the South Summit. While climbing the last three hundred meters below the Main Summit, we had overtaken a mountaineer from Zimbabwe going it alone. In the tradition of the Great Messner, he was without oxygen equipment. When he saw us, he rolled his eyes and obviously took us to be an hallucination.

"Yeti," he croaked, and his dark face was gray with horror and exhaustion. Mercifully, driving snow then hid us from view.

Admittedly, we were a little breathless when we reached the summit. It was then that I understood what the veteran mountaineer had meant when he said that a person must get to know his own limits before he can know himself.

Here we were standing in the diffuse light like two hairy old apes gasping their lungs out. We'd made it, we'd managed the entire 8,848 meters by virtue of our own strength—by fair means! After all, our full inner potential had been mobilized.

We enjoyed the isolation of the summit while waiting for our mountain comrade from Zimbabwe to arrive. The clouds opened and the sun broke through. We brushed the snow off each other's fur.

We had to wait until the cameramen arrived in the helicopters and filmed us. Rich Wolsley waved through the window and made a V for Victory sign. We unrolled the Union Jack and flourished it energetically before packing it into the special container on the summit. We then entered our names in the summit book as successful ascents, nos. 3763 and 3764, while a Chinese helicopter hovered above us to document sovereign rights. The mountaineer from Zimbabwe did not appear. We heard later that he had turned back after seeing us.

We then made our descent.

We've been in Darjeeling ever since. The monsoon has begun. Water gurgles through the eaves, a curtain of cloud hangs over the mountains. Professor McKillipson and his assistant, Dr. Dearslay, Jr., have long since departed—shrugging their shoulders. A few days ago, Wolsley left, too, after handing us each a check for over 100,000 pounds and clapping us encouragingly on the shoulder. His hand withdrew a little from the physical contact.

I shave my face three times a day, tear in desperation at the thick, black fur on my chest and shoulders, and look uncertainly at myself in the mirror. Temporary modification! None of the antidotes have worked either. I'm convinced that my lips are gradually turning blue and that my eyeteeth are already noticeably longer.

Wisps of cloud hang over the terraced tea plantations. Outside on the wooden veranda under a jujube tree sits a discontented ape, slurping his tea. From time to time, he pushes back the old creaking wicker chair and paces silently back and forth, his claws clicking on the boards. When there is a momentary pause in the frogs' chorus and everything is perfectly silent, I sometimes hear sobbing and, looking through the window, see him drying his tears with his long, hairy forearm.

Translated from the German by Sally Schiller and Anne Calveley

Demons Aren't a
Girl's Best Friend

by
Greg Costikyan

Magic by itself isn't funny. People by themselves aren't funny. Society considered differently isn't funny. But put them all together in the right way (with a twist of lime, perhaps) and you have something that's not only amusing but intriguing.

When compiling this anthology I received numerous stories that weren't funny, and a number of strung-together gags that didn't work as stories. Efforts that worked both as humor and as involving stories were a true rara avis. *I was in fact becoming more than a little desperate when the following narrative arrived. Yes, it was amusing, and yes, it was a story. But it also possesses that simultaneous great virtue and disappointment of good writing.*

It's over too soon.

Even in the lambent afternoon light, the house of Elias Entwhistle was an eldritch structure. It stood alone in a weed-covered lot and was the only structure for dozens of cubits in any direction. The architecture was bizarre: The roof was held up by pillars at each of the four corners, each pillar consisting of four demons, one standing on the head of the next; and the eaves were gargoyles, arms linked, heads bowed under the gutter.

Carstairs had been here before, so he wasted no time looking for a knocker or doorbell, but spoke to the gargoyle affixed to the face of the heavy wooden door. "I say, my good thing, is Magister Entwhistle about?"

The gargoyle opened one eye. "Who shall I say is calling, sir?" it said.

Carstairs harrumphed. "My card." He extracted a small piece of white pasteboard from a silver case and held it up to the gargoyle. The gargoyle's eyes crossed as it tried to read the thing.

The door flung open; Carstairs had to leap back to avoid being struck. In the doorway stood a dark-skinned young woman, less than five feet in height, wearing a grayish wrap and carrying a feather duster.

"Who the hell are you?" she demanded.

Carstairs peered at her through his monocle. "Where the devil do you get your manners, wench? Major Joseph Carstairs," he said. "Ninth Montieval Fusiliers, Retired. Please inform Magister Entwhistle of my presence immediately."

"What do you want with that parasite?" she snapped. "I got cleaning to do." She slammed the door.

The monocle fell from Carstairs's face, to dangle at the end of its chain. He turned a mottled red and white in rage, and lifted a hand to pound on the door.

"Sorry, old man," muttered the gargoyle.

There was a muffled shout from the other side of the door: "What by the sixteen planes of hell do you mean by turning away my visitors?" It sounded like Entwhistle.

"You miserable skunk!" yelled the woman. "Too damned lazy to get one of your damned demons to do the wash. That's all it is! Laziness. And when are you going to start teaching me magic?"

The gargoyle chuckled to itself, eyes closed.

"I tell you, you must master the transformations before—" Entwhistle bellowed.

"Hah! What does it take to prove that I've mastered them? Last week, I—"

"Once is not adequate. Listen, you bint, back to your wash or I'll—"

"You'll what? What? I'm a free woman. You pig. I should never have listened to you!"

Entwhistle opened the door. With his closely trimmed beard and dense mustache, he might have looked rather Mephistophelian if he hadn't looked so disheveled.

"Come in, come in, old man," he said.

" 'Show you the seven worlds on chariots drawn by winged demons from the sixteenth hell,' you said," shouted the woman, waving her feather duster. "Ach, I can't believe I fell for this crap. That's my problem, I've always been a sucker for a pretty line."

Somewhat shamefacedly, Entwhistle led Carstairs through the foyer and down the hall. The woman pursued them, brandishing her duster menacingly.

"Bastard! Took me on to have something in your bed and to make you breakfast, more likely."

Entwhistle opened a door, pulled Carstairs inside, and slammed it. "It's about bloody time I started to see something tangible from this relationship," the woman screamed through the wood. Entwhistle rolled his eyes and went to the sideboard. He poured himself a stiff drink. "Get you something, old man?" he asked. Carstairs accepted a sherry.

The walls were lined with bookshelves. In the center of the room, inscribed in the floor, was a metallic pentacle. Inside it hung purple smoke. It was the first cloud of smoke Carstairs had ever seen with eyes and horns. The eyes followed Entwhistle as he moved. Something malicious glinted in their depths.

The woman muttered something beyond the door and moved off.

"Really, Entwhistle," said Carstairs, "I can't imagine why you put up with that."

"My apprentice," said Entwhistle miserably, his nose in his drink.

Carstairs raised an eyebrow. "Why don't you discharge her if she's so difficult?"

Entwhistle sighed. "Hoist by my own petard," he said. "One of the first things a summoner learns to do is make binding pacts. Can't control demons if you can't bind them to an agreement."

"I don't follow you."

"I vowed to take her on for seven years—the usual apprenticeship period. The vow is binding. If I break it, all the contracts I've made, all the magic I've done, comes undone."

"How did she ever talk you into that?"

Entwhistle sighed heavily and took another slug from his drink. "Damned if I know," he muttered.

The smoke in the pentacle gave a deep, slow, booming laugh. Entwhistle's face twisted. "That's enough from you!" he shouted, and snapped his fingers. The laugh cut off, and the smoke curled as if in pain. The eyes glinted in hatred. Entwhistle regained his composure.

"But come, come," he said, moving to a desk. "You didn't visit to discuss my amours, I'm sure."

Carstairs harrumphed again and sat in an armchair. "Indeed not," he said. "I believe I have heard you talk of Magister Thaumus without pleasure?"

Entwhistle scowled at the name. Despite the fact that he and Thaumus were among Montief's most prominent wizards, or perhaps because of it, there was no love lost between the two. "It would be no surprise to me if you had," he said.

"Good," said Carstairs. He paused for a moment, as if wondering how to proceed. "You are a sporting man, are you not, Magister Entwhistle?"

"I have been known to back a horse or two," said Entwhistle.

"You may recollect that tomorrow is the Iron Tusk Cup."

"So it is," said Entwhistle. The Iron Tusk was not a horse race, but a railroad one. Mammoth trainers brought their best beasts and mahouts; the line between Montief City and Saucisson was cleared, and trains were dispatched, each with a standard load, down the tracks toward Saucisson, at half-hour intervals. The team with the best time was awarded the Iron Tusk trophy, which was worth a great deal to the breeders of the winning beasts, in terms of publicity and sales to the railroads over the following year. "I fail to see—"

"Magister Thaumus has entered a novelty in this year's competition," said Carstairs. "An 'Incendiary Engine,' he calls it; a steel-wheeled thing, powered somehow by fire."

"That is his discipline," Entwhistle allowed. He himself was *Magister Demonis,* a summoner; Thaumus was *Magister Igniti,* with power over the element of fire.

"I have seen the Incendiary Engine in its trial runs; over brief distances, it runs at nearly double the speed of a brace of mammoths."

Entwhistle smiled faintly. "So?"

Carstairs coughed, took out his handkerchief, and polished his monocle. "This is a matter of some delicacy," he said.

Entwhistle chuckled. " 'Delicacy,' " he said. "Wonderful word, I've always thought; very flexible. You mean you want me to fix Thaumus's wagon, I take it. Fixing a race is not only highly improper but quite illegal, you know."

Carstairs put his monocle back in and stood up hastily. "Quite so, quite so," he said. "Good heavens, one couldn't possibly envision such a thing. No, no, I say, look at the time."

"Oh, sit down, Joseph," said Entwhistle. "Who've you got your money on?"

Carstairs swallowed. "The Masters & Baleham team," he said. "Excellent breeders; taken three of the past ten Iron Tusks. I've seen the beasts in training; dashed great creatures. Three to one against, even before Thaumus's damned entry, but I'm a dab hand at this sort of thing; I'd lay those odds the other way round, if I were a bookie. But Thaumus has everything with legs beat. The Incendiary is the odds-on favorite now, and old M&B is up to twenty-to-one."

"I see," mused Entwhistle. "You're in for a pretty penny, I take it?"

"Up to my neck," said Carstairs.

"And stand to make a twenty-fold return if something should happen to Thaumus's wagon."

Carstairs smiled faintly.

"Goodo," said Entwhistle briskly, standing up and rubbing his hands together. "My fee will be one hundred pounds."

Carstairs looked as if he were about to swallow his monocle. "Great thundering gods," he choked.

"Take it or leave it," said Entwhistle. "I'm a busy man, you know."

Carstairs's face was losing that dangerous crimson color; he was no longer quite on the verge of apoplexy. "A hundred quid," he complained.

"Consider the risk I'm running," said Entwhistle with irritation. "Good heavens, to be caught fixing the races; I'd be ostracized from one end of this town to the other. It's a small enough fee—"

"Yes, yes," said Carstairs. "I'll pay the damned hundred quid, gods help me."

"Fine," said Entwhistle, standing up to show Carstairs out. "Good luck to you, then."

Afterward, he lay back in an armchair, put his feet up on the ottoman, and closed his eyes. A hundred pounds was all very nice, but there were other possibilities here. He supposed he could bet on the race, but he had not Carstairs's confidence in his chances of picking the right mammoth. On the other hand—

There was a copy of the *Fen Street Journal* on Entwhistle's desk; he took it every day. He picked it up, opened it, and ran his eyes down the figures. Yes, he was right: Shares in the major mammoth breeders were all down in the past fortnight, no doubt on speculation that Thaumus's damned Engine would cut into sales to the roads. Now, suppose the Engine were not merely to fail, but to fail in spectacular fashion, proving the dangerousness of the technology? Judging by the price/earnings ratio, Masters & Baleham's shares could double overnight.

The first order of business was obviously to visit his broker.

Morning sun slanted into the rail shed through high, enormous windows. The air of the shed was redolent still with the smell of mammoth, for it had housed those great elephantine creatures before it had been rented by Magister Thaumus. A painted machine, gold and red, all steel and iron and circular wheels, sat at the shed's center, on the switching rail; it was the Incendiary Engine, Magister Thaumus's pride and joy, the device that proposed to send the mammoths back to their northern plains. Into the air, from beneath the great steel machine, curled a tendril of smoke; not woodsmoke, nor that of coal, but the smoke of a pipe.

"All right, guvnor?" said an aproned workman. His balding pate was smeared with grease, and a massive black spanner was held in one hand.

Thaumus pulled out from under the Engine, his corncob clenched in his teeth, and sat up. He rubbed one grimy hand across a muttonchop. "Yes, Jenkins," he said. "I've probed the boiler tubes with an awl, and I don't find any obvious flaws; but mind you watch the steam pressure during the race. Three tubes ruptured during tests, you remember; can't have that happen today."

"Never you fear," said the engineer. "I know this old gel like the back of me hand."

"Indeed," said Thaumus, standing up, and clapping the workman on the shoulder, "good man."

About the shed bustled a dozen men, checking the piston fittings, giving the valves a last oiling, filling the tank with water. "You remember the grimoire, now, Jenkins," Thaumus said. "If for any reason I can't make it to the starting line, you're to read the incantation on page sixteen—"

"Aye, sir," said Jenkins. "To summon the fire elemental. But ye'll be there, never fear."

"I shall certainly endeavor to be so," said Thaumus. "There

have been two attempts on my life in the last three days."

"Sir!" said Jenkins, shocked.

"The Mammoth Mahouts' Guild is not fond of me," said Thaumus dryly, "nor the breeders. And fixing the Iron Tusk is virtually a tradition—"

There were three sudden booms, kettledrum sounds; Thaumus whirled to face them, recognizing the sound of a teleport. Workmen shouted in fear and scurried for cover; three demons stood within the shed. One recognized demons mainly by their enormous disparity in form; creatures of chaos they were. One was a thing like a fuzzball with teeth; one, a patch of purple smoke, with eyes and horns; one, a winged and fanged monstrosity. They were hunting about the shed, looking for something. For Thaumus?

There was a sudden roar of flame, Thaumus's defenses kicking in. Thaumus had prepared a ward-triggered spell against just such a magical assault. Two pillars of fire twisted within the shed now; fire elementals. Each elemental spun to engage a demon.

The winged demon was instantly incinerated, but the fuzzball was tougher; it danced aside and spit out a long stream of liquid, which struck one of the elementals. The pillar of flame screamed, an unworldly, high-pitched sound.

The smoky demon had spied Thaumus and was flitting directly toward him. The wizard began to shout a spell—but the demon was on him in instants.

Thaumus choked, purple smoke burning like acid in his lungs; the smoky demon gave a deep, bass, unsettling laugh. Jenkins reached for Thaumus, an expression of concern on his face, but the whole scene was fading out, outlines becoming fuzzy, the world a place of purple smoke, consciousness slipping away . . .

Suddenly, Thaumus was breathing air. He wheezed deeply.

He was lying on something; a floor. Checkered parquet, he noted. He rose unsteadily to his feet. He was in the center of a room, apparently the parlor of a town house, converted to a study. Two long windows let in the morning sun; the walls were covered with bookcases. Above the mantel hung a rather garish oil of a nude and a framed diploma; Thaumus couldn't make out the name, but it was a Sabreheim University degree. He curled his lip; Thaumus was a Montief Polymagical man.

Thaumus was standing in the center of a silver pentacle inlaid in the parquet. Tentatively, he tried to push a finger out of the area demarcated by the pentacle; the finger rebounded, as if it had run into a glass wall.

The smoky demon hung in the pentacle with him.

There was one other person in the room, a man, of average height, with a well-trimmed black beard and heavy mustache. "My dear Magister Thaumus," he said.

"You have the advantage of me, sir," Thaumus replied.

Elias Entwhistle's face fell. "You don't recognize me?" he said. "We met last year, at the Beltane Ball. I was wearing peach velvet . . ."

"Ah, yes," said Thaumus, reaching for his pipe. "I remember, vaguely. Quite vulgar, I thought. I remarked on it to the Baroness Claudette. 'There goes new wealth,' I said. 'Completely tasteless,' she replied. Discerning woman, the Baroness."

"Shut up, you," snarled the demonologist. "Ma'omfelemars!"

Thaumus blinked at this non sequitur.

"Yo," boomed a deep voice. Thaumus realized it was the demon who shared the pentacle with him.

"Where are the blueprints?"

The demon laughed its slow, disconcerting laugh.

Entwhistle shouted a Word of power. The smoke curled, and the disembodied eyes winced.

"Didn't find it," boomed the demon.

"Idiot!" said Entwhistle.

A woman's voice came from the room's closed door. "What's going on in there?" it said. "Can I watch?"

Entwhistle turned to the door and snarled silently. "Finished the cleaning, tart?" he demanded.

Thaumus grinned. This was beginning to be entertaining.

"Yes, I finished the bloody bedamned cleaning!" the woman shouted. "Let me in."

"Go practice your transformations," said Entwhistle.

The woman shouted an obscenity that made Thaumus start.

Entwhistle addressed the demon. "Where are the others?" he said.

The demon's eyes studied the bookshelf.

"Answer me!"

"You talking to me?" boomed the demon.

"Yes, you jackanapes!"

Thaumus watched the door with interest. The heavy bolt that barred it slid slowly back.

"Answer you what?" boomed the demon innocently.

Entwhistle ground his teeth. "Ma'omfelemars, where are the others?" he said, biting off the words.

"What others?"

"The other two demons!" shrieked Entwhistle. Thaumus looked at him askance; either Entwhistle was having a particularly frustrating day, or the man was more than slightly mad. Probably, he reflected, both; dealing with demons was a chancy business at best.

"Oh, them," said the demon. "What about them?"

"Where are they?"

The door's lock clicked, and clicked again. It opened a crack. A small, dark-skinned woman thrust her head into the room. Thaumus winked at her and lit his corncob, flame emitting from his forefinger. She opened the door a little wider.

Entwhistle noticed the open door, and Seema within it. "I thought I told you to practice your transformations," he said.

"She did," said Thaumus, puffing serenely. "She practiced them on your lock. Very nice job, too." Seema smiled.

"All right, all right," said Entwhistle, throwing up his hands. "You might as well sit in." He whirled on the demon. "Well?" he shouted.

"All right by me," it boomed.

Entwhistle's forehead was beginning to turn a dangerous red. "I wasn't asking for your permission," he snarled. "I was asking you where your miserable companions are."

"Oh," said the demon.

Entwhistle balled his fists and did a little dance.

"You see, demoiselle," Thaumus said conversationally to Seema as she took a seat on the couch, "one must be precise with demons. They are a contrary race."

"Watch it, man," boomed the demon, sounding faintly insulted.

Entwhistle let out a long breath. "Ma'omfelemars," he said with dangerous calm.

"Yo," said the demon again.

"Where are Bradackfolaren and Joss'tetsekou?"

"Right now?"

"Yes!" Entwhistle practically screamed.

The smoke seemed to shrug. "Beats me."

Entwhistle gave a whimper of frustration.

"The one with the wings is dead," said Thaumus. "I didn't see what happened to the fuzzball, but he was pretty badly burned by the time we departed." He puffed.

"Thank you," said Entwhistle testily. "And where are the blueprints?"

Thaumus smiled. "I shan't say," he said.

"Not you! Ma'omfelemars!"

"Yo."

There was silence for a moment.

"Ma'omfelemars, where are the blueprints?"

"Don't know."

"You didn't see them at the shed?"

"No."

"Did you search for them?"

"No."

"Why not?" Entwhistle yelled.

"Hey, fella," protested the demon. "They killed Joss'tetsekou. I didn't feel like hanging around."

Thaumus cleared his throat. "I can't imagine what you hope to gain from the blues," he said. "My patent is on file with—"

"Shut up, you!" yelled Entwhistle. He paced around the room. "Damn," he said finally. "I shall just have to do without." He stared out the window and twirled his mustache contemplatively. "In the meantime, we shall have to put you on ice. Can't have you nobbling the fix."

Thaumus contemplated the mustache. He wondered whether Entwhistle had adopted the mannerism because he wished to be considered villainous—certainly the pointed beard lent a certain sardonic panache—or if the gesture was unconscious. "Ah," he said dryly, "the sort of sportsmanlike ploy one would expect of a Sabreheim man."

Entwhistle merely grinned and pronounced a spell.

Thaumus found himself on a featureless plain under a featureless sky. The light was dim.

The demon was with him.

His pipe was still alight; that was some consolation.

"Where are we?" Thaumus asked.

"Zezemachnotran," said the demon.

"Very enlightening," said Thaumus sarcastically.

"Sixth demonic plane," said the demon. "Dullsville. Do you play whist?"

"My personal and financial future is about to be sabotaged by that cretin Entwhistle; I'm stuck in another dimension; and you want to play whist?"

The demon produced a deck of cards. "You prefer cribbage?"

Entwhistle attracted some attention as he strolled through the crowd. It was not his person that elicited comment, nor his garb; the more conservative sort might consider his mauve hose a bit déclassé, but that was perhaps more a judgment on the taste of his valet than on Entwhistle's, and in any event, his dress could be forgiven for a man spreading a bit large at the races. Rather, it was the fact that he bore a three-cubit-long canvas bag, circular in cross section, over his shoulder. Some gentlemen, to be sure, brought folding chairs or one-legged stools to the races, to line the track itself, rather than sit in a box at the starting line; but one would, of course, expect a personal assistant or gentleman's gentleman to carry such a burden. Alas, Entwhistle had no humans in his employ, and while Stossmekoloren or one of the other demons would have been quite capable of carrying the bag and negotiating the crowd, the appearance of such a monstrosity would have attracted undue notice, and Entwhistle wished to preserve a certain element of anonymity.

It was a gray day, a little chill; the seer in the morning paper had predicted rain, and consequently many were carrying umbrellas. But despite the prospect of precipitation, the crowd was gay. A brass band played patriotic marches down at the starting line, women wore elaborate and brightly colored hats, and vendors of sausages and roast pigeons moved through the crowd, calling their wares. The lines at the betting windows were long, but Entwhistle was not thither bound. He had no money on the race, unless one counted the heavy investment he'd made in mammoth breeders' shares.

Entwhistle walked down the line to the rail yard. A high picket fence cut off the rather unsightly view from the surrounding neighborhood. Entwhistle walked along the fence, whistling a bit to himself, until he found what he was looking for: a gate.

A guard stood there, in the uniform of the Montief and Elven. "No admittance, guvnor," he said as Entwhistle approached.

"Ah, my good man," said Entwhistle, reaching out to shake the guard's hand with a five-pound note folded up in his own, "I appreciate the need to keep out the riffraff; but I have only the purest intentions, wishing merely to examine the respective beasts in order to judge their merits."

The guard took Entwhistle's hand, shook it, and, in pulling back, sneaked a glance at the bill that had been transferred to his own. Entwhistle had been careful to fold it in such a way that the "£5" was visible. The guard pocketed the bill, then glanced up and down the fence. "In you go, guvnor," he said in a low tone, unlocking and opening the gate. "Step lively, now."

Entwhistle hustled inside.

A whole series of rail lines paralleled the fence; at one end of the yard, they curved in, eventually joining together in a single track that led out of the yard and toward the stands. At the other end, a series of switches, slanting across the rails, made it possible to move a train from one track to another, or to transfer cars from train to train. Several lines led out that end of the yard, curving away to the roundhouse and the mammoth sheds.

A series of crossties were stacked against the fence; Entwhistle stored his bag there, then strolled out, across the lines.

Several trains were already made up, each sitting on its own section of track; mahouts and hostlers were getting ready for the early heats of the race. Each team consisted of two cars, each car with a standard load of grain. Each train was pulled by two mammoths, in most cases a bull and a cow. The bulls were larger and stronger, but would fight if yoked together; one of the trains, Entwhistle saw, was pulled by a bull and meer, a sterilized male. Meers were stronger than cows, but the bulls tended to be irritable even with them. For this reason, bull-meer teams were rarely used commercially, but some handlers preferred them for the races.

The ground was carpeted with dung. They wet the rail yard daily, Entwhistle knew, to keep the dung down. Even so, hostlers moved about with wheelbarrows and shovels, picking up the stuff when a beast let fly, both for reasons of hygiene and because there was a market for the stuff. Mammoth dung was highly prized by fruit and vegetable growers.

Not ten cubits away, a bull trumpeted, startling Entwhistle. The creature's trunk was curled, and its piggish eyes were staring malevolently at the wizard. A mahout, atop its back, shouted something and struck at the back of the mammoth's ear with a pick; when irritated, the beasts sometimes forgot their training and left the track, derailing a train. They hadn't put blinkers on the beast yet, Entwhistle saw.

He stepped gingerly over a rail and started off across the yard.

His shoes were soon coated with dung, but there was no stopping that. He saw the Incendiary Engine at last, on rail three.

Entwhistle cursed; he had half hoped that removing Thaumus would force the team to scratch, as they no longer had the wizard to prepare whatever spell motivated the device. Obviously, Thaumus had prepared for the eventuality of his absence.

Well. That was why Entwhistle was here. He removed the signet ring from his left hand and approached the Engine.

One man was busy washing dung off the Engine, no doubt wishing it to make as fine an appearance as possible before the spectators. Another was under the machine, between the wheels, banging away at something; and a third was at the rear, half inside an open hatch.

"I say," said Entwhistle, approaching the open hatch. "The fabled Incendiary Engine. A beauty, I must say."

The man in the hatch pulled out, standing on a short ladder leading up to the place. Entwhistle saw that the hatch was surrounded with symbols that, to the untutored eye, might have appeared mere design; he knew them as protective runes. The man was smiling, obviously proud of his machine.

"Aye, that she is, sir," he said, stepping down. "And she'll have no problem today, I'll warrant ye that."

"Glad to hear it," said Entwhistle heartily, "for I have a dozen guineas on her. May I see?" Before the man could quite prevent it, Entwhistle scrambled up the ladder and peered into the hatch. There was a spherical chamber within, walled with thick steel, tubes and valves of unknown purpose opening off it. Entwhistle carefully and quickly placed his ring in one of the tubes, out of sight.

"I say, sir, we really can't have—" said the workman, placing a hand on Entwhistle's shoulder.

"I'm sorry," said Entwhistle. "Am I presuming? Tell me, how does she work?"

"A fire elemen—look here, sir, you really shouldn't be in the yard."

Fire elemental, eh? Very interesting, thought Entwhistle. Although, to be sure, he had suspected as much. "Yes, quite right," said Entwhistle apologetically. "But I couldn't resist the opportunity to see her at close quarters."

"I appreciate that, sir," said the workman, "but there have been threats, and—I really must ask you to leave."

"Oh," said Entwhistle, doing his best to sound slightly put out. "Very well." He strode stiffly off.

He retrieved his canvas bag before leaving the yard. Distant thunder rumbled, and a few drops of rain pattered onto Entwhistle's hat. He opened his bag and took out an umbrella.

Entwhistle's study was quiet. It was deserted of both human and demonic occupants. The windows were open slightly, and a damp breeze redolent of bracken and brush blew the curtains aside. The room was lit only by the gray light that shined through the windows; dark carpets, dark paint, and the dark spines of books lent it a somber and civilized air.

The bolt on the door slid slowly back. The lock clicked, and clicked again. Seema opened the door a crack and peered within.

She half expected to be attacked by some demonic form. Entwhistle had made it plain she was to steer clear of his study. That was why he'd locked the door. It would have been like him to leave a trap for her.

But nothing happened. She pushed the door open and, gaining confidence, went to the desk, walking carefully around the pentacle. She sat down in Entwhistle's chair, grinned, and put her boots on the desktop. She put her hands behind her head and looked around the room.

Then she got up, went to a bookshelf, and pulled down a tome, essentially at random. She flipped through it, skimmed the contents page, and put it back.

Working her way around the room, she began to get a glimmer of Entwhistle's organizational scheme. She came across a volume that seemed more promising: *Fiat Law Made Natural, or, The Bindings, Oaths, and Contracts of Summoners' Lore.*

She went to the desk and began to study the book. She realized the light was dim and, looking up, noticed an oil lamp on the desk. She hesitated, then decided to attempt one of the transformations she'd been practicing. Clearing her thoughts and summoning power, she willed the wick to flame.

And it did.

Emboldened by her success, she began to read more confidently.

As much as Entwhistle may have regretted swearing to instruct her, she regretted having sworn to obey him more. She had a romantic image of magic: she wished to sweep across the skies, borne up by the backs of demons, to conquer kingdoms with her powers, to have numerous suitors contend for the favor of the mighty wizardess' hand, to rescue friends and slay foes. She had been educated well, though her parents sought nothing more for her than a favorable match, and she was familiar with literature and the arts; but, prior to her apprenticeship, she had no direct experience of magic, her knowledge of it deriving mostly from fiction.

Elias seemed to spend his time burning things in braziers, breathing noxious fumes, and reading, endlessly reading. She yearned for adventure, not for scholarship; and she was more than tired of the menial tasks to which Elias put her—especially since the man had demons aplenty to do the selfsame jobs.

Elias intended her to learn humility, as hubris is a dangerous trait in any demonologist: one must never summon anything one isn't sure one can control. Seema didn't feel humble; merely humiliated. She wanted out of her bargain.

And so she studied her book assiduously. But it was written in a dry, indirect style, replete with the jargon of the discipline. She had difficulty following even the sense, and the nuances of much it said escaped her. She grew irritated with it. In a way, she was correct to do so: the author wrote as he did to impress his colleagues and mystify those unacquainted with his art. The information he had to impart could have been stated in a far clearer and simpler way. But mystification increases the awe of the uneducated and makes those who understand feel pride in their own abilities; most of the books on Entwhistle's shelves were written in similar fashion.

When she came to an enchantment described as "a ritual of unbinding," she seized on it. She resolved to use it. She would be free of her obligation to Entwhistle, whatever it might cost.

"Pine pitch," she read. She pulled open all the drawers in Entwhistle's desk and found the one he used to store his essences. There was indeed a bottle of pine pitch.

She loaded the fireplace with coal and sprinkled pine pitch atop it. Using the same transformation that had lit the lamp, she lit the coal as well.

While it burned and the fire began to penetrate the coals, she read further in her book. She stood behind the desk, the fire to her back, and did as the book said, as if she were a cook following a recipe.

She made a cutting motion across her face, the palm of her hand open downward. *"Mondrarok,"* she said. *"Mokalor morkath."* She clenched her fist, then opened it, her fingers now pointing upward. *"Avgenii voglapan amenish."*

There was a creaking noise. She flipped the page.

"The 'gesture of disavowing'?" she said. "What the hell is that?"

There was another creaking noise, this one a little higher pitched than the last. She looked about, uneasy, then quickly went on. *"Ahntoe! Ahntoe! Y krakatoe!"*

A wind swirled through the room, and she reached down to hold the page in place, then raised both hands overhead as instructed. *"Na glamish! Na kriptoy! Na namblor!"*

A chunk of plaster fell from the ceiling. She looked up in dismay. As she watched, a large crack split the plaster. She wondered desperately whether she should complete the spell or break it off here. She could feel the power thrumming through her; if she did not release it, what would happen? She'd better continue.

But the next instruction made no sense. Under "Gesture," there was some kind of bundle of lines. If she'd been better taught, she'd have recognized it as a Klath diagram, used by sorcerers to describe complex ritual gestures in a compact form. She could make neither head nor tail of it.

And under "Incantation," the book merely said: "appropriate similarity elements, tort descriptors, or clausal references, followed by spirit invocations (see page 76)."

As more plaster began to fall and horrendous creaking noises and sounds like firecrackers reverberated through the building, she desperately flipped to page 76 and read the first thing that sounded like it might apply: *"Spiritus, Plani, Elementi Physici, Nomeni, Linguae, Dei, Tribi, Et Cetera"*—thus stating that the Ritual of Unbinding was to apply to all spirits, planes, physical elements, names, languages, gods, tribes, and so on—the author's far-from-exhaustive list of possible similarity elements.

The power flew from her, and she nearly collapsed on the table. The general nature of her spell dissipated the energy instantly; and, since its targets had been so generally stated, it had little effect outside of the immediate vicinity. She did not free every bound spirit in the city, nor did she free the planes from their mooring in the multiverse, nor the physical elements from their appointed role in the cycles of nature; it would have taken a god to make so drastic an unbinding.

The effects on Elias Entwhistle's house were, however, quite drastic enough.

The plaster in the walls and ceilings disintegrated into its constituent parts, the lime no longer binding together the sand and horsehair. The nails shot forth from the timbers and laths, the sandstone lintels crumbled, the pegs shot from their holes, and books separated from their bindings; the furniture fell into its component parts, the mortar ceased to bind the bricks, the joists separated from their beams, the window glass turned to sand, the flooring turned into sticks of disconnected wood, and the pentacle came to pieces; and, last but far from least, the sixteen demons that formed the load-bearing members of the house and the gargoyles that made its soffit awoke from their long torpor.

The house came tumbling about Seema's head. Timbers, sticks of furniture, and roofing tiles plunged past her. As she crouched timorously, a beam swung toward her, but, inches away, exploded, the residual effects of her spell unbinding it to splinters.

After seconds that seemed like hours, she crouched in the rain, atop a pile of rubble in a weed-grown lot. Pages unbound from their volumes fluttered on the breeze, and plaster dust swirled in the air. The only sounds were the patter of rain and the hiss as the coals from the fireplace drowned.

Four tall columns stood where the building corners had been: four columns, each of four demons, standing one atop another. For a long moment, these held high. Slowly, then with gathering speed, the columns fell and slammed into the ground.

Seema looked about her, still too stunned to think. Slowly, with creaks and groans, the demons stood. They looked around, they examined the rubble, they looked at each other, they rubbed their shoulders and their arms.

And then they turned on Seema and gave her hideous grins.

"Five years," said one. "Five years as a bleeding doorstop."

Around them, the gargoyles, too, were beginning to stand.

"Five years with pigeons shitting on my nose," said another.

"Look, guys," said Seema nervously. "I'm sorry. Okay?"

One took a step toward her. "Someone's going to pay," he said, his eyes glowing red in rage.

"Look," said Seema, backing off. "I mean, I freed you guys. Right? Like, you should be grateful."

One gave a slow, booming laugh, which reminded her of Ma'omfelemars. They all moved toward her.

"Let's eviscerate her," said one.

"No," said another. "Let's rend her limb from limb."

"No, wait," said a third. "I know this great pit of fire in the Slough of Despond, over on the third demonic plane. We can—"

"Ma'omfelemars!" shouted Seema, naming the only demon who had ever shown her kindness (mainly, she suspected, to spite Elias). And she shouted the Words of summoning she'd heard Entwhistle use so many times.

"Twenty points behind," said Thaumus morosely, gathering up the cards from the featureless plain.

Ma'omfelemars began to turn even more transparent than he already was. "I'm being summoned," he said. "Ciao."

"Take me with you," said Thaumus hastily.

The demon hesitated, then said, "All right." A smoky tendril grabbed Thaumus's arm, and the sixth demonic plane began to fade.

It was raining. Thaumus was getting wet. He hated the rain. He glared at the sky.

He was standing near a pile of rubble in a weed-covered lot. Ma'omfelemars was with him. Quite a lot of demons he hadn't met before were standing around. They looked peeved about something.

Seema was a few feet away. "Good day," said Thaumus. "Or rather, not. Dreadful weather. Is it still the tenth?"

"Yes," Seema said nervously. "Ma'omfelemars! You've got to help me. These guys . . ."

"Don't get involved, smoky," said one of the demons, one with big fangs and small flames coming from his nostrils. "She's dead meat."

"What happened?" Ma'omfelemars asked.

Seema was embarrassed. "I botched a spell."

Thaumus looked around and grinned. "Some spell," he said. "It was a ritual of unbinding."

He cocked an eyebrow. "Oh? Hmm."

The demons moved toward them. Thaumus picked up a floorboard and quickly sketched a pentacle in the earth, protecting Seema, Ma'omfelemars, and himself. He spoke a Phrase of power.

The demons halted. "Now then," said Thaumus.

"I bet if we all rush at once the pentacle won't hold," said one demon.

"Look," said another. "It's in the dirt. The rain will erase it given enough time. We just have to wait."

Thaumus looked down. They were right. Raindrops were already blurring the lines.

"Thanks," Seema said to him.

"Do you know where Entwhistle is?" Ma'omfelemars asked her.

"Yes," she said.

"Tell them," he said, nodding his horns toward the other demons. "They'd rather have him than you."

She turned to them and tried to speak. "I . . . I can't," she said.

"Conscience got you?" said Ma'omfelemars nastily. "Remember, the man thinks nothing of turning intelligent creatures into architectural embellishments. He—"

"It's not that," she said miserably. "I'm still bound by my oath."

Thaumus laughed. "Is that what you were trying to do? Unbind the oath? And you unbound them, instead, eh?" He shook his head.

Seema was abashed. "I'll never make a sorceress."

"On the contrary," said Thaumus. "If you can wreak this much damage, you must have a certain degree of innate talent."

"I must?"

"Without question. I would suggest you ask Entwhistle to free you from your obligation and apply to one of the universities."

"I don't have the money for—"

"There are scholarships for the gifted. I'll sponsor you myself."

"I . . . I'll think about it," she said.

"If," said Ma'omfelemars, "you're still alive in fifteen minutes." They studied the demons, who grinned back.

"Can you banish them?" said Seema.

"Only if they're fire-aligned," said Thaumus. "I have no particular power over demons." There was silence for a moment, save for the patter of the rain. Then Thaumus slowly asked, "Why isn't Entwhistle here?" He hoped Seema's oath wouldn't stop her from speaking; the information was presumably nonprejudicial in itself.

"The race," she said. "He . . ." She put her hands to her mouth, realizing what she'd done.

"Thank you," said Thaumus. "Ahem. My good . . . entities."

"What do you want?" said one of the demons.

"If I tell you where the man who bound you is at present, will you agree to depart from this place and harass us no further?"

"Yes," the demon said.

"No!" said another.

"I say yes," said a third.

"Maybe, if . . ." began a fourth.

"Ah—can I ask you to work this out among yourselves?" said Thaumus.

The demons huddled. It took them a few minutes to decide. The humans eyed the blurring line of Thaumus's pentacle worriedly.

The demons broke huddle. "All right," said one, evidently their spokesdemon. "If you agree never to summon or bind any of us," he said to Seema.

She blinked. "Demons in general?" she said.

"Huh? No, the sixteen of us. And the gargoyles, too."

"Oh. All right."

"Are we agreed?" said Thaumus. The demons all nodded.

"Right," he said. "I believe you can find Elias Entwhistle at Montief Central."

"Where's that?"

"Eh? The railroad station." Noting evident incomprehension, he elaborated. "You take Carchemish Boulevard to Marshmuddle and Brandywine, then you . . . look, I'm off there myself. Why don't I lead you there?"

The demons seemed amenable.

"My best wishes, demoiselle," said Thaumus, raising his hat, "but I have a race to win."

Seema looked unhappy, but had no response.

"If you wish to take me up on my offer, simply leave a message at the Thaumaturge Club for me," said Thaumus.

"I'll think about it," said Seema. "Gods, what is Entwhistle going to do to me?"

A winged demon grabbed Thaumus by the arms and bore

him away through the rain. "I say, put me down!" shouted the wizard.

"Faster this way, pal," the demon said. "We got a bone to pick with Entwhistle. Let's go!"

"I wouldn't worry too much about Entwhistle," Thaumus shouted to Seema over his shoulder. "He won't be doing anything to you, until this lot is through with him. Which may be a good long time."

One of the monsters gave a long, braying, hyena-like laugh.

Nervously, Jenkins completed the words of the spell, shouting them into the rain-laden air. He felt power discharge, and there was a *whump!* as something appeared in the boiler chamber. Abruptly, the open hatch radiated heat like an oven.

Jenkins slammed and dogged the hatch and gave a thumbs-up to the other men. He clambered up into the cab, where Marks, the engine-mahout, waited. Jenkins went to the engineer's station and pulled down on the water lever.

Water trickled into the boiler, flashing instantly to steam. The fire elemental gave a howl. Jenkins felt a momentary cringe of empathy at that, but dismissed it; Thaumus had assured him that the elementals had no souls, were barely self-aware. Surely this was no worse than mammoth training, a task which involved a certain degree of cruelty.

The pressure gauge rose into the amber zone. Jenkins engaged the piston release, and steam hissed from a vent under the carriage. "Steam's up, Mr. Marks," he said formally. "Ye may take her away."

"Aye, Mr. Jenkins," said Marks, and released the brake. There was a *SHOOMP* as the piston opened, releasing steam; the wheels began to turn. *SHOOMP . . . SHOOMP . . . SHOOMP*— they turned with gathering speed. Mammoths on an adjoining track trumpeted at the unaccustomed noise. Marks tugged on the steam whistle, which Thaumus had installed in imitation of that very trumpeting sound—and for the first time, Montief City was treated to the *TOOOOOOOOT* of an Incendiary Engine.

The men tossed caps in the air. The Incendiary Engine moved down the track, curving across the switch toward the single egress. Marks saw they were going a little too fast—no need to gain full speed until start time—and feathered the steam. The Engine passed through the gate and into the station.

Folk in the stands craned for a better view. Marks gently applied the brake, and the Engine slowed, coming to a complete stop just before the great banner that marked the start line.

One of the race officials came out, with a pocket watch. "Two minutes fourteen seconds, gentlemen," he said.

"What's the best time today?" asked Jenkins.

"Masters & Baleham," said the official. "Forty-eight minutes thirteen; but Flying Oliphaunts is twenty-two forty-nine at Little Queeling." Little Queeling was an intermediate station, roughly halfway down the line to Saucisson; Flying Oliphaunts was the team that had left Montief a half hour earlier.

"We'll run up their heels," said Jenkins, grinning.

The official shook his head skeptically. "One minute thirty— mark," he said.

"Damnation," said Entwhistle, whanging away at the flint with his piece of steel. He had dry cotton as tinder, which ought to work fine, except that it wasn't particularly dry, not in the rain. There was not a minute to spare, and he desperately needed to get the charcoal brazier burning.

He stood atop one of the mammoth sheds, sheets of rusty steel roofing sloping gently away toward the gutter. He'd positioned himself carefully; he could see the Incendiary Engine at the starting gate; he could see the rail line extending off toward Saucisson, but he was hidden from view of the stands. Oh, one of the gawkers along the line might notice him, but he was sufficiently far away that he trusted to distance and the rain to hide his presence.

"Catch!" he said with fury, virtually smashing the flint. "Catch, I say!"

A tiny point of orange light glowed in the cotton. Entwhistle snatched it up and blew, gently at first, then with greater force. The cotton caught, and Entwhistle shoved it into the brazier, snatching up the bellows and working them. Gradually, the charcoal began to smoke. There was no chance he'd get a full blaze in time, but a little heat was all he needed, enough to vaporize the rather volatile essence of cinnamon he'd brought.

The brazier lit, he dived for his open canvas bag and snatched out his folding pentacle, cursing his own luck. He'd been spotted skulking around the barn by one of the railroad dicks, and it had taken him a good hour to get rid of the man. He needed a line of sight to the Engine, and he needed privacy, and this was the only place that looked like it afforded both. It was not an ideal place in which to work; Entwhistle was soaked to the bone, his legs ached from standing on the slope, and the air was foul with the stench of mammoth manure, which was heaped up in a great pile against the base of the barn.

He unsnapped the pentacle, rods of silver folding out into a five-pointed shape. He'd had the thing hand-made and found it very useful when traveling. He laid it on the sloping roof and stepped within it. At last, he was ready. He took out the bottle of cinnamon oil and sprinkled a few drops on the brazier.

He had less than a minute, by his watch.

"*Avramet!*" he shouted. "*Kastalor avramet, mektor felahnk.*"

Power drew about him. His arms writhed in complex gestures. His hair rustled with static electricity.

Down there, in the boiler of the Incendiary Engine, was his own signet ring, probably red-hot now with the elemental's fire. Entwhistle had worn the ring for nearly a year; it was therefore associated with him magically—similar to him, as it were. Therefore, he could do magic through it, transfer his power.

He felt a connection with the ring click into place . . .

Thaumus and the demon that bore him aloft had outdistanced the others, who followed, more sedately, at ground level. Where another man might have suffered vertigo, flying through the air with nothing beneath his feet, Thaumus felt exhilaration. This was better even than railroading, although the rain did put a bit of a damper on things. Thaumus yearned for an umbrella.

Montief Central Station hove into sight. The demon flitted down to a perch atop the tiled roof of the station itself. Several people in the stands craned to watch them; wizards borne aloft by demons were not an everyday sight.

"There's the Engine," said Thaumus proudly. "Good man, Jenkins."

"But where's that creep Entwhistle?" demanded the demon.

"He's got to be about," said Thaumus.

"Maybe so," said the demon. "I bet there's a thousand people down there. How are we going to find him?"

"Hmm," said Thaumus. He found his corncob and his pouch of weed—the pouch was waterproof, luckily—and began to fill his pipe.

*   *   *

"Kambellar kankratchee, sekundar floret," shouted Entwhistle. Below him, below the shed, was Earth, the world; earthly things fall, seeking to return to their appointed sphere. Betwixt Earth and Air is Water, pooling in oceans and lakes; rain falls from the sky, seeking to return to its own sphere. Above Water is Air and its breezes, both gentle and strong; its sphere is betwixt Water and Fire, explaining why bubbles rise and flames leap upward. And above Air is Fire, peeping through the great barrier called Sky, which prevents the instant incineration of the world; peeping through the holes called Sun and Moon and Stars.

Each element has its elementals, beings of pure matter. And a mage trained to control a particular element may summon elementals of his own sphere. Entwhistle was a summoner; his greatest power was the domination of demons, but he was capable of summoning any magical creature, elementals of fire included.

Suppose the one elemental within the boiler of the Incendiary Engine were joined by a second; and a third; and possibly, if necessary, a fourth. What then?

Perhaps the boiler would explode; perhaps it would simply melt into slag. Whatever happened, thought Entwhistle, it should be satisfyingly messy—and a satisfying demonstration of the superiority of mammoth-drawn conveyance.

"Sstothenes malakar sstothentares," shouted Entwhistle, arms wheeling in ritual gestures, opening a gateway to the Sphere of Fire.

As Thaumus lit his pipe, his finger suddenly flared, the tiny flame becoming a good-sized torch. Thaumus waved his finger out, eyes widening.

Someone had opened a gateway to Fire, someone nearby; he could feel the magical thread, upward toward the sky. The flare of his finger had been spillover, an epiphenomenon. He could sense the thread of power, from—

"Over there," he said, pointing toward the mammoth sheds. "I can sense him."

The demon left off scanning the crowd, grabbed Thaumus, and instantly flitted thither.

Now, thought Entwhistle, it was merely a matter of summoning the elemental and dispatching it down the link to his ring.

"Ignis, scarleth somenetes, abjuretione," he said, sprinkling mineral oil on the brazier; the fire blazed up. *"Afrait no—"*

Entwhistle received a buffet to the side of his head, knocking him sideways and almost out of the pentacle.

"Take that, you bounder!" shouted Thaumus as the demon lowered him to the sloping shed roof. Thaumus had kicked Entwhistle in passing.

The demon hurled itself toward Entwhistle, snarling, claws outstretched, but rebounded off the barrier around the pentacle.

"How the devil—" said Entwhistle, rubbing his head.

There was a *WHUMP*. The interior of the pentacle was suddenly filled with flames. Entwhistle had broken off his spell, uncompleted, and the elemental appeared in the pentacle with him, not down the link to the Engine.

Entwhistle screamed as fire played over the body.

"Oh, bother," said Thaumus, reached a hand into the pentacle, and pulled Entwhistle out. The elemental, imprisoned within it, screamed in rage.

There were blisters on Entwhistle's face, burns on his hands. "Thank you," he gasped.

"Don't," said Thaumus, pity in his voice.

The demon pounced on Entwhistle, its hyena-like laugh announcing its triumph. The space around Entwhistle and the demon became curiously vague, the forms fading away, Entwhistle screaming imprecations at the demon as both faded into insubstantiality—and then they were gone.

Off, presumed Thaumus, to one of the demonic planes.

"TOOOOOOOT," went the Incendiary Engine; the crowd applauded.

Thaumus turned, and watched as his little red and gold machine made off, with gathering speed, down the track, steam hissing from the vents, steel wheels clacking along steel rails.

Seema turned before the mirror, checking the fit of the dress. It swept down in graceful lines toward her feet, bustle at the back, the front betraying a slight décolletage. It was, thought Seema, ravishing.

"Keep it, then," said Amelia. "Heaven knows, I won't wear the thing."

"Amelia!" said Seema. "It must be worth ten pounds if it's worth—"

"Bother," said Amelia. "Father will keep on giving me these things."

"You're sure you won't come?"

"You know I can't abide receptions, parties, and balls, dear," said Amelia. "Dreadful things. I shall stay here and plow through my quadratics. You can do me one favor, however."

"Yes?" said Seema.

"Do see if you can get me an invitation to look at the Incendiary Engine," said Amelia.

"Of course," said Seema.

"That's all, then," said Amelia. "I'm off to tea with the philosophy department. If you need anything, let the maid know." And she let herself out.

Thank heavens for Amelia, thought Seema, studying herself in the mirror again. They had met at finishing school, which both, for not wholly dissimilar reasons, had detested; but Seema had not kept up the friendship afterward. It was very good of Amelia to have taken her in when she appeared on the doorstep, bedraggled and woefully wet. But Amelia had never been conventional; she seemed to have no interest in suitors, none in the city's social life, and a passionate devotion to her studies. Perhaps she, too, could put in a good word with the university, if Seema decided to take Thaumus up on his offer.

And it was good of Amelia to offer her the loan of this dress; certainly, Seema could not have appeared at the Iron Tusk Reception in her soaking gray wrap.

As it was, she would be gate-crashing, and scandalously without male escort.

On her back, Seema felt the cool, fresh breeze of the evening, blowing through the open window she could see in the mirror. And through the mirror was climbing . . .

Seema whirled. "You!" she gasped.

Entwhistle was dressed in a black cloak and boots. "You miserable bitch," he said in a low, furious voice. "What by all the hells did you do? Do you know how much that house cost me? Do you know what it took to get free of those damned demons?"

"Hurt—hurt me and I'll scream," said Seema.

"Hurt you? Hurt you!" Entwhistle's voice was rising almost to a shout. "I *can't* hurt you, you pathetic skink! No matter how much you hurt *me*! *You're my apprentice!* And I could kill myself for having agreed to—"

"Look, Elias," said Seema, "you don't want me. I don't want you. Can't you discharge me?"

Entwhistle blinked, as if this were unexpected. "I can, with your agreement," he said.

"I'll agree if you won't exact retribution," she said.

Entwhistle ground his teeth, then looked at the window furtively, as if fearing something outside. "Very well," he said at last. "Certainly I'd like to eat your liver, but being shot of you is an enormous step in the right direction."

Rapidly, as if fearing she might change her mind, Entwhistle spat the Words of a spell. It was, Seema saw, the same Ritual of Unbinding she had attempted, executed competently.

"That's it," he said. "Goodbye." And he began to clamber out the window.

"But what about—"

He peered over his shoulder at her, one leg over the railing. "About what?" he said. "Madam, a good dozen demons with a collective chip on their shoulder the size of Mount Marena are combing the city for me even now. And I have an appointment with a maggot named Carstairs, Major Jos., who is attempting to welsh on a debt. I haven't the time to chat."

"Never mind," said Seema, relieved. And she went to the railing, to watch him clamber down the ivy and out into the night.

Faerie lanterns hung everywhere about Montief Central, the fays within glowing their dim, greenish light. From inside the station, the sounds of a dance band played. Seema's hansom moved forward a few feet, as the next carriage in line reached the station entrance and disgorged its load of well-dressed men and women, who strolled up the steps toward the gaiety and bright lights. At last, it was Seema's time to step out, and she did, tipping the hack. "Thank ye, miss," he said, touching his cap, even though her tip had been nothing more than the usual.

The entrance was flanked by a heavyset man in the uniform of the Montief and Elven, all blue and green and gold braid. "Name, miss?" he said, holding up a sheaf of papers.

"I'm afraid I've no invitation," she said apologetically.

The guard's expression of deference changed instantly to sternness. "Sorry, miss," he said. "I can't admit you."

She gave him an ingratiating smile. "Good my sir," she said.

"Here it is, a clear spring night; adventure beckons. Surely you remember the days of youth, when—"

The guard looked acutely uncomfortable, but motioned to two men wearing the batons and caps of rail-yard dicks. "I'm sorry, miss," he said. "There are to be no exceptions."

Damnation. "See here, my good man," Seema shouted. "I have no intention of going outside to the guard station with you alone. I can't imagine what you're suggesting." If charm didn't work, perhaps embarrassment would.

On the floor, people turned to stare at the guard with undisguised loathing. The man was turning a definite puce.

"I never!" he protested. "Markham! Nath! Escort this young lady—"

Thaumus appeared, in very proper dress: maroon hose, gray kilt, lace shirt. "What's this?" he said to the guard. "She's on the list."

"She is?" said the guard, looking as if he were about to swallow his Adam's apple.

"Of course," said Thaumus. He took the guard's papers and flipped them over. "There, 'Seema Last Name Unknown.'"

"Why didn't you say so, miss?" asked the guard, looking woebegone.

"Sorry," she murmured, taking Thaumus's arm and gliding into the station.

"What is your last name, by the way?" Thaumus asked.

"Haladji," she said.

"Ah," said Thaumus. "I had intended to hold the reception at the engine shed," he told her conversationally, "but Entwhistle's demons left it in too much of a shambles. The railroad was kind enough to lend this space."

Along the walls, white-coated servants poured champagne from an apparently inexhaustible supply. Others wandered in and among the guests, with platters of hors d'oeuvres and canapés. The band played, and a space had been cleared before them for dancers. But the focus of admiration was obviously the Incendiary Engine, silent and cold now, gleaming red and gold on the nearest track.

"Congratulations, Magister Thaumus," said a fat man in a crimson waistcoat. "Twenty minutes ten! I wouldn't have thought it possible."

"It would have been faster still, my lord," said Thaumus, "if they hadn't halted the Engine at the Little Queeling signal. They were afraid we'd rear-end the Flying Oliphaunts, we were running so quickly."

The fat man smiled. "We shall have to talk," he said.

"My offices will be open tomorrow," said Thaumus. The two men nodded, and he and Seema drifted away toward champagne. "Lord Cavendish of the Klontarr Road," he told Seema.

"I've decided to take you up on your offer," said Seema.

"Excellent," said Thaumus. "If Montief Polymagical isn't interested in someone of your ability, I'll be greatly surprised. And Entwhistle?"

"He's released me," she said.

Thaumus raised an eyebrow. "Really?" he said. "I hadn't expected him to escape so soon."

Seema shrugged. "He's really quite good at what he does."

Thaumus inclined a head. "Perhaps so," he said. "My offer, however, comes with one condition."

Seema looked at him warily as she accepted a glass of champagne. "And that is?"

Thaumus coughed, and looked away. "That you might consent to dine with me," he said, a little awkwardly. "From time to time. To—to discuss progress in your studies."

"And other matters?" she asked, smiling.

"Other matters, of course," said Thaumus, smiling back.

The Broad in the Bronze Bra

✧

by
Esther Friesner

You get up in the morning and you go to work and generally it's not at all funny. It's serious business, what you do for a living, and you take it seriously. Nothing funny about it.

If you happen to be, say, a mercenary instead of a shoe sales-man or an auto mechanic or a stockbroker, you probably take it more seriously than most people take their profession (well, maybe not if you're a stockbroker). Killing people is serious business, and you take it seriously, and . . .

There's entirely too much seriousness about this. Leave it to Esther Friesner to point out why, while incidentally skewering assorted other sacred cows along the way. I mean, in today's tough job market, you take what you can get.

"Nine-letter word for *slave* (obs.)." Tiffany took alternating nibbles at her pencil eraser and the frizzly ends of her streaked red hair. "S-E-C-R-E-T-A-R-Y," she spelled aloud, writing the word into the puzzle pattern with absolute assurance. None of the letters fit with those already on the grid, but she knew what she knew.

The intercom from Mr. Carlson's office buzzed. Tiffany sighed. It had been a quiet morning at Carlson and Carlson, Perfect Place-ments. It usually was. A fine patina of dust had settled over the file cabinets, where folders empty of hopeful employment-seekers' résumés vied for space with folders empty of potential employers' requirements. What few headhunting calls came in were thanks to those firms relying on blanket computer listings. These included every employment agency in the city, from powerful to pitiful. Carlson and Carlson fell into the latter category.

Tiffany jabbed the Speak button on her unit. Annoyed, she noticed that this week's manicure had chipped already. If she was lucky, maybe all Carlson would want out of her was a quickie. Then at least she'd be able to bargain him into giving her the rest of the day off so she could go get her nails done.

"Yes, Mr. Carlson?" she asked, doing her best to purr.

"Get in here. Now. And bring your pad."

"Well, awright." Tiffany pursed her lips, vexed. A request for her steno pad boded very ill. It meant real work. Tiffany didn't have anything against real work, and was very good at it when forced to perform—150 wpm dict./85 wpm type was nothing to sneeze at—but on the whole, she'd rather be in Club Vortex, trying to catch the eye of something male, especially if it wore a suit that cost more than her weekly take-home pay.

Steno pad in subtle use as a push-up device for her unhaltered bosom, Tiffany opened the office door. The pad, the bosom, and her jaw all fell at the same time.

"Oh, my *Gawd*!"

"Shut your gawp, creature, or he dies." Wild hair, the shade and abundance of a small haystack, tossed backwards over sun-browned shoulders. Huge blue eyes with their own inner glow of hot flint shot flaming daggers at the dumbstruck Tiffany. A sword whose steel edge winked a wicked blue-white lay just beneath the second of a series of chins pertaining to Mr. Carlson, and the whole picture was drawn together by a small, wiry woman whose chief article of clothing was a string bikini.

On second glance, Tiffany saw that it was not made of string, but metal. Not even gold lamé picked up that much luster from the light.

"Do as she says, Tiffany." Mr. Carlson's words came out as a ghastly croak. Obediently, Tiffany snapped her mouth shut and bent to recover her pad.

"Your concubine?" the woman demanded of Carlson, giving her sword an encouraging little twitch to speed his reply.

"I never laid a hand on her! I'm a married man! I didn't touch her! She is only my secretary, honest, really, I swear, you've got to believe me!" Carlson's excuses finally dribbled to a stop. Out of steam, he meekly inquired, "You one of those libbers, huh?"

"Speak you to me of *livers*, wretch?" The lady gave Carlson a stiff knee-jerk to the kidneys. "My liver will smoke on the blade of a better man than you. Look to it!"

"I didn't mean anything by that, not a thing, honest, I swear, nothing!" A slug-trail of saliva shone from one corner of Carlson's mouth. Tiffany observed his desperate squirmings and decided that there *was* something she enjoyed watching more than *Dallas*.

The lady snorted in disgust and let the sword descend from her captive's neck. "You are pathetic." Moodily she spat in Carlson's eye, to emphasize her point. He made no protest, and even gave her a furtive *May I?* glance before daring to dab off the gob. "Pathetic," she repeated. A sigh heaved the considerable bosom so precariously contained in its glittering cups. Twin gilded dragon-heads with ruby eyes roared silent warning over her nipples. "Truly Oustrav has chosen his curse with care—may a thousand scorpions infest his loins! To send me to this heartless, gutless world, where men are crippled sheep, and women"—she regarded Tiffany with exquisite scorn—"women are too ugly to bed."

"Hey, you cut that out!" Tiffany squealed. "You just watch who you're calling ugly, okay? I mean, you're not any prize yourself." She returned fire with a scorn of her own forging—perhaps not so exquisite as the lady's, but possessed of a raw animal vitality nonetheless. Her flawlessly glossed upper lip lifted in contempt. "*You* don't even know enough to shave your legs, I bet. That's why you wear those goalie pads." One chipped nail haughtily indicated the visitor's snake-embossed greaves.

The lady drew back, astonished. Carlson cringed. "Tiffany, for God's sake—" he hissed.

"Silence, worm." The lady smacked him across the breadbasket with the flat of her sword. The wind rushed out of him and he groaned. The greaves jangled a bit as their owner strode forward to clap a hand on Tiffany's shoulder.

"You surprise me, wench. You have blood in your veins after all, instead of puppy-spew. I like you." She smiled.

"Goody." Tiffany didn't sound convinced.

Somehow the lady's sudden camaraderie worked a wondrous change on Mr. Carlson. Still puffing a bit from recent assault, he bustled over to join the womenfolk. "Well, well, well, isn't this nice?" His custom-made benevolence and officiousness would have whisked him through any TV preacherman audition in town. "Just like I always say, it takes a woman to understand a woman."

"Now just a minute, Mr. Carlson," Tiffany protested. "You oughta know *very well* that I do not swing that way. Even the time you said you'd give me a raise if we did a threesome with—"

"Tiffany, Tiffany, Tiffany." Mr. Carlson chuckled at the dear child's notions. "If a raise is what you want, a raise you shall have—and a promotion! And all you have to do is . . ."

"You're *real* sure you can't type, Mila?" Tiffany asked for what seemed like the hundredth time.

A massive wrist cuff of enameled bronze smashed down onto the delicate table, denting the black lacquer finish badly. "Have I not told you the same repeatedly, *Tee-Faan?*" Tiffany's given name underwent a creepy metamorphosis in the lady's mouth:

Tiffany as a name implied cuteness, cuddliness, accessibility, the need to be protected and adored, and could provoke the desirable subconscious connection-making-with-large-expensive-diamonds potential to the ear of any innocent male. This was good.

Tee-Faan sounded too frigidly competent for comfort, a person capable even of handling snotty headwaiters and back-zip dresses solo; sort of like *Ethel*. This bit it raw.

Tiffany had no time to waste on correcting Mila's elocution. She had bigger fish to stir-fry. "Yeah, well, I just kinda hoped— It would make it so much easier to get you a job if you could type. You *do* want a job?"

"You doubt the given word of Mila, daughter of Handrad the Magnificent, first swordswoman of Queen Ulioni's Companions?" The table got another bash. Taking Mila out to lunch had not been one of Tiffany's brighter notions, even if Mr. Carlson had given her an unlimited expense account. Her face went red as she felt the eyes of a dozen Japanese waiters bore into the back of her skull. She knew they were staring—after Mila's series of outbursts, how could they not? They were much too courteous— or much too scared—to say a word, but they would remember. The next time Tiffany wanted to eat at Sakaki, she knew how polite yet how firm a refusal she would get.

"Hey, look, chill out, okay?" The thought of her impending

ban from a high-class sushi joint like Sakaki got Tiffany's dander up. "I was just double-checking. You can't kill a girl for double-checking."

"I have," Mila replied.

Tiffany decided to let it slide. "So awright, you don't type, you don't take dictation—"

"*No one* dictates to Mila, daughter of Handrad the Magnificent, first swordswoman of—"

"Yeah, yeah, yeah. But you need a job and you don't have any skills. Super. We're screwed."

Mila scowled. "Already? In my land, we have lunch first." Her eyes swept the line of hovering waiters. "Very well, if I must. I'll take the short one with the big nose."

Tiffany managed to grab Mila by the scabbard as she lunged for her chosen man. "Sit *down,* dammit. I didn't mean it that way. Jesus Christ, I wish I could get my hands on the bozo who wished you on us. I'd tighten his nuts for him."

Mila subsided. "I would prefer to cut them off, but if fortune permits me to face the vile Oustrav again, I shall reserve the honor of his nuts for you, Tee-Faan. As for my skills, get me but within sword's reach of Oustrav and you shall see what I can do!"

Tiffany patted Mila's hand in sisterly sympathy. "Honey, I know you're good at what you do, but trust me: There's not much call for castration in entry-level jobs."

The swordswoman appeared to absorb her companion's ineffable wisdom. "Is it so?" Her eyes unsuccessfully fought to contain a fat pair of tears. "Has the scum Oustrav indeed found me a world where all my accomplishments are counted as naught? Alas! Still I hear his evil voice, exulting as I stumbled into his trap. How could I know the meaning of the arcane designs he had gouged into the floorboards of his noisome lair? How could I guess that once within their unholy compass, I was his captive, subject to the terms of the great spell he laid upon me?"

"I dunno," Tiffany admitted. "That's men for you. Wait until you think you know the rules and then they switch the game on you. Here, have some more *sake.*"

Mila belted back the meager contents of the porcelain cup, then chugged hot rice wine straight from the stone decanter. Only the jeweled "slave" bracelets bedizening hand and wrist stopped her from wiping her mouth on her arm.

"Oh, the cunning of the misbegotten fiend!" Mila cried. "He

might not kill me, for I wore the Talisman of Yumph where no man may see it and live—unless I am fond of him—yet he was free to exile me. 'This be your doom, Mila!' he cackled. 'That you must walk an alien world, where you must prove your worth beyond doubt to the inhabitants thereof. Thrice may you attempt to fulfill this condition, but no more. Aye, thrice only, and unless your end-devour is crowned with success—"

"Your *what* is crowned?"

"—unless you gain full *ass*-ken-dansy over your ant'*ago*-nints—"

"Whose ass?"

"—until you may carve out for yourself a nitchy—"

"Neesh!" The secretary fairly bellowed the correction into the swordswoman's face. "What you carve out is a *niche*! Jesus Christ, even *I* know that." Mila might have a blade as long as a walrus' wingle, but Tiffany had her limits. She leaned across the table, chin on palm, and in a more civilly modulated voice said, "That isn't really what he said to you, is it." No question was implied or allowed. "All that high-sounding talk is something you read somewhere, right? Or else you'd know how to pronounce the words better."

Mila gaped, then lowered her head in shame. "The Great She truly works in wondrous ways, to have brought my unworthy self into your wise keeping, Tee-Faan. Yes, it is as you have so correctly divined."

She reached inside her wide swordbelt and produced a folded vellum broadside. Tiffany could not read the strange sigils written thereon, but the page was amply illustrated. A gorgeously gowned woman with excellent upper-body development had her arms around a doe-eyed youth in a silken doublet and filmy harem pants. She was tearing the bodice of it away with her teeth while her captive went into a swoon of ecstasy and full cooperation. In her heart of hearts, Tiffany had the conviction that, if translated, the larger characters across the top of the broadside would read: *Passion's Purple Plaything,* or similar.

Mila retrieved her prized reading material. "What Oustrav really said was that I could come back either after I saw how far I could get on a world where swordswomanship is worth beaver turds—his foul curse granting me just three tries to make good—or when I was ready to perform *pemsquatz* upon his revolting person."

"Pemsquatz?" Tiffany's lovingly brushed and penciled eye-brows rose. "Honey, that's not translating at all."

A deep flush darkened Mila's cheeks. She beckoned the secretary nearer. Tiffany inclined her head above the *sake* cups and Mila whispered a thoroughly detailed, aptly translated description of *pemsquatz* (active, passive, and corporate forms) into her companion's dainty ear.

Tiffany paled. When Mila said, "Of course it must be done differently if the katydids escape, or the sheep is bilious . . ." she excused herself from the table hurriedly.

She returned from the Little Geishas' Room slightly green and shaky, but with enough inner vitality to exclaim: "Ga-*rose!*" She took a supportive belt of *sake* and slammed her cup down with a force of personality behind the gesture to equal Mila's. "*Pemsquatz* my ass!" she declared.

The swordswoman sighed. "For starters, perhaps. But Oustrav has never been one to stop at starters. It is not *pemsquatz* in and of itself I dread—except perhaps the corporate form, as who would not?—but the humiliation that awaits me when I must give in to Oustrav."

"Give in? Uh-*uh!*" Tiffany was in grim earnest. "No way are you going to give Oustrav anything but big, dripping gobs of grief."

Mila nodded slowly. "I have some experience with big, dripping gobs. But we have only three chances, and then"—her voice hoarsened with unaccustomed fear—"*pemsquatz* willy-nilly. So it mote be."

"*I'll* nilly his willy for him, the big bully." The battle-light burned brightly in Tiffany's eyes now. Oustrav might belong to realms and dimensions alien from her own, but she knew the cut of his jib well enough. He was the big ol' spiritual great-granddaddy to Mr. Carlson and his numerous, verminous ilk. Her life thus far had appeared to prescribe a course of judicious appeasement when confronted by members of the opposite sex holding the job market High Country.

And what of her supposed sisters in the ranks? How peculiar. Time and again Tiffany had witnessed the weird skin change that overtook any female who managed to climb out of the primordial ooze of the secretarial pool and evolve lungs and a business suit. They always wound up treating the remaining secretaries worse than did the Carlsons and the Oustravs. At least with a male bully, you got dinner and a movie before you got screwed.

The opportunity to strike back at the bastards would not come soon again. She'd take it while she could—which just about summed up Tiffany's whole life(style) philosophy. The chance for vicarious vengeance rammed right through her pineal gland and made her giddy. "You leave it to me! Mila, you're gonna carve yourself a nitchy in this world like there's no tomorrow, and it won't take anywhere near three stabs to do it. And without getting anything yucky all over your sword, either!"

"Is it so?" The swordswoman's eyes widened with amazement tinged with just the merest hint of hope.

"I'll stake my lifetime subscription to *Cosmo,* it's so," said Tiffany. "*Plus* my supply of Retin-A."

Mila was solemn. "For this promise, Tee-Faan, I and all of my descendants, dependents, apprentice swordswomen, and household toadies shall call you sword-sister to the end of days."

"Super. Just don't call me late for dinner." Tiffany giggled.

JOB ONE.

"Your trapezius," Mischa breathed, his eyes igniting with the unholy flame of obsessive artistry. "I must have it."

"*Mis*ter Colinero!" Tiffany drew herself well out of the client's reach. "I'm not that kind of a girl."

"I can fix that. Airbrushing works wonders." Lithe as a weasel, he slipped around the table, his perfect teeth bared in a wolfish grin.

Tiffany was no friend of wildlife, even when it did have a chest expansion to leave Schwarzenegger looking like a rachitic chicken by comparison. This was business, spelled W-A-R. Before the athletic artist could reach her, she swung her attaché up and back sharply, the way a lesser being might twiddle a switchblade or toy with the safety on an Uzi.

The attaché had brass-bound corners. Mischa Colinero did not. He took the hint and retreated. Feigning abrupt disinterest he asked, "What brings you to my humble atelier, my dear?"

In her best Boardroom Bitch voice, Tiffany replied, "I represent Carlson and Carlson, Perfect Placements. I—my secretary talked to you on the phone about our new modeling agency subsidurry."

"So she did." Mischa turned back to the table and idly picked up a thickly encrusted palette. "It was, I confess, a fortuitous call.

Your discount was quite tempting, and of course I am always looking for fresh . . . talent." He pronounced it *meat*.

"I'm just checking to see how things are working out for you and—uh—" She pummeled her brain, seeking the alias she'd bestowed upon Mila after the office computer barfed when she tried cramming Daughter-of-Handrad-et-cetera down its electronic craw. "Millie Hanks."

Mischa's dynamic nostrils flared prettily. "What can I say? See for yourself." He motioned Tiffany nearer to the work in progress on his easel. When she hesitated, he gallantly assured her that he regarded her trapezius to be as sacred as his own.

The canvas was grandiose in theme and conception, an epic poem to rippling thews, straining sinews, burnished flesh, and minimalist metal fashion. Against a sketchy background of tumbled treasure chests and deceased giant reptiles, Mila loomed supreme. Tiffany stared, speechless. Although the artist had provided his model with a tatty prop shield that looked like a gold-dipped hubcap, everything else about the alien swordswoman was felicitous, apropos, and her very own. At her feet was the incompletely limned figure of a handsome, black-robed man with a complexion like cottage cheese gone bad. His cowering stance suggested a person whose life-style options had been suddenly reduced to Cringe, Grovel, or Die. Even the mystic sigils on his robe seemed to writhe in abject terror.

"Oh, wow," Tiffany breathed. "She's, like, perfect."

"Isn't she." Mischa folded his arms. He didn't sound as happy as he should.

"Is something wrong?"

"Wrong? Nothing. Only I'm afraid I shall have to cancel her contract forthwith, discount or no discount. I'm sure you understand."

"Understand what? If there's nothing wrong—"

"Not a thing, unless you wish to count the loss of my best male model." Mischa sighed dramatically and gestured at the partially painted pseudo-sorcerer. "You told me she was not widely experienced, but I have never dealt with such unprofessional impulses. Not even at science fiction conventions. If she had only waited until his part of the painting was finished! Without him, I'll have to chuck the entire canvas as a dead loss."

Tiffany cast a nervous glance at the oil painting of Mila Rampant. "She didn't *kill* him?"

"Kill him? Why would you think—?" Mischa regarded the canvas, then bestowed a dry, condescending laugh on Tiffany's apparent credulousness. "Really, my dear, just because I illustrate fantasy doesn't mean I *live* it. Eccentric Ms. Hanks may be, but hardly the sort to go about slitting any throat she fancies."

Tiffany, knowing the truth of matters, kept mum. "So then how—?"

Mischa tossed back a tumble of sleek, blue-black hair from his lofty brow. His high cheekbones reddened considerably. He beckoned Tiffany nigh, and whispered discreetly in her ear.

"She did *WHAT*?!"

"If he did not desire my attentions, he should not have dressed in that provocative manner." Mila poked her pasta salad with a callused forefinger and sulked. "He was *asking* for it!"

Tiffany rolled her eyes at the ceiling and for the fifth time explained, "He was in the bathroom, changing from his costume into his street clothes. *With the door locked!* Busting in like that and catching him in his skivvies was no excuse for you ravishing—um—taking advantage of—uh—doing what you—" A weensy frown momentarily twisted her mouth. "How *did* you manage to do that to a man? If he didn't want it, I mean."

Mila shrugged. "Deep down, they all want it. Most thank you for it later. The details are mere philosophy and stage dressing."

"This is not good." Tiffany gnawed one fuchsia fingernail, despite the fact that her manicure was fresher than the arugula on her plate. "That job was *made* for you, and you blew it."

The swordswoman's eyes filled with melancholy. "I know," she said. "It has always been the shame of my family, that we are dragged down by our baser impulses. Was not my blessed mother, Handrad the Magnificent, first swordswoman of Queen Ulioni's Companions, done to death in a tavern brawl over the favors of a common hoochy-boy?" She dashed away a tear. "It was not worth it."

"I guess it wouldn't be," Tiffany said, patting Mila's hand in sympathy.

"I did not even find him to be that great a lay, after. Still"—she brightened—"it *did* get me that promotion in the Companions."

Tiffany withdrew her hand and made a silent promise to call her mother more often.

* * *

JOB TWO.

Tiffany lay on her belly across the front seat of her Hyundai and cautiously raised her head to peer out the side window.

"I do not see why you refuse to let me defend myself with honor," Mila grumbled from beneath the pile of dry cleaning in the backseat.

"Shh!" Tiffany ducked back down. "There's still one of them circling the block." It was hard to whisper with a mouth furry from fear.

"She is not even armed!" Mila had no more qualms about raising her voice than she did about raising her sword. The blade impaled Tiffany's best rayon skirt, the point wrapped and tangled in the Kut-Rate Kleeners plastic bag. It looked like some amok Freudian adman's creative concept for a Safe Sex campaign.

"I said *shhh*! She doesn't need weapons." Tiffany stole another peek at the grimly pacing figure in front of the Cheerful Chipmunk Childcare Center. "She's a mother."

As they waited for the lady in question to tire of her search and go home, Tiffany had more than enough leisure to review her latest bad judgment call. It all came of minimalist thinking. If Mila had no acquired skills to make her a job-market catch, surely she must possess some *congenital* quality that could be exploited for hire? And what profession was it that all women were born for?

Tiffany made her suggestion.

"What?" Mila's hand clenched the hilt of her sword automatically, tiny sparks glimmering between her grinding teeth. "After what I have told you of *pemsquatz*, you would suggest that I, Mila, Daughter of Handrad et cetera, lower myself into the abyss of degradation, sell my soul for the tawdriest of returns, drag my spirit through the noxious slime and stinking offal of the common gutter by accepting such—such—*pah!* I will not even dignify it by calling it employment."

"Jesus, you'da thought I was asking you to turn tricks!" Tiffany protested.

"Turn—?"

"Hook. Whore. Mattress dance for money."

"Hmmm." For an instant, Mila misplaced her anger. "Now, *there's* a possibility, only . . . No, no. One of my clients might request *pemsquatz,* and then I would have to cut off his *slobasuks* and beat him to death with them." Her ruminations ceased as her eyebrows whip-snapped back into their initial scowl. "Whelp-tending," she sneered.

"Child-care," Tiffany amended. "Everyone knows women are perfect for a job like this. It's instinct, you know? Like being able to tell if the guy's lying when he says he's not married. I just happened to hear from my old friend Doris that the place she farms out her rug-rats is real shorthanded and *desperate*. Okay, so it's in Brooklyn, but you'll get over it. You'll just be an aide. Who needs a degree to see that the kids drink their milk and eat their cookies? We'll find you a decent outfit for the interview and you'll be in like Flynn."

"Then let Flynn mind the fucking brats," Mila growled. But Tiffany hung in there, wheedling for all she was worth, and at last her persuasive talents triumphed.

Now, huddled in the Hyundai, she wondered whether she were perhaps *too* good a salesperson. "Everything was going so good. How'd you manage to screw up this time?"

"I was doing my *job*." Mila made the word sound like a lower invertebrate. "In truth, it was not quite so revolting as I initially feared. These children were different from the ones I knew back home, at least so far as drool, snot, other excretions, and general level of vermin infestation was concerned. There was something almost appealing about the little buggers."

Peeping through the break between the two front seats, Tiffany saw that Mila's eyes were growing misty. "I guess you like kids after all, huh?"

The mist burned off at once. "In collops. But for those miserable beasts, I would still be employed, and on my way to throwing Oustrav's failure in his teeth!" Her passions were too much for the dry cleaning to contain and the warrior woman sat bolt upright.

"*There she is!* There's the creature who corrupted my little Ashley!" The woman on the sidewalk froze in mid-pace and began gesticulating wildly. The bright red door of the Cheerful Chipmunk Childcare Center burst open and a horde of her sisters in maternal outrage spilled into the street. Behind them came an obstreperous passel of preschoolers, looking no different from any of a thousand other such groups. They were smiling, gleefully untidy, manically energetic, boisterous, rebellious, and merrily determined to get their own way no matter what.

Their unique nature became apparent when the casual observer saw that every single one of them was armed to the teeth: small socks weighted at the toe with God-knows-what collection of heavy objects to make improvised blackjacks; Tinkertoys and Erector sets forged into any number of stabbing and jabbing configurations; rubber bands and marbles used for long-distance aggression; safety scissors broken into their component halves, the edges whetted sharp, and plastic rulers snapped in two, the better to take full advantage of the resulting jagged points.

One extraordinarily creative tot had made a catapult out of Lego blocks and was using it to lob the disembodied heads of Barbie dolls deep into the enemy ranks.

The enemy was by definition any mother or caregiver fool enough to suggest that the children cease this fascinating new game and come home.

Tiffany saw no choice but flight. She wrenched the ignition key and gunned the Hyundai out of there, taking out her right headlight on the left taillight of the car parked in front of her. As they raced away, Mila stuck her head out the window and shouted, "The Great She be with you, you mangy urchins! And Mila's thanks for paying so much attention to me during Show and Tell!"

"Keep the dress *on,* I said." Tiffany grabbed Mila's hand and yanked her into the restaurant. "As long as Carlson's got me on an expense account, we're going to soak him for plenty. This place costs a zillion dollars plus your grandma's virginity, but I'm hungry and he's paying."

"My grandmother—" Mila began.

"I don't want to hear about it. And *stop* tweaking at your hem."

"I can't help it." The warrior woman had lost some of her ginger. She was no math whiz, but she could count to three and the fact had just come home to her that she had one—count it—one chance left to overcome Oustrav at his own game. She was almost whining when she said, "I'm not used to having so much cloth between my hand and my sword."

"I'd put a goddamn wall between you and that blade if I could," Tiffany replied. "Now sit down, shut up, and eat."

First, though, they had to order. Their waiter was the chirpy sort. "Hi, I'm Brad! Our specials today are blackened redfish, venison pâté, and roast Long Island duckling with pink pepper-corn sauce." He tossed a cottony candytuft of blond hair out of his eyes and delivered his wine recommendation in the voice most advertisers reserve for their feminine hygiene product commercials.

Mila ordered foreskins on toast and he went away.

Freed from the presence of Glynda the Good Waiter of the North, the ladies got down to business. That is to say, Tiffany announced, "We're screwed," and Mila broke down and cried.

It was pretty shocking. Tiffany had been expecting curses, threats, even a little crockery-smashing. Instead, Mila just put her head down in the whole-wheat rolls and sobbed.

"Gee, honey, don't have a cow." Tiffany patted Mila's hand and wished to heaven the swordswoman would stick a cork in it. People were looking, not even bothering to pretend it was an accidental glance. Since this eatery was the fifth most expensive in New York, they figured it was safe to risk eye contact. It was all goddamn embarrassing. "We still have one more chance. This time I'm gonna really think hard about it and—"

"Can you not understand, Tee-Faan?" Mila lifted her head and honked like a croupy seal. "The insidious wiles of Oustrav will not be gainsaid. Well does he know how dearly I seek to avoid all possibility of *pemsquatz* with him. Thrice must I fail to find gainful employment in this, my exile, else he has me. Think, Tee-Faan! If I fail twice, how might I most certainly avoid a third cock-up?"

Tiffany thought. She also passed Mila a pack of Kleenex. Eventually she concluded, "If you don't try the third time, you can't fail and he can't get you. Jesus, that's a loophole the size of Godzilla's asshole." She looked at Mila. "He plugged it, huh?"

Mila nodded. "To the hilt. I did not wish to tell you ere this. I feared the added burden of a time limit would hurry you into poor decisions. Alack, it no longer matters. The full terms of Oustrav's curse conclude that I must find my place in your world either within three tries or by midnight of the day sacred to my birth."

"The day—? You mean your birthday?" Again Mila nodded, and her expression left Tiffany with the uneasy yet positive feeling that it was much too late to do any shopping for the occasion. "And that day is—today?"

Mila howled.

Brad came skimming over with their salads. "Is something wrong, ladies?" He gave the sniveling swordswoman a look that diagnosed her condition as PMS with a pinch of Manhattan psychosis thrown in to make it interesting.

"Woe!" Mila bellowed at the ceiling fans. "This very day was I born!"

"Oh," said Brad, cocking his head to one side in that beguiling way which was guaranteed to sell many, many bottles of men's liquid grooming aids if he ever got out of this dumb temporary job waiting tables and back to modeling which was his *real* calling; after acting, of course. He walked off with a determined mien which the bawling Mila did not notice but which Tiffany did. She was no ace at drawing conclusions, but plain city instinct warned her that a waiter-with-a-mission was to be regarded as charily as a pit bull with a wagging tail.

And lo, so it mote be, as Mila would put it. For just as Tiffany was on the point of suggesting that Mila try to make an optimistic list of all the *positive* qualities a purely *pemsquatz*-based relationship might have to offer ("Lust Is My Copilot," *FEMALE! Magazine,* September 1990), Brad returned with their entrees. He was accompanied by three of his lithesome cohorts. All four of them flexed, preened, and shot smiles at any diners who looked even marginally likely to be connected with the modeling or entertainment fields, then cleared their throats and—

"Oh, no," Tiffany whimpered.

Oh yes indeed.

"Happy birthday to you! Happy birthday to you! Happy birthday, dearrrrr—?" One waiter gave Tiffany an inquiring look while the others held on to the note for dear life.

"Mila," she whispered. Tiffany's knuckles were white as she clutched the edge of the table and watched her dining companion. At the first sweet burst of song, the barbarian swordswoman had raised her head like a wolf scenting the nearest Hopelessly Crippled Old Mooses' Home. Tiffany knew the End of the World when she saw it coming.

"Meee-laaaaaaaaaaa!" the waiters warbled. "Happy birthday toooo yooooooooooooouuuuuuu." They beamed when the other diners applauded.

Mila's chair scraped back one inch; no more. Oblivious, the waiters returned to their stations. Mila watched them go, lower lip firmly clamped between her teeth. Her bosom rose and fell to the tempo of a funeral march. There was a hot, opaque quality to her eyes. Something dire was most definitely pending.

This was not the optimum time for Brad to return with a

peppermill the size of a Percheron's leg and brightly ask, "So, the big three-o?"

Mila's sword tore its way through her dress and still had enough momentum left to sever the peppermill in twain. Peppercorns like organic buckshot arced forth, clattering down into the plates of all nearby.

"Swine," Mila gritted, allowing the tip of her blade to dribble playfully down Brad's shirtfront until it reached the top of his fly and paused, awaiting further orders. "Where I come from, we have ways of dealing with men who ask a lady's age. For this base mockery of my plight, you shall pay!"

There was a loud rustling as the other patrons hastily flipped up their menus, fixed their eyes on their meals, or feverishly consulted their Week-at-a-Glance daily planner, all this without acting as if anything untoward were happening. Acknowledging imminent mayhem was one step away from becoming that most endangered of species, an urban witness. Brad rolled his eyes like a horse with a spring of holly under its tail, but his fellow waiters were equally busy pretending that the only thing about to be skewered in their restaurant was the orange roughy *en brochette.*

"Please, please don't hurt me!" Brad blubbered, wringing his hands. "At least nowhere visible."

Mila's lip curled in scorn. Unfortunately, her stay on this world had evoked so many uses of that contemptuous grimace that she promptly got a cramp which froze her mouth into a pretty good Elvis impression. On her, it looked silly.

This was not the wisest time for the pudgy suburban matron at the legendary table-by-the-kitchen-door to look up, behold, and get the giggles. Tiffany heard the titter and cringed. Mila heard too. Her ice-cold eyes passed over the entire population of the eatery, seeking the guilty party.

"I am about to have the freedom of my body abrogated by a despicable and noxious creature," she informed the assemblage, her voice chill and bitter. "He means to subjugate me not because he so craves my obvious physical attractions, but simply because it is within his power to compel what love may freely request. He intends to conquer and possess me as if I were a *thing* which has captured his fancy, not a *person,* with her own wishes and desires. All this awaits me momentarily, with a life of utter and total sexual enslavement and personal degradation that shall shatter my spirit and break my pride. *And you laugh?*"

The silence was awesome. Not awesome enough, though. From her table in the Outer Darkness the suburban lady rose up, leveled a finger at the swordswoman, and bleated, "Are you one of those libbers?"

That was when Mila threw the first bowl of cioppino. Followed by a chair. Followed by one of her pet daggers. "Swine!" she bellowed. "Crow-leavings! You are unworthy of a quick death by honest steel!"

"Then what's this? *Pâté de foie gras?*" the housewife gasped, pointing at her double helping of Chocolate Decadence, now pinned to the table by the aforementioned dagger.

"Bronze doesn't count, sow," Mila replied, and sheathing her sword, she lunged for an unattended Caesar salad-making cart. The first-strike capabilities of anchovies were about to be put to the test. A fresh, unsevered peppermill fairly leaped into the swordswoman's hand, a bludgeon with which to reckon. The *maître d'* groaned as he realized that Doom needs no reservations.

Still, each crisis makes its own cowards and heroes. The waiters grabbed trays and improvised a shieldwall to protect the heavy tippers. Brad dove for cover. Those few diners nearest the exits used them, including the suburban *Frau* who beat it into the kitchen. Those customers cut off from retreat set up a brave counterattack using whatever was to hand. Roast Long Island ducklings achieved flight in the afterlife. Tofu took a grim toll. Delicately sauteed milk-fed lamb chops presented with a bouquet of lightly steamed seasonal baby vegetables and a raspberry *coulis* hit the fan.

Tiffany didn't want to see culino-military history in the making. Her dry-cleaning bill was big enough already. She slipped inconspicuously to the floor, and from under the peach-flounced tablecloth heard Mila taking out her pre-*pemsquatz* frustrations on anyone within reach. Screams, shrieks, and the sound of shattering glass and china formed a series of constant, gentle suggestions that Tiffany remain right where she was.

"Spirited wench, isn't she?" said the gnarled old man beside her. He had not been there a moment ago. In fact, Tiffany could not recall having seen anyone like him in the restaurant before Mila's little snit.

"Hey! How did you get under here?"

"I have my arcane ways."

"I don't care what kind of cane you use; find your own table," Tiffany sniped.

"Oh, I'd like to," the old man answered. "I suppose this is one of those worlds where you have to be escorted to a seating place by a snotty minion?"

"Headwaiter, yeah." Tiffany squinted at him. It was difficult to see, what with the tablecloth and the slowly accumulating pile of bodies cutting off what little light sneaked in under the hem, but on second glance the old man didn't seem to be all that old. His hair and beard were a little grizzled at the edges, but both were elegantly clipped. This was the hallmark of no common barber, no ordinary hairdresser or *coiffeur;* this 'do was pricey enough to have been the work of an Executive Individual Hispidotechnologist. His hands were long, the fingers thin and perfectly manicured, each one adorned by one or more thick gold rings. Emeralds, rubies, and diamonds glowed with their own inner light even in the sub-table gloom. Tiffany had made a part-time study of the Seven Warning Signs of Cash (*INDULGE! Magazine*, February 1988) and this guy had them all. Even the strange smoky-spicy cologne he affected was probably called Liquid Assets. It smelled like money burning a hole in someone's pocket.

Or was that brimstone? Tiffany sneezed.

"May the Seven Underfed Demons of Bangrak's Abyss not tear your soul out of your nostrils and carry it away with them," he said politely.

If that was his version of *"Gesundheit,"* Tiffany knew that a formal introduction was not going to be necessary after all. "Mr. Oustrav?"

The wizard blinked, taken aback. "Why, yes. How do you know my name?"

Tiffany gave him her most bewitching smile and tried real hard not to get any drool on his jewelry. "Oh, I have my own, uh, whatyousaid-cane ways."

A blue-white light flared at the tips of Oustrav's fingers. By its radiance, Tiffany saw that he wore a lush, heavy-handed blue silk gown embroidered with gold and silver signs of cosmic significance. (Maybe not the cosmos that daily told Tiffany she was about to Meet New Friends and Tread Warily with Regard to Financial Matters, but a star is a star.) Thoughts of taking him shopping for a decent suit (and maybe just one itsy-witsy designer original dress for Tiffi-wiffi, hmmm?) set up a fearsome jangle in the tender young cash register of her heart.

"Speak, child," Oustrav said. "Do not fear to tell me all." He didn't sound like a debauched, *pemsquatz*-obsessed fiend; more like a kindly grandfather.

The clangor of battle on the other side of the tablecloth was dying down a mite, so Tiffany spoke quickly and to the point. She finished by saying, "I guess you've come to collect on the deal, huh?"

Oustrav nodded. "A bargain is a bargain. Her time has elapsed. Hm. It sounds as if Mila is about done out there." He reached for the edge of the tablecloth.

"So are you gonna do it the way with the sheep or the way with the three cabbages and an acrobat in mufti?"

Oustrav dropped the tablecloth and fell back with a horrified gasp. "You *know* of—of—of—?"

"Pemsquatz?" She saw him wince. "Well, yeah. Some."

"Knowing this, you can even speak of the cabbages without— without—?" He did an elaborate pantomime of being violently ill.

Tiffany shrugged coyly. "I gotta admit, when Mila first told me, I did sort of toss my tortillas. But after, when I got to thinking about it . . . You ever actually *try* the corporate form? I mean, I once read this article in *Responsive Woman* that told about this really incredible new position that sounds an awful lot like it and it's guaranteed to give the woman at least seven simultaneous— or was that subsequent?—anyway seven *guaranteed* . . ."

It was some time later that Tiffany became aware that the katydids had escaped. Someone was nudging her in the shoulder with a sandaled foot. Through a mighty pleasant haze she heard Mila exhorting her to come forth and rejoice amain. Tiffany feared that if she rejoiced any further, her spine would turn into a strand of loosely strung worry beads, but she managed to crawl back into the daylight. Oustrav remained hidden, not so much out of fear as of exhaustion.

It went without saying that the restaurant was a shambles— albeit a high-fiber, low-cholesterol, heart-smart shambles. In the midst of devastation, Mila stood like the statue of some proud conqueror, dollops of meringue, custard, and whipped cream taking the place of pigeon droppings.

She did not stand alone. By her side, one arm about her waist, was a dashing young man wearing a suit now jointly designed by Armani and Betty Crocker.

"Behold, Tee-Faan!" Mila exulted. "Behold the one strong and cunning enough to best Mila in single combat!"

"It was nothing," he said. "I just happened to be seated near the dessert trolley, that's all."

"Is he not wonderful?" Mila demanded. "The modest ones are usually the best in bed, too. But he is more than that! He has saved me from the clutches of the vile Oustrav by promising me gainful employment as well."

"Doing what?" Tiffany asked, although her recent experience turned every vowel she uttered into a diphthong.

"Executive manager in charge of permanent personnel association terminations and immediate workplace relocations," the man told her. Grinning like a love-struck shark, he translated: "Hatchetman. Woman. Person. Whatever, she's perfect for the job, and she starts *right now*. Anyone with the *cojones* to make a waiter leave you alone with that goddamn peppermill is someone my company needs!"

"Is that what you like best about me, Mila's little snuggie-dragon?" the swordswoman wheedled, plucking bits of watercress from his hair. "My *cojón*-wonies?"

Tiffany was still making gagging noises when Mila pounded her on the back and said, "I owe you thanks. My neesh is secure, my body my own, Oustrav's curse impotent."

"Oh, I wouldn't say—"

"Nay, speak not. I shall find the means to repay you. I am in no hurry to leave this world now." She gave her new plaything a carnivorous glance. "I shall have my people call your people. The Great She ordains that we shall do lunch!"

"Okay, I guess." Tiffany did not sound overly enthusiastic. "Only you won't be able to reach me at Carlson and Carlson anymore."

"Is it so?" Mila's brows rose. "You quit?"

Tiffany licked her lips. "Let's just say I have finally, uh"—she cudgeled her brains for the exact wording of the *SEIZE! Magazine* article on self-restructuring, remodeling, redirecting, and telling the boss to shove it—"discovered and actualized the true depths of my professional careerpath employment potential."

"Oh," said Mila. "You quit."

*   *   *

The office intercom buzzed, interrupting Tiffany's perusal of the crossword puzzle. "Ms. Mila of Microtechnocybertronics Inc., on line two," the receptionist said. "She's terminated another dozen software engineers and wants you to know she referred them to our agency. Will you take the call?"

"Have her hold a sec, Dawn, honey." Tiffany set down her puzzle and thought hard. Another *dozen*? The fees they'd collect for finding those diskette jockeys new jobs would be fat ones, but still, a dozen? Good thing that Oustrav and Oustrav, Perfect Placements, was so very good at knowing what to do with wizards, computer or otherwise. Mila probably thought she was doing her old pal Tee-Faan a favor. She'd have to be told to slow down.

Which message Tiffany would deliver just as soon as she finished up this puzzle. There was only one clue left: "Eight-letter word for state of bliss, extreme felicity or delight. Begins with a P." She touched the pencil point to her tongue, then wrote P-E-M-S-Q-U-A-T-Z. She had to cram two letters in one space and hardly any of the others besides the initial P fit with those already on the grid, but she knew what she knew.

How well she knew, how very, very well . . .

The Final Apprentice

by
Steve Rasnic Tem

And so to bed. With what profound cogitation, I mused, should I finalize this tome? With what abstruse speculation should I conclude? How can I best serve you, the reader, in your perpetual and unending quest to improve, enlighten, and otherwise raise up your querulous self? As fellow participants in what recondite epic shall we turn together the last pages of this folio, for which some transitory, straight-boled, cellulose life-form on a pulp farm in south Georgia has sacrificed the sum total of its brief existence?

Aw heck. Or as Margaret Ball and Greg Costikyan might say, piffle! Peruse the following, which shall be last.

Then go out, rent Sullivan's Travels, *make some popcorn, and laugh yourselves stupid.*

The tiny creature struggled mightily between the narrow arms of Andrew's forceps. With a slight tremble in his pudgy hand Andrew held the magnifying glass for his apprentice to see (again his final apprentice was reminded of the great age of this, the last wizard of the world, semi-retired). "There boy—identify that one for me."

Apprentice (still wearing "the horns of befuddlement" Andrew had awarded him the week before) sidled slowly over and bobbed his head dumbly like a reluctant steer at a Texas barbecue. He draped one bloodshot eye over the glass. "Ummm . . . ummm."

"I'm waiting, Apprentice."

"Well . . . he's approximately two inches high, I'd say. His coat is covered with several dozen patches of bright colors. His face is withered, wrinkled, a lost, panicked look to the eyes . . ." He straightened suddenly. "I swear, Master Andrew, Lord of the Pierced Earrings, Enchanter of the Fifteen Speedy Laundrettes, Vizier to the Sweaty But . . ."

"Apprentice, *please* . . ."

"Oh . . . well, he appears to resemble the former president."

Andrew shook his head. "All presidents look like that once they're out of office. It's all the acrobatics, I hear. But his identity, Apprentice? Of what species is this particular elf?"

Again Apprentice leaned over the glass. By now his breath had quite fogged it, but he did not dare tell Andrew this. He absently stroked his horns. "Massariol?"

"Apprentice! Massariol come a foot high with red knee socks!"

"Ummm . . . ummm. Salvanel? Bwbach?"

"Apprentice!" Andrew's great beard unfurled in anger. He took a sudden step toward him in his baggy green overalls.

"Barabao? Giane? Follet?"

"Apprentice!" Andrew's beard curled and uncurled like a party horn.

"Kobolde? Pixie? Rutabaga? Republican?" Andrew started swinging his arms in rage, the magnifying glass in one hand, the elf-between-forceps in the other. "Castanet? Calliope? Kristofferson?" Andrew started chasing Apprentice around the room, the horns of befuddlement catching on beaker stands and distillation tubes and pulling it all crashing down. "Diehard? Veg-o-Matic? Energizer?" Andrew threw up his arms and the magnifying glass wedged into one eye socket like a monocle. "Brassier? Brisket? Bluebird? Brownie?" The elf-between-forceps flew end over end and landed with a tiny but fruitful thud. "Magpie? Mistress? Misogyny?" Apprentice had no opportunity to avoid it. "Diaphra . . ." *SPLAGG!* And suddenly Apprentice's feet had left him and were flying south for the winter.

Andrew attempted to follow them but couldn't quite attain departure speed, his own feet snared by the horns of befuddlement which, for the first time, he regretted having given his apprentice. Suddenly he was draping Apprentice like a rug woven by Persian opium addicts.

Avoiding eye contact with his all-powerful mentor, Apprentice poked a finger into the sticky mess in his right palm and stirred it. "Of course!" he cried. "It's a Portune! And here I thought they were extinct!"

Apprentice mopped the specimen room wearing the long, tattered "ears of the hopeless" (the horns of befuddlement were currently keeping his boss the last wizard Andrew entertained—even now he could hear from down the corridor the hatchet ringing off those noble branches of bone, punctuated by his master's shouts of glee). An open copy of *The Field Guide to Elves, Dwarves, and Others of Abbreviated Stature* hung suspended from a stiff wire that curved over his head and attached to the back of his collar. He had to turn the pages with his tongue. He observed that the colored illustrations tasted not unlike his mother's home-baked matzo. So Apprentice mopped and read and toiled with tears in his eyes, now and again pausing to wipe his nose with one ragged, hopeless ear.

"Hey, burro-head, got a match?"

Apprentice looked warily at the row of cages lining the far wall. Leprechauns, Goat People, Fountain Women . . . all the bigger types were quartered there. Then he noticed the one who had spoken to him: fiery red eyes and eagle-taloned fingers, protruding teeth and that unmistakable red cap. Like one of Santa's elves the day after the Christmas Eve keg party.

He wasn't supposed to speak to the Red Caps. Ever. "Fairy-punks," Andrew called them. They lived only in places with a history of violence, like fortified castles or discount stores. They dropped great stones on the salesmen who came to their doors and dyed their caps with the blood. And on top of that they wouldn't even return their victims' sample cases. Their filthy chambers were littered with desk calendars and ballpoint pens. They also could foretell disasters by making a loud noise like three cats Scotch-taped to the vanes of a ceiling fan (as part of his home-study course in wizardry Apprentice had tried this out just so that he might recognize the sound—now and then his pets still thanked him for this experience with small aromatic gifts left in his sock drawer).

The Red Caps were a sturdy, gray, and exceedingly cranky breed of elf.

"Come on, kid. Bloody hell. I'm dyin' in here."

Apprentice could see that the nasty-looking creature had at least seven or eight cigarettes shoved into his wide, tooth-studded maw. "Don't you know that besides being bad for you, smoking is terribly out of fashion now?"

"Bloody hell. We Red Caps are from the British Isles. Scottish, mostly." The Red Cap wiggled his heavy eyebrows. The cigarettes bobbed up and down like albino porcupine quills piercing his lips.

"*Oh . . .*" Comprehension dawned so unfamiliarly across Apprentice's face he had an urge to run and wash it off. Then he frowned. "No. I'm not supposed to talk to you. I'm in enough trouble already."

"Is this the way you treat a guest? No towels, no little soaps, no mints on the pillow?"

Apprentice patted his pockets. "I've got a little piece of Baby Ruth here somewhere . . . it's a little linty . . . er . . . the lint is probably green . . ." He wrestled not to look confused and lost the match. "But you're a prisoner."

"Iron bars do not a prison . . . oh, forget it. What's your name, kid?"

"Apprentice."

"I didn't ask you what you did for a living."

"No . . . Apprentice."

"Funny name to give a kid, even one with long ears."

"My mother had very definite vocational plans for me."

"Mothers are like that. Unrealistic. It can be pretty traumatic for a kid. Mine wanted me to be a Boston Celtic."

"Is that like a Druid?"

"Forget it, kid. Don't strain your ears. What's that book you got?"

"An identification manual, for you little people."

"That's very politically correct of you. I bet in private you refer to us as *shrimpy bastards* or *elven scum,* right?" Apprentice did his best to look indignant. "What's the matter? Stomachache?" Apprentice buried his face in his guidebook, stroking the pages with his tongue (and wincing at another paper cut), pretending to read. "You should try that with some ketchup."

"We're collecting you, I suppose you know that." Apprentice peered around the edge of the book, looking for the Red Cap's reaction.

"Yeah, I figured. I used to collect you big guys, but I had a problem finding large enough jars."

Apprentice leaned forward on his mop, then struggled to remove the handle from one nostril. "Thish ismot . . . *ah* . . . this isn't something to joke about, you know. Master Andrew, Keeper of the Jerusalem Stringball, Protector of the Westminster Pail, Litigant in the Superior Court of the State of New York, Finder of Lost Loves, er, and many other things too numerous to mention in this particular bit of dialogue, is the world's last remaining wizard and I am his final apprentice and it is our task now that magic grows old-fashioned and passé to capture every last remaining sprite and elf of whatever stripe . . . er, *some* of you are striped, I'm sure of it . . ." He fumbled uselessly with his guidebook. " . . . after which time there will be no more magic or fantasy to . . . well, to confuse the issue."

"He, this Andrew-of-the-tortured-explanation, *he* taught you this?"

"Er . . . yes."

"And what, pray tell, is to replace magic and elves in this new world order?"

"Well, *science,* of course, and domestic services. That sort of thing. Of course, we already *have* science—rockets and electricity and gravity and all that stuff—but so many people still believe in magic and fairies and other superstitions things. Master Andrew says science doesn't work as well as it ought to and so now it's time to get rid of all that other stuff and as the world's last wizard the responsibility has fallen to him and it's a lousy job but the benefits aren't so bad."

"Bloody hell, I'm a *superstition*?"

"Well, you have to admit you *do* look like one."

The Red Cap nodded as if in grudging agreement. He wiggled his cigarettes again. Apprentice was amazed at the elf's talent. *He* could never have talked so clearly around that many cigarettes and protruding teeth. "Your Master Andrew wears green overalls."

"He's preparing for a life after magic. He's been taking a correspondence course in Electronics and Small Appliance Repair. He says green overalls are a more fitting uniform for the new age."

"His green overalls are baggy. They're not 'fitting' at all."

"Master Andrew says comfort in the seat area helps him to think."

"He *must* be in control of a powerful magic, if he hasn't broken down and turned you into a doorstop yet."

Andrew thought this might be the famous Red Cap sarcasm he'd heard so much about, but wanted to see the elf's face to make sure. He moved his head to the side quickly, hoping to get a better look at the Red Cap, but the book sprang immediately to partially block his view. He jerked his head back and forth several times in this manner, until finally the book shot back violently and slapped him in the face. "I'mb sborry," he mumbled through his bleeding nose. "That bwas siblly."

"Your Master Andrew doesn't look like much of a wizard to me."

Apprentice was seriously offended, a difficult feat to manage with a bloody nose. "How can you say that?"

"He's, well, a bit on the chubby side for a wizard, isn't he?"

"He likes chocolates. He says they help him focus."

"Well, Mr. Accessory . . ."

"Apprentice."

"Everybody knows you should never trust a fat wizard. It shows he's been spending more time with the cakes and custards than with his studies. They say the more rib that shows, the wiser the wizard." By logical progression, of course, this meant that the wisest wizards were the dead ones, but Apprentice said nothing. After all, the Red Cap's teeth *were* sharp. "*You,* at least, study hard, I hope."

Apprentice casually reached up and rubbed from his chin the white sugar left over from his late morning snack. "Hard as a Poltersprite."

"Ah, they just like to make noise. A wizard has to be more than that. A wizard is a self-starter like, well, like a pig on hot asphalt."

Apprentice blushed. His master had told him this very thing many times. Apprentice himself was not so enterprising. Sometimes it was necessary to light a fire under his feet, and in fact oftentimes Master Andrew had cheerfully obliged. But the blisters felt much better now. "Master Andrew always says mosquitoes would make great wizards—that is, if they weren't so small and if they weren't insects and if they didn't die so quickly and all . . ."

"A wizard has to be forceful, determined," the Red Cap continued, "and bondable. To the talented wizard, nothing can ever be totally unexpected, except perhaps finding a chicken with decent athletic ability."

Here, the evil imp had hit a sore point. Many had been the hours Master Andrew had laughed out loud while perusing this very same volume, and yet he selfishly refused to underline the good parts for Apprentice.

Apprentice raised his hand, dropping the mop handle. "Wizards know how to *transubstantiate*! Oh, they're *big* on that. You know, base metal into gold, water into wine, vast forests into knickknack shelves, that sort of thing . . ."

"A wizard understands everything about spirits and their doings. He knows their abilities, their tricks, their secret savings accounts. A good wizard can play a spirit like Eric Clapton plays guitar, although perhaps with a little more bass."

"Oh, and don't forget their knack for finding magical objects: amulets, lamps, swords, crotchless panties, potions . . ."

"They tend to be loners. Now, occasionally they might attend an office party, but they always leave before those funny games with the photocopier begin . . ." The Red Cap stopped. "You know, I *like* you, kid."

Apprentice looked down, embarrassed. Not only because unsolicited expressions of endearment made him shy, but because he had just discovered he had one foot wedged inside his mop bucket. "Well . . . maybe you Red Caps aren't so bad, either." He tittered softly.

"How about that match, then? You know me . . . I'm not going to *bite*." The Red Cap laughed, too vigorously it seemed. But Apprentice made himself laugh too.

"Sh-sh-sure. Why not?" Apprentice walked over to the cage, lit a lint-encrusted match that had been resting in his pocket for years it seemed, and lit each of the Red Cap's cigarettes in turn.

"Apprentice?"

"Yes, Mr. Red Cap, sir?"

"You just lit three of my teeth."

"Oh, sorry . . ."

The Red Cap leaned back against his cell wall, sighing, blowing smoke, and wincing from the pain, although not necessarily in that order. "By the way . . . did your Master Andrew explain to you how, after he collects us all, he's going to get rid of the various members of fairydom?"

"Well, not exactly."

"Guns or poison, probably."

"Oh! Of course not!"

"Bloody hell. Sounds like a little fairycide to me, leprechaun-lynching, dwarf-butchery, coup de gnome. Many names, but the results are always the same."

"Never! Never!"

"Well, enough of *my* problems. You have your studies to complete, right? Read me a little from your guidebook. After all, I *can't* know *everybody*."

Apprentice ventured to formulate a studious expression, but as in most of his attempts to strike a particular pose, he looked to be in the throes of indigestion. "Well, let's see, there's the Giane from Sardinia. Wood spirits with long breasts who occupy themselves with spinning and memorizing soup can labels. Despite their talents they have difficulty finding dates on the weekends."

"Maybe if they memorized the sports page . . ."

"It says here they sing sweet lullabies in their caves to men who fall in love with legumes and are brokenhearted when these haughty legumes refuse to wear the lingerie the men have ordered specially for them from mail-order houses in California."

The Red Cap nodded sagely. "The Giane have lost all interest in normal sexual relations, I hear, nine of ten greatly preferring animal husbandry."

"Then you know them?"

"Not intimately. I assume you've captured these creatures?"

"They're in the back playing poker with the goat people."

"Then I hope it isn't too friendly a game. What's in it for you, anyway, 'Prentice?"

"I get to become the next wizard, after."

"After what?"

"After all the magic is gone."

"Isn't that a little like being made captain of the ship after it's been left permanently in dry dock?"

"It's not all magic, being a wizard, you know."

"Enlighten me."

"Wizards get to know things. I like knowing things. Master Andrew, Grand Dragon of Small Appliance Maintenance and Repair, is learning all about televisions, radios, microwaves, that sort of thing. I'd like to know things like that. I'd like to know anything, Mr. Red Cap."

The elf looked at the guidebook in Apprentice's hand. "You know your elf and fairy families, or at least you're *working* on it."

"But what good is that going to do?" Apprentice blushed. "I'm sorry, Mr. Red Cap, but all you folks are going to be gone soon. Remember science? Maintenance and repair?"

The Red Cap smiled, his countless huge teeth practically exploding up out of his gums. "Bloody hell, Apprentice. I have an idea."

"Apprentice! Apprentice, where are you?" Master Andrew splashed across the wet floor. He had been unable to find his assistant anywhere. And worse, all their specimens were gone, every last variety of dwarf, fairy, elf had vanished. "Oh, damn!"

He didn't really care all that much, actually. It was a new world out there. There was no place for a fairy kingdom anymore. They had lost their ecological niche. He and Apprentice had been feeding and sheltering most of them for years. They wouldn't be able to last more than a few days on their own.

He stopped and stared at the counter that ran across the back of the room. All the cages for the smaller sprites had been removed and the space had been filled with a variety of electronic gear instead. Upon closer examination he discovered they were some of the televisions, stereos, home computers, CD players, and VCRs from his shop upstairs, the ones he hadn't yet been able to figure out how to repair. They were all plugged in to the strip of outlets above the counter.

He walked up to a stereo and turned it on. Beautiful, almost unearthly music flooded the chamber.

He flipped on a TV. Cowboys rode across an endless range of variegated browns, a sunset of reds, blues, and greens sweeping the background.

He pushed a button and the computer beeped into life. He poked and stroked VCR and CD player controls. Lights blinked. Motors whirred smoothly.

"They're all in perfect working order, sir," Apprentice said behind him.

Master Andrew turned to his apprentice, who wore identical green overalls to his own. "Very impressive, Apprentice," he said. "I didn't even know you were studying such things."

"I . . . I seem to have a natural affinity for the work."

"Yes . . ." Master Andrew gazed about at the happily humming machinery, filling the air with the warm aroma of electrified chips, diodes, and resistors. "Very impressive. There are more upstairs . . . I'll bring them down to you straightaway." He started toward the staircase, then turned. "The fairies, Apprentice? The elves? What did you do with them all?"

Apprentice smiled and laughed softly. "Never-never land, boss. Never-never land." Then he winked.

Master Andrew laughed with him. "Ah, yes, never-never land. I didn't think you had it in you, Apprentice." Then he climbed the stairs.

Apprentice went over to the stereo and peered closely at the speaker cloth. The voice inside was unearthly. With his eye up to the loose weave he could just barely make out the tiny siren within, its head thrown back, mouth open to expose a throat that plunged deep into the heart of fairyland.

He moved to the television and lowered his head as close as he dared to the screen (he knew he would never be able to quite trust the radiation given off by such things). The tiny cowboys inside turned on their horses and waved to him, the artificial sun in the distance reflecting off their elven smiles.

Finally he stood by the desktop computer. A toothy grin filled the screen. "What did I tell you?" The Red Cap's voice was static-filled, but recognizable just the same on the cheap speaker. Tiny puffs of cigarette smoke exploded rhythmically from the disk drive door. "A little cramped, but still . . . I don't mind calling it home. Certainly better than the alternative."

"There's some dirt on your little window thingie," Apprentice said with concern. He raised the mop that had been leaning against the wall. "Let me get it for you."

"Apprentice . . ."

Too late the mop slopped over the screen, water sloshing into the ventilation grille. The screen made a popping noise, and there was a soft scraping from somewhere deep inside the computer and the straining sound of something winding down.

"Bloody hell," the speaker said softly. "Bloody hell."

Classic Science Fiction and Fantasy

__ **THE WOODS OUT BACK** R. A. Salvatore 0-441-90872-1/$4.99
Bestselling author R.A. Salvatore creates a world of elves and
dwarfs, witches and dragons—all in the woods behind Gary
Leger's house. There Gary discovers he is the only one who
can wear the armor of the land's lost hero and wield a magical
spear. And if he doesn't, he can never go home again...

__ **DUNE** Frank Herbert 0-441-17271-7/$5.99
The bestselling novel of an awesome world where gods and
adventurers clash, mile-long sandworms rule the desert, and
the ancient dream of immortality comes true.

__ **STRANGER IN A STRANGE LAND** Robert A. Heinlein
0-441-79034-8/$5.99
From the New York Times bestselling author—the science
fiction masterpiece of a man from Mars who teaches
humankind the art of grokking, watersharing and love.

__ **THE ONCE AND FUTURE KING** T.H. White
0-441-62740-4/$5.99
The world's greatest fantasy classic! A magical epic of King
Arthur in Camelot, romance, wizardry and war. By the author
of The Book of Merlyn.

__ **THE LEFT HAND OF DARKNESS** Ursula K. LeGuin
0-441-47812-3/$4.99
Winner of the Hugo and Nebula awards for best science fiction
novel of the year. "SF masterpiece!"—Newsweek "A jewel of
a story."—Frank Herbert